Praise for *The Bone Curse* by Carrie Rubin

"A tense, perceptive tale of an investigation into a terrifying threat."
—*Kirkus Reviews*

"A teeth-grinding story of ancient curses and mystical remedies...*The Bone Curse* will keep even the most skeptical reader awake long past midnight."
—**Andra Watkins, *New York Times* bestselling author of *Not Without My Father* and the Nowhere Series**

"A cursed medical student... a vengeful Vodou priest... a vast subterranean Parisian catacomb with more secrets than the bones that rest there... what could go wrong? Take note medical thriller fans, the genre has a new contender, and her name is Carrie Rubin."
—**Larry Brooks, *USA Today* bestselling author**

"From the first page to the last, the tensions never let up ... Bravo to Rubin for creating another fast-paced medical thriller that both keeps you turning pages and opens a window into a world most of us have never considered."
—**Audrey Kalman, author of *What Remains Unsaid* and *Dance of Souls***

"A sizzling slice of Vodou served alongside methodical medical science. What's not to love? Unique characters, a plot that galloped along, and some damn fine writing, too."
—**G.M. Barlean, author of The Rosewood Series**

Praise for *Eating Bull* by Carrie Rubin

"A deftly crafted novel of suspense and a compelling read from beginning to end...Very highly recommended."—***Midwest Book Review***

"...bought the book, read the book, loved the book..."
—**Larry Brooks, *USA Today* bestselling author**

"A solid thriller that manages to infuse one boy's coming-of-age with a whole lot of murder." —*Kirkus Reviews*

"Each of Rubin's characters is carefully developed and believable."
—*Akron Beacon Journal*

"Rubin is a masterful storyteller who weaves her medical knowledge into a gripping thriller, diving head-first into a meaty subject that has been ignored for far too long. *Eating Bull* paints a disturbing portrait of a society in denial and delivers characters that get under your skin and stay there."
—**Dianne Gray, award-winning Australian author of *Soul's Child* and *The Everything Theory***

PRAISE FOR *THE SENECA SCOURGE* BY CARRIE RUBIN

"Rubin masterfully blends medical thriller, mystery, and sci-fi into a thoroughly enjoyable read."

—**Audrey Kalman, author of** *Dance of Souls*

"This fast-paced, beautifully written medical thriller glues you between its covers and will not set you free until the final page!"

—**Frederick Anderson, author of** *I Am Cara,* *The Butterfly Man,* **and** *Hallbury Summer*

"*The Seneca Scourge* grabs you by the throat and doesn't let go until the last page."

—**Elizabeth Hein, author of** *How to Climb the Eiffel Tower* **and** *Overlook*

THE BONE CURSE

THE BONE CURSE

CARRIE RUBIN

SCIENCETHRILLERS MEDIA

SCIENCETHRILLERS MEDIA

THE BONE CURSE. Copyright ©2018 by Carrie Rubin. All rights reserved. For more information, contact ScienceThrillers Media, P.O. Box 601392, Sacramento, CA 95860-1392.

www.ScienceThrillersMedia.com
Publisher@ScienceThrillersMedia.com

First edition, 2018

Library of Congress Control Number 2017960505

FIC031040 FICTION / Thrillers / Medical
FIC031070 FICTION / Thrillers / Supernatural

ISBN 978-1-940419-97-8 (hardcover)
ISBN 978-1-940419-98-5 (trade paperback)
ISBN 978-1-940419-99-2 (ebook)

Cover design by Lance Buckley (Envelup Design)

For my sons, who brighten my day with laughter

"Ah, foolish one! Why thinkest thou that thou shalt live long,
when thou art not sure of a single day?"
—Thomas à Kempis, inscribed on the Imitation Pillar, Paris Catacombs

PARIS
TUESDAY, JUNE 23
10:40 A.M.

Within the suffocating stairwell of the catacombs, something happened to Ben. He'd expected dizziness. Distress, even. The pragmatic med student had battled claustrophobia before. But this feeling? This was more like despair. Seeing millions of bones two hundred feet below Paris no longer seemed worth the agony.

He gripped the railing and focused on his spiral descent, counting the steps to distract himself. The rest of the tourists were far ahead, and though his friend Laurette was only a few feet behind, he felt utterly alone.

"Eighty-seven, eighty-eight, eighty-nine."

An invisible hand squeezed his throat. The shock of it threw him off balance, and he stumbled several steps before regaining his footing. He pressed his body close to the stone wall and willed himself to calm down. Just keep counting, he thought. You'll be at the bottom soon.

"Ninety-six, ninety-seven, ninety-eight."

Ghost arms cinched his chest, and air rushed from his lungs. He faltered a few more steps. Behind him Laurette's Caribbean accent surfaced. "Are you okay? Something is not right. I feel it too. Please, Ben, *arrêtes*." As a native of Haiti who spoke more French than Haitian Creole, Laurette was telling him to stop.

He wanted to. Dear Jesus he wanted to. Especially for the woman who'd given him this free trip to Paris when her brother had backed out last minute. But something wouldn't let him. Something drove him onward, his shoes smacking the concrete steps as though he were a marionette. Losing control troubled him on a good day. Losing it in an underground graveyard terrified him.

He tried to call out to Laurette, but his jaw snapped shut. Only a wheeze whistled through. On his second attempt, fingers seized his brain. They squeezed and pressed and jumbled his thoughts. Reasoning slipped away and time lost all meaning. No more counting steps. No more efforts to turn back. Whenever a snippet of rationality surfaced, some unseen force pushed it back down.

When his body finally reached the quarry, the dank tunnels of the catacombs welcomed him. Though aware of his surroundings, compelled by them really, he slipped further away from his cognitive self and shuffled through the earthy corridors, their limestone walls and pebbly pathways a cumin haze of dust. By the time he reached the first burial site, the bones took over completely.

Reaching as high as the ceilings, organized piles of abandoned tibias and femurs supported rows of human skulls. Some of the ossuaries were narrow and musty, barely clearing his six-foot frame. Others were roomier. Save for a few sconces, all of the chambers were dark.

Empty eye sockets, browned and desiccated with time, stared out at Ben at chest level. You're almost there, they whispered.

Cool water plopped onto his hair and dripped down his stubbled cheek. With the mindlessness of a robot, he wiped the moisture away and zipped his hoodie higher. With each step his urgency grew. At times he was aware of Laurette's growing concern, her pleas to turn back, her insistence that a dark presence was controlling him, but he was incapable of responding. Instead he kept winding through the ossuaries. The deeper he weaved into their shadowy maze, the calmer he became. When he tried to reason why that was, the dead air hushed him. At last he spilled into a spacious room with a stone altar. His body halted and his power of speech returned. Any lingering fear vanished.

"We're here," he said, excitement buzzing inside him.

To his left lay a collection of bones. Engraved in stone next to the osseous pile were the words: OSSEMENTS DU CIMETIÈRE DES INNOCENTS DÉPOSÉS EN AVRIL 1786.

"No. We must keep going." Spirals of ebony hair coiled around Laurette's cheekbones, her expression a tight mask. One hand grasped a limestone pillar, the other clutched her bronze locket.

"It's just another pile of bones. You saw worse as a nurse in Haiti."

"We must not stop here. I feel something *mal*, something bad. Let us catch up with the others." She released the pillar and grabbed his arm, trying to lead him onward.

He pulled away and approached the billboard-sized heap of bones.

You are very close now, they whispered.

Chilly, underground air crept inside his sweatshirt and enveloped his clammy skin. Water dripped softly in the corner. He barely noticed. He had to see these bones.

"I remember this room from your guidebook."

"Please, Ben, your voice. It is scaring me. I fear something evil wants you."

"These were the first bones transferred to the catacombs, back in 1786."

From his peripheral vision he saw Laurette trembling.

Do not worry about her.

"Your book said patients who died at the *Hotel-Dieu* hospital were taken to the Holy Innocents' Cemetery and dumped into mass graves." He spoke mechanically, an unknown presence demanding he voice the ossuary's pain.

"Please. We must go."

"But the cemetery got so crowded, the bones were exhumed and moved to the catacombs." He shuffled closer to the skulls. "Just think. All those people sick with disease, suffering, getting terrible treatment in an overcrowded hospital, only to be dumped in a mass grave when they died, as if they were no better than the rats and fleas that infected them."

"This is not you talking. I am frightened. Let us—"

"Give me a minute." His rebuke made her jump. She pressed her body against the stone pillar, hands shaking, locket clutched to her fleece jacket.

A flash of reason blipped in his brain. *What's happening? Go to her. She needs you.*

We need you, the bones sang, and like a siren and a thief, they stole his attention back. He wanted only to be in their presence. To look at their porous marrow. To smell their earthiness.

And to touch one. A special one.

A bone on the right seemed to signal him. He shifted his stance. Behind him Laurette called out, her cry a million miles away. A tug on his hood tried to pull him back, but his feet were bricks.

He lifted his arm.

A bone. A femur. Brownish and old, its osseous surface cracked and nicked over the centuries, buried with a tale it could never tell.

His hand reached up.

"Ben, no!"

Like finally scratching a relentless itch, he wrapped his fingers around the femur.

For a moment time stood still, the air as dead as the human remains around them. Then pain stabbed his palm, and an electric current shot through his body. His back arched, and his jaw jutted forward, as if being wrenched from his face.

Laurette shrieked and wrapped her arms around him. The shrillness of her cry and the immediacy of her touch broke Ben's rigor. His muscles relaxed, and his stupor ended.

He snatched his hand away from the bone and blinked at the blood flowing from his palm. Crimson drops plopped onto his heavy-toed shoes and the chalky ground around them.

His heart raced and his chest heaved, but his mind recovered. He returned Laurette's embrace with his uninjured arm. "Oh, thank God," he said. She gulped air and cast an anxious glance his way. "Shh, shh, it's okay. I'm okay now." Aside from his bleeding palm and dizziness, he was.

After a moment's hesitation, she grabbed his chin and stared into his eyes, as if needing reassurance.

"I promise I'm okay. I'm so sorry. I don't know what came over me."

Once she calmed down he looked back at the offending femur but saw nothing to explain the cut. No spur, no sharp edge, no barbed border.

Pressing his bloody palm against his jeans to stanch the flow, he couldn't understand what had happened. Couldn't sort out his bizarre and uncharacteristic behavior. So it wasn't long before the thirty-year-old prag-matist in him resurfaced.

Just a severe reaction to claustrophobia, he decided. Like that panic attack when he got trapped in a service elevator years ago.

Bleeding hand pressed against his thigh, he gently guided Laurette into the next tunnel. "Let's get out of here. I owe you better than this on our last day in Paris."

Her high-arched brows wrinkled with worry as she kneaded her locket, a protective amulet given to her by her brother before she'd left Haiti for Philadelphia. "But do you not see? Something now runs in your blood. I don't know what, but I feel it. I—"

"It's just a little cut. I'll be fine." And by the time they exited the catacombs and reemerged in the blinding sunlight, he truly believed that.

Because the only things running in Benjamin Oris's blood were practi-cality, logic, and reason.

1

Growing up, Ben had only wanted to be one of two things: a carpenter or an orthopedic surgeon. Both jobs pounded and sawed hard surfaces. Both jobs mastered mechanical forces. But only orthopedics nourished his love of science.

At six fifteen in the morning, with his landlady's cat in his lap, Ben ate breakfast and reviewed an article on infective endocarditis. Toast crumbs littered its pages and coffee stained its corner. If he didn't get the disease's criteria down pat before rounds, Dr. Smith would crucify him. Then it would be a life of carpentry after all.

He stroked the tabby's fur. "What are those painful lesions on the hand and feet called?" The cat didn't answer. Neither did the kitchen's 1970s appliances or pea-green cabinets. He grabbed the article and flipped through it. "Osler's nodes, Izzy. Osler's nodes."

Izzy purred and blinked. Ben nuzzled her to his face, her whiskers tickling and smelling of tuna. "At least I'll still have you if Dr. Smith gives me the boot."

The cat jumped off his lap and slunk to the open basement door, heading back upstairs to her mistress.

Et tu, Brute? Ben thought.

He gave up on the paper and tossed the rest of the toast in the trash. His appetite wasn't the same since he'd returned from Paris. Neither was his energy level. He'd been suffering headaches too. Considering he'd started his first clinical rotation only nine days earlier, he wasn't surprised. Internal medicine was one of the toughest clerkships.

Especially when his attending blamed him for her stepson not getting into med school.

After making sure Izzy's tail was in the clear, he closed the basement door and stepped into the living room, its garish carpeting a burnt-orange shag nobody in their right mind would choose. Before he could retrieve his backpack from the tattered sofa, his phone buzzed in the pocket of his chinos. A text from Laurette: *You left yet?*

Soon. If don't get pre-rounds done before report Smith'll kill me, he replied.

Laurette typed back: *Sounds drastic. Give her a goat.*

Goats don't fix everything.

So I should not give Edith one?

Ben smiled and texted: *No she'd just cook it.*

Laurette was referring to Edith Sinclair, Ben's landlady of ten years, who'd only agreed to rent her brownstone's basement to him when he promised he kept to himself and didn't party. Though cordial to Laurette, the seventy-eight-year-old woman squirmed at the idea of Ben having a black girlfriend, and for that reason alone he never bothered to tell her their relationship was platonic. The same tight smile appeared whenever Ben mentioned he was raised by two dads.

But despite the fact Mrs. Sinclair and her decor were stuck in the seventies, he liked living there and was more than happy to repair her broken shutters or damaged drywall. He did his best to repair her loneliness as well, stopping by for visits whenever he could.

Lunch today? Laurette texted.

Ben's thumbs hovered over the phone. Their face-to-face interactions had been strained since they'd returned from Paris. Laurette was convinced something was wrong with him, and he didn't want to rehash it. He rotated his right palm and examined the spot where the bone had cut him. A purplish, rubbery papule the size of a baby pea had formed there.

Sure, he finally typed. Her text humor suggested she was getting back to herself, which was good because he missed her jokes. Though not his girlfriend, she was his best friend, and he remembered how quickly he'd bonded to the public health student two years his senior when they met in epidemiology class a couple years before.

A glance at the time told him he'd better hurry. He typically biked to the hospital which, traveling from Wallace Street to downtown Chestnut, took anywhere from twelve to fifteen minutes. Though driving might be quicker, there was no point in wasting money on gas or parking. On the coldest days, he took public transit.

Grabbing the stuffed backpack off the couch, he heaved the bag over his shoulder and winced when the strap scraped his hand. He looked at his palm again. Red droplets sprouted around the lesion. Though the papule had occasionally itched and tingled, up until now it hadn't rebled.

With no bandages in the medicine cabinet or elsewhere, he cursed and grabbed a wad of toilet paper to blot the area. A knock on the door interrupted him.

"Helloooooo. Are you in there?"

Ben closed his eyes. The sing-songy voice was unmistakable.

"It's Kate, sweetie. Hope I haven't missed you."

Shit.

Kate Naughton. Mrs. Sinclair's twice-divorced, forty-three-going-on-seventeen-year-old daughter. What was she doing there so early? Probably just coming in from a night of drinking, her mom's place a shorter drive from whatever bar she'd holed herself up in. But what did she want with him?

He never should have slept with the woman. Either time.

For an introvert, he really needed to learn to keep his pants on.

Eighty-proof breath accosted him the moment he opened the door. He stepped back, his eyes watering. "Hey, what's up? I have to get to the hospital."

The woman teetered in, closing first the door and then the distance between them. Her honey-wheat hair was matted on one side and poufed on the other. Smeared mascara rimmed her lower lids. Cleavage ballooned from her silky blouse, and a dark stain dotted the left shoulder.

Even drunk and disheveled, she looked … tempting.

Ben backed up, images of an inflamed Dr. Smith realigning his priorities. When he reached the wall, the glassy-eyed woman had him trapped. The scent of his sandalwood body wash mixed with her boozy fumes.

"Aren't you a doctor yet, honey? You've been at this school thing a long time."

"I'm sorry, but you can't stay."

Kate's left hand plopped onto his pec and her right onto his bicep. His backpack fell off his shoulder and thumped to the floor. She gave his bicep a squeeze. "Money for tuition isn't the only thing construction work's given you."

She winked, and her hand slid down his chest and onto his abdomen. Her fingers danced their way to his belt. Despite his resistance he felt himself getting hard. Gently but firmly he pushed her away with his uninjured hand, the right one still clutched in a fist over the wad of now-bloody toilet paper.

"Kate, I have to go."

Her grabby hands flew back to his chest, where she kneaded his muscles. "And to think you came from gay fathers. Did Mike … er … Mark … er, what's the dead one's name again?"

"Max." Ben's voice tightened and his erection fizzled.

"Yeah, that's it. Did Max ever finish that gene … geneo … oh, shoot, what's that thing called? Your mom mentioned it to me."

"A genealogy, and no." Ben guided her away, more forcefully this time. He picked up his backpack and opened the door, pulling her into the stairwell with him. One of the most regrettable moments of his life was when Kate had befriended Harmony, his mother (though that was using the term loosely). Harmony had showed up at the worst possible time: when Kate was still in his bed. Just thinking about Harmony made his head hurt.

"Oh, don't get all mad." Kate's tone became impish. "I know what'll make you feel better. It's been too long since we've, *you* know." Red acrylic fingernails tapped his tie.

Seven months to be exact. Seven months since he'd vowed it would never happen again. And it wasn't her age. It wasn't even his noncommittal relationship with Melissa, his ex-girlfriend. It was Kate's batshit craziness.

"Kate." Firm now. "Let me lock the door."

But before he could pull out his apartment key, she was all over him. Hands on his chest, his shoulders, his ass. Lips and tongue on his mouth.

"No, we're done with that." He pushed her away, and to keep her from charging again, he grabbed both her hands before they made it to his chest.

The bloodied tissue fell to the floor, and even in that heated moment he was surprised by how saturated it was.

Kate leaned in again, but then she too saw the blood. "Ooh, you're bleeding, baby." Swaying from inebriation, she held up her left hand, his blood leaving a moon-shaped smear on her palm.

"I'm sorry," he said, his tone softer. "Let's go up to your mom's to wash it off. I need to bike to the hospital, and I'm already late." As he turned to lock the door, Kate let out a whoop that made him jump.

"Well, that's what I came to tell you, doctor man." Her eyes seemed to float in their orbits, and she had to grab the handrail for support. "Your bike. I just crushed it with my car."

2

Ben swerved his black '96 Mustang into the entrance of the visitor's parking garage and snatched a ticket from the dispenser. According to the fee board, he'd be twenty dollars poorer by the end of the day. But it was the closest lot to the hospital, and if he didn't get his ass moving, he'd have bigger problems than parking debt. Morning report started in ten minutes. He'd either have to skip pre-rounds to attend it, or skip morning report to pre-round. Though both options would piss off Dr. Smith, being ill-prepared on his patients would be the bigger sin.

Pre-rounds it was.

After finding a tight space on the sixth level, he sprinted down the stairwell to the second level walkway connecting the visitor's lot to the main building of Montgomery Hospital. His backpack thumped against his shoulder blade, and his shirt clung to his already perspiring chest. Another scorcher of a day ahead.

The medical complex consisted of a cluster of brick buildings covering three blocks of downtown Philadelphia. Some were connected via walkways on their second floors. Others required crossing the street. Most of the specialty clinics, research facilities, and academic offices had parking areas of their own.

The main hospital with its arched entrance and expansive windows contained several floors of inpatient wards and the emergency room, or emergency department as Ben was learning to call it. To do otherwise was to annoy Dr. Smith. Though Ben spent most of his time in that building, he still attended daily after-lunch lectures in the Southeast Pennsylvania College of Medicine, easily accessed via a detour through the Talcott Center, which housed the labor and delivery unit. Ben enjoyed seeing the swollen bellies and happy faces of the women in the waiting room. It was a nice break from the pain and disease on the internal medicine ward.

But there'd be no time to cross over to the medical school to retrieve his white coat from the student lounge that day, even if it meant a pile of hurt from Dr. Smith during rounds later on. "I expect you all to look like professionals," she had said the first day of his clerkship. "Men, that includes a tie and white coat. You're aspiring doctors, not vagrants."

Damn Kate.

How the woman had managed to mangle his bike when he'd chained it to a tree near the berm was a mystery. She'd dragged him outside to look at it, the Philadelphia street springing to life with people exiting their red-bricked row houses on their way to work or out walking their dogs. Given that his landlady frowned upon having a bike in the house, he always left it out on the berm. The thing was a piece of junk, so he'd never had trouble with anyone stealing it. Still, seeing its squashed front tire and twisted handlebars beneath Kate's Taurus had disheartened him. Piece of junk or not, it was his primary means of transportation.

Putting the morning's rough start behind him, he skidded into the main hospital complex, a large, open design with an atrium that reached nine stories above to a glass ceiling. Skipping the crowded foyer at the west bank of elevators, he darted toward the stairwell and galloped three steps at a time to the sixth floor. As soon as he got there, his cell phone buzzed in his front pocket.

Though Ben managed many things well, getting off schedule wasn't one of them. Pressure squeezed his chest, and acid reflux (a recent development, compliments of Dr. Smith's clerkship) burned his throat. He could hear his father's voice in his head: "Can't be so rigid in life, son. Things don't always go as planned."

Ignoring his phone, he hurried on. The closer he got to 6 West, the greater the antiseptic smell and the more crowded the hallway. A trio of surgical residents brushed past him, their white coats swishing against their scrubs. They barely acknowledged his lowly med-student presence, even though he'd seen a couple of them on the ward for consults. He was probably older than all of them too.

Just as he was about to enter the unit, his phone vibrated again. With a grumble he checked it. A voice message from his dad. He wished Willy would text instead of call, but the day Willy sent a text message would be the day something was wrong.

Slipping into a small waiting room just off 6 West, Ben listened to the message, his gaze focused on a pile of tabloid magazines littering a central table. "Hey, Benny. The store had a little break-in. Nothing to worry about, I'm fine, but I could use your skills fixin' the window. I know you're busy. Hate to trouble you."

Sweat dripped between Ben's shoulder blades as he sank onto a maroon chair. Someone broke into Willy's Chocolate Chalet? Located on South Street, the store had never had any trouble in the past.

He closed his eyes. His body temperature rose even more. First the bike, now the shop window. When would he find time to repair them? He had five patients, two sets of rounds, a couple lectures, and a whole lot of studying ahead.

An elderly man with a cane and movements suggestive of Parkinson's disease shuffled into the waiting room. He gripped the armrest of a chair opposite Ben and struggled to sit. Ben jumped up. "Here, let me help you." He grabbed the man's arm to steady him.

Once comfortably positioned, the man said, "Thank you. Very kind of you."

Ben nodded and asked if he needed anything else. When the man assured him he didn't, Ben headed to the ward, whipping off a quick text to his father to let him know he'd stop by after work and seal the window until they could get new glass. Willy might not send texts, but at least he read them.

As for the bike, it would have to wait until the weekend. He'd pick up new parts and do the repairs himself.

In between his mountain of studies.

Ignoring the growing ache in his temples and the squeeze in his chest, Ben spent the next forty minutes checking in on his patients while the rest of the team was at morning report. The work distracted him, and he started to relax.

Maybe Hard-Ass Smith wouldn't even notice his absence.

=╟=

Having finished informal team rounds with the senior resident two hours later, Ben waited near the central work station for his attending's arrival, his throat dry and his fingers fidgeting with the bandage he'd found in a supply cart and stuck on his injured palm. The staff area, a large square made up of three adjoining counters and a back wall fronting a supply closet and break room, had long since come alive with hospital personnel. Across from the work station, patient rooms lined the periphery, their numbers spanning from W664 to W684.

At nine thirty sharp, Dr. Taka Smith burst through the automatic doors and marched down the stark hallway, its monotony broken by oak wall guards, a red emergency phone, and an automated external defibrillator. A group of nursing students parted like the Red Sea for Moses when the diminutive attending barreled past them, her lab coat flapping around her tailored suit and her pumps clicking on the tile. Glossy, bobbed hair framed her delicate face.

To an outsider she might appear sweet—even docile—but Ben knew the Japanese-American was more samurai than geisha. One of the few people he'd seen her cater to was her stepson, Joel, and in her mind, if it weren't for Ben's deferment year to earn money for med school, Joel would have gotten the last spot in the class. Then he would be the one rounding on patients instead of toiling in the biochemistry lab a block away, working on his master's degree. It didn't seem to occur to them that maybe Ben was the better student, and maybe the admissions committee figured he was a good enough candidate to let him defer a year.

The un-Japanese name of Smith came from her neurosurgeon husband whom she married eighteen years before. Ben knew the details because the accomplished husband-and-wife-physician duo was the subject of the hospital's most recent quarterly newsletter.

Waiting with the gathering team members, he watched Dr. Smith stride toward them, her lined eyebrows raised and her lips a tight line. "How nice of you to join us, Benjamin. Hope you enjoyed your sleep-in while the rest of us were at morning report."

The rest of "us" included the senior resident, three interns, a diligent fourth-year student acting as an intern for her sub-I month, and two other third-years besides Ben, including Melissa Horner, an athletic, pixie-haired blonde who happened to be his former girlfriend. Bonus stress in an already stressful rotation.

Ben swallowed. The burn in his throat returned, and before he could answer the attending, she continued. "Please, share with us what was so important."

What could he say? He was late because his bike got smashed? He was late because, unlike the others, he didn't have an unlimited gas allowance? He settled on, "Sorry. Transportation issues. It won't happen again."

Dr. Smith peered up at him, as if disappointed in having no better excuse to shred. She wrinkled her dew drop of a nose and glanced at his cheap, charcoal tie, and then his short-sleeved shirt. "I see donning a lab coat was too difficult a chore."

Ben said nothing. What was the point? The sooner they moved on, the better.

Sighing, the attending shifted her focus to Jamal Brooks, the senior resident. "Who's first?" she asked.

Like a school of fish, the group trailed after their two superiors to room W668, where a thirty-nine-year-old man with endocarditis lay febrile in bed. A repeat of *Friends* blared from the television, but when the rounding team shuffled in—their entrance order determined by hierarchy—the patient muted the TV and turned his flushed face to them.

Customarily the intern assigned to the patient presented to the attending, and the senior resident chimed in when needed. For the most part, the medical students were ignored, their input sought during informal rounds with the senior resident instead. That didn't stop Dr. Smith from "pimping" Ben though, an ugly term for aggressive quizzing of medical trainees. While Tim Cho, the intern, presented the endocarditis patient and the plan for the day, Ben braced himself for what would follow.

Sure enough, moments later Dr. Smith cut the intern off and homed in on Ben. "Based on what Tim presented, what Duke criteria, both major and minor, qualify this patient for a diagnosis of infective endocarditis?"

Ben cleared his throat. Lacking a tablet like the rest of the students, he gripped his clipboard of notes. "He has two major criteria: more than one blood culture positive for *Strep viridans* and an oscillating mass on his aortic valve. Although those two alone are enough for diagnosis, he also has the minor criteria of fever and a positive rheumatoid factor." He exhaled more loudly than he would've liked but held Dr. Smith's stare.

Uncomfortable silence followed, and then the petite attending nodded and said, "Correct."

After finalizing the treatment plan with Tim and Jamal, the team moved onto the rest of the patients. Dr. Smith seemed to forget about Ben, perhaps mollified by his endocarditis response, so he finally relaxed. While the interns presented their patients, Ben's mind—and gaze—wandered to Melissa. When a portly man walked by with his buttocks exposed through his gown, Ben caught his ex-girlfriend's eye and smiled. At first, the corner of her mouth lifted, but then she gave Ben a chilly look and redirected her attention to Dr. Smith, who was listening to the sub-intern present a patient with chronic *C. diff* infection.

She hates me, Ben thought.

Could he blame her? He'd known she wanted more than an occasional romp, and yet he couldn't seem to give it to her. He kept ducking and deflecting until she finally gave up. A few weeks later she walked straight into the all-too-eager arms of Joel, Dr. Smith's stepson.

Talk about a hospital soap opera.

Ben trailed the rounding group out of the *C. diff* patient's room and followed them around the corner into another room.

He should've been honest with Melissa. Admitted how much he liked her, how much he *still* liked her. He should've confessed his reluctance to take it further was because he needed to focus on school. He'd worked too hard to get where he was to risk backsliding. Instead he'd clammed up, always leaving the discussion for another—

"How do you feel about her decision, Mr. Oris?"

Ben startled at the sound of his surname. The rounding team returned to the hallway, and Jamal pulled the patient's door closed behind them. Dr. Smith crossed her arms and waited for Ben's response. The air around them thickened, and his breath caught in his throat. "I'm sorry, what was that?"

"I asked how you feel about her decision."

"Uh … what decision is that?" Blood rushed behind his eardrums.

Dr. Smith assumed a staccato tone. "Her decision to forgo all future treatment for her colon cancer and her insinuation she'd like someone to help her die."

Max popped into Ben's mind. His non-biological father, stage-four colon cancer, lying in a hospital bed, emaciated, feverish. Although Max's suffering had ripped Ben's heart in two, Ben had sought all last-resort treatments, anything to give him more time with his father.

Before Ben even realized he was responding, he said, "I think it's wrong." Behind Dr. Smith, Melissa's wide-eyed gaze finally caught his. In it he saw *shut the hell up*. And yet he didn't. Instead he remembered the trial drug he'd fought for that put Max in remission and gave Willy and Ben six more good months with the man. "I think people should fight 'til the end."

Dr. Smith drummed her fingers against her arms, the pen in her coat pocket jiggling from the motion. "Well, wouldn't it be nice to live in Benjamin's world where everything is so cut and dried? Where Western medicine has all the answers and any other avenues are wrong."

"Well, I didn't exactly say that."

"If you expect to make it as a doctor, you better expand your viewpoint. Learn that life isn't packaged into neat little boxes." His ears burned, but the attending wasn't finished. "Clearly you could use a brush-up on ethics, particularly on patients' rights to terminate care. I'll email you literature this afternoon. Tomorrow after rounds you'll grace us with a ten-minute talk on the subject." Leaving no room for discussion, Dr. Smith darted off, the rest of the fish swimming after her, no doubt grateful to be out of the flotsam.

Crap.

More papers to read. More research to do. A shattered window to repair. A bike to fix.

He scratched his palm, dropping his clipboard in the process. It ricocheted off the floor and flew three feet down the hall. Melissa left the group to retrieve it. When she handed it to him he snatched it back, ripping his bandage off and sending loose papers to the ground. He smashed the bandage back in place before the lesion had a chance to rebleed.

"Ben," she said, her head tilted in sympathy.

"Spare me your pity, princess." He bent down to rescue his patient notes, avoiding Melissa's eyes until she scampered away in her Jimmy Choo flats. He knew both his tone and his use of the label she detested had just severed their connection for good.

Crap.

3

Lunch tray in hand, Ben weaved his way between cafeteria tables, care-ful not to let the rolling apple knock over his cup of water and sop his burger. Cascading sunlight from the atrium's glass ceiling warmed his scalp and worsened his headache. The cerebral ache had sprouted shortly after noon when Dr. Smith's ethics articles popped up in his email. Seven papers in all. Christ.

He spotted Laurette at the end of the room, and his mood started to lift. Near her left, a plant-studded divider separated the dining area from a long hallway of administrative offices. A hospital gift shop lay ahead.

"Nice blouse." He sat down across from her. "Crimson's a great color on you."

"*Merci*, but what's wrong, my friend? You look like a man who has lost his farm."

Ben raised an eyebrow and took a bite of his burger.

"Perhaps you are not getting enough sleep. As we say in Haiti, 'It is the owner of the body who looks out for the body.'" Laurette bobbed her head in a goofy fashion, and her coiled hair bounced off her chin.

Despite his stress, Ben laughed. "Don't worry about me. I'm fine."

"Well, maybe this will make you finer." Laurette lifted a brown bag from the floor and pulled out a plastic sandwich container. When she opened it, the scent of cinnamon and coconut filled the space between them.

"Oh wow, you made me *tablet kokoye*?" Ben reached into the container and pulled out a baked good that looked like peanut brittle. He popped the whole thing in his mouth and moaned as he chewed the sweet Haitian treat. When he swallowed the last of it, he took a sip of water and said, "You're too good to me."

"It is nothing." Laurette brushed the compliment off. "I want for you to find your farm."

"I have no idea what that means, but you're a good person, Bovo." The nickname stemmed from his fumbled attempt at her last name, *Beauvais*, the first time they'd met. When she waved him off again, he picked up his hamburger and shifted gears. "How's your summer course going?"

"Great. It is advanced epidemiology with Dr. Reeza Khalid." She folded up the brown bag and placed it to the side.

Ben paused mid-bite and removed the burger from his mouth. "Whoa, *the* Dr. Khalid? She's big doings."

Laurette's face broke into a radiant smile, making every angle of her exquisite bone structure a lesson in geometry. "Incredible, yes? And she has agreed to mentor my capstone project."

"No shit?"

"No shit." When Laurette said the words, they came out *no sheet*.

Ben smiled. Between his friend's good news and her tasty tablet kokoye, his blood pressure lowered ten points. "That's awesome."

They ate in silence for a while until Laurette wiped her mouth with a napkin and cleared her throat. Her fingers fluttered to the bronze amulet around her neck, the same one she'd worn in the catacombs. Embossed with a star and faux emerald, and stuffed with a potpourri of dried plants, her brother had offered it as protection, though protection from what she'd never said.

Now, all traces of joy left her face. Even the air seemed to change around them.

Ben leaned back. He knew where she was headed. Smack dab into a discussion he'd avoided since they'd left Paris. "Haitian sweets and epidemiology aren't why you asked me to lunch, are they?" Mealy hamburger clogged his throat. A drink of water did little to clear it.

Laurette rubbed the locket's emerald, her fingernails the color of her blouse. "I want to make sure you are okay. We have not talked about what happened in the catacombs. Not really, anyway." She studied his bandaged palm. Ben closed his hand and put it in his lap.

"There's nothing to talk about, other than to apologize again for being such a dick. I wish I could take it all back."

"I don't seek apologies. You were not yourself. Do you think I could not see that?"

Images of beige limestone tunnels and powdery bones flooded Ben's brain. Fear and shame washed over him, and for a moment he was back in the claustrophobic stairwell. He dug his blunt nails into his flesh. His insistence on touching the bone and his willful disregard for his friend's concern (*no, let's not kid ourselves, Benny Boy—her absolute terror*) were as mysterious to him now as they had been then.

"I'm fine," he simply said, pressing the bandage under his fingertips.

"You do not look fine. You look tired. You look ill." She glanced at the half-eaten burger on his plate. "And you do not eat much."

"Because I've just started my first clinical rotation and I have an attending from hell. Guess I'm not myself right now."

"That is my point. Something happened to you in the catacombs." She squeezed her amulet. "I do not know how to say it without you thinking me *fou*. You know the word? Crazy."

Ben didn't, but he did now. "I don't think you're crazy. You're one of the most reasonable people I know. But you're imagining things that aren't there."

Laurette pushed her own partially eaten sandwich aside and leaned closer. "I have been having dreams, you see. Dreams of you …" Her voice trailed off when a surgical nurse walked by with a slice of pizza.

Ben wiggled an eyebrow.

"Not those kinds of dreams. Don't tease. I mean something bad." She dropped her voice to a whisper and leaned in so close Ben could see the mocha-colored specks in her irises. "Something evil. There is blood and there is evil."

Despite Ben's dismissive grunt, hair prickled on the nape of his neck. "Come on, you don't believe in that spirit nonsense. I know your brother is a bigwig voodoo guy in Port-Au-Prince, but you told me you don't practice it."

Laurette chewed her lip, as if trying to decide whether to be insulted or not. After a heavy exhale, she sank back against her chair. "We call it serving the *Lwa*, not 'spirit nonsense'. *Vodou* is a religion, the practice of ceremonial rituals to bring good fortune. It is not the Hollywood version of voodoo dolls and zombies. And my brother is a *houngan*. A priest."

"Sorry."

"If not for Guy, I would not be in Philadelphia. He encouraged me to come live with my Auntie Marie and get a degree in public health so I can better serve our people."

"And if it wasn't for Guy, I would have never been able to see Paris."

She gave a small smile. "It is pronounced *Ghee*, not *Guy*."

Though Laurette had been disappointed her brother couldn't go to Paris like the two had originally planned, she hadn't hesitated to take Ben in his place. Despite the trouble at the catacombs, they'd had a great time, and he hoped she knew how grateful he was.

But her lightheartedness was fleeting. "There are some things you do not see. Things you refuse to see." She glanced at his right hand, which had resurfaced and was twirling his water cup. "For instance, why you still need a bandage."

She reached out to inspect his palm, but Ben buried it in his lap before she could. "I reinjured it. Not a big deal."

"But it has been over two weeks. It should be better by now. There is something bad inside you, I feel it."

Ben clenched his jaw. The topic was getting old. "I can't make our Thursday night run tonight. My dad's store was broken into. I have to fix the window."

"*Mon Dieu.*"

Ben knew that expression. It meant *my God*, and *by* God, Ben's news put Laurette into a tizzy. Her hand shot back to her amulet, the sudden movement lifting Ben's tray and pitching the apple to the floor. It rolled and came to a stop next to a child's foot one table over. "Do you see? Things are not as they should be."

Ben cracked his neck, a longtime habit from a long-ago construction injury. He stared up at the glass ceiling to the blue depth beyond and wondered where his level-headed friend had gone. If he wanted histrionics, he'd hang with Kate. Or Joel. "Come on, you're stretching things."

"But I am frightened. My dreams—"

Before she could work herself up again, Ben snatched his lunch tray and stood. "I gotta go. Lecture at one." He squeezed her shoulder. "Look, everything's fine. I'm fine. Just trying to adjust to this hellish rotation." He snorted a laugh. "Maybe it's me who should be serving your Lwa. I could use all the help I can get." He gave her shoulder another squeeze, grabbed the tablet kokoye, and walked away.

With just a few minutes to spare before his one o'clock lecture on inflammatory bowel disease, Ben crossed from the main hospital to the Talcott Center via a second-floor walkway. Through its plexiglass windows, he surveyed the congested avenue below. Honking cars, bicyclists, and pedestrians competed for space on the narrow, downtown street. He tried to focus on the readings he'd done for the lecture, but his thoughts cycled back to Laurette and her words: *Something evil. There is blood and there is evil.*

A chill fluttered through him, the air-conditioned hallway of the Talcott Center too frigid for his short-sleeve shirt.

There are some things you do not see. Things you refuse to see.

He had to get her out of his head. In all the time he'd known Laurette, she'd hardly mentioned Vodou once.

The hamburger rumbled like an earthquake in his belly, and his forehead ached. He remembered his out-of-body experience in the catacombs, his cruelty to his friend, his inexplicable need to touch that bone.

Ridiculous, he told himself. It was just a stress reaction from the claustrophobia.

He rolled his neck and cracked his knuckles, then shifted the backpack to the other shoulder and strode across Labor & Delivery's waiting room—or L&D as it was called. The unit's décor was a far cry from the stark whiteness of the main hospital. Soft carpeting absorbed his steps, and powder-blue walls invited his gaze to framed photographs of smiling babies in a rainbow of ethnicities.

When he reached the stairwell door to descend to the street level and cross over to the med school building, a tiny voice howled behind him. He glanced over his shoulder to see a fallen toddler being scooped up by his mother. Then he did a double take.

A woman in a maternity sundress had just entered the unit's door next to the reception desk. Though Ben had only seen her from behind, her short, chestnut hair and wedge heels triggered recognition.

Sophia.

He stared at her empty wake. Couldn't be. He shook his head and entered the stairwell. Though he doubted it was her, thoughts of the dark-haired beauty he'd met eight months ago warmed his chill.

Sophia Diaz. First encountered during Intro to Clinical Medicine in his second year. As a cancer patient in remission, she had agreed to let her oncologist—Ben's preceptor for the course—use her office visit as a teaching opportunity for the students. A few weeks later, Ben had spotted her at a pub. After a few beers, ethics took a backseat to lust.

Maybe he needed to read Dr. Smith's ethics articles after all.

Med student and cancer patient had ended up back at her place. Sophia swore she'd never had sex with a stranger before, and judging by the giant crucifix on her bedroom wall and the picture of Jesus on her nightstand, Ben believed her. But she said she was celebrating life that night, and "when life brings you a good-looking guy and an opportunity, you seize it."

Ben had seized it all right. Twice that night and once in the morning. Though he was with Melissa at the time, she and Ben had never been exclusive. Still, the athletic blonde had surfaced in his mind, so when Sophia didn't offer her number the next day (an omission that stung, frankly), he hadn't offered his either.

It was a memorable one-night stand, that was all. One night of celebration for Sophia and her remission. One night of questionable, though not entirely atypical, behavior for Ben.

No harm, no foul.

4

Willy's Chocolate Chalet was located in South Philly on the south side of South Street, but standing on the sidewalk that night, Ben saw shards of glass from the store's front window scattered in all four directions.

Like the three-story buildings on either side, white-wood paneling fronted the store's ground floor exterior. Orange-red brick made up the upper two levels, which housed a photography studio and an accounting office. Green shutters framed all but the street-level window, its pane shattered at the exact spot where a giant chocolate truffle once lay. Along with the missing truffle, most of the store's calligraphy letters were gone too. Only *halet* remained.

Inside stood the central counter, its glass intact and its chocolaty concoctions unscathed. Behind that was Willy's shiny equipment, from tempering and panning machines to enrobers and cutters, where melting, churning, coating, and clumping produced an endless array of fragrant, mouth-watering treats.

Willy used to like having customers see him at work behind the counter. "Makes the chocolates taste sweeter to see the care that goes into them." But ever since Max died, Ben's father seemed more interested in getting the job done than in delighting his patrons. As soon as he could, he'd shuffle home to his townhouse five blocks away, leaving his assistant manager to keep the store running until close. Other times he'd walk for hours or hide away in a darkened movie theater.

Sweat trickled down Ben's forehead, and his hair matted against his scalp. Though the sun had begun its salmon-pink descent, the thick heat stuck around and clung to him like a leather cloak. He'd stopped by his apartment to grab his tools and change into jeans and a T-shirt, but he was wishing he'd donned shorts instead.

After his apartment he'd gone to the hardware store, where, based on the window measurements Willy had provided earlier, Ben had cut out two pieces of plywood and charged them to his already bloated credit card. The double reinforcement would offer more security until the window-repair guys could come on Monday.

With pecs and biceps flexing, Ben hoisted the outside piece of plywood and leaned it against the store window next to a short ladder he'd retrieved from the storage room. With the back of his hand, he mopped off another round of sweat from his brow. "Hey, Dad, I'm ready for you."

Within moments his father appeared in the doorway.

Shorter than Ben but with an equally thick head of dark hair, albeit graying around the temples, their relation was obvious. Same caterpillar eyebrows, strong jaw, full lips. Only their noses differed. "Thank God you never got my honker," his father liked to say.

Willy grabbed one end of the smooth plywood. Though his waist had thickened over the years, he hadn't lost his upper body strength. "How'd you get these over here? No way they fit in your Mustang."

"Jimmy was getting off shift. Drove them over in his truck."

"Still straddling two worlds, huh? As comfortable in a hardware store as a hospital."

Ben grabbed the other end of the plywood. "Maybe I should stick with hardware."

The two men hefted the piece over the outside window. "Everything going okay in school?"

"Yeah, no worries."

"You know, son, if you need a loan. For school or to fix up your place, I can—"

"Thanks, I'm good." Truth be told, Max would groan from his grave if he knew Ben still lived in Mrs. Sinclair's nightmare of a basement. Several times Max had offered to help Ben decorate the place "so a person's first instinct isn't to vomit." But Ben had always refused both of his fathers' money. During bad years their chocolate shop barely stayed afloat. Ben wasn't about to squander any extra dollars they made during the good ones. "What about you? You doing okay?"

"Oh, fine, fine."

Masters of communication they were not.

Ben maintained his grip on the sheet of plywood with one hand and reached for his drill from his tool belt with the other. "Think you can support this in place while I drill in the screws?"

Willy shifted position and weighted his upper body against the center of the thick panel. "You still seeing that cute blond gal?"

The power drill whirred to life, saving Ben from an answer. He drilled a screw through the plywood and into the lower left window frame. He completed the same action on the right, balancing precision with speed so he could free his father from the panel's weight. Swinging out his right leg, he pulled the ladder closer with his foot, then climbed it and drilled screws into the upper corners as well. The work relaxed him, the drill as comfortable in his hands as a double boiler was in his father's.

Ben stepped off the ladder. "You can let go now. Those four will hold while I add a few more. Then we'll do the same on the inside."

"You were always good with your hands." Willy watched Ben drill. "Your high school trainer was smart to steer you to bone surgery. Saw how smart you were. Now you can drill and hammer on people." A rare smile of late softened Willy's face. He puffed out his chest. "My son. The doctor."

"Well, I'm not there yet. Have to survive internal medicine first." Ben descended the ladder and leaned against the plywood, a bubble of acid rising at the thought of his academic workload. He pushed away from the temporary window. "Let's go inside and attach the other sheet."

With the scent of freshly made fudge perfuming the air, they secured the inside piece of plywood. The fudge was maple walnut, Ben's favorite. Normally he couldn't resist its salty richness, but thoughts of vandalism, Laurette's weird dreams, and an ethics presentation he hadn't yet started trampled his appetite. Thanks to the air conditioner, his body heat lessened, but his damp shirt still clung to his chest, and his palm was so moist the drill grip ripped off his bandage.

"Crap."

"You hurt yourself?" Willy glanced up at Ben on the ladder and eyed the sore on Ben's hand.

"It's nothing." Ben pressed the bandage back in place, hoping it would hold.

Finally, with the last screw in place, he once again descended the ladder onto the tiled floor, and the two men admired their work.

"That'll hold you over 'til Monday. Houdini himself couldn't get through this. Is your alarm system up and running?"

Willy nodded. "Not like it did any good. The guy was in and out before the police got here."

Ben leaned against a glass counter full of colorful candies and surveyed the room and its shelves of knickknacks. Mugs, glass figurines, humorous plaques, even water and food bowls for pets. Nothing seemed to be missing or broken, and Willy had straightened and cleaned everything by the time Ben had arrived. "You sure they didn't take anything?"

"Like I said, the register has scratch marks near the drawer, like someone tried to pry it open. 'Course it was empty, seeing as how I hadn't opened the store yet. They tossed some stuff on the floor, broke a few chocolate pizzas, even messed with my desk in the back room, but I can't see that anything was taken."

"That doesn't make sense." Cold air from the overhead vent ruffled Ben's hair and goosebumped his flesh. "They didn't try your office safe?"

"Not that I can tell. The painting hiding it didn't look touched."

Ben glanced around the shop one more time. He dug in his pocket for his keys. "Well, I better take off. Lots to do."

"Sure, sure." Willy stroked his five-o'clock shadow. "Say, I meant to tell you, your moth—um, Harmony—phoned me. She says you haven't been returning her calls."

"Dad, don't start."

"I'm not starting anything, but she'll be coming to town soon. She wants to see you."

"And as always, I'm supposed to drop everything." Ben gathered his tools and stuffed his leather belt with more force than was necessary.

"She cares, Benny. She always has. It's just that life's been a struggle for her."

Ben headed to the door. "Call me if you have any trouble with the window." Before he walked out, he swallowed his irritation and turned back to his father. "Sorry I've been a lousy son lately. Just really busy."

Willy blinked. "Aw, you couldn't be a lousy son if you tried."

They gave each other awkward nods, and Ben stepped out into the darkening evening. On the sidewalk, he almost collided with a man wandering by. Ben excused himself and tried to pass, but the guy planted himself in front of Ben.

"It is no problem, sir." The stranger's accent was similar to Laurette's, and the fact he was Haitian, or at least sounded so, made Ben take a closer look. Dreadlocks, narrow eyes, well-muscled though shorter than Ben. An herbal scent wafted from his black tunic and jeans.

The man knocked on the plywood. "You have a break-in?"

"Yes." Caution in Ben's voice.

"The world is a dangerous place, no? Everyone wanting something." Like the flick of a match, his face broke into a smile. Then he turned and left.

Ben frowned. Willy materialized behind him.

"You know that guy?" Ben asked.

His father peered down the sidewalk at the departing figure. "Hmm, looks like the man who helped me carry deliveries into my office a few days ago. I recognize the weird shirt and accent. Nice guy. In fact, he asked about you."

"Me?" Ben couldn't have been more surprised if Willy had just told him he'd coated an elephant in chocolate.

"Saw your college graduation picture in my office. I told him you were going to be a doctor."

Ben flipped the Mustang's keys in his hand. "You're too trusting, Dad."

"And you're not trusting enough."

His father didn't say anything else, but he didn't have to. "Fine. If Harmony calls again, I'll answer." Ben raised a hand to hold off his dad's forthcoming gratitude. "If I can."

After a parting nod to his father, Ben headed down the sidewalk toward his car. He could still see the man with the dreadlocks ahead, turning to cross Lombard Street. A sense of unease tingled Ben's spine. He should've warned his dad to be careful. Something about that stranger seemed off.

5

At the conclusion of formal rounds almost one week later, Dr. Smith dismissed the residents to chart notes and write orders. Before Ben could join them, she ordered him and the two other third-year medical students to follow her. Like an empress dressed in pink Chanel with matching pumps, the internist led Ben, Melissa, and Farid through a perfumed wake to room W676 at the far end of the ward. Beyond the glass in the closed door, a woman lay asleep, pale arms resting on top of the blanket, an intravenous line coiling around her left hand and a pulse oximeter tethering the right.

Even without entering the room, recognition slapped Ben like a wet towel. His eyes widened and his lips parted into a surprised, "Oh."

"Our newest admission," Dr. Smith said, twirling the Rolex on her wrist. "An interesting case that came up from the ED during rounds, so no one from the team has seen her yet. Farid, look up her name on your tablet."

But Ben already knew her name.

Kate.

Kate "The Bike Crusher" Naughton.

He almost said it out loud but instead stood mute and dumbfounded while Farid pulled up the patient's file.

How was this the same woman Ben had fended off in his basement apartment a mere six days ago? The one who'd set him back fifty bucks for a new tire and chain, plus an hour of banging out kinks and straightening handlebars?

Her body looked lifeless in the hospital bed, honey-wheat hair flattened against the pillow and face ashen in the morning sunshine. Gone were the eye shadow, mascara, and blush. In their place, a sheen of sweat and sunken orbits. Though Ben could hear nothing through the closed door, her breathing seemed labored, neck muscles straining with each breath. Even in sleep, her mouth bore an uncomfortable frown.

"I'd like to take this patient," he blurted, realizing too late he'd interrupted Dr. Smith.

"Maybe you'll allow me to finish speaking before making your demands?"

Ben attempted an apology, but having a woman he'd slept with a few feet away, one who resembled a corpse, made concentration difficult.

"As I was saying," Dr. Smith continued, her focus back on the others, "four days ago, Ms. Naughton developed a headache and fatigue. By Monday she was experiencing weakness, fever, arthralgia, and muscle aches. She thought it was the flu, but by Tuesday she developed vomiting and diarrhea with severe abdominal pain, and early this morning she noted blood in her vomitus and stools. She took a cab to the emergency department, where she then developed double vision. We're still waiting on her lab results."

Ben thought back to the previous Thursday. Was Kate contagious when he saw her? Would he catch it? Not likely, given her symptoms started three days later. But what about his landlady, Kate's mother? He'd hate to see Mrs. Sinclair get that sick.

Ben tuned back in. Dr. Smith had just asked Melissa for a differential diagnosis for Kate's symptoms. His ex-girlfriend's expression suggested she wasn't sure.

"*Salmonella, Shigella, E. Coli* ..." Melissa's voice wavered, and she looked to her colleagues for help.

"*Campylobacter?*" Farid said, more question than statement.

"Of course." Dr. Smith tucked her manicured hands into her lab coat pockets. "An infectious disease is most likely, particularly with an enteric organism like the ones you mentioned, but we must also think outside the box. Mr. Oris? Suggestions?"

Ben's thoughts raced. An idea came to mind, and although he was no more confident than Farid had been, he answered as though he was. He'd learned long ago that supervisors, whether they were construction bosses or attending physicians, hated wimpy responses.

"Ebola," he said. A nurse passing Kate's room smirked, and somewhere behind him a male voice snickered. He ignored the mocking and pushed on. "It's true, we haven't seen Ebola in the U.S. for a while, but we now know it can come here."

Dr. Smith crossed her arms in front of her. Instead of berating him like he'd feared, she nodded. "Yes, unlikely, but we need to file the possibility in our minds and find out if she's traveled recently, especially given her symptoms. She's under contact and droplet precautions for now. In the meantime, assuming a more obvious infection, what should we treat her with?"

Another nurse with a tray of meds passed by, her shoulder brushing Ben's. He felt on fire beneath the white coat, especially with Dr. Smith's laser-sharp attention on him.

Think, he told himself. Gram-negative bacteria. "A third-generation cephalosporin while we're waiting on cultures." Again, he spoke with more confidence than he felt.

Dr. Smith's chin rose higher. "Besides stool and blood cultures—and though overkill, an Ebola test—what else should we check for?"

"*Clostridium difficile.* If she's been on recent antibiotics, she's at risk for it. Even if she hasn't been, she could still get it."

"Why is that?"

"Because it's becoming more common in the general population, not just in hospitalized patients."

"And what would we treat *C. diff* with?"

"Vancomycin."

"What else should we give her besides meds? Probably the most important thing of all."

"IV fluids." Ben was still on fire, but this time in a good way. With each serve the attending lobbed, he cleared the net with a correct response.

Dr. Smith paused, uncrossed her arms, twirled her watch. Melissa and Farid stood silent by Ben's side. "Since you seem to be on a streak, Benjamin, tell me what might the double vision imply?"

A moment's hesitation. "Um … that she could have central nervous system involvement, like meningitis or encephalitis. *Salmonella* can cause meningitis." He exhaled through parted lips and silently thanked Jamal for the article on enteric infections. It was one of the many papers the senior resident had given them at the onset of the rotation. Judging by Melissa's and Farid's blank stares, they hadn't yet read it. Not that Ben was trying to show them up. Far from it. He was merely trying to survive the clerkship.

After a few seconds, as if tapped of further questions, Dr. Smith nodded. She turned to Melissa. "I want you to take Ms. Naughton as a patient. She'll be a great teaching case. Maybe the best one this month."

Ben's cheeks flushed. He'd answered every one of Smith's questions correctly, and yet she was giving Melissa the patient? His fingers found the purplish wound on his right palm and dug. Since the lesion hadn't bled in days, a bandage was no longer necessary.

Despite his better judgment, he spoke up. "Could I follow the patient instead?" He was about to add he knew Kate but figured that would hinder his cause.

"No, Melissa will."

Ben's nails drilled deeper into his palms. When Dr. Smith reached for a gown and mask, Melissa doing the same, words tumbled out before he could stop them. "Technically it's my turn for a new patient. Isn't that how we do things? By rotation?"

Silence swallowed the room. Melissa paused, one arm in the yellow gown, the other suspended in front of her. A nervous laugh escaped her glossy lips. "It's okay. Ben can have her if he wants."

Dr. Smith grabbed a mask and thrust it at Melissa. "No, it is not okay. I will assign the patients how I see fit."

Ben's jaw clamped shut.

Don't do it. Don't do it.

He did it. "With all due respect, Jamal assigns the patients. That's what it says in our clerkship syllabus."

Upon hearing his name, Ben saw the senior resident look up from his huddle with an intern a few patient rooms down. His expression suggested Ben close his trap, and judging by Dr. Smith's death grip on her gown and mask, Ben decided that was a good idea. As they so often did, Max's words echoed in his brain: "You know, Ben, for a guy who doesn't talk much, you really need to learn when to shut up."

Before Ben could apologize, his tight-lipped attending stepped closer, so close he could smell the mint on her breath. Her brown-eyed gaze burned up at him. "Let's get something straight. You're not building a backyard deck here. You're not laying bricks, or shingling a roof, or cleaning out gutters. You're taking care of people's lives. So I suggest you learn to follow orders or else march your steel-toed boots right out of this hospital."

In the stillness Ben heard someone pour tap water from the supply room behind the front counter. In the opposite direction, an IV pump alarmed, signaling an empty fluid bag. Everywhere else was a tomb.

Finally, he averted his gaze. Dr. Smith pivoted toward Kate's room and indicated with an arm flap that Melissa resume gowning, masking, and gloving. She gave Ben no further mind.

Flushed from humiliation, he turned and walked away. She might as well have just called him white trash and been done with it.

6

Taking the elevator meant more risk of running into Dr. Smith, but Ben was too worn out for stairs. Although he knew his attending would pop a blood vessel if she caught him in Kate's room, no way could he leave for the day without seeing his landlady's daughter. They shared a history, and he owed her that much.

He exited the sixth-floor elevator bank in front of the central windows and allowed himself a glance at the atrium below. Carefully tended trees and plants skirted the cafeteria tables, most of which were filled by a growing dinner crowd. From Ben's elevation, the diners looked like action figures. If he strained he could hear their muted conversations punctuated by an occasional laugh or cough. Luckily he couldn't smell their food, because despite his lagging appetite, the thought of pizza and pasta made his mouth water and his empty stomach howl in protest.

He pulled away and headed to 6 West, where the smell of patient dinner trays was less enticing. Outside Kate's room, the odor shifted to human waste.

She must've soiled herself again, he thought, his heart going out to her. He knew how much she would hate that. She cared so much about her physical appearance.

From what Melissa had told him earlier, Kate's vomiting and diarrhea had worsened, blood still coloring both. But his ex-girlfriend had also said the Ebola PCR came back negative. Though Ben was relieved Melissa was speaking to him again, her tone had been cool and professional, not the playful teasing she used to dole out.

Something else in Kate's lab tests had the ward team buzzing as well. A sky-high eosinophil count. Normally that type of white blood cell measured less than five hundred, or at least that's what Ben's lab app said, but Kate's level was over nine thousand. Ben knew allergic diseases or parasites could spike the blood's eosinophil count, but he didn't know what else did. He better find out. His patient or not, Dr. Smith would pummel him with questions.

He bit the inside of his cheek. Kate should have been his patient. A flake or not, he cared about the woman, and seeing her so frail in there made his breath catch.

After one more glance around the ward, making sure none of his team was there, Ben donned a mask and gown. The fabric was snug around his shoulders, and the mask smelled like manufactured fiber. Even though the Ebola test came back negative, the protective precautions hadn't yet been lifted. They still didn't know what they were dealing with.

Once inside Kate's room, Ben gagged. The smell of feces overpowered him, and he had to take tiny inhalations through his mouth before he could resume nose-breathing. Kate, having heard the door open, flopped her head to the side, face pasty, lips cracked, no recognition in her hollow eyes.

Ben stepped closer to the bed, his nostrils threatening to seal up. "Kate, it's Ben. Ben Oris."

At first the woman merely blinked, but after a few seconds, awareness surfaced and she managed a curl of a smile. "Hey handsome," she croaked. "I was wondering if I'd see you." She tried to scoot herself up but failed. She smoothed her hair instead, a feminine but pointless gesture that only deepened the ache in Ben's chest. "Shit, I look horrible. You shouldn't see me like this."

"Come on, you're as sexy as ever. How you feeling?"

"Like that bike of yours I crushed."

"Yeah, smooth driver you're not." That got him another tiny smile. "Sorry it took so long for me to get here. I wanted to come sooner, but another med student got assigned to you."

"You're sweet to come at all. My mom was here. They let her visit once the Ebola test was cleared." Kate's voice weakened with each word, but she managed to add, "And your mother called. She's stopping by tomorrow."

"Harmony? How'd she know you were here?" A bad taste in his mouth rivaled the fecal scent in the air.

"She called my mom, looking for you."

Super. Willy had said something about Harmony coming to Philadelphia, but with all Ben had going on, he'd forgotten. "You and Harmony friends. Now that's messed up."

"Remember when she stopped by your place and caught us screwing like rabbits?"

He blushed. He remembered.

Kate's expression sobered. "You were always nice to me, Ben. Listened to my rants. Gave me the time of day." Despite her dehydration, tears formed in her eyes. At least the medical staff were keeping up with her massive fluid losses so far. "Will you check in on my mom if I … well, if I …"

Ben shuffled closer, his body hot in the protective gown, his chin moist from breathing inside the mask. He grabbed her hand and felt it tremble in his own. "Hey, don't talk like that. We'll get you tuned up."

"They don't know what I have, and my vision's shot to hell."

"We'll figure it out."

She started to say something else, but her lips pursed and her eyes grew wide. She flapped her arm at the emesis basin lying on the bedside table, her IV tubing swinging wildly. Ben snatched the pink, kidney-shaped receptacle and raised it to her chin while gently pushing her torso forward so she wouldn't aspirate.

Blood-streaked vomit erupted from her mouth. Most of it landed in the basin, but a few drops spattered the bedspread. "Shh, it's okay." Ben rubbed her back as she continued to vomit. "We'll get you better." God, he hoped they'd get her better.

Thoughts of Max surfaced, his father weak and pale after failed rounds of chemotherapy. Ben focused and pushed them away.

After four rounds of retching, the last two yielding only a few squirts of pinkish secretions, Kate nodded and allowed Ben to ease her back against the pillows. With his free hand, he reached over and grabbed a fistful of tissues from the bedside table. He dabbed at her mouth and arms where vomitus had splashed.

"Jesus Christ, the last thing I want is sexy carpenter man seeing me like this."

Ben squeezed her hand, her flesh hot against his gloves. "Don't worry. You'll be batting those big greens in no time." He rose and crossed to the bathroom where he emptied the emesis basin into the toilet and rinsed it out in the sink, just as he'd done many times for Max.

He stepped out of the bathroom. "There. Good as—" His heart leaped to his throat.

Through the glass in the hospital door someone watched him. A petite woman in a pink Chanel suit. Raised eyebrows, pursed lips. Not particularly angry looking but not pleased either.

How long had Dr. Smith been there?

Before Ben could leave the room to explain, she turned and walked away.

Moments after Ben stuffed his white coat inside a locker in the med student lounge, his cell phone buzzed in his back pocket. It was already past seven, and he was eager to get on his bike and head home to study. He saw the caller was Willy.

"Hey, Dad, what's up?"

A week had passed since Ben fixed the store window. He'd meant to have dinner with his father but hadn't had time. Guilt walloped him, and he trudged to one of two leather couches beyond the bank of lockers and collapsed onto it. While his dad thanked him again for his help and told him about the new window now solidly in place, Ben studied the far wall of cubby-hole mailboxes, one for every student. Why, in the era of texts and emails, did they even bother?

"What I'm calling about is, I did find something missing from the store after all. And I'm kind of sick about it."

Ben sat up straight. "What is it?"

"The weirdest thing. You know that framed baby picture of you? The one with your bronze shoe on the marble base along with a lock of your hair?"

Ben smirked. "You mean the one your employees give me grief about?"

"It's gone. Someone took it."

"What do you mean, 'took' it? Who would take it?" Ben stood up and crossed to his mailbox. He pulled out a handful of fliers and memos—mostly reminders about lectures and social gatherings, the latter of which he ignored.

"I don't know, but I can't find it anywhere. They probably stole it during the break-in, but why? It's of no value to anyone but me." Ben heard a catch in his father's voice.

"Maybe you took it home and don't remember."

"No, I know it was here. Remember that guy outside the store last Thursday when you put up the plywood? The one I told you helped me carry boxes into my office a few days before the break-in?"

Ben's shoulders tensed. He remembered the strange man. "What about him?"

"He saw your college graduation picture on my shelf. I bragged to him about you becoming a doctor. And that picture was right next to the baby one. So I know it was there before the window was smashed, but it's not there now."

"You think the person who broke into the shop took it?" Ben tossed the fliers into the trash, his neck tight, his senses on high alert.

"Yes, and it breaks my heart. Why would somebody do that? Makes no sense."

Ben had no answer for his father, but he agreed. It made no sense at all.

7

Once they hit Walnut Street, Laurette slowed her pace to match Ben's, concern knitting her brows. "You are okay, yes? Am I going too fast for you?" The two were jogging along Rittenhouse Square, an enclosed park of nearly two city blocks.

"Don't flatter yourself." Ben upped his pace, ignoring the burn in his chest and the hitch in his side. His sneakers thumped the sidewalk around the park's perimeter. Though Laurette was in great shape, Ben could easily surpass her on their twice-weekly runs. Until today.

He was off his game. His endurance was crappy, his fatigue and headaches persistent. Lack of sleep and too much work, he supposed. The heat didn't help either, but he'd jogged in worse.

But despite his malaise, he'd looked forward to the evening run. He wanted to tell Laurette about Kate. Maybe she could consult her adviser. See if the epidemiologist had any insight as to what was going on with his landlady's daughter.

Together they rounded the northwest corner of the park. Tourists filed in and out of the upscale hotel across the street, some unfolding paper maps, others taking a more twenty-first century approach and looking at their phones. When Ben gawked at a curvy woman in a halter top in front of the hotel's shrubbery garden, he lost his footing and stumbled into the park's iron fence. Metal scratched his skin and dripping sweat burned his eyes. He was almost too exhausted to be embarrassed.

"Let's take a break," Laurette said, slowing even more.

"I'm fine." Ben's tone was sharper than intended, but he matched her slowed pace anyway, relieved she didn't rib him about it. Instead she teased him about needing to save face in front of the pretty blonde.

He wheezed out a laugh. "Yeah, that wasn't too smooth, was it?"

"Like a goat in high heels."

He smiled, and they jogged in silence for a few minutes. When he caught his breath again, he said, "You remember Kate Naughton?"

"Your evil landlady's daughter?"

"Mrs. Sinclair's not so bad. She just doesn't like me bringing women into her house."

"Especially black ones."

A glance at Laurette as they rounded the southwest corner reassured Ben she was teasing. "Guess she's not as progressive as her free-spirited daughter. But she's really sick."

"Your landlady?" Surprise in Laurette's voice.

"Her daughter, Kate."

"What is wrong with her?"

"What isn't?" Ben relayed Kate's symptoms, his voice breathless and choppy despite his attempts to steady it. "Antibiotics aren't helping, and so far her stool, blood, and spinal fluid cultures are negative. She's still vomiting and crapping blood, and today she's confused and lethargic."

"That is horrible."

"The weird thing is, her eosinophil count is really high. Everyone's stumped. I was hoping you could run it by Dr. Khalid. See if she has any other ideas. A rare zebra diagnosis we haven't thought of."

"*Bien sûr.*"

Having heard the phrase before, Ben knew it meant *of course*. Not only did Laurette make him tasty tablet kokoye, she was schooling him in both French and Haitian Creole. He thanked her, and then, hoping she wouldn't notice, slowed their pace even more. When they rounded onto South 18th Street, he had enough wind to speak again. "It's weird to think she could be so sick. She looked perfectly normal when I saw her a week ago. In fact, she was all over me."

His friend clutched his arm, bringing their jog to a halt and causing Ben to nearly trip again. A scowling jogger swerved onto the curb to avoid crashing into them.

"What's wrong? You look like me after a round with Dr. Smith."

His humor did little to subdue her. Her dark eyes had become two black pools of panic. Though alarmed, Ben was grateful for the respite. So were his heaving lungs. He dragged his friend to the nearby park entrance and leaned against a concrete pedestal next to a flowering shrub. She seemed hardly aware they'd moved.

"What's wrong? You're creeping me out."

When she spoke, her tone was sinister. "You saw Kate before she fell ill?"

"Yeah, so?"

"And she came to the hospital less than a week later?" Laurette's hands flexed and unflexed by her sides. She reached for her amulet strap and pulled the bronze locket out of her tank top. Her fingers grazed the embossed star, its central emerald catching the setting sun and momentarily blinding him.

Seeing Laurette's growing fear made Ben's scalp prickle, as if someone had doused his head with ice water. "What are you saying?" But he was pretty sure he knew what she was saying.

"*Mon Dieu. Il est vrai.*" Laurette snatched Ben's right hand and rotated it upward, ignoring his request for translation. "It is true. It's happening."

"What's happening?" Ben tried but failed to retrieve his palm from her tight grip. Passersby started to stare.

Laurette studied the purplish papule on his hand, oblivious to his annoyance. No bigger than a baby pea, and yet, by the look on her face, one would think it was the size of a tennis ball. She didn't touch the area, just gripped around it, forcing his palm into hyperextension, so much so his hand muscles cramped in protest.

"I know, I know, I should get it checked out. But who has time for that?"

"My visions." She paused, and when she saw his expression, said, "No, do not roll your eyes at me, for they are visions, not just dreams. I see you in them. I see blood. Yours and the blood of others. Blood of people you have hurt."

"Hurt?"

"*Oui.* Not on purpose, but somehow you have hurt them."

Ben protested, but she cut him off.

"I did not believe at first either. It sounds *fou*, you know? But now a woman you touched is near death. I cannot ignore the visions any longer."

An ache blossomed between Ben's temples. "Visions. Right. Here, drink some water. You're clearly dehydrated and delusional."

With the hand she wasn't gripping like a rock climber, he pulled a water bottle from the running belt around her waist and tugged her across the grass to the closest bench. Together they sank to the hot seat. When Laurette started to speak, he thrust the bottle her way and ordered her to drink. She finally let go of his hand and complied. He grabbed his own water and did the same. Sweat dripped from their noses onto the plastic containers, though while his could fill a bucket, hers would barely top off a thimble.

When they finished, her focus on him was as intense as before. "I have tried to keep these visions from you—you are so set in your beliefs—but you must hear me now."

"I don't—"

"I spoke to Guy. And to my Auntie Marie."

"Oh, come on."

"I told them ever since we entered the catacombs, something was not right. Something dark and evil wants you."

Ben scoffed and looked away. A mother walked by, her toddler scurrying two feet ahead on a wrist leash, a cinnamon churro in his fist.

Laurette carried on. "You were cut by that bone, and nothing has been okay since." Ben stood, but she pulled him back down. "Please, you must listen. Do you think I like saying these words? Do you not know how foolish I feel? It is my family who thinks these thoughts, not me. My brother, the priest in Haiti. My mother who works by his side. My other brother in West Africa. My sister the teacher. Though many in Haiti have given up Vodou and converted to Christianity, my family has not. Even the man I was to marry practiced Vodou." Laurette blinked as if sand were in her eyes. Ben knew her fiancé had died in the 2010 earthquake, but she rarely talked about him. Once she'd composed herself, she continued. "Only my father and I see the practice as folklore, but that does not mean we do not believe *others* believe. And that belief is a powerful thing."

"So you're saying I made Kate sick? Because of some bone in the catacombs?" Ben tried to laugh, but it didn't come. Only nausea. And the pounding headache. His own recent dark dreams surfaced, but he buried the images, refusing to play the ridiculous game.

"I don't know exactly, but my brother has told me about curses, curses that sit idle for a long time, only to come alive years later."

Ben jumped to his feet. A pigeon quickly claimed the spot he'd abandoned. "Oh for God's sake. This is stupid. I have too much to do to sit and listen to this."

She grabbed his arm. "I believe you sense the darkness, but your—what is the word? Pragmatism? Yes, your pragmatism does not allow you to admit it. I see you are not feeling well. I see the shadows under your eyes. I see your fatigue, your short temper. This is not the Ben I know."

"Well, Jesus, look at the hours I'm keeping."

"No, it is more than that."

"Then how come no one else is sick? I've been around plenty of people."

"I don't know, but Auntie Marie told me about a *mambo*, Mambo Tina, a priestess who might be able to help us see more. The mambo's assistant is a clerk in Uncle Trey's pharmacy. We can contact her through him."

Though Ben wanted to bolt, his knees trembled and betrayed him. He plopped back down on the bench. The pigeon flitted away. "You're saying there's voodoo in Philadelphia?"

"Not voodoo. *Vodou*."

"Whatever."

"There are many Haitians here. Believers do not stop believing just because they have left their homeland. And we need their help."

Despite his best effort Ben's limbs continued to quake, but whether from anger or exhaustion—or yes, even fear—he wasn't sure. He needed to get home. "Listen. I'm fine. Everything's fine. Let's go get some pizza and call it a night."

Laurette reached up and grasped his face with both hands. "You must let me help you. You are in danger. There are others in my visions. A man. A dark man. Not only in skin but in spirit. Darkness all around him. And blood. And ..." Her voice trailed off, and her throat seemed to constrict.

"And what?" Despite the shade of the tree, Ben felt more overheated now than when he'd been jogging. And so weak and nauseated.

"Beneath all that blood in my visions, I see a ..." Her voice dropped to a whisper. "I see a baby."

"A baby," Ben said blankly.

That was it, he'd had enough. But when he tried to free himself from Laurette's grip and rise from the bench, he couldn't. Because something blipped in his brain, something that kept him rooted to the spot. A tiny nibble he couldn't grasp. A tiny speck of recognition floating around in his cerebral ether, its meaning evasive and vague, yet terrifying all the same.

But though his mind couldn't clinch it, his gut did, and before he could stop himself, he leaned over the side of the bench and retched. Not once, but twice. Park dwellers' stares burned into him while Laurette rubbed his back, just as he'd done for Kate a day earlier.

When he finally sat up, face flushed, pride wounded, he eyed his stomach contents on the grass. He pictured Kate in her hospital bed.

No way.

No way could Laurette's words be true.

8

"You gonna stick me or keep stroking my hand like a queer?"

Ben gave another tap to the web of veins on the back of the patient's gnarled hand. Embarrassed to have zoned out, he tried to focus on the man's IV placement, but the fog in his mind remained. Ever since the run with Laurette the night before, he'd been distracted and out of sorts.

A curse. How naive could she be?

"Jeez Louise, would you hurry it up? Why do I always get stuck with the trainees?"

Babies and blood.

Ridiculous.

Another thought nagged at Ben, a thought he now blamed for making him toss his cookies in the park. It was far more realistic than Laurette's macabre fantasies, but he hadn't dared dwell on it.

It was only one night.

Max's exasperated sex talk echoed in Ben's head, a talk that had come with a box of condoms after Ben lost his virginity to a chocolate store employee at the age of fifteen. "It only takes one tiny sperm to seal the deal, for heaven's sake. If you can't keep your pants on, at least use one of these. Gorgeous Max is too young to be a grandpa."

Conjuring all his psychic might to push the intrusive thoughts away, Ben glanced up at the surly patient. The man needed an IV for his acute diverticulitis. Any minute the nurse would pop in with his med bags. "We'll use this one." Ben tapped the least torturous vein he could find.

The patient grunted in response.

Moisture collected inside Ben's gloves. His hands itched, and the papule on his right palm pressed against the snug covering.

That woman only looked like Sophia. No way it could be her.

He shifted his position on the rolling stool, cracked his neck, and swabbed the man's skin with an alcohol wipe, its gauze cool on his gloved fingers and its fumes tickling his nose. He grabbed the IV catheter. "You ready?" Without giving time for an answer, Ben squeezed the guy's hand so firmly his wrinkled eyes widened in surprise. "And don't use the word *queer* around me again."

Once the patient's surprise faded, he mumbled something that sounded like *homo*, but though Ben's upper lip twitched, he said nothing more. Growing up with gay fathers had pelted him with a steady stream of anti-gay rhetoric, and he'd long since learned once an asshole, always an asshole.

"You done many of these things be—?"

Ben punctured the skin with the needle and deftly slid the twenty-gauge catheter into the vein.

No, he hadn't done many IVs before, but it had taken only a few tries before he'd mastered the procedure. To Ben, the skill came easily. He'd performed carpentry tasks that required more precision than sliding a needle into a vein.

Not that it mattered. Dr. Smith would ignore his prowess like she ignored everything else he did right. But Jamal, the senior resident, hadn't ignored it. He'd taken to calling Ben the IV King, and it wasn't long before Ben's vein-blowing classmates were seeking his help, too intimidated to ask the nurses.

A baby. One night.

The old guy watched Ben tape the IV in place.

Just go to Labor & Delivery and find out. Put the stupid notion to rest once and for all.

Ben flushed the IV to confirm good placement. The saline flowed easily. He scooped up the paper trash generated by the procedure and placed the needle in the sharps container. A glance at the clock above the bed told him he had thirty minutes before radiology rounds at three. Plenty of time to stop by L&D.

"Well, look at that," the patient said. "Mr. Short Coat got the IV in on his first try. Sometimes surprises happen when you least expect them."

Ben ripped off his gloves and exited the room. As he headed to the Talcott Center where Labor & Delivery was housed, he prayed the man was wrong. A surprise from a pregnant woman was the last thing Ben needed.

Ten minutes later in the busy L&D unit of the Talcott Center, Ben tried to waltz up to the ward station as if he belonged. Nurses hustled back and forth between rooms, med students and residents tapped at computers behind the counter, and excited fathers scurried out of delivery rooms to follow freshly birthed babies to the newborn nursery. Amid the chaos, Ben felt as out of place as an atheist at a tent revival, but other than a bespectacled ward clerk, no one questioned his presence.

"Can I help you?" she asked.

"I'm just here for a consult." The lie chafed his tongue.

She waved to the bank of occupied computers. "Join the club."

Ben scanned the U-shaped desk. The fact he'd be violating patient privacy laws if he pulled up Sophia's chart made his stomach flip, but he had to find out. Unfortunately, every terminal was in use. Just as he was about to give up, a stocky fourth-year med student Ben vaguely recognized shoved away from a monitor and hurried down the hall to an attending who'd called him over.

Before Ben could chicken out, he grabbed the vacated chair and plopped down, the seat warm beneath his gray chinos.

He studied the screen. The departing student had forgotten to log out. Ben considered doing it for him but then changed his mind. Electronic medical records were monitored, and if Ben signed in and accessed L&D charts, he'd risk detection. His rotation was internal medicine, not OB. On the other hand, if the fourth-year student, whose name on the screen read Pete Sampson, was currently rotating through L&D, he'd be expected to look through charts.

After a furtive glance around the unit, Ben inhaled and clicked open the patient census, the computer interface no different from internal medicine's. He scanned the list of admissions.

His stomach lurched. Sophia Diaz. Room 216. The woman he'd slept with several months before.

His palm hovered over the mouse. He didn't know whether to click or run. Did he really want to know the truth?

Behind him, the pneumatic tube system spat out a pharmacy delivery with a sonic *ffffwwwit*. To the left someone shouted a stat order for a glucose level.

With acid burning his throat, he replayed the night in question.

Saturday, November 22nd. He remembered the date because he'd just finished a block of exams the day before. Exhausted yet wired, he was picking up takeout at a pub not far from his apartment. While he sipped a beer and waited for his food, he spotted Sophia, a patient he recognized from his Intro to Clinical Medicine class. In remission and sporting a new crop of dark hair, its stark shortness in no way diminishing her almond eyes and full lips, she'd played into Ben's hands as much as he'd played into hers. It wasn't long before they tore up her quilt-covered bed, where neither hanging crucifix nor framed Jesus could dampen their enthusiasm.

Ben leaned back in the L&D chair, its wheels squeaking. He'd used a condom. He always did. From his grave, Max was probably fist pumping the air in victory. But a spark of memory kindled Ben's anxiety: a torn condom on the third go-around the following morning. He'd felt the tear, had even seen it, but he'd rationalized it away. Figured he'd torn it while removing it. Besides, he reassured himself now, Sophia had been on chemo. Her chances of fertility were low.

But staring at the undulating letters of her name on the L&D computer screen, he knew he was selling himself a load of crap.

He clicked open her chart. The moment he did, Pete Sampson returned. "Hey, I was using that terminal."

"Sorry. Find another one." Ben sensed Pete's ire behind him and imagined the guy's face flushing a port-wine hue. But bulk didn't scare Ben. Over the years, he'd landed as many punches as he'd taken.

The fourth-year student stomped away, leaving Ben free to scan Sophia's personal information, starting with her address. Juniper Street. Definitely the same Sophia Diaz. He grabbed a sticky pad an arm's reach away and jotted down her address and phone number. Then he slipped the note into his wallet. Scrolling down the screen he found the section for *Father's Information*. The words *none listed* filled the space.

Ben's gut expanded like a balloon. Desert sand coated his mouth.

With sweaty fingers, he gripped the mouse and clicked open Sophia's medical information, starting with her admission history and physical. Admitted eight days before for preeclampsia at thirty-four and a half weeks gestation. That must have been when Ben saw her entering the unit. She was discharged after twenty-four hours but then readmitted yesterday when a follow-up in her obstetrician's office showed a dangerously high blood pressure. The obstetrician started her on an antihypertensive along with magnesium, which Ben thought was to prevent seizures but couldn't remember for sure. He knew preeclampsia was bad news though. It could mean early delivery if not controlled.

He switched over to the daily progress notes. Sophia had now reached over thirty-five and a half weeks gestation, and since her blood pressure was stable, the doctors were continuing to monitor her. They wanted to get the baby to thirty-seven weeks before delivery if possible. That would avoid most perinatal complications. But according to the record, her actual due date wasn't until August fifteenth.

A cramp in Ben's neck forced him upright, and he rotated his shoulders to release it. His gut balloon was now a hot-air balloon. One terminal over a sleepy resident typed a patient note. "Hey, do you have one of those birth wheels?" Ben asked her.

"Be a lot easier to google a pregnancy-date calculator." The droopy resident yawned, but when she looked up and saw Ben in more detail, her posture straightened, and her face blossomed.

Ignoring her flirty smile, Ben pulled out his phone. With shaky hands that couldn't be trusted, he googled a pregnancy calculator. There were two choices for calculating due dates: *Date I Conceived* and *Date of Last Menstrual Period*. Not knowing the latter, he plugged in November 22nd for *Date I Conceived*, which was the night they had sex.

A due date of Saturday, August 15th spit out.

The gastric hot air balloon burst.

Fuck.

The only way the numbers could come out that perfectly was if Sophia, too, knew the conception date. And unless she was a get-around-town kind of gal, which he doubted given the religious symbols plastering her bedroom, Mr. Benjamin Oris was the father.

His windpipe narrowed, and the room spun around him, its occupants blurring. Laurette's words flashed in his mind, the ones she'd spoken in the park right before he'd puked: *Beneath all that blood in my visions, I see a baby.*

His sweaty hands fell from the keyboard. He had to get out. He had to breathe.

He reached out to log off Pete Sampson, but in doing so, his right hand snagged a metal clipboard next to the monitor. The papule on his palm scraped open, and a drop of blood beaded its surface. He grabbed a tissue to stanch the bleeding and stumbled away from the counter, the flirty resident now gone.

This can't be happening. I can't be a father. Not now.

"You okay?"

Ben turned toward the voice. A nurse stood in front of the printer near the workstation exit. Her youthful face bore a combination of concern and hurriedness, and a name tag on her flowery scrub top read *Tanisha, RN.*

"Do you need help with something?"

Ben found his balance and shook his head. "No, sorry, I'm good, but do you happen to know who's taking care of Sophia Diaz?"

Tanisha studied his short white coat. "I am. Why? You the student assigned to her?"

"She's a … she's a friend of mine." It was the best response Ben could muster. He backed up, grabbed another sticky note from the pad he'd used earlier, and jotted down his cell phone number. "Would you call me if anything comes up with her? You know, early delivery, any problems, that sort of thing?"

"'Cause I've got so much free time on my hands?" But she took the sticky note, and her expression softened. "Yeah, I will. That girl needs a friend. Poor thing's on her own. Family's strict Catholic, I guess. Wrote her off when they found out she was pregnant." The young nurse clapped a hand over her mouth. "Oh, shit. Did I just violate privacy laws?"

Not nearly as bad as I did, Ben thought, his heart skipping a beat. "Don't worry. It's our secret." He thanked her and headed toward room 216 on legs that wanted to go anywhere else but there.

He slowed to a stop.

I could just walk away. Sophia would never know. I could head straight to radiology rounds where I belong.

This time it was Willy's words that echoed in Ben's brain. "Always be the man who sleeps easy at night, Benny Boy. Do the right thing."

Exhaling pent-up breath, Ben marched toward room 216. The door was slightly ajar. A hospital phone flanked one side of its frame, a photograph of a smiling baby the other.

But what about med school?

Images of a crying infant, unread papers, and a crossed-arm Dr. Smith swirled through his head, followed by getting tossed out of med school and driving an excavator for the rest of his life.

Despite the grim pictures, he couldn't walk away.

Inhaling the last of his breath, he knocked lightly and pushed open the door.

There on the bed, dressed in yellow pajamas and writing in a baby book covered with storks, was an obviously pregnant Sophia. The same Sophia he'd slept with eight months ago but hadn't spoken to since. Her chestnut hair was longer—just past her chin in a layered style—and her heart-shaped face a little fuller, but the almond-shaped eyes and full lips were the same.

She glanced up when he entered. The smile she was wearing as she'd jotted in the book faded. Her expression shifted from surprise to fear to worry.

It was a look that no doubt matched his own.

9

"Relax, I don't expect anything from you."

Ben teetered on a narrow, convertible chair-bed in Sophia's hospital room, barely registering her words. His eyes fixated on the continuous strip of paper spitting out of the fetal heart rate machine next to the wall, its sensor strapped around Sophia's rounded belly.

Christ. He was going to be a father.

The *blip blip blip* of the monitor was as unsettling as the silence between them, and he finally tore his gaze away. He surveyed the room, its offerings a far cry from the extravagant delivery suite he'd seen at a private hospital when he and Melissa had visited a postpartum friend of hers. No wood paneling, mosaic tiling, or Ethan Allen furniture for Sophia. Instead she got stark walls, gray vinyl flooring, and a small bathroom in the corner, just like all the other rooms at Montgomery Hospital. The only difference from them was the bed. Sophia's would convert to a laboring one. Just drop the bottom, pull up the stirrups, and push.

Nausea washed over him. His face blanched.

"I mean it. I don't need anything from you. And yes, I'm one hundred percent sure it's yours," she added, even though he hadn't asked. No need to. Based on her dates, he was one hundred percent sure too.

She pressed her lips together and raised her chin. "I didn't tell you because you didn't ask for this. Just leave and pretend you never saw me."

Ben choked out a laugh. His jaw stiffened, and his mouth curved into a strained grin. "You think I could do that? Wow, guess I didn't make much of an impression on you."

Sophia looked out the window, beyond which a brick building stood. "I won't be responsible for ruining your life. I can do this myself."

"Yourself? Really? From what I heard, your family jumped ship." Ben glanced at the gold cross hanging around her neck.

Though Sophia continued to stare out the window, Ben saw her body tense.

"I'm sorry. I didn't mean to sound flippant." He massaged his forehead, the ache ever present. "I'm just … oh, man, I don't know what I am." He caught a glimpse of the clock on the wall above her head. "Other than late for radiology rounds, that is." Was that what his life would become? Missed lectures? Missed rounds? A moan he hadn't intended slipped out.

Sophia shifted her position and leaned toward him, the baby's heart-rate blips accelerating in response. With her pajama-clad arm, she grabbed his right hand. "Look, this is a lot to take in. We only had one night together." She blushed and lowered her eyelashes. "A pretty great night though."

Despite his whirling thoughts, Ben raised an eyebrow. "You'll get no argument from me there."

"But that's all it was. I don't expect you to pay for it the rest of your life. Literally or figuratively. I'm at peace with where I am." She released his hand and sank back against the propped-up pillows. She raised the gold cross to her lips and kissed it. "Given my cancer, my chemotherapy, my lack of frozen eggs thanks to my family's objections—it's 'unnatural' they said—I think this was meant to be." With tender strokes she caressed her belly above the monitor's sensor. "Meant to be for *me*, not you."

When Sophia raised her hand from her belly, Ben noted a streak of red on her yellow top. He glanced at his palm and saw the blood was from him. He tried to apologize, but his tongue was frozen and his mind too caught up in what she'd just said. She was giving him an out. A chance to escape.

"Now go. Get back to your work."

Again he wanted to protest, but again the words didn't come.

"Please, go now," she ordered. "Before you commit to something you'll regret."

With his head pounding and his nausea mounting, he stood. Though he knew he should say something, something like *I'll be back later* or *I won't abandon you*, he didn't. Instead he walked to the door and exited the room, leaving not even a trace of commitment behind.

Disgust filled his mouth, his throat, his esophagus. Self-hate weakened his gait. There was no sinking lower than he just had.

Ben made it as far as the small waiting room outside of 6 West before collapsing onto a chair against the wall. The otoscope in his overstuffed coat pocket clunked against the armrest, and the vinyl seat cushion wheezed under his sudden weight. Across the room, a gum-popping teenager looked up from her textbook.

Sitting in the same spot as last week when he'd learned about the chocolate store's break-in, he wondered what would smack him in the face next. Maybe Sophia's baby would be an alien.

Our baby.

He groaned out loud and sank deeper into the chair. The teenager gawked at him.

Recognizing he was losing his shit, he attempted a smile, but his lips seemed cast of plaster. His heart galloped against his ribs.

He was going to be a father.

And he'd just abandoned the mother.

He moaned again, and the blood drained from his face.

"Hey, you okay?" The teenager shot forward, the textbook sliding off her lap. "Need me to call someone?"

Ben shook his head. He mumbled something about being fine and leaned against the wall. With pain blasting his temples, he closed his eyes to block out the blinding sunlight from the window on his left and the flashing images from the muted television above the girl's head. He heard rather than saw the teen go back to her seat. After several deep breaths, his equilibrium returned and his heartbeat slowed. He lifted his head and blinked.

A baby.

Any day now.

Finding a weak smile to offer the girl, he stood, smoothed his lab coat, and thanked her for her concern. Under the sudden attention, the teenager blushed, the pinkness in her cheeks matching her bubblegum.

After one more deep breath, Ben stepped out of the waiting room and pushed through the double doors of 6 West. Halfway down the hall, the clipped voice of his attending brought him to a halt. Dr. Smith, dressed in a blue linen suit, was exiting a patient room to Ben's left. Jamal was behind her.

"Why Benjamin, I didn't know you were already an expert on MRIs and cat scans."

"I'm sorry I missed radiology rounds. Something unexpected came up." *Like cribs and diapers.* He did his best to maintain eye contact.

"Oh, by all means, don't let pesky things like patient care and learning disrupt your life. We're here to serve you, Mr. Oris. Just let us know what we can do." Shiny, bobbed hair danced around the attending's chin, and her eyes feigned reverence.

"It won't happen again."

"We've heard that before," Jamal said. "Get your act together." The senior resident's reprimand stung worse than Dr. Smith's. He'd been quick to praise Ben in the past couple of weeks, and it hurt to disappoint him.

The internist let the issue go and indicated with a flap of her hand that Ben follow them. Her tone thawed, but her gait accelerated. "The radiologist showed us Kate Naughton's head CT. The intern ordered it, given her seizures and confusion. Since you seem to have an interest in the patient, I thought you'd like to know it was normal."

Ben hustled behind Dr. Smith, his heavy coat pockets flapping against his thighs. If she was upset he'd been in Kate's room two nights before, she didn't show it. Unsure whether her newfound cordialness was an olive branch or a trap, he responded with hesitation. "Actually, I was just about to check on her. Melissa told me Kate's ... er, Ms. Naughton's ... liver and kidneys are failing."

"And why do you think that is?" Having reached the ward counter, Dr. Smith leaned her back against it and crossed her arms. Jamal began swiping his tablet's screen beside her.

"Could be the infection. Could be poor perfusion. Could be the start of sepsis." At Ben's answer, Jamal looked up and nodded, a faint smile on his face, his earlier irritation seeming to fade.

"And the high eosinophil count? What's the differential diagnosis for that?" Dr. Smith asked.

"Allergic disorders, parasitic infection, autoimmune disease, neoplasms, hypereosinophilic syndrome, and sometimes even Addison's disease or fungal infections." Ben paused for a breath. He'd been waiting for that question.

"Bravo." Jamal grinned. He placed the electronic tablet under his arm and applauded. "You read the article I gave you. The only one who has, I might add."

Dr. Smith wrinkled her nose and formed what almost passed for a smile. "Remember to use proper precautions when you visit her," was all she said.

Ben nodded and hurried off to Kate's room before the attending could change her mind. He plucked a gown from a nearby cart. When it was halfway on, a woman burst out of Kate's room. A scent of sickness and disease trailed her. "Benny," she cried.

Ben froze, recognizing both the hyper voice and the auburn curls. *Harmony. Shit.*

Staff at the counter glanced their way, and from behind a computer terminal, Ben's fellow third-year, Farid, mouthed the word *Benny* and grinned.

With arms still trapped in his gown, Ben was helpless to fend off Harmony's enthusiastic embrace. He hoped Dr. Smith wasn't witnessing the display. If she found out Ben's connection to Kate, she might rescind her permission to let him follow her on the side.

Harmony squeezed him in a massive hug. As he always did when blasted with her exuberance, he wondered whether she was taking her meds. When she finally pulled away, she gripped his ungloved hands in her own. "It's so good to see you." Her smile faltered, and she added, "But I'm sorry for Kate. She looks terrible."

Ben had barely opened his mouth before Mount St. Harmony erupted again, this time peppering him with questions about Kate, school, girlfriends, and Willy. The best Ben could manage were a few vague comments and nods before he wrestled his hands free. When he yanked them away, moisture dampened his palm. A quick look told him Harmony's manic grip had caused the papule to bleed for the second time that day. He'd have to hunt down a bandage and leave the thing on.

"Listen, I gotta go." He closed his hand to avoid bloodying his pants or white coat.

"Oh, okay, let's grab dinner tonight, I know this place—"

"I've got a lot of studying to do."

"Then we'll do lunch tomorrow. We could go out or I could meet you at the hospital or—"

"Probably won't have time."

"Breakfast maybe or even a quick chat in the hospital lobby or …" Her words finally tapered off, and though her lips held a smile, her eyes lost their sparkle.

"Yeah, I'll call you." After a short goodbye, he hurried away, not taking the time to check on Kate or chat with any of his amused team members. He wanted only to flee.

But he knew he wouldn't call her. In the past, every time he'd tried to rise above his graveyard of grudges, Harmony's history of constant absences, missed holidays, and skipped graduations pulled him back down. As a child there were times he went months—years, even—without hearing from her. Now, at thirty years old, he was fine with the long intervals, but not so much when he was an eight-year-old kid staring at his Power Rangers calendar, waiting for the promised visits that never came.

Storming out of the exit doors like a rodeo bull, he wondered how his life had derailed so quickly. He wanted to go back to his routine, back to studying and patient care and away from babies and bipolar mothers. When he almost slammed into a respiratory therapist in the hallway, he knew he needed to calm down. He veered toward a patient-consultation room a few yards away from the waiting room. At least Harmony wouldn't spot him in there when she exited the ward, and maybe he could find something to cover his bleeding palm.

When he swung open the door and charged into the carpeted room, he stumbled to a stop and nearly tripped over his feet. There, in front of a small couch, two people were kissing. Passionately. Pawing at each other in a way that suggested they'd soon make use of the sofa. Surprised by his sudden entrance, they pulled apart.

Joel and Melissa.

Ben turned to stone, both hands hardening into fists.

10

Taupe walls with framed landscapes closed in on Ben. Melissa's cheeks flamed, and she lowered her eyes. She stepped away from Joel, but the grad student smirked and pulled her back.

Ben pressed his fingertips into his flesh, barely cognizant of the blood oozing from his palm. For a moment he couldn't speak. Couldn't move. He stared at his ex-girlfriend: deep blue eyes, tousled blond pixie cut, smart, witty. Why hadn't he fought to keep her?

The baby. Harmony. Now this. Not since he was nine years old had he been so overwhelmed and frustrated by a day's events, back when he'd tried to build a hope chest for Max and Willy for Christmas. Willy had found him sobbing amidst piles of wood and scattered tools, the project too big for a kid. "Benny, here, here, come to me," his father had said. "You're too hard on yourself. Some things are out of our control. Sometimes we just have to let life happen."

Over the years, Ben had tried to do that, but on days like this, it never came easily.

A ceiling fan fluttered above. Dizzy, he rested against a central table. He shouldn't have skipped lunch.

"Are you okay?" Melissa stepped toward him.

"I'm fine." Ben's hand squeezed the table's edge.

Joel leaned against the wall and crossed his arms. His jeans probably cost more than Ben's rent. "You look a little rough, buddy. What's the matter? Internal medicine tougher than building warehouses?"

"Joel, don't start." Melissa shook her head in warning. "Maybe you better get back to the lab."

The grad student was referring to a warehouse construction job Ben had worked during his year of deferment from med school. A big job with great pay, enough to put a dent in Ben's future debt and enough to convince the admissions committee to give him the year of deferral.

Ben gave Joel an icy stare. "Get over it. I got in, you didn't. Not my problem you were last on their list and got booted."

Joel pushed away from the wall, a flap of gelled hair falling onto his forehead. "They just needed a little diversity, that's all. A redneck with gay fathers checks off two boxes. In fact, maybe you got a little Brokeback Mountain in you too."

Ben shortened the distance between them. "Why don't you ask your new girlfriend how Brokeback I am? Didn't hear her complaining."

"Stop it." Melissa's tone was sharp as she glared at both of them.

Joel closed the remaining gap. He was so close, Ben could smell Melissa's raspberry lip gloss on him. "You might've got the med school spot, but I got something better. She practically dived into my arms."

Ben fisted and unfisted his hands. His temples throbbed, and his jaw clenched.

"What, you want to hit me? Brilliant. That's just what a redneck would do."

"Enough." Melissa grabbed both of their arms. "You're acting like fourth graders. I'm not a trading card, Joel. And Ben, quit egging him on."

Melissa was right. Ben was too old for schoolyard fights. Why was he letting the idiot get to him?

He puffed out his cheeks and exhaled. He extended his right hand in apology but switched to his left when he saw the fresh blood. "She's right. This is stupid. Let's put it behind us."

Joel shoved Ben's arm away and mumbled something Ben didn't catch. The grad student headed toward the door. "Come on, Melissa."

She started to follow, but once Joel cleared the room, she stepped back inside. "Did you even like me? Or was I just convenient?" When Ben didn't answer right away, her lips formed a tight line. "That's what I thought."

"No, it's not like that. I did like you. It's just …"

She waited, but when nothing followed, she shook her head and stepped out.

Ben reached and grabbed her arm before she could take off down the hall. Ignoring Joel and his scowl, Ben pulled his ex-girlfriend back into the room. "I'm sorry. I know I was a crappy boyfriend." Her cherry-blossom perfume teased his nostrils, and his muscles weakened at the familiar scent. "Maybe we can try again."

"How dare you?" Melissa's expression was one of confusion and anger, but Ben saw longing there too. "I finally get on with my life and you want to screw it up again? Do you have any idea how much I liked you? How long I waited for you to act like you gave a shit about us? But you never wanted an *us*, did you? That didn't fit with your life plan."

She pulled free from his grasp. Blood streaked over her skin as it passed through his palm.

When he saw it, he grew even more contrite. "God, I'm sorry. Let me clean that for you." He rushed to a tissue box on the end table by the sofa. When he turned around, she was gone.

11

Morgan Pharmacy was located on Cecil B. Moore Avenue, just over a mile north of Ben's apartment. Its gray exterior offered no awning, leaving Ben at the mercy of the sun while he chained his bike to one of the metal bars covering the store's window. Above his head, an aged sign boasted *Locally Owned* and *We Compound*.

He pulled the bottom of his Phillies T-shirt up and wiped his face with the damp fabric. Then he raised his arms to remove his helmet. Trapped sweat dripped down his cheeks. A few blocks back, a bank's time and temperature display had flashed ninety-five degrees. Ben felt every bit of it.

Smoothing back his hair, he entered the store. Though he welcomed the blast of arctic air-conditioning, he could have done without the eye-watering combination of drugstore perfume and compounded medicines.

He scanned the place for Laurette. Thanks to a run-in with a teary Mrs. Sinclair on the way out of his apartment, he was late. He couldn't rush his landlady though, not with her daughter so sick in the hospital. And truth be told, anything that distracted him from his obsessive thoughts about Sophia and the baby was a blessing. All weekend long, images of fatherhood had swirled through his mind. To shove them away, he dived deeper into his studies or did pull-ups on his door-mounted bar until he was so exhausted his brain followed suit.

When Laurette had called earlier and asked for his help on a paper she was writing about over-the-counter drugs and the public's misconceptions about their safety, he'd leaped at the chance. Anything to get away from his worries. Had he not been so eager for a distraction, he might have wondered why she hadn't asked her Uncle Trey instead. After all, the man was a pharmacist at the drugstore. But there had been other things on Ben's mind than the oddness of her request. Things like being a father, abandoning the mother, an upcoming dinner with his own mother, an ex-girlfriend's broken heart, and an ex-lover near death.

But he wondered about it now.

Walking past shelves of snack foods and stationery, he spotted Laurette in front of a magazine rack, browsing a glossy, home-decorating journal. Unlike him, she appeared cool and dry, though her linen shorts and lavender top were wrinkled and creased from the heat.

When she saw him, she lifted the magazine. Its cover showed a palatial home with stately gardens. "Imagine what this would look like to the Haitians living in tent cities. It has been several years since the earthquake, and still people live under tin and tarp with no electricity. And the toilets? Do not get me started."

Ben had no intention of getting her started. As tough as he had it financially, it was nothing compared to her countrymen and women. He was a privileged white boy in comparison, though she'd never made him feel that way. Having a government official for a father had made her life more comfortable too, and Ben knew she felt guilt over it. "You'll make a difference when you go back."

She shook her head and replaced the magazine. "I don't know. I want to think so, but perhaps I will just be a nurse with a fancy degree when I return to Port-Au-Prince. How much can one person do in the face of poverty like that?"

Before Ben could respond, she shifted gears and thanked him for coming. The way she fiddled with her handbag made him sense something was wrong. It was the purse she'd splurged on at a Paris boutique. Seeing its yellow leather and shiny clasp conjured the catacombs fiasco in his mind.

He blinked the image away. "Are you okay? You seem nervous."

"Oui, oui, I am fine."

Her purse squishing suggested otherwise, but he let it go and headed toward the over-the-counter medications in the back aisles of the store. "Should we start with pain relievers or cough-and-cold meds?"

No answer from his friend. He turned around and found her staring past him toward the back counter. Her striking eyebrows folded in consternation, and her hand found her amulet. "Let us go in the back perhaps? There is a room my uncle gives us permission to use."

Ben's internal radar picked up a signal, though from what, he didn't know. Before he could question her again, she grabbed his arm and led him down an aisle. Contact lens solution, adult diapers, and skin creams passed by in his peripheral vision.

Behind the counter, a tall man with a deep voice and a white coat helped an elderly woman with a prescription. Another patron waited in line behind her. Though Ben had met Laurette's Aunt Marie in the past—a rather cold woman who didn't seem to like him much—he'd never met Laurette's uncle. On the few occasions Ben had been to Laurette's home (she lived with her aunt and uncle), Trey had been gone.

"Is that your uncle?" he asked as she dragged him to a door near the medication counter.

Laurette nodded but didn't stop for introductions. Instead, she exchanged a look with the man. He buzzed the back door open in response.

"Uh, what's going on, Bovo?" Ben's hair follicles pricked up in warning

Averting his gaze, Laurette held the solid door open and pointed to a room at the end of the hallway.

When Ben started to protest, she said, "It is fine. More privacy to work back here."

He hesitated, then went through the door. He told himself his recent turn of events was making him paranoid.

Memos, notices, and an old-fashioned time clock hung on the scuffed hallway walls. A small restroom on the left read *Employee Use Only,* and next to that a fire alarm. At the end of the hall, right before an emergency exit, stood a closed, gray door.

Outside the room, Ben's voice took a sharper edge. "This isn't about your paper, is it."

Laurette smiled weakly and turned the doorknob. "It is nothing. You will see."

She nudged Ben inside a typical break room with a fridge, microwave, and sink. Bulletin boards tacked with more memos hung on the walls. Also inside were two men seated across from each other at an oval table. A half-empty yogurt container sat in front of one of them, while a black cloth was folded in front of the other. Noticeably absent were over-the-counter drugs or other materials Ben might use to help Laurette with her paper.

Ben studied the men, both of whom now stood and smiled, though one's glance flitted around the room, much like Laurette's had in the pharmacy proper. Both men had closely cropped hair and both were slender, but the one standing to Ben's left near the fridge was taller and more muscular than the one standing in front of a bulletin board to Ben's right. The latter had keloid scars over his arms extending all the way up inside his polo shirt. The other was dressed in black jeans and a dress shirt and wore more confidence in his wide smile and dark, playful eyes than the nervous one did.

Ben didn't mind being the only white person in the pharmacy, but he sure as hell minded being the only person without a clue as to what was going on. He looked at his friend. "Okay, what's happening here?"

The door *whooshed* shut behind him. Laurette's expression, not unlike that of a child who's been caught shoplifting, was answer enough.

They weren't there to work on a paper. And judging by the bulky contents hidden inside the black cloth on the table, they weren't there to talk about drugs.

"You need to tell me what's going on." Ben's torso grew rigid. He planted his foot back slightly, ready to bolt from the room. The refrigerator hummed beside him, and the scent of warmed-up lunch lingered in the air.

Laurette exhaled slowly, as if trying to find her nerve. "Ben, meet David Alcine." She lifted her hand toward the man with keloid scars and nervous eyes. Upon hearing his name, he shoved forward from the bulletin board. A blue sticky note wafted to the floor behind him. "David is from Haiti too. He's a clerk in the pharmacy and a friend of my Auntie Marie."

Ben nodded a tentative hello. David Alcine didn't extend his hand in greeting and neither did Ben.

"And this is Jean Miot." Laurette waved her other hand toward the man in black jeans. "He knows my brother in Haiti. They have worked together, yes?"

Jean Miot's smile widened. Though the relaxed nature of it put Ben more at ease, he remained poised for a quick exit. Unlike David, Jean extended a hand. Ben held back, pointing to the bandage on his palm as if that were the reason for the snub. In reality, he was too confused and wary for a friendly greeting. His conversation with Laurette in the park three nights before popped into his head, as did her words of dark dreams and Vodou. And babies.

Beneath all that blood, I see a baby.

How had she been so prescient the night of their jog? How could she have known about Sophia's baby, a baby he still hadn't told her about?

He blinked the nonsense away. Coincidence, that was all.

And yet a nauseating lump rose in his throat.

"… happy to be of help to you," Jean Miot was saying, his accent more pronounced than Laurette's and his teeth nowhere as nice. When he smiled, blackness gaped where two molars should be. His eyes, however, were large and intoxicating, and Ben imagined women falling for their lure.

"Help me with what?" Ben turned toward Laurette cautiously.

A nervous smile flitted on and off her face. She squeezed her amulet and glanced at Jean, who stepped up and took over. "Please, sit. I know you have questions. I hope for you to have answers, Mr. Oris." It came out *Meester Orees.*

Ben cast another sour look Laurette's way. She took a seat at the far end of the table and indicated Ben do the same. "Please listen before you judge," she said, her eyes pleading.

Though he hesitated, Ben's curiosity trumped his internal alarm, and he sat at the head of the table, his butt barely resting on the edge of the chair and his limbs ready for flight. The two men joined them, one on either side. Jean Miot placed his hands on the black fabric in front of him and slowly unfolded it.

Several small, colorful cloth bags with drawstrings lay inside the fabric, as did a black candle, a white candle, a small skull, and a cluster of necklaces made of tiny brown shells flecked with black.

Ben frowned and raised his eyebrows, but Laurette said nothing. He kneaded his temples. Five minutes. He'd give her five minutes.

The man with the confident smile lifted a small blue bag and began to speak. Ben raised a hand and silenced him. "No, I want to hear from Laurette first."

The three Haitians exchanged glances. Jean sat back and gave a go-ahead signal to Laurette. The anxious, scarred man to Ben's right remained silent.

Laurette cleared her throat. Her fidgeting fingers shifted from the bronze and emerald amulet to her onyx ring, and her eyes fell upon the quiet man. "David is not just a pharmacy clerk. He is a *houngan si pwen* ... an assistant priest. A trainee, you might say. He works with a respected priestess here in Philadelphia who goes by the name of Mambo Tina. I mentioned her to you the other night in the park."

Ben's top lip curled like a German shepherd about to sic, but Laurette rushed on before he could speak.

"I wanted to consult Mambo Tina for your experience in the catacombs, so I—"

"You did what?"

"Please, let me finish."

Though it took every ounce of his patience, Ben decided to hear her out. She deserved at least that considering everything she'd done for him, from running his errands when he was swamped with exams to saving him money by sharing her leftover home-cooked meals at lunch. Not to mention keeping him sane with her dumb goat jokes.

So for her, he would listen. At least for now.

He nodded, and she continued. "I wished to consult Mambo Tina about your cut from the bone and the strange illness of your friend, Kate. Your poor health too." She must have seen his oncoming denial, because she added, "You are not yourself. You are tired, pale, and grumpy."

Ben ground his teeth. Laurette sharing his personal information with strangers pissed him off, but he allowed her to go on.

"I thought perhaps the mambo might have answers, but Auntie Marie and my brother think Monsieur Miot is a better place to start. You see ..." Her lips quivered, and she twisted her ring more persistently. She glanced at Jean Miot, as if seeking encouragement, but Ben saw doubt in her eyes too. Jean, still clutching a cloth bag, its string cinched tight around the opening, smiled and nodded for her to continue. She looked back at Ben. "You see, Monsieur Miot is not a trained Vodou priest. He is a *bokor*. That means he ... ah ... he handles things priests and priestesses will not."

"What kind of things?" Ben asked slowly. Jesus, what had she gotten him into?

Laurette clasped and unclasped her hands. "Dark magic. He performs dark magic. It is for this reason Guy and Auntie think he is best to—"

Ben shot up. His chair lurched backward and screeched against the lino-leum. "Seriously? You dragged me here for this? Come on. You're too smart for this shit."

Laurette stood as well, her tone no longer timid. "It is *because* I am smart I do this." Passion replaced fear, and her dark eyes sparked in indignation. "Something is not right. Whether or not you admit it, you know it's true. Something happened in the catacombs. Something dark has traveled back with you. Let Monsieur Miot try to learn of its nature."

"A voodoo—excuse me, *Vodou*—intervention? Really?" Ben shook his head and fisted his hands so hard his fingertips went numb. "Call me when you've come to your senses."

He pivoted and whipped open the break room door, its handle banging the counter and rattling the coffee pot. He bolted out of the room, but not before catching Jean Miot's grave warning.

"There are evil forces in this world, Mr. Oris. It is only dark methods that stop them."

12

Slouched on a leather sofa in the med student lounge, Ben scanned a paper on the pathological findings of inflammatory bowel disease, hoping to cram in last-minute details before pathology rounds at four. Two other third years lounged on the couch across from him. One had her eyes closed, a laptop on her lap. The other typed with two sausage fingers on his iPad. A third student snarfed down a pungent pizza roll while sorting through his mail cubby.

Try as he might, Ben couldn't concentrate. His thoughts kept cycling back to Laurette and her ambush in the pharmacy two days before. He hadn't spoken to her since, hadn't even returned her texts, making it the longest they'd gone without communicating in some form. Even at their busiest, they texted each other jokes or funny memes, but he was still too pissed to talk to her.

There are evil forces in this world, Mr. Oris. It is only dark methods that stop them.

"Bullshit," Ben mumbled.

The chubby student looked up from his iPad. When he realized Ben was speaking to himself, he went back to typing.

Eyes back on his paper, Ben once again tried to focus on the words in front of him, but his mind kept wandering, this time to Kate. During rounds that morning he learned she'd deteriorated the evening before, with worsening organ failure and the development of disseminated intravascular coagulation, or DIC as everyone in medicine called it. Ben knew from his basic science classes that in DIC, clotting proteins got all messed up, putting the patient at risk for serious bleeding.

According to Jamal, who'd been on call the night before, Kate had started bleeding in the early morning hours, first internally and then externally from her nose, ears, and eyes, prompting transfer to the ICU. The look of fear in the senior resident's eyes had unnerved everyone at rounds. "God, I've never seen anything like it," he'd said. "And I pray I never do again." Ben just hoped the ICU staff would be able to treat her.

Focus, he told himself, returning to the journal article's long passages about intestinal skip lesions and fistulas. His cell phone buzzed, relieving him of the tedium. The phone's display told him the call was from a hospital number. Keeping his voice soft to avoid waking the dozing student, he rose and stepped away. "Hello?"

"Hey there, it's Tanisha, the nurse from OB/GYN? You asked me to call if anything changed with your friend. I wanted to let you know her blood pressure's been unstable today."

Though Ben had made it as far as the L&D ward yesterday, he'd chickened out before he got to Sophia's room. He hadn't been by to see her since learning the bombshell news about the baby five days ago. His baby.

Guilt washed over him. "Are they going to induce her? She's about thirty-six and a half weeks now, so the baby should be okay, right? Right?" His voice rose, and the slumbering student blinked open her eyes.

"They're not inducing her yet, but that'll be the next step if they can't stabilize her. I thought you should know since the poor woman hasn't had many visitors." She paused, then added, "Haven't seen you around lately either."

Ben swallowed a lump the size of his fist. He thanked Tanisha and hung up. Crossing over to the bank of lockers, he couldn't control the swarm of thoughts in his head. Unfortunately none of them had to do with pathology rounds. For someone who'd always avoided drama, he was suddenly a lightning rod for it.

Knowing he couldn't afford to miss path rounds, not after his promise to Dr. Smith and Jamal that it wouldn't happen again, he shoved the medical articles into his locker next to his backpack. When he turned to exit the lounge, the door flew open, and a flushed-face Joel stormed in.

"I've been looking all over for you." The grad student's eyes were cobalt flares and his mouth a trembling scowl. He planted his feet in a wide stance and blocked the exit.

"Yeah, what for?" Ben had no time for another adolescent skirmish with the guy. Too bad the biochemistry lab was so close to the hospital.

"She's sick and it's your fault." The words came with a spray of saliva.

Ben wiped his cheek. Behind him, he felt the gazes of the other students, the sleepy one no doubt now wide awake. "What are you talking about? Who's sick?" For a moment, Sophia flashed in Ben's mind, but he dismissed the thought. Joel didn't know about her. Or at least Ben hoped not.

"Melissa. Who do you think?"

Ben's hackles lowered. "She was fine in rounds this morning." She'd been quiet, but Ben assumed it was because of their recent brush in the consultation room.

"Well, she's sick now. Thanks to you."

"Sick with what? Why is it my fault?"

"Headache, low-grade fever, body aches. Just like that patient."

"What patient?" Ben waited for clarification. Then his jaw sagged, and before Joel even said the name, Ben knew.

"Kate Naughton. The patient who was supposed to be yours but Melissa got instead. She told me all about it."

Ben was about to mention it was because of Joel's stepmom that Melissa got saddled with Kate, but he held back. The guy was upset enough. Instead, he tried to get the grad student to move out of the way. They could finish talking in the hall, away from the three sets of listening ears.

Joel wouldn't budge. "If she gets sick like that patient, I swear I'll—"

"Melissa could be sick with anything. She takes care of lots of patients." But even Ben heard the uncertainty in his voice. Hands inside his coat pockets, he squeezed his stethoscope and otoscope. "Probably just a cold." The words trickled out so weakly, he wasn't sure he even uttered them.

Joel's eyes blazed and then moistened. He swiped the back of his hand over them. "You better sure as shit hope so, because my mom told me Kate Naughton just died."

⊐⊏

Forgetting all about pathology rounds, Ben bolted from the College of Medicine and sprinted across the street toward the Talcott Center, his shortcut to the main hospital building. The afternoon sun blinded him, and he barely dodged a Jeep in his haste. Ignoring the blaring horn, he leaped to the curb, sidestepped a man in a wheelchair on the sidewalk, and threw open the building's heavy glass door. He raced to the second-floor walkway leading to the hospital, his overstuffed pockets pelting his hips and his thick-soled shoes squeaking on the glossy tile.

If Joel was correct, Kate was already dead, but if her body was still in the intensive care unit, Mrs. Sinclair might be there at her daughter's bedside. He imagined how frightened and alone she would feel. If he got there in time, he could comfort her.

He couldn't believe Kate was dead. Didn't want to believe it. Kate the eager beaver. Kate the cougar. Kate the middle-aged party girl was dead.

And no one knew why.

Sprinting up the last stairwell to the fourth-floor ICU, Laurette's words echoed in Ben's brain: *Something dark has traveled back with you.*

He pictured Kate in his basement apartment less than two weeks ago. Pictured her hands all over him, her lips smothering his, the smear of blood he'd left on her palm.

He pushed the ridiculous notion away, angry at himself for letting Laurette get inside his head. Kate had suffered a horrible infection, that was all.

After ripping open the stairwell door, he finally slowed his step. Uncomfortable with his first visit to the ICU, he straightened his tie and adjusted his short white coat. When he passed through the unit's automatic doors, a grieving, middle-aged couple plodded out, arms around each other, tears in their eyes. Ben stepped aside for them, and his own chest filled with dread. How would he face Mrs. Sinclair? He'd always known he would encounter death in medicine, but he hadn't expected to confront it so soon, especially with someone he knew.

At the bustling ICU counter, he asked a tall woman in scrubs if Kate Naughton was still in the unit. The woman glanced at his student ID tag and pointed across the hall. A ringing phone stole her attention before he could ask anything else.

Ben swallowed the fireball in his throat and crossed over to Kate's room. Peering through a six-inch gap in the window curtain, he saw her lying in the bed, her mother by her side. Even from a distance he could see dried blood around Kate's nose, mouth, and ears.

A nurse and doctor in full protective gear stood near the head of the bed, removing tubes and pulling out lines. The nurse intermittently patted Mrs. Sinclair's hunched back. She, too, was masked and gowned, strands of unwashed gray hair poking through the mask's ties. Her body shook with sobs, tears staining her powder-blue mask.

Seeing his landlady's grief paralyzed him. What would he say to her? He had no answers. No one did.

Shifting position, his view of the room expanded, and he saw two other people at the foot of the bed. Despite their protective clothing, he recognized one of the women. He couldn't have been more surprised if Kate had just sat up in bed.

Laurette? Why was *she* there? An alarm wailed from somewhere behind him as he tried to digest her presence. Her world was classes, practicums at the public health department, and research projects. Not clinical medicine.

But then he remembered he'd asked her to run Kate's condition by her advisor, Dr. Khalid. The epidemiologist must've thought the case was worth looking into.

As if by telepathy, Laurette looked up and caught Ben's eyes through the window. She nodded, said something to the dark-haired Dr. Khalid, and started removing her protective gear near the door. While Ben waited for her to come out, he watched the nurse pull a catheter from Kate's bladder. Bright red urine swished inside the attached bag.

His body went cold. He'd talked to this woman. Laughed with her. Slept with her. Now she was dead.

And Melissa was sick.

Laurette stepped out before he could expand on the daunting thought. The removal of her gown had lifted the collar of her blouse toward her chin, and her familiar citrus scent sweetened the air. Though still irritated with her, he was grateful to have her near.

After a pause, she said, "I am sorry for your loss. You were good to Kate."

"Did Mrs. Sinclair recognize you?"

"No, I don't think so. She bears too much grief to see others. No parent should lose a child."

And no child should be abandoned by his father.

The thought of Sophia and his desertion of her filled him with self-loathing. He did his best to push it away. "Thanks for talking to Dr. Khalid about her. Does she have any idea what caused this?"

Laurette shook her head. "When I mentioned her symptoms and the high eosinophil count, she was … oh, how do you say … intrigued? Yes?" Ben nodded and his friend continued. "She phoned Dr. Smith, who invited us to come. This is our second visit, but when we came before you were not speaking to me." Ben's cold shoulder after the pharmacy stunt hung in the air. "I will share with you if she has any theories."

"You look skeptical she will."

Laurette scanned the area. She took Ben's arm and escorted him off to a dark corner of the unit, its overhead lighting either turned off or burned out. She lowered her voice. "I know you are angry with me. I'm sorry. But I'm not sorry for wanting to help you. I can no longer ignore my fear." Lifting Ben's right hand, she pointed to the bandage on his palm. "That cut cursed you, and now you are cursing others."

Ben jerked his hand away. Too discombobulated for anger, he slumped against the wall and rubbed the stubble on his chin. "I can't do this again. Don't you see how crazy you sound? People don't talk about curses here. You've got to stop this."

"Then why do you still wear the bandage?"

He opened his mouth. Closed it. He had no answer. The papule hadn't bled since Friday, so why *was* he still covering it? He should've found time for a doctor's appointment and had the thing removed. Surely Dr. Smith would have allowed that, and it would have ended Laurette's flight of fantasy. Of course, with nothing but catastrophic health insurance to cover him, a thousand-dollar dermatologist bill would sink him.

"There will be others who fall ill," Laurette warned. "More who will bleed. My dreams have shown me."

Ben's intestines swirled. He blinked Melissa out of his mind. "You're insane, Bovo. Kate had an infection we haven't identified. Yet. This is the real world, not a fairyland."

Laurette glanced over her shoulder. Dr. Khalid was exiting Kate's room. With haste, his friend yanked something out of her skirt pocket and stuffed it into his hand. "Here. Take this."

He glanced down. A sharp, gray object attached to a leather strap lay coiled on his palm. "What the heck is this? A bone?"

Dr. Khalid scanned the room for Laurette, who quickened her speech. "Yes. An animal bone from my brother, given to me when I was a child. Guy blessed it for protection."

Ben thrust the object back in Laurette's hands. "Jesus, I don't want that."

"You need it, my friend. And so do those around you." Her dark eyes implored him.

"No."

She tried to stuff it in his coat, but Dr. Khalid approached and called out before she could. Laurette crammed the amulet back into her skirt pocket. Before turning to her advisor, she whispered words that both terrified and comforted Ben. "I will not abandon you, my friend. Not while this curse eats your soul."

13

Ben slogged through the parking garage, relieved to be leaving the hospital. Since he'd agreed to have dinner with Willy and Harmony, he'd opted to drive his car that morning. Though the parking ticket was an expense he didn't need, in his exhausted state, he was glad to have a ride that didn't require pedaling.

Tap, tap, tap. Hard soles on the concrete behind him.

He twisted around, wondering if someone was following him. A figure slipped behind an SUV.

Just someone heading home. God, he was getting paranoid. Thanks to Laurette and her far-fetched delusions.

Navigating Philadelphia's streets during rush hour did little to improve his mental state. Horns blared, pedestrians mobbed, trucks blocked the intersections, their exhaust fumigating his car. By the time the Mustang turned onto South 22nd Street, Ben was ready for three fingers of whiskey and a schooner of beer.

Make that four fingers. Harmony was coming for dinner.

A beat-up Impala plastered with bumper stickers pulled out of a coveted spot across the street from Willy's complex. Hardly believing his luck, Ben claimed the space, maneuvering his Mustang into a bumper-to-bumper, parallel-parking masterpiece. Farther down the street, Max's silver Mazda sat idle. Other than mandatory moves for street cleaning and snow removal, the vehicle saw little road time. Since Willy was close enough to walk to the chocolate store, he didn't have much use for a car, let alone a second one. Ben knew his father would never sell it though. Not until Ben forced the matter, anyway.

Behind the steering wheel, Ben's face softened into a smile. He recalled Max in the back seat when Willy had first taught Ben how to drive. Max, overly dramatic in times of stress but determined not to miss Ben's first session, had squealed and averted his eyes, lamenting they'd all end up in an ambulance. Willy and Ben had just laughed.

What Ben wouldn't give to hear that squeal now, or to see Willy tease Max in response. But that Willy no longer existed. The closest he came to his old self was when Harmony visited.

Leaving his backpack behind, Ben exited the car and headed toward the white-brick building, passing a dog walker and his panting pug along the way. Colorful flower boxes decorated the first and second story windows of the neighbors' units. Willy's remained bare.

Inside the oat-hued hallway of the four-condo complex, scents of thyme, oregano, and garlic greeted Ben. At least his father hadn't abandoned cooking. His homemade spaghetti sauce made an evening with Harmony almost worth it.

Ben rapped a quick knock on his father's door before entering. Inside the foyer voices traveled from the kitchen, its view blocked by the living room wall.

Still wearing his white coat, his mind so full of worry he'd forgotten to leave it in the student lounge, he peeled it off and tossed it over a wingback chair. He glanced into Max's study across the hall. As always, its glass French doors were closed. Beyond them, the desk remained untouched.

Every time Ben had offered to sort through Max's things, Willy refused. He wouldn't even look at the genealogy study Max had been working on before he died. It was a gift for Willy, though Max hadn't been able to complete it. Whenever Ben raised the subject, Willy just nodded and waved his hand, indicating it was a matter for another time.

Ben's stomach rumbled. He exhaled and headed toward the kitchen, entering just in time to hear Harmony ask Willy, "Does he still get stressed when things don't go as planned?"

"Pretty much," Ben said dryly.

The two turned toward him, their surprise obvious. A granite bar with a plate of hors d'oeuvres separated Willy from Harmony, Willy on the side with the gleaming appliances and walnut cabinets, Harmony on the side with the table. The pale yellow walls seemed unfittingly cheerful.

His father and Harmony exchanged embarrassed glances. Willy's eyes seemed more hangdog than normal and his crow's feet more pronounced. As usual, he wore jeans and a checkered shirt with a T-shirt underneath.

"Oops," Harmony said, her ring-adorned hand flying to her mouth. She flitted forward in a gauzy skirt and silk tank top and gave Ben a hug. Given how he'd treated her at the hospital four days before, he reciprocated, though his movements were wooden and his muscles tense. When she pulled away, a collection of gold bracelets snagged her long, auburn hair, and she freed herself with a giggle.

"Some wine?" she asked, reaching for a glass. Her fingers trembled, and Ben wondered whether from nerves or medication.

Willy plucked a bottle of locally brewed ale from the fridge. "Benny's a beer guy."

Ben took the bottle and thanked his father, then sat down at the table. Willy went back to the stove, and for a few moments bubbling marinara and humming appliances were the only sounds.

The lack of noise was strange. Usually Harmony prattled on about her recent travels or her man du jour, who, last Ben had heard, was a rich guy from India. Onset of a depressive state, maybe? But she rarely visited them when she was "under the wool blanket," as Willy liked to call it.

Ben watched the woman who'd given birth to him nibble a cracker, put it down, pick it up again, then drop it. She shook her head and went back to her wine.

Though Ben had never met her parents, he knew her birth name was Patricia Claxwell, the name *Harmony* a creation of her own. From what Willy had told him, upon learning of his unwed, twenty-one-year-old daughter's pregnancy, Dr. Claxwell had been furious. He'd wanted her to abort the fetus or give the infant up for adoption. He'd envisioned a prominent life of academia for her, just like his own. When she chose to quit school—not so much because of the baby but because she'd grown "bored of classes and pompous professors"—her father threatened to desert her, demanding his wife do the same.

Ben had always suspected there was more to the story. Twenty-one was young, but it wasn't unheard of, and single women had babies all the time. Despite Harmony's gift of the gab, however, she never talked about her parents and bristled whenever Ben raised the subject. "Oh, let's talk about something fun," she'd say. So he'd learned to quit asking and, truth be told, rarely thought about it anymore.

Studying the woman now in the brightness of Willy's kitchen, he could tell something was off. It wasn't just her uncharacteristic silence. Her complexion was pale, sweat beaded her forehead, and her hands displayed a fine tremor when she eased her way back onto the barstool.

Cycling down. That had to be it.

Perhaps sensing his scrutiny, she raised her chin and smiled, though the levity didn't reach her hazel eyes. "So how's Kate?"

Ben took a sip of beer. It tasted like shock and disbelief. "She died today."

"Oh how horrible." Harmony rushed to a stand but weaved unsteadily. She fell back onto the stool.

Willy remained at the stove but pivoted his body toward them. "I'm very sorry to hear that."

"Did they find out what caused it?" Harmony's tone was breathy.

According to my best friend, it was me, he wanted to say. Instead he shook his head.

More silence, the three of them inhaling the Italian spices, lost in their own thoughts.

Unaccustomed to Harmony not guiding the conversation, Ben was at a loss for what to say. The quiet so unnerved him, he almost considered telling them about Sophia and the baby. He squashed the notion. Telling Willy would be difficult enough. He couldn't handle Harmony's emotion to boot.

His father came to the rescue. "I told Harmony about the store's break-in."

"Yes, how odd." Harmony swirled wine in her glass, its ruby hue imparting some much needed color to her complexion. "Why would anyone steal your baby hair and bronze shoe?" She turned toward Willy, who munched on cheese squares while shaking a strainer full of cooked noodles over the sink. "Remember when we put that keepsake together? I sent Ben's shoe, picture, and hair to that company whose flier was in our hospital bag. Remember how worried you were they'd get lost in the mail?"

Willy smiled at the memory. He dumped the pasta back in the pot and stepped forward to grab Harmony's hand, her presence, as always, appearing to lift him.

Ben gripped his beer bottle, not buying into the happy-family illusion they were selling.

He knew the history of his conception. Willy was thirty-two at the time, still in the closet and desperate for a child. One night at a party thrown by a mutual friend, he met Patricia Claxwell. The young college student, in the throes of untreated mania and three days without sleep, deduced Willy's homosexuality and uncovered his desire to father a child. She decided right then and there in all her unmedicated glory to give him one, no strings attached. Willy, in his inebriated state, thought it a grand plan. They had sex that night and decided if she got pregnant, it would be fate. Well, hello fate. Nine months later, Willy was a father. Two years later he met Max Towner and officially came out. Together they created a family unit of three. Though Harmony requested to stay in Ben's life, she kept her word and gave up all parental rights. Just like that. Signed, sealed, and delivered. Had she stayed away completely, Ben might have adjusted, being no more the wiser, but as a child, her impossible-to-track and often ill-timed visits confused instead of comforted him.

"Why doesn't she want to be my mom?" he'd asked Willy when he was barely six years old, fighting back tears and trying to pretend it didn't matter.

Ben cracked his neck and took another swig of beer.

Once, when he was fourteen, he'd entered a woodworking contest. For whatever dumb reason, he'd decided to build a jewelry case for Harmony. Maybe he'd hoped she'd be so impressed with his hard work and diligence, she'd never leave again. He'd painted the box black and stenciled it with red roses. Inside, he built three sliding drawers with different-sized compartments to hold her vast jewelry collection. His effort to detail paid off: he won second place. Seemingly delighted, Harmony had promised to come to the award ceremony, but on the day of the event, she no-showed. Trying to comfort his son, Willy made up an excuse about a delayed flight, but Ben would have none of it. Drowning in a sea of acne and adolescent hormones, he pushed his father away and yelled, "You might as well have screwed a whore."

That was the one and only time Willy had struck Ben. Shocked into silence, Ben had rubbed his stinging cheek. "Don't you ever talk about your mother like that," Willy had sputtered. "You don't know the whole story. You have no idea what she's been through."

And apparently Ben never would, because the subject remained an unspoken barrier between them.

"… with cheese or without?"

Ben blinked. Willy looked at him expectantly.

"Sorry?"

"I asked if you wanted cheese on your garlic toast."

Before Ben could answer, his phone vibrated in his pocket. He mumbled "cheese" to his father and pulled out the phone with his free hand, his other one still gripping the beer bottle. Resting his elbow on the table, he read the text message.

Tanisha here. Ur girl got induced, laboring fast, already 6 cm. So if ur really her friend, get ur ass over here.

The bottle nearly slipped from Ben's hand, its edge striking a stoneware plate. The clatter made both Willy and Harmony swing their heads his way.

He stared back at them, mouth open and heart breaking into a sprint.

He was about to become a father.

14

Ben burst through the door of the med student lounge, his nerves like live currents of electricity. Around a small table three second-years slurped noodles from takeout boxes while quizzing each other from note-cards. Soy and Szechuan sauces peppered the air. The students swiveled in his direction, nodded, then returned to their own worlds.

In his haste to leave Willy's and get to the Talcott Center, Ben had forgotten his white coat. Figuring he'd be less conspicuous in L&D wearing one, he stopped in the lounge to grab a spare. There were always some lying around. He had to hurry though. Tanisha's last text said Sophia was already at eight centimeters.

He'd mentioned nothing about the baby to Willy and Harmony. Couldn't bring himself to share the news. Instead he blamed his abrupt departure on an ailing patient.

Three coats hung on a rack near the lockers. He tore one free and checked the inside collar for size. Seeing it was a large, he slipped it on, wrinkling his nose at the eau de BO that came with it. No time to be choosy.

Feeling close to spontaneous combustion, he bolted for the door. Before he got there, something in his mail cubby caught his eye. As soon as he realized what it was, he cursed under his breath.

Laurette had stopped by in his absence. And she'd left him a present.

He snatched the object out of the cubby and stuffed it in his pants pocket, hoping none of the other students had seen it. His finger grazed the sharp tip, and he jerked his hand away. A pink scratch, but thankfully no blood.

If he had wanted Laurette's superstitious necklace, he would have taken the damn thing in the ICU when she'd tried to foist it on him. As if a bone blessed by her brother could offer protection. The only protection Ben needed right now was protection from screwing up his kid's life.

And his own.

He ripped open the door and raced to Labor & Delivery.

"Push," the doctor and nurse barked in unison.

Ben gripped Sophia's hand as she strained and groaned through another contraction. Perspiration dotted her forehead, and pain etched her face. The metallic scent of blood clung in the air, and whenever Ben moved, body odor from his loaner lab coat rose to join it.

"You're doing great," he said, tucking a clump of short, sweaty hair behind her ear. Despite his outward composure, his insides floated in a cloud of disbelief. A woman he barely knew was having his baby. What was more, she'd absolved him of all responsibility. He could still walk away.

And yet he rubbed her shoulders, wiped her brow, and gave her pep talks.

"One more push and your baby greets the world." The doctor's sandy locks were tucked inside a surgical cap, and her blood- and fluid-streaked gloves were crossed in front of her blue gown. Sophia started to push, but the doctor shook her head and smiled. "Not yet. Wait until the next contraction."

Sophia exhaled, her flushed cheeks glistening, her long lashes moist. She turned toward Ben as he eased her back against the pillow. "You don't have to be here," she said, panting.

"What? And miss the excitement?" He winked and grabbed her hand again. "There's nowhere else I wanna be." Despite his paralyzing doubts over what the future held, he meant it.

Whether she wanted it to show or not, Sophia's relief was unmistakable. Then her abdomen stiffened and contracted, and that relief morphed into pain.

"Okay, this is it." Ben helped lift her upper back off the bed. Her gold cross got tangled in its chain, and he smoothed it back down. "You can do this."

More cries to push from the doctor, more enthusiastic encouragement from the nurse, more murmurs of reassurance from Ben. When the head emerged, the doctor directed Sophia to quit pushing and gently glided the rest of the baby out.

Up to that point Ben had remained at the head of the bed near Sophia and hadn't witnessed any of the birth. When the doctor and nurse fiddled with cord clamps and cut the cord, he saw pink, slimy flesh emerge from the blue drapes around Sophia's legs. Arms, legs, head, buttocks. All parts seemed to be there.

Ben swallowed. His throat constricted. His chest squeezed in a way it had never squeezed before.

The doctor handed the somewhat limp baby over to the nurse, who scooped it into a blanket and put it on the warming bed. When she stimulated it with drying, the infant started to cry. A rousing cheer erupted from the nurse.

The doctor beamed at Sophia. "Congratulations, Ms. Diaz. It's a boy."

When the doctor finished suturing the episiotomy and the nurse completed the newborn assessment, they allowed Sophia a few minutes with her baby.

"I'll come back for him in twenty minutes," the nurse said before leaving. "He looks great, but he's just over thirty-six weeks, so we'll want him in the nursery soon. Make sure his temp and vitals are good. You can put him to breast if you like. Sometimes trying right away makes things go smoother."

Sophia promised she would. "Do you want to hold him?" she asked Ben once the nurse stepped out. She raised the swaddled bundle toward him.

Ben sucked air through his teeth. "Oh, I don't know." His shirt stuck to his torso, and the stinky lab coat he'd draped over the armrest brushed against his elbow.

"You don't have to." Sophia caught his gaze and held it. "I meant what I said. No pressure. I can do this on my own." Her attention returned to her infant. The expression on her face was pure bliss. "This little guy is all I need." The mother's lips swept her son's forehead, just below his thick crop of dark hair. The baby opened his eyes and blinked. Sophia's face lit up like an angel's.

An unfamiliar pang welled within Ben's chest. "Well, maybe just a quick hold. If I'm not a third wheel, that is."

Before he knew it, his son was in his arms. Small eyes searched his own. Pursed lips opened and closed. Tiny limbs wriggled within the blanket. The boy was perfect. Nothing squashed or molded. Nothing bruised or discolored. Only a faint vascular marking between his eyebrows, like a salmon-hued Rorschach inkblot.

An image of Willy holding his grandson flashed in Ben's mind, and out of nowhere, a sob strangled his throat. He blinked like a man with pepper spray in his eyes and hoped Sophia hadn't noticed.

A pink arm flipped out of the blanket, and five perfect fingers startled open. Ben grabbed the hand in his own. So tiny. So warm.

His phone vibrating in his front pocket broke his wonder. Its persistent tremor suggested a call rather than a text. He ignored it but handed the baby back to Sophia nonetheless. He didn't dare hold the boy any longer. Didn't trust himself to think clearly while swimming in a sea of emotion.

Sophia nuzzled her nose against her son's cheek and spoke directly to him. "Two years ago I thought I would die from cancer, but here I am, cancer-free, and here you are, perfect and healthy." She grabbed the cross around her neck with her free hand and pressed it to her lips.

Ben's phone rang again, and again he ignored it, simultaneously marveling and panicking at the sight before him. He didn't know Sophia. Not really. Nor did she know him. Maybe she'd hate him. Maybe she'd think him too rigid and distant like Melissa did. Maybe she was hoping he'd take her suggestion and bow out of their lives completely.

"Have you decided on a name yet?" he asked.

Another nose to cheek nuzzle. "Not yet. I want to get to know him first." Then, startling Ben, she lifted her gown and exposed a breast. Ben's cheeks flushed, and he averted his eyes, but he looked back when he heard her laugh. "He's latched on already."

"That's because he's brilliant."

"Like his daddy." Sophia beamed down at her child.

And that was all it took.

Like ocean waves, blood rushed behind Ben's eardrums. His heartbeat sped up, and he leaned closer to the bed. Just as he was about to tell Sophia he was all in, his phone vibrated again. A short blip this time, indicating a text.

"You better get that," she said. "Maybe it's Dr. Spock." She giggled at her own joke and stroked the baby's face.

Ben pulled the phone from his pocket. Willy.

His dad never texted.

Ben read the message. He shot up in his chair, startling both Sophia and the baby, who pulled away from the breast.

Call me! Now! the text practically screamed.

"What is it?" Sophia asked in concern.

Ben shook his head and called his father. He stood and paced the room. Willy picked up on the first ring and started talking before he even confirmed it was Ben. "It's Harmony, she's not well, something's wrong, she—"

"Dad, slow down."

Though still anxious, Willy's voice slowed to coherence. "I thought she was heading into a depression. She seemed off tonight, you know?"

Ben did know. He'd thought the same himself.

"But she wouldn't eat dinner, and when she stood up from the table, she nearly fainted. Said she wasn't feeling well. A stomach ache."

Ben's shoulders relaxed. "Just give her some fluids. I'm sure she'll be fine."

"But she visited that woman in the hospital. Kate. The one who died. And now I'm worried she …" Willy's voice tapered off.

The tension in Ben's shoulders returned. Kate had been sick. She died. Melissa had taken care of Kate. Now *she* was sick. Harmony had visited Kate five days ago. Could she have the same thing?

"Oh, God," Ben said, not realizing he'd spoken aloud.

"Son? Son, are you there?"

"I'm here. Sorry." Inhaling, Ben settled himself down. Lots of people got sick from lots of different things. *Relax.* "Where is she now?"

"She just left in a cab to go back to her hotel. I tried to call you before she left, but you didn't answer. I suggested she go to an acute care clinic or the ER, but she refused. I'd take her there myself if she'd let me, but, well, you know how I feel about hospitals."

Ben did. Nothing like a dying partner to sour a person on hospitals.

"I was hoping you could check on her."

"I'm not a doctor yet."

"Please, Benny. Just call and make sure she's okay. What if Kate infected her?"

Laurette sprang to Ben's mind. Her accented voice. Her frightened but firm words: *That cut cursed you, and now you are cursing others.*

"I'm sure she's fine, but I'll give her a call."

"Thank you. Just want to be safe."

Father and son said good-bye. Ben opened his palm. Saw the bandage was gone, probably sweated off during the delivery. Dried blood crusted the lesion. When had he reinjured it?

Was it possible? Could he have picked up an infection from that catacomb bone? Not a curse for God's sake, but some type of infection?

Ridiculous. Those bones were ancient. They couldn't harbor infectious organisms.

"Everything okay?" Sophia asked again.

Before he could answer, the nurse popped in for the baby. While she tended to Sophia and the newborn, Ben said a quick goodbye and promised to return. The skepticism in Sophia's face suggested she didn't believe him.

15

A few hours after leaving Sophia and the baby, he was still a tangle of nerves. Back in his apartment, seated at his desk in his living room, he searched online tips for new fathers in hopes of calming himself down. Knowledge was power after all. Instead it had the opposite effect. Colic, cytomegalovirus, newborn fevers, Sudden Infant Death Syndrome, blocked intestines. So much could go wrong. How did people do it? Just reading about SIDS made his throat collapse.

At least Harmony was okay. He'd called her hotel room after he left the hospital, and she assured him Willy was overreacting. "I'm fine. Just a little tired."

Leaning back in a wooden chair not meant for comfort, he ran his toes through the shag carpeting and his fingers through unusually thick stubble. Had he even shaved today? One room over in the unfinished part of the basement, the spin cycle of his landlady's washing machine kicked in. The machine heaved and shook, clothes twisting and thumping inside. Normally Ben wouldn't do laundry this late, but the grieving Mrs. Sinclair was staying across town with relatives. She'd left Izzy behind. Cat-sitting was the least Ben could do.

He got up and entered the laundry room, his bare feet a human broom across its dusty floor. He'd promised Edith he'd take a look at the broken-down relic, but he never got around to it. Too busy with his clinical rotation.

And now her only child was dead.

"Shut up," he hollered at the old washer. It ignored him and bucked like a seizing Transformer. He kicked it. Hard. When it kept rocking, he reached out and punched the power knob. The machine fell dead. Ben dropped to the concrete floor and leaned against the silenced appliance.

His mind raced. Sophia. Their baby. Surviving med school and residency as a father. Kate. Melissa sick. Maybe Harmony too. Laurette's foolish belief Ben was behind it. Earlier, he'd texted and called Melissa but got no response. No surprise there.

He put his head in his hands and squeezed. Sleep. That was what he needed. Pre-rounds were in seven hours. But he knew sleep would never come, not if his mind flipped and dinged like a pinball machine all night.

As if feeling his pain, Izzy sauntered in and nudged her head against his thigh. He picked the tabby up and clung to her, grateful to have another beating heart next to his own. After a few minutes of purring on her part and strangled breathing on his, he stood and turned the washing machine back on. Its rocking and chugging sent Izzy darting back upstairs. Ben returned to his living room. On his laptop, the last article he'd accessed remained on the screen. Newborn circumcision. He winced and closed the internet browser.

Minutes on the computer clock ticked by. Unable to think clearly or move, he watched them like a corpse. Then an idea surfaced, one that gave him a chill. He clicked the browser back open, hesitated, and then typed the words *Haitian Vodou*.

From a handful of websites, he learned the following:

> *By the end of the 1700s, hundreds of thousands of slaves had been plucked from West Africa and transplanted to Saint-Domingue in the Caribbean, a French colony that would later become Haiti. The slaves were sent to work the land's coffee and sugar plantations, but given the brutal conditions on their voyage across the Atlantic, many died en route. Others perished within a few years of relocation.*
>
> *With them, the Africans brought along their ancestral practice of Vodun. Over time, African Vodun fused with the religious practices of the Saint-Domingue indigent tribes, along with the Catholicism of the land-owners, which was forced upon the Africans. The result of this spiritual fusion was Haitian Vodou, a practice the slaves tried to keep secret from the plantation owners. In 1804 the Vodouisants (Vodou practitioners)*

credited Vodou for allowing them to pull off the only successful slave rebellion in the history of the world.

With his interest piqued, Ben clicked to a new web page. He rubbed his eyes and read on. Just as Laurette had said, Vodou appeared to be more a way of life than a religion.

Believers perform different rituals for their ancestral dead and family spirits. These spirits are known as Lwa (or Loa) and are considered angels who work for Bondye, the God deity who created and maintains the universe. In addition to ancestral Lwa, everybody has their own personal Lwa to serve in order to bring good fortune to their lives. Failing to serve results in bad fortune. Vodouisants make altars and perform ceremonies to communicate with their Lwa. They offer gifts to appease the spirits and then consult them for healing, divination, or advice. These gifts include the blood of sacrificed animals.

At that point in Ben's reading, a photograph showed two men near a tree holding a goat with a slit throat. Blood drained from the dead animal's neck into a bowl. A few crimson drops splashed onto the surrounding dirt. Ben grimaced and rolled his neck, massaging the tense muscles. He hunched back over and read on.

The Lwa answer their servants through messages, dreams, and sometimes through temporary possession—mounting—of a human body. The possessed person is known as a chwal, *a horse, because it is as if the Lwa rides him or her.*

Though Vodou is meant to be used for good with the aid of trained—initiated—priests (houngans) and priestesses (mambos), some uninitiated priests and priestesses, known as bokors, use it for evil and are frowned upon by initiated houngans and mambos.

Like an inflatable toy taking shape, Ben rose up in his chair until his spine was ramrod straight. Pinpricks of electricity buzzed through his hairline.

Bokor.

He recognized the word. Laurette had mentioned one of the men in the pharmacy was a bokor. The one with the big eyes and charismatic smile. Jean Miot.

With growing alarm, Ben opened a new website. Mentions of zombie curses, human sacrifices, sexual dances, and the devil. And blood. Everywhere the word *blood*.

He scrolled through endless links, each site spiking his heart rate with graphic images of dead-eyed zombies and blood-spurting animals. Then he realized the disturbing images referenced voodoo, not Vodou, a distinction both Laurette and the other sites he'd visited had been quick to make. He relaxed somewhat. According to an earlier web page, voodoo was a popularized and often fictitious practice associated with Louisiana. It was the subject of sensational Hollywood movies and lurid novels, not real life. Its claims of zombies, bizarre rituals, and infant sacrifices were folklore and had nothing to do with Haitian Vodou.

Ben exhaled and stretched his back, arms folded behind his head. Almost one in the morning. He had to get some sleep. But just as he was about to close the internet and shut down the laptop, his finger froze above the mouse. In the corner of the screen, two words in a creepy, blood-red font held his gaze: *Vodou Curses*. Ignoring the warning bells going off in his head, he clicked open the link.

Lacking the graphics of the other websites, the page was more like an imageless Word document, with densely packed paragraphs against a white background. The words told of notorious Vodou curses placed throughout the centuries by uninitiated bokors for nefarious purposes. In other words, evil practitioners who cast spells to seek revenge, inflict bodily harm, or gain control of another. Or to kill.

How this was done varied. Sometimes, through the use of neurotoxic powders, the bokor rendered his victim into a coma and buried him alive. After many hours, the victim was dug up and given an antidote that revived him but left him dissociated from his former self, essentially a zombie. The process of zombification left a person's soul displaced from his body, condemning him to an enslaved state where he'd spend the rest of his life doing the bidding of another. Other times the cursed individual developed a sickness, either a permanent ailment or a fatal affliction. Or maybe the target was not the accursed person himself, but rather his loved ones, who then suffered severely for his misdeeds, a punishment oftentimes worse than his own death.

Dust coated Ben's mouth. The muscles in his neck and back screamed, and his heart raced uncomfortably. Laurette and her warnings flashed in his mind.

Bullshit. It was all bullshit. He just needed a good night's sleep. Slumber to clear his overtaxed brain.

But yet he read on.

More words about assuming powers, taking blood, inflicting suffering. Then a line made him catch his breath.

The blood of an accursed man's offspring may be more powerful than that of his own. For through an infant flows the purest blood of all.

Ben aspirated pooled saliva. Sputtering, he coughed to clear it. His palm grew cold and clammy on the mouse. It was horse shit—of course it was—but his thoughts flew to his newborn son nonetheless. No wonder Laurette was always clutching her damn amulet. If he believed those things, he'd never dare leave the house.

Grateful for his place in time and geography, he came to his senses and shut down the laptop, but he'd be lying if he said the late-night stillness didn't bother him. He hoped for a passing car outside the basement's hopper window, a barking dog, even the banging of the washing machine, which had long since fallen dormant. Anything to remind him he wasn't alone in the world.

Trudging off to bed, he assumed he'd never find sleep. He did, but it was a fitful sleep, filled with zombies, tunic-wearing Haitians, and curses.

And babies. Babies and blood.

In the worst of the nightmares, the tip of a knife grazed unblemished, newborn skin. Before it could pierce the flesh, Ben bolted awake, his heart thundering and his sheets drenched in sweat.

When he recovered enough to move, he whipped off the covers and stumbled to the closet, where he slid open the wooden door panel so forcefully it slipped off its metal base and clattered against his worn-out treadmill. In the dim light of a street lamp outside his tiny window, he reached for the pants he'd worn that day, He dug around in their pockets until his palm closed around something cold and sharp.

He pulled out the bone amulet Laurette had left in his mail cubby and slipped it over his head. Then he sank to his bed and willed his pulse to slow down.

16

In standard hierarchal fashion, Ben hustled down the emergency depart-ment corridor behind Dr. Smith, Jamal, and Kelly, one of the interns. Each face was somber, but none so much as Ben's. Disbelief and panic squeezed his chest.

Melissa Horner was in the emergency department. His ex-girlfriend. The perfectly lovely woman he'd left dangling on a relationship string for months. And now she might have what Kate had.

Upon reaching the main counter, Dr. Smith stopped in front of a man with wire-rimmed glasses and jet-black hair. According to the embroidered name tag on his white coat, he was Dr. N. Amin, one of the ED attendings. He was discussing medication orders with a curly haired nurse who jotted the instructions on a clipboard. Near the nurse's left elbow a phone went unanswered, and in a room behind her, an alarm wailed. A blur of blue scrubs ran to its source, and from the maelstrom, a female voice barked something about paging the trauma surgeon. The scents of floor polish, sweaty bodies, and plaster for orthopedic casts commingled in the air.

The two attendings greeted each other. Judging by the warm smile Dr. Amin gave Dr. Smith, he was in her good graces. He even used her first name—Taka—to address her, his accent more British than Indian.

"We came to see 6 West's newest admission," Dr. Smith told him, her bobbed hair skimming the collar of her azure blouse.

Bushy eyebrows rose above Dr. Amin's wire frames. "All of you?"

"She's one of our medical students. We didn't want to wait until she reached the floor." Dr. Smith's jaw slackened, and though she quickly resumed a professional countenance, Ben hadn't missed the flash of worry in her eyes. She glanced at a sheet of paper in Dr. Amin's hands. "Is that Ms. Horner's blood count?"

At the mention of the CBC, Ben tensed. Would Melissa have eosinophilia too? The only clue they'd had of Kate's illness was her sky-high eosinophil count, even though they had no idea what caused it. He bit his lower lip and prayed Melissa's would be normal.

The ED doctor nodded, the top of his head level with Ben's forehead. "It is, but there was a problem with the sample. They have to rerun it."

Ben's teeth sank deeper into his lip. It took all his willpower not to sprint to the lab and run the test himself. Not that he'd know how.

"What's going on with our young colleague?" Dr. Smith glanced over her shoulder, and when she did, her eyes softened.

Ben turned to follow her gaze. About twenty feet behind them on the right, Joel sat on a stool, holding a patient's hand. Ben assumed it was Melissa's, but with the curtain drawn, only a forearm was visible. As if sensing their presence, the grad student looked up. His fear shifted to contempt upon spotting Ben.

Without thinking, Ben placed his hand over the bone hidden beneath his shirt and tie. Though he'd dismissed last night's dreams as absurd, he couldn't bring himself to remove Laurette's childhood amulet.

"Miss Horner came to the ED this morning." Dr. Amin leaned against the counter, his white coat bunching up at his sides. "Mild symptoms yesterday: headache, low-grade fever, body aches. But all worse in the last twenty-four hours."

Tentacles of unease wormed around Ben. He waited for the doctor to go on.

"Now she has vomiting, diarrhea, and severe abdominal pain. Specks of blood in her last stool too. Her exam and electrolytes support dehydration, and since she can't keep down fluids, we need to admit her. We figure she has gastroenteritis, but her boyfriend—your stepson, I believe—mentioned her caring for a recently deceased patient with an unknown illness."

Dr. Smith nodded and turned to Jamal, who proceeded to fill Dr. Amin in on Kate's hospital course, including her deterioration into shock, clotting abnormalities, and diffuse bleeding. "An autopsy will be done," the senior resident added.

The grip on Ben's insides tightened. He tugged on his tie, its snugness suffocating him. Between morning report and rounds, and now Melissa's pending admission, he hadn't had time to see Sophia in L&D. He'd called her room during rounds when Dr. Smith was preoccupied with a phone call, but the new mother didn't pick up. He'd just started dialing her cell phone, using the number he'd jotted down when he perused her chart the week before, when Dr. Smith finished her own call and eyed him impatiently. He'd stuffed his phone back in his pocket before reaching Sophia. What if she thought he'd taken her advice and abandoned them?

Inhaling deeply, he returned his attention to the group as they headed to Melissa's bedside. Once there, Dr. Smith did the talking, leaving Ben and the two residents standing quietly next to her, Jamal periodically stepping aside to allow the nurse access to Melissa's monitors and IV line.

Seeing his ex with tubing in her arms and sensors on her skin tore at Ben's heart. Her short, blond hair was flattened against the pillow, and dark circles rimmed her sea-colored eyes. Despite her obvious malaise, she put up a good front and answered Dr. Smith's questions. Ben knew her well enough to know having her colleagues see her like that was the last thing she wanted.

Dr. Smith promised Melissa they'd take good care of her. The internist rested a hand on Joel's shoulder, as if to reassure him, but he shook his head and glared at Ben.

"It's his fault. Kate Naughton should've been his patient, not Melissa's."

Ben bit back the urge to defend himself. He could see Joel was hurting.

"No one's at fault." Dr. Smith blushed and seemed embarrassed by her stepson's accusation, offering the first glimpse of vulnerability Ben had seen from the woman. "Melissa most likely has a stomach bug. You know that. Some IV fluids and she'll be good as new."

Melissa offered a small smile and patted Joel's hand, but the grad student remained poised to pounce.

"Lots of people interacted with Ms. Naughton during her hospitalization, Benjamin included." Dr. Smith nodded Ben's way. "The nurses were especially involved in her care, and none of them are sick. There's nothing to suggest it was contagious or even infectious. It could have been immune-mediated for all we know. But just to be safe, we'll put Melissa in isolation." Joel's eyes widened, and she quickly added, "Only as a precaution."

Ben told himself to relax. Even Dr. Smith didn't think the two cases were related. He'd let Laurette fill his head with foolish fears.

And yet you wear her amulet, Benny Boy.

Finishing their assessment, the group shuffled away. Before they reached the ED doors, Dr. Amin hurried over, waving a sheet of paper. "Wait. I have Miss Horner's CBC results."

Ben clenched his hands. Images of Melissa puking and stooling blood flooded his brain as he waited for the bespectacled doctor to continue.

"It appears her eosinophil count is off the charts," Dr. Amin said.

17

Ben didn't finish his ward work until after five. He was tired and hungry, having missed lunch when the team admitted Melissa from the ED. Two fruit-and-nut bars from the vending machine at three thirty had been a poor substitute, but he couldn't waste time eating now. If he didn't visit Sophia and the baby soon, he'd explode.

Backpack over his shoulder and white coat in his locker, he headed to Labor & Delivery in the Talcott Center. Since he was coming from the med student lounge in the College of Medicine, he had to cross the street instead of using an upper-level walkway. In his preoccupied state, he barely registered the late-afternoon heat or the tumult of rush-hour traffic.

When he reached L&D's automatic doors on the second floor, he jumped back in surprise. The last person he expected to see was coming out: Joel. The two men eyed each other, confusion on both their faces. A businesswoman carrying a huge balloon decorated with trains and trucks shuffled past them.

"You here to congratulate Amy too?" Joel's tone suggested he'd rather eat shit than talk to Ben.

"Amy? Who? No, I …" What could he say? He didn't want Joel knowing about Sophia. He'd blab to his stepmom that Ben was a new father, making Ben's chances of surviving internal medicine even slimmer.

"Amy? The grad student I work with?" Joel mimed a monkey face, as if to say, *Are you stupid or something?* "She just had her baby. I stopped by while

Melissa's getting an x-ray." Ben had no idea who Amy was, and in his silence, Joel raised his chin and narrowed his eyes. "What are you doing here, then?"

The doors whirred open, and a man wearing an *I'm a New Grandpa* T-shirt walked out. Ben shifted gears. "Look, I'm sorry about Melissa. At least she's doing okay so far."

Joel's Hollywood face shifted into a Neanderthal glower. "You don't get to say her name. You treated her like nothing but a convenient—" His voice broke off, as if he couldn't bring himself to say it. "She's none of your business now." He pushed past Ben, thumping Ben's shoulder with his own. Before walking away, he turned around and stabbed a finger in Ben's chest. "There's something up with you, man. I don't know what it is, but I don't trust you for a second."

He huffed away, leaving Ben rubbing his shoulder, wondering how in the world his tidy life had become so messy.

A few minutes later he entered Sophia's room in time to hear a nurse asking, "How's your head and stomach ache? Getting better?"

"What? Are you sick?" Ben dumped his backpack on the chair and hustled over to Sophia.

She smiled, her arm extended, a blood pressure cuff encircling it. "I'm fine. I just had a baby, remember?"

The RN's ponytail swished back and forth as she moved around and checked Sophia's vitals. "You men. Always nervous about this baby stuff." She redirected her attention to Sophia. "Okay to talk with him in here? You were in the shower when the doctor stopped by, and she asked me to pass on the evening's plan."

Sophia nodded. "Yes, Ben here is the ... he's my friend."

The digital blood pressure device beeped its reading, and the nurse recorded the number on a piece of paper, which she then stuffed into her scrubs pocket. She pressed gently on Sophia's abdomen. "Your doctors are going to continue the magnesium for now. They keep it onboard for twenty-four hours after a delivery to prevent seizures."

"Seizures?" The back of Ben's shirt had come untucked, and he pulled out the front to match. "The doctor thinks she might have seizures?"

"No, it's just a precaution with preeclampsia." An alarm on the infusion pump sounded. The nurse unkinked Sophia's IV tubing and pushed a button to silence the beeping. Addressing Sophia, she said, "Your blood pressure's still acting up so they want to watch you. I'm sure you'll be fine."

"What about the baby?" Ben asked.

"The pediatrician wants him in the nursery for now. The little guy's having trouble keeping his temp up, and he's still a poky eater." The RN must've seen the worry on Ben's face, because she added, "That's all to be expected. He's a bit early. At least he's latching onto the breast well."

Sophia fiddled with the cross around her neck. "He's safe in there, right? I just wish he could be with me all the time."

Ben patted her shoulder. "He'll be fine in there. A newborn nursery's tougher to escape than prison."

A laugh from the nurse. "He's right about that." Her hands fell to her ample hips. "Tanisha will be taking over at seven, but I'll be back tomorrow. Maybe you'll have a name for the little guy by then."

Sophia merely smiled.

After the nurse left, Ben moved his backpack to the floor and sat down on the chair. He extended his weary legs and tried to put Melissa and her high eosinophil count out of his mind, at least for a while.

"You didn't have to come," Sophia said.

"Hey, I'm only here for the ambiance." He fanned an arm at the drab walls and scuffed vinyl flooring. When Sophia laughed, he felt five pounds lighter.

"Whoa, so you do smile," she said, seeing his momentary mirth. "That's the first genuine one I've seen from you since I've been here. It's nice. You should do it more often."

"Just tired. Tough rotation." Needless to say he omitted the part about Vodou dreams and bone amulets.

"I meant what I said yesterday. I don't expect anything from you. I—"

Ben put a finger to his lips to silence her. He reached for her hand but remembering his bandage, which he'd taken to wearing permanently to avoid bleeding on everyone like a sacrificed goat, he drew back. "I'm not going anywhere."

"You say that now, but what about in three weeks? Three months? Three years? What about when you're on call all night and have to deal with an irritable infant or toddler the next day? No, you have a life plan. I heard all about it the night we hooked up. I won't take that from you. I won't trap you into this."

"Hey, hey." Ben gently tugged her short hair. "I don't know what's going to happen, but I know I'm not walking away. Neither financially nor parentally." Though he presented a reassuring front, a tsunami of anxiety swirled within him. He couldn't even commit to Melissa. How was he going to commit to being a father? Not to mention cash flow. He'd have money one day, but he sure didn't have any now.

Sophia turned toward the window and stared at a neighboring building. Her eyes blinked, and Ben suspected his words were what she wanted to hear. To break the awkward moment, he told her about Willy. Then, to his amazement, he told her about Max's death, his childhood, even Harmony's abandonment. By the time he'd finished, his hands were shaking and his mouth was as dry as the stupid bone pressing into his chest.

"Thank you for telling me that," Sophia said. "I can tell it wasn't easy. And thank you for being here. I know we hardly know each other, but we can do it, right?" She laid her head back against the pillow. "Weird how life works. One moment we're practically strangers, the next we're forever connected."

Ben smiled, but the comment sat in his gut like an anchor.

With his appetite mollified from the bread roll and vegetable beef soup a vegetarian Sophia had shared from her dinner tray, Ben stood in front of the newborn nursery and stared at his son through the glass. Though he had studying and an upcoming presentation to prepare that night, he needed to see his son first.

Watching the baby sleep, swaddled in blue blankets and nestled in a bassinet, Ben's heart swelled and a lump formed in his throat. At that moment he knew. Knew he was all in. He'd find a way to make it work. Maybe Willy would help. Maybe he'd be horrified. Either way, Willy would be there. And most times, that was enough.

With reluctance, Ben tore himself away. When he turned to leave, he did a double-take.

A figure dashed down a perpendicular hallway and disappeared. Ben thought he recognized the guy, but with the fleeting glimpse, he couldn't be sure. A hospital employee maybe? No, someone else.

Bothered, but still at a loss five minutes later when he reached the hospital's bike rack, he unlocked his bicycle and helmet. Though the evening was still warm, it was loads better than the oppressive swelter of the past few days. On the sidewalk, people flocked about, grab-on-the-run Philly cheesesteaks or pizza slices clutched in their hands. Ben nearly trailed like a slobbering dog behind their intoxicating scents.

Instead he put on his helmet, popped the U-lock in his backpack, and hoisted the bag over both shoulders. As soon as he mounted the bike, planning to spring for a sandwich from the vendor down the street, his phone rang. Worried it might be Sophia, he planted his feet on the ground and pulled out his phone. Willy again.

"Hey, Dad, what's up?"

"Benny, listen, you gotta come to Harmony's hotel. She doesn't look good. Says she's just feeling blue, but this is more than her usual wool blanket. She's really pale. I tried to get her to drink some water, but she can't keep it down." *Water* came out *wooder* in Willy's Philly accent, a pronunciation Ben sometimes got caught with too.

He waited before answering, legs still straddling his bike, a fire hydrant near his right foot. Willy was uncomfortable with sickness. It was Max who'd nursed Ben through strep throats and stomach flus. Willy tended to worry that every symptom, no matter how small, was one step away from death, especially after Max got cancer.

On the other hand, Ben knew Harmony had visited Kate. Assuming it was nothing felt risky. God knew what was going to happen to Melissa.

"Does she have anything else going on? Cold symptoms, fever, nausea, stom—"

"Oh, God. Oh shit."

"What?" Ben nearly toppled over. He repositioned himself over the bike's bar.

"She just vomited blood."

Ben's grip on the phone tightened. "I'm on my way. Call 9-1-1. And Dad? Be careful. Wash your hands and try not to touch her."

Racing off through the narrow streets, he dodged cars and insults like only a seasoned city biker could. As he pedaled, the backpack pulled his shirt tightly against his torso, pressing Laurette's bone amulet deep into his flesh. He swore he could feel it burning. Almost as if it were branding him.

18

Ben sat in an empty hallway behind the emergency department, hardly believing the news. Across from him, a row of darkened ultrasound rooms extended to automatic doors on both ends, the outpatient radiology staff having long since departed for the day. Not keen on hanging out in a crowded waiting room with its coughing and weeping masses, he had dragged a chair from one of the deserted rooms and isolated himself in the hall.

Harmony was getting transferred to 6 West.

Though in the ED she'd told Ben to go home and get some sleep, he didn't feel comfortable leaving her until she made it to the ward. He would visit her there soon, but first he needed a moment to regroup. Needed to figure out how to explain his relationship with Harmony to the 6 West staff. They'd no doubt ask about his presence. Medical students weren't on call past nine p.m. Plus, Kelly was the intern on that night, and considering her fondness for chatter, she'd want his family dynamics spelled out in detail, which she'd then happily spill to the rest of the team in the morning.

The automatic door whirred open. Ben expected to see a staff member come through, but to his surprise (and relief, despite their recent argument in the ICU) it was Laurette.

"Ah, there you are, my friend. Someone told me you were hiding back here."

"How … what are you doing here?" Ben jumped up to give her his chair.

"Take a tired man's chair? That I cannot do."

When Ben insisted, she thanked him and sat, her empire-waist blouse drawing his eyes to her cleavage. He checked himself and looked away.

"Your father phoned and told me an ambulance was bringing Harmony to the ER, where you would join them. He did not want you to be alone."

"He doesn't much like hospitals."

"That I could tell."

Ben sank to his haunches and leaned against the wall, his head in line with the wooden guardrail. "I'm sorry I haven't texted you. You just caught me off guard in the ICU yesterday with all your ... well, you know."

She patted his knee. Gone was the crimson nail polish. In its place, an elegant seafoam, once again matching her blouse. "No worries. How is Harmony? Your father mentioned she visited Kate, yes? Do you think it's the same illness?"

Ben shrugged, the amulet shifting with his chest, the bone plastered to his skin. He needed a shower. Between the stress of the day and his mad bike ride to Harmony's hotel, he smelled ranker than spoiled meat. "Probably," he said. "Same symptoms of weakness, fever, vomiting, diarrhea. She saw Kate six days ago, which fits the same time frame as Melissa. Plus, her eosinophils are high." He rocked back and forth. "Fuck." The word echoed in the empty hall. "Sorry."

"Shh, it will be okay."

Laurette rubbed his back, and despite his penchant for physical boundaries, he melted into her touch. "She's going into isolation like Melissa. Suddenly everyone's donning gowns and masks like the plague has come to town. They ran an Ebola test on Melissa even though Kate's was negative. Melissa's was negative too."

Laurette nodded as if the news was no surprise to her. Ben knew what she was thinking: *It is not Ebola, Benjamin Oris. It is you.* He felt a sudden need to defend himself. "Kate was around a lot of people before and during her hospitalization, but only Melissa and Harmony caught it. That means the infection isn't very contagious and certainly not airborne."

Laurette stopped the back rub and stared at a crash cart across the hall, her coiled sprigs of hair falling as motionless as her body.

"But that doesn't surprise you either, does it?"

"No."

Ben shifted off his haunches and dropped all the way to the floor. Like a dejected rag doll, he let his legs splay out in front of him. "Believe me, I know it's strange. The three sick people are all linked to me. But they're also linked to each other. It could just be a coincidence."

"I don't think you really believe that."

"I don't know what to believe. I know you think something happened to me in the catacombs, and who knows, maybe it did." He rubbed the bandage on his palm, feeling the mounded lesion beneath it. "Maybe I did get infected with something. Maybe I'm passing it on to others. But even if I can accept that, I *can't* accept anything about curses." He didn't tell her about his internet research nor that he was wearing her amulet. He also didn't fess up about Sophia and the baby. He wanted to, but he felt an inexplicable need to keep his two worlds separate, as if mixing them would somehow bring harm.

"We come from different places. We see through different lenses. But that does not change the issue, does it?" She reached down from the chair and grabbed his hand, turning it palm upward. Dust from the floor powdered his fingers. "Whether your version or my version, something bad is in you and now it is in those around you."

Ben freed his hand and rubbed off the dirt. "I've decided to talk to Dr. Smith tomorrow."

Laurette raised her eyebrows, clearly surprised.

"No, I'm not going to say anything about curses. I'm not an idiot. I'm going to tell her I might have caught something from an old bone."

"That is not the best way. Let me help you instead."

"You can help by letting Dr. Khalid know. See what she thinks as an epidemiologist and infectious disease specialist. Maybe there are pathogens old bones carry."

"Yes, I will ask her, but that is not the kind of help I meant."

Ben leaned his head against the wall and closed his eyes, softly at first then so tightly he saw bright lights. He knew what kind of help she meant. The first offerings of it already hung around his neck.

But he had no clue how to accept help like that. And judging by the sickening twist in his gut, he sure as hell didn't want to.

19

"Melissa Horner, hospital day number three. Overnight she—"

"Let's have Benjamin present Melissa today." Dr. Smith cut Kelly off, leaving the intern's mouth open midsentence. "After all, she's his patient too." Dr. Smith lowered her eyes and brushed something off her linen skirt.

Standing outside Melissa's room in a sea of white coats, stethoscopes, tablets, and clipboards, the rounding team turned to Ben, no doubt as surprised as he was to deviate from the routine. Interns always presented at formal rounds. Had he been lured to a trap?

Regardless, he was ready. He'd been following his ex-girlfriend's hospital course so closely he could recite every drop of her output to the exact milliliter. God, how she must hate that, her colleagues discussing her urine and stool output as if discussing how she takes her coffee.

And though he hadn't yet been able to voice his concerns about his role in the infection to Dr. Smith (she'd been away at a conference the day before), he *had* managed to get caught up with both his readings and his sleep in her absence. He'd gone on his routine Thursday night jog with Laurette too, finally telling her about Sophia and the baby. Her subdued response was what he'd expected.

Ben glanced at his notes on Melissa and started to present. "Melissa's bloody emesis and stools increased, so the on-call team bumped up her IV fluid rate. She remains febrile and developed confusion overnight, just like Harmony two rooms down."

As if a synchronized school of fish, the medical team looked in that direction, giving Ben time to clear his throat before the shock of everything closed it for good. Both Melissa's and Harmony's rooms had silver carts stocked with yellow robes positioned nearby. Boxes of gloves, blue respiratory masks, and a few goggles for those performing more invasive measures were stockpiled as well. A red octagon sign warning *Contact Precautions* was taped to each door, along with illustrations depicting proper gowning, masking, and gloving techniques. An epidemiologist and infectious disease specialist continued to be on the case.

Judging by the pocket of silence surrounding the team, they all shared the same thought: Kate had grown confused too. Then she went downhill and started oozing blood from every orifice and died.

"Shall we?" Dr. Smith's chin lifted, as if she, too, needed to mentally prepare to enter her student's room. "But given the infectious disease precautions, only those who need to be there will go in." With manicured nails, she pointed to Jamal, Kelly, and Ben, all of whom proceeded to gown, glove, and mask.

Inside the room, Joel slumped forward in a chair next to Melissa's bed, his head buried within his gowned and gloved body as if resting. When the door clicked open, he sat up. His eyes blinked above his mask. Melissa lay asleep, face toward the window, skin the same ashen hue Kate had worn a few days before.

Joel's eyes pinched into a tired scowl, and he pointed at Ben. "Not him. I don't want that scumbag in here. He's the one—"

"Enough." Dr. Smith's sharp tone quieted Joel, clearing up any doubt he fully accepted the woman as his mother. The grad student huffed back against his chair.

The attending's rebuke had roused Melissa, and the normally chipper woman rolled a sluggish, perspiring head across the pillow, her blond pixie matted against her scalp. Licking her lips, she opened her eyes and muttered something.

"What's that, baby?" Joel leaned forward. He lifted Melissa's limp hand as if it were blown glass.

Ben's heart cinched. A dollop of guilt measured in too. Asshole or not to Ben, the guy treated Melissa like a goddess, far better than Ben ever had.

But despite soothing his girlfriend, Joel's touch had the opposite effect. Melissa arched her back, rolled her eyes up, and stiffened like petrified driftwood.

"She's seizing," Jamal called out, rushing to her right side.

Joel jumped up and stumbled back, his gloved hands covering his mask, panic in his eyes. On instinct, Ben claimed Joel's vacated spot and shoved the visitor's chair out of the way with his foot. While Jamal called to the charge nurse, Ben turned Melissa onto her side so she wouldn't aspirate if she vomited. Her body convulsed, arms and legs jerking rhythmically and jaw stiff. When he heard the senior resident bark for an order of lorazepam, Ben shouted, "No, not lorazepam. She reacted to that during a knee arthroscopy three years ago. It's in the chart."

Jamal froze and looked at Ben. He raised his eyebrows above his mask then nodded. Before he could say anything else, Dr. Smith stepped up, her gloved hands clasped together in front of her yellow gown. "What would you like to give her instead, Benjamin?" Her voice was calm, almost encouraging.

"Maybe phenytoin would be better."

"Dosage?" Dr. Smith asked. Though Jamal seemed antsy to call out the next order, he applied an oxygen mask to Melissa's face and indicated with a nod that Ben continue. By then, a nurse had arrived and was checking Melissa's monitors and vitals. Kelly, the intern, was at the bedside as well, making sure Melissa didn't lose her IV lines during the rhythmic convulsing.

"Ten to fifteen milligrams per kilogram." Ben remembered something he'd read and quickly added, "But no faster than fifty milligrams per minute."

The attending nodded. "Okay people, you heard the man. Let's get that drug here. Remember, a few minutes of a seizure isn't going to hurt the patient. Just monitor her vitals while we wait for the meds and make sure she doesn't aspirate. She might even stop on her own."

Dr. Smith moved toward her stepson, who had backed up against the wall. Though no longer in Ben's line of vision, he heard the frightened grad student's continuous loop of, "Please, please let her be okay."

"She'll be fine, Joel," Dr. Smith said, a note of impatience in her voice.

All the while Ben remained at Melissa's side, helping Kelly and Jamal keep her stable until the medication arrived.

＝╠＝

Thirty minutes later, Ben sat behind the ward counter and entered a note on Melissa in the computer. Though student updates weren't part of the patient's formal record, the neophytes still wrote them daily to practice the skill. Farid, Ben's fellow third-year, tapped at the keyboard next to him, while two of the interns printed out lab reports for an old-fashioned gastroenterology attending who refused to look at anything digital. All four trainees were quiet, absorbed in their work and sober from knowing one of their own had just had a seizure down the hall.

Every few seconds Ben glanced up to the far end of the counter where Dr. Smith stood talking to the gastroenterologist. Ben wanted to catch her before she darted off. Though his palms grew moist at the thought, it was time to speak up about his role in the infection, even if she thought him an idiot.

He needn't have worried about missing her. She was the one to approach him, her expression neutral. "Can I have a word with you? In private?"

"Sure." Ben scrambled to collect his belongings, stuffing his small clipboard into his coat pocket along with his stethoscope. Straightening his tie, the hidden amulet shifting as he did so, he followed Dr. Taka Smith into an empty room.

Inside W672, Dr. Smith closed the door. The last thing Ben saw was Farid behind the counter, looking in their direction, raking his finger across his throat in a *you're dead* gesture.

"Sit." The attending pointed to a cushioned chair by the window. She perched her own bottom on the end of the bed, her tiny form barely indenting the white blanket.

Though Ben's heartbeat was somewhere north of his Adam's apple, he tried not to show it. Through the wall, an alarm in the next room was quickly silenced.

Dr. Smith fiddled with her Rolex, smoothed her skirt, then refolded her hands in her lap. Finally, she looked at Ben. "I'm sorry for how my son treated you in there. Whether he's here in the capacity of a frightened boyfriend or not, that was unprofessional. He should know better."

Ben opened his mouth, then closed it. That wasn't what he was expecting.

"You showed good thinking in there, Ben." The fact she'd addressed him as Ben instead of a clipped *Benjamin* or *Mr. Oris* surprised him as much as the compliment. She leaned forward and crossed her legs at the ankles. "Thinking on one's feet is critical in medicine. With Melissa's seizure, you've shown you can do it. For a third-year student just starting his clinical rotations, that's a rare quality. Maybe it's because you're older than most of your classmates, maybe it's just a gift. Either way, it's impressive."

"Thank you," was all he could think of to say.

The internist examined a thread on the bed and picked at it. "I know I can be a difficult attending, but you should understand I'm hardest on those who I think can take it. Certain rotations, internal medicine included, have to weed out the weak. That may sound paternalistic, and Human Resources would probably have my neck for saying it, but in my opinion it's true." Her gaze caught his. "And you, Ben—you deserve to be here."

Though she left it at that, not bringing Joel's deferment into the conversation, Ben caught the undercurrent of her words. "Thank you," he said again.

The internist gave a sharp nod, popped off the bed, and told him to get back to work.

"Wait," he called out before she opened the door. She waited for him, her fingers clutched around the handle.

For a few seconds his lips moved, but nothing came out. He stood and wiped his palms on his chinos. "I think I'm responsible for making these women sick."

Dr. Smith removed her hand from the door and cocked her head. "Explain please."

Over the next five minutes, Ben told her about having contact with all three women, first Kate in his basement apartment (though he left out their past sexual hook-ups), then Melissa, and finally his estranged mother, Harmony. He then told her about his visit to the Paris catacombs a month before and showed her the unhealed papule on his hand, explaining how it had rebled a few times. He omitted Laurette's Vodou nonsense—he wasn't insane—but nonetheless said he worried he was patient zero.

It was at that point Dr. Smith smiled, amusement flickering in her brown eyes. She raised her hand to interrupt his rambling. "Are *you* sick?"

"Me? No. I mean, I've been a little tired and have an occasional headache, but—"

"Are you febrile?"

"No."

"Vomiting?"

"No."

"Having bloody stools?"

"No."

"Seizures?"

"Noooo," he said, drawing the word out.

She stifled a laugh. "Sorry. I'm having a little fun at your expense. Look, both Melissa and Harmony were exposed to Kate. Kate is patient zero. Well, maybe there's someone else out there we don't know about, but she was the first to come to our attention."

"Yeah, but—"

"There isn't a medical student alive who hasn't suffered from medical-studentitis. Do you know what that is?"

Ben's hands retreated to his coat pockets. He fiddled with the bell of his stethoscope inside the left one. "I think I do now."

"It's when students are convinced they have the disease they're studying. No doubt your colleagues are convinced they have ulcerative colitis, lymphoma, rat bite fever, you name it."

"Still, don't you think it's odd I know all three patients?"

"Odd? No. A coincidence? Yes. You knew the first one, and she infected two more women you know. That's all." Dr. Smith must have noticed his lingering hesitancy, because she added, "If it will make you feel better, I'll give you an order for a complete blood count."

A *eureka* moment hit Ben. Why hadn't he thought of that? So simple.

"If your eosinophil count is normal—which it *will* be—you can quit worrying. Will that make you feel better?"

Sighing in relief, he told her it would.

"Good. I'll sign a written order when I get back to my office and have my secretary run it to your student mailbox. That way you can take it to the lab at your convenience, and if you change your mind there won't be an electronic order waiting."

"Thank you," he said for the umpteenth time, still trying to process the shift in her demeanor toward him.

As they exited the room, she patted his shoulder. "A normal lab is the quickest cure for medical-studentitis. You'll see. But get that palm lesion looked at before it *does* get infected."

His taut muscles finally relaxed, and he trailed out the door behind her. Still, trepidation remained, and he rested the tips of his fingers on the hidden amulet. Hopefully his blood count would be normal.

20

With his laptop resting on his thighs, Ben looked up from Laurette's email, his neck so cramped it was as if someone had jammed a knife into the muscle. He kneaded the area and sank back against his lopsided sofa. The heat from his laptop practically shrink-wrapped his shorts, and the dread he felt made him sick to his stomach.

And to think he'd finally relaxed after talking to Dr. Smith the day before. Had put his fears about infecting the women to rest and instead spent the evening checking in on Melissa, followed by Sophia and the baby, who still weren't ready for discharge. Although Dr. Smith's CBC order wasn't in his mail cubby when he'd left the hospital—and given the weekend, probably wouldn't be until Monday—he'd been reassured enough by her words to not sweat it.

Until he'd read Laurette's email.

Now, unable to stop himself, he cut short his neck massage and read it again.

> Dear Ben,
>
> Please read this email carefully and then meet me in Rittenhouse Square at noon, near the Duck Girl sculpture in the park. This is very important! I received this information from my brother. As you know, I have spoken to Guy about you before. Yesterday, I told him about the three sick women and also that you have a new son. Please do not be

angry. I know you are a private man. But I need my brother's counsel. Auntie Marie's too. This is not something I understand like they do. Although Guy is in Haiti, he has passed time in Philadelphia, and he knows houngans and mambos who practice here.

Vodou is very secretive. Stories, treatments … even how to cast a curse … are passed down from generation to generation. They are told with the tongue and rarely written down. That keeps outsiders out. Guy is one of the most learned in our city, perhaps even our country. I tell you this by email, because I worry you will not listen to me in person. This is what my brother knows:

Upstairs, Mrs. Sinclair's pattering footsteps interrupted Ben's reading. He heard her call Izzy for lunch, perhaps needing the cat's company. Despite the gravity of the email, his thoughts drifted to the woman. When he'd stopped by to see her the night before, he was distressed by her disorientation and grief, as if she had no idea what to do with herself now that her daughter was dead. Ben had seen that look before on his father. To think he might be responsible for it made him sick.

The footsteps stopped, and the creepy silence returned. He read on.

In the eighteenth century, a powerful mambo named Nasicha Boro was enslaved on a sugar plantation on Saint-Domingue, the colony that later became Haiti. A Frenchman, Pierre Marcel, and his son ran the plantation, and both men were known for their cruelty.

According to the story (but understand I cannot confirm its truth), Nasicha had a fifteen-year-old daughter named Kalifa whom the slave owner claimed for his own. Night after night he violated the poor girl until soon she became with child. Shortly after, the Frenchman took both the mambo and her pregnant daughter back to France for a visit, where he expected them to continue their servitude in the slavery-free France. While on the ship, Nasicha had little contact with Pierre, though he repeatedly called for Kalifa. Distraught and wanting to save her daughter, it is rumored the furious mambo cast a curse within Kalifa, one that would not harm the girl but would pass through her fluids to the slave owner the next time he assaulted her. Once cursed, Pierre Marcel would inflict a sickness on those he loved, and before his eyes he would see their bodies rot from the inside out. Any future offspring would carry the curse as well.

But according to the story, there was never a next time. Whether the Frenchman was repelled by the girl's growing belly or whether he took sick is not known. It is only known that when they arrived in France, Marcel's wife learned of her husband's betrayal. Livid over Kalifa's pregnancy, as well as her husband's obvious affection for the girl, the slave owner's wife poisoned Kalifa in hopes of causing an abortion—or worse. Sadly, the girl became gravely ill and was only hospitalized because a neighbor woman took pity on Nasicha and her daughter. But in the hospital, she died.

A dog yelped outside the window behind Ben's head. He jumped, and the laptop slid off his thighs. He righted it, and when his heart descended from his throat, he returned his gaze to the email.

The dying, pregnant girl had been sent to the Hôtel-Dieu, the oldest hospital in Paris. (And Ben, here is where I did my own research to collect the facts. I know you are a man of facts, and so I give them to you now.) The year was 1771, and at that time, the care at the hospital was poor. Not until a fire in 1772 did the organization change. But when the slave girl was there, the place was overcrowded and many people died. Many of the dead were buried in a mass grave at the Cimetière des Saints-Innocents, a cemetery closed in 1780 for lack of space. (And from here Ben, you must pay close attention. I know you think me fou—crazy, yes?—but the following should strike fear in you. Or at least caution.)

The bones from this mass grave were exhumed and were the first to be moved to the Paris catacombs in 1786.

Do you remember, Ben? These were the very bones we stood in front of. These are the bones you ran your hand over. AND THESE ARE THE BONES THAT CUT YOU.

Do not stop reading here, Ben, I implore you. I know this email is long, and I know what I say is hard to believe. I can see you shaking your head now and scrunching your face like you do when you do not agree with someone. And then you roll your eyes and puff out your cheeks as if what they tell you is fou, as if there is only black and white and nothing in between.

Ben exhaled, his cheeks indeed puffed out, even on the second read-through. Laurette knew him so well it was eerie. He shifted the laptop toward his knees to dissipate the heat and steadied himself for the last part.

This is why I take the time to write these words out. It will give you time to process them. You are a visual person, yes? Because the next part is very important.

My brother believes you were cut by the cursed girl's bone. Her remains have lain deep in the ground below Paris for over two centuries, holding a curse that never took root. Two hundred years for it to fester, to seethe, to gain power. And finally, someone came along and disturbed it. Cut himself on it and absorbed its fine dust into his blood, where it is now finally free to do what it was meant to do.

Do you not see? What was meant for the slave-owning Frenchman has come alive in you. You, Ben. It is not Pierre Marcel whose loved ones will fall ill and die from rot. They are long gone. It is you. It is your loved ones who will die from the touch of your hand. From that cursed boil that pulses there.

I know what you are saying here. You are saying, "Kate is not really my loved one. Why is not Willy sick? Why are not you sick, Laurette?" But Ben, I tell you, it may only be a matter of time. Are you willing to risk Willy? Sophia?

Your son?

So please, now that you have read my plea, meet me in the park to talk more. I will tell you the next step to take. I am not a stupid little girl with fanciful stories. I am not naive. I may not know all that my brother knows, but I know when something evil is near.

Your friend always,
Laurette

The knife was back in Ben's neck. He pushed the laptop onto the couch cushion and stretched his head all the way back. When that didn't relieve the cramp, he plopped to the floor and lay supine, willing his body to relax. Raising his right arm, he removed the bandage from his palm and studied the violaceous papule. The damn thing was still the size of a small pea. Hadn't changed at all. He stroked the fleshy surface. Rubbery, firm, not tender. He'd make an appointment with a dermatologist. It might take a while to get in, but at least he'd have it scheduled, and now that Dr. Smith knew about it, she'd give him the time off.

He thought back over the last couple of weeks. Tried to remember touching the women who'd fallen ill. Kate had grabbed his hands in the stairwell of his landlady's home, he remembered that. She'd had her hands all over him, and she got his blood on her palm. And in the patient consultation room outside the ward, he'd grabbed Melissa's arm, right after Joel had stormed out. In his mind's eye he could see the blood trail his papule had left behind on her skin.

What about Harmony? He closed eyes and replayed their interaction on 6 West after she'd visited Kate. She had embraced him, embarrassing him in front of the staff.

His eyelids flipped open. Yes, Harmony had grabbed his hands. That was what had restarted the bleeding before he saw Melissa.

Jesus. It couldn't be.

"Medical-studentitis, that's all. Dr. Smith said so." He spoke aloud, hoping to lessen his fear, but instead he only managed to spook himself more in the graveyard silence.

Sinking deeper into misery, he replayed Laurette's warning words in the email: *Are you willing to risk Willy? Sophia? Your son?* He wondered why she'd excluded herself. She was every bit as important to him as the others.

His stomach swirled, and his flesh broke out into goosebumps. Any muscle relief lying down had granted disappeared. He pushed himself up to standing and tugged his sticky T-shirt from his chest, the amulet scratching his skin below it. Fou or not, he knew where he had to go.

Despite the scorching noon sun and near ninety-degree temperature, Ben wasted no time pedaling to Rittenhouse Square. Sweat-soaked and steeped in adrenaline, he secured his bike to a rack inside the park and made his way to Laurette at the Duck Girl statue, a bronze sculpture of a young girl in toga-style clothing holding a duck in her left hand. It stood on a stone pedestal in the center of the Children's Pool, into whose waters Ben wanted to dive and never come out.

The two students greeted each other with tentative hellos before moving to a bench near the stone balustrade. Though an overhead tree granted some respite from the sun, the air was breezeless, making the many park-goers as listless as the bushes around them. As usual, Laurette looked remarkably fresh, her Haitian roots having long ago acclimated her to heat. While Ben's shorts bore elliptical sweat stains around his groin and his T-shirt stuck to him like sap, her jean shorts and red tank top appeared clean and dry. Even her minimal makeup was unmarred.

"And that is why I think we should seek a divination," she was saying, her fingers massaging the faux emerald in the center of her bronze locket.

"A divination. Gee, that sounds science-based."

"It's often done with cards." Her eyes traveled to Ben's chest, and he knew she spotted the amulet's bulge beneath his shirt. She said nothing, and for that he was grateful.

"I'll probably regret asking this, but what's it do?"

"It allows the houngan or mambo to find the root of your problem. Then he or she can help you find a solution."

"And *poof*, just like that this whole mess is solved. Nifty." Ben mopped his brow. He craved water, but he'd already drained his bottle on the ride over. He slouched on the bench and stared at his friend, childishly pleased to see a line of sweat trickling down her cheek.

"I think you know it's not that simple, but it is a place to start."

He snorted.

"I thought perhaps we should see Mambo Tina, the priestess I told you about at the pharmacy, but Guy feels a … a bokor is better suited for this … curse."

"That Miot guy? You said your brother knows him?"

"Yes, Jean Miot." Another line of sweat dampened Laurette's cheek, and she wiped it away. "But there is something else I must tell you."

"Beyond me being cursed by an ancient slave girl? Tough to beat that one, Bovo."

"Jean Miot, the bokor, would like to see your baby when he gets out of the hospital. He says he will need to—"

Ben shot up on the bench, his sudden movement startling a nearby squirrel that darted off to another tree. "*Hell* no. Man, each time I think you're sounding sane again, you lose another marble."

Laurette didn't appear to be listening. Her attention was focused on something behind Ben, and with a worried expression, she nodded at whatever it was.

Ben turned around and watched a male figure emerge from between two trees. The man wore khaki shorts and a muscle shirt, and as he got closer Ben recognized the closely shaved hair and large, dark eyes. Anger bubbled up inside him. "You invited Jean Miot here without telling me?"

"Guy says we need his help."

"No. I agreed to let *you* help me, not him. You think I'd bring my son to a stranger? To a voodoo worshipper, for Christ's sake?"

Ben hopped up, and Laurette did the same. When Jean Miot joined them, the three formed a silent triangle in front of the bench. A group of preteen girls carrying jump ropes strolled past, and when they were out of earshot, the bokor smiled and extended a hand.

Just like in the pharmacy, Ben didn't shake it. Instead, a sudden recollection surfaced in his brain. "You were outside my son's nursery last week." He moved forward until he was barely inches from the bokor's face. "Are you following me?"

Jean took a step back. "I am here to help you. You *and* your baby."

Ben's face flamed red but not from the heat. He looked to Laurette. "I can't believe you'd do this. Have some stranger stalk my infant son?" Ben raised a fist in the air. "Enough, goddammit, enough. Curses? Vodou priestesses? Dark magic? Forget it, I'm out of here."

He started marching away, but Jean glided forward so quickly he caught Ben by surprise. "Evil is in you, Mr. Oris. Running through your veins. Coursing through your blood." The man gripped both of Ben's arms and squeezed, a feverish look in his eyes. "Do you not feel it? Do you not want to save those around you? Bring me your son. I will help you."

Ben ripped free from the bokor's grasp, passersby staring in their direction. The two men's height differed by at least two inches, to the other man's advantage, but they were of equal bulk, and Ben was not intimidated. He got up into Jean's face again, his words spitting out in staccato beats. "Stay the hell away from my son."

Ben gave Laurette a final look of betrayal and stormed away. His shoes pounded the concrete path with such force, even Duck Girl looked shaken.

21

After inhaling a ham sandwich from a vending machine on the main floor, Ben vaulted five flights to the inpatient ward. Dividing what little free time he had between his harem of hospitalized women, he'd been rushing around to the point of exhaustion. Today's thirty-minute lunch break would go to Harmony, but whether out of guilt or a sense of obligation he couldn't say. Despite their issues, seeing her in a hospital bed shredded him. Her auburn hair was dulled by dehydration, her skin bruised from needle pokes, and her face creased in pain.

It was the sixth day of hospitalization for both Melissa and Harmony. That morning, Melissa had been transferred to the ICU after vomiting a crimson river into an emesis basin during rounds. Joel remained by her side, both of them shells of what they'd been a week before. Despite the grad student's lassitude, angry vapors emanated from him whenever Ben entered the room, like tiny molecules of hate diffusing through Ben's protective gear.

Dr. Smith had pleaded with Joel to leave Melissa's room, fearful he too would get sick, but Joel refused, saying he'd rather stay quarantined with his girlfriend than leave her by herself. So there he sat and slept, sweating for hours underneath his own mask and gown. Ben had to give the guy props. His love for Melissa was obvious. If she died, which was a thought that made Ben's heart split in two, he had no idea what Joel would do. But he had a pretty good idea who he'd do it to.

Fortunately, both an infectious disease specialist and Dr. Khalid agreed the contagiousness of the unknown infection was low, considering only three cases existed with no new ones in six days. A colleague of Dr. Khalid's at the CDC agreed. With continued strict isolation and proper staff protection, they were cautiously optimistic the mysterious illness was contained.

Though their reassurances seemed to calm everyone else, the lack of spread beyond Ben's personal world heightened his own panic. One minute he was fretting over Laurette's email; the next he was telling himself he was an ass to get caught up in it. Still, the encounter with Jean Miot two days ago had him rattled.

After rounds that morning, Ben had reminded Dr. Smith about the CBC order. She apologized and promised to get it to him later in the day. Deep down he was relieved she'd forgotten. No test, no proof he was responsible.

When Ben hadn't been stressing over Melissa and Harmony, he stressed over Sophia. Though the baby's ongoing hospitalization wasn't surprising given his mildly premature delivery, it *was* concerning that Sophia was still hospitalized. She'd been in for almost a week now. Her blood pressure had climbed again, and she continued to have abdominal pain and headaches, prompting a more thorough workup. Of course, that made Ben terrified he had infected her, so to be safe he no longer held their baby. When Sophia questioned him about it, he claimed he didn't want to expose the infant to hospital germs. During his trips to L&D, he also scouted the area for Jean Miot, making sure the bokor didn't rear his dark-eyed head. Whatever game the guy was playing, Ben wanted no part of it.

The only bright spot was that Sophia had finally named the baby.

Maxwell Diaz-Oris.

Thinking about it now in the stairwell made Ben smile. He'd barely been able to speak when she told him, so touched she'd named the baby after the father Ben had lost. He hoped Willy would be equally pleased, but for now the man remained in the dark about his grandson, too torn up about Harmony for Ben to introduce more chaos into his life.

There'd be time for that conversation later.

At least Ben hoped there would.

⊒⊨

Harmony was asleep when Ben entered the room, but she roused when his elbow accidentally bumped the bedside table near the visitor's chair.

Blinking, she raised her head. Pale fingers flicked at the oxygen prongs in her nose. "Sorry, honey. Dozed off. Sweet of you to come again."

Ben pulled the chair closer, his personal protective gear hindering his movement. "I've got a few minutes before my one o'clock lecture."

"My son, the doctor." When she smiled, blood oozed along her gum line.

At the sight, words caught in Ben's throat. It was only a matter of time before she joined Melissa in the ICU, and like Kate, once the two women reached the full-blown bleeding of DIC they would likely die.

She seemed not to notice his despair. "You'll call Willy and let him know I'm okay? He gets so worried. Max dying … it was too much for him."

"Of course." Ben closed his jaw and swallowed.

For a few moments the only sound was the hum of the IV infusion pump. When Harmony tried to speak again, a trickle of blood flowed from her nostril.

With his gloved hand, Ben snatched a tissue from the box on the side table and dabbed above her upper lip. "Shh, we don't have to talk."

Her eyes widened, as if the idea distressed her. "But there are things I want to say. You think I abandoned you." When Ben protested, she raised a freckled arm and feebly waved him off. "You know you do. I understand. It must seem that way. But there are things I never told you." She caught her breath, and in the pause Ben heard a muffled call for a food tray from someone in the hallway. "My father was a cruel man. To my mother. To me. He … well … let's leave it at that." Pain filled Harmony's face, but there was something more. Shame? Fear? "Throw in a daughter with mental illness, and you're headed for trouble." She tried to laugh, but only a dry hack and another dribble of nasal blood came out. "My bipolar has always been nasty. Hard to treat, even with drugs. Leave it to me to be the brittle case, right?"

Ben dabbed at her nose again, too disturbed by her sudden confession to speak. Never before had she talked like this. Not of her mental illness, her father, her poor mothering skills.

She knows she's going to die.

"Taxed my parents so much. Getting pregnant was the last straw. He threatened …" Harmony's voice faded off, and she stared at the ceiling, the whites of her eyes two capillary road maps. "Said he wouldn't support a twenty-one-year-old nutcase and her 'bastard son.'" Harmony attempted quote marks with her fingers but only managed to dislodge the pulse oximeter probe on her finger.

Repositioning it, Ben let her continue. He needed to get to lecture but was too riveted to move.

"I considered running away with you, you know." Tears dotted her pale lashes. "But I was crazy, not dumb. Knew I wouldn't last a day as a mother, not with my illness. Needed my father's money for treatment. Knew it was the only way to get better. For you, you see?"

All Ben could do was nod.

"Thank God for Willy." A smile reached her sunken eyes. "Such a good man. Never left my side when I was pregnant. And when you were born, never did I see someone fall so much in love with a baby." Another pause for breath. "I knew you'd thrive with him. He was everything I wasn't." She raised an arm, and Ben grabbed her trembling, feverish hand and lowered it to the bed in his own. "I did my best. Someday I hope you'll see that." Tears plopped down her cheeks. "What a crybaby I am."

"Don't worry about it. It's a good sign we're giving you enough fluids."

Seriously? A medical update? Ben winced at his own stupid words.

Tell her about your new son. Tell her she'll be okay. Tell her you forgive her.

But he could do none of those things. Her sudden intimacy along with his years of childhood self-pity had paralyzed his tongue.

Harmony's hand went lax in his own, and her chin dropped. Her gaze became unfocused, and her eyes glassed up. Her next words came out jumbled. "Judge, don't. Willy. Had to ..."

Confused, Ben squeezed her hand. "What was that? Harmony, I didn't under—"

Her body stiffened and her back arched, and just like Melissa, she started convulsing.

At first Ben froze, but then he remembered what he was and stepped into action. Careful to keep her IV and nasal cannula in place, he turned her onto her side and pushed the nurse call button. While he waited for help, her body jerked beneath his own. Why hadn't he apologized for his own childish behavior? Why hadn't he offered his forgiveness? That was clearly what she sought.

Pride and pigheadedness, that was why. Maybe that was his real curse.

22

Bathed in fading sunlight, Ben pressed against Willy's granite counter with one hand and shoveled Salisbury steak into his mouth with the other. Despite his father's good cooking, the oniony meat was tasteless on his tongue.

You shouldn't be here, he thought.

Though reason and logic suggested Dr. Smith was correct and the infection had nothing to do with him (*curses aren't real, Benny Boy*), he hated to take even the slightest chance of making his father sick. But in Willy's distress over Harmony, he had pleaded with Ben to come over, and Ben would rather take a nail gun to the chest than desert his father.

In his back pocket, Dr. Smith's CBC order burned. If only he'd gotten to the outpatient lab before it closed.

"How're the potatoes?" Two barstools over, Willy salted his spud. "Not sure I baked them long enough."

"They're fine."

Silverware clanked against plates. Mouths chewed. Fresh cubes plunked in the refrigerator ice maker.

"I should be there with her." Willy spit out the stem of a green bean. "What kind of a man is scared of an ICU room?" He took a drink of his ale.

"There's nothing you can do for her. She understands."

"You're spending time with her?"

"I am." Ben pictured the blood oozing around Harmony's gums. Dropping his fork, he reflexively placed his right hand over the bone amulet hidden beneath his shirt. He'd left his tie and white coat back in his locker, along with his backpack. Since he planned to return to the hospital to check on the women, there was no need to tote the heavy bag around.

His father's brow relaxed a bit. "Thank you. I know that's hard for you." Willy reached over the empty stool and gave Ben's shoulder a rough squeeze. "Hey, what the …? Your hand's bleeding, son."

Before Ben could register the words, Willy grabbed Ben's hand off his shirt. Blood stained the white fabric and streaked across Ben's palm, where it seeped out from beneath the bandage.

"No!" Ben jumped off his barstool and leaped away from his father.

But it was too late. Willy's fingers were smeared with red.

Seemingly confused by his son's outburst, Willy grabbed a napkin and wiped his skin clean. "It's no big deal."

But Ben barely heard him. He barely heard anything but the blood rushing through his head, like a swift river of death.

Ben pedaled his bicycle like a madman. Frustrated by the city traffic, he bypassed his apartment on Wallace Street and headed northwest toward Fairmount Park with its unfettered biking and walking trails. On his left, the sun's red orb descended behind pink-tinged clouds. The air, still warm, smelled of grilled meat and diesel fumes.

With the tails of his dress shirt flapping around him, he knew he looked foolish, but after seeing his blood on his father's hand, he needed to escape. Needed to fly. Needed to feel air blast his face with so much force it stole his breath.

Massive trees, immaculate lawns, and pungent flower beds blurred by in his peripheral vision. Sweat soaked his clothes, and his palms sopped the hand grips. His abrupt departure had alarmed his father, but Ben had to flee.

Laurette was wrong. She had to be. If not, what did it mean for his father?

A salty sting burned his eyes. No. It couldn't be. He wouldn't believe Laurette's crazy ideas.

When his chest nearly burst from exertion, he stopped, his bike tires squealing on the park trail's pavement. A child picking a dandelion from the grass berm looked up in alarm. She dropped the weed and ran to her mother and brother who were seated at a picnic table on the other side of the path.

Ben pedaled a few feet farther to put distance between himself and the family. Then he pulled the bike off the trail and leaned it against a tree. Moving to the other side, he fell back against the trunk and stared at the open greenery of Fairmount Park. Philadelphia's skyline shimmered in the background a few miles away.

After a few minutes he felt better. The mad sprint had cleared his head and made him realize he was being a fool. He was not the cause of this. He pulled his phone from his pants pocket to call his father. He owed the guy an apology for scaring him to death. Before he unlocked the mobile, a woman he recognized from previous runs trotted toward him slowly. She flicked her ponytail and gave him a flirty grin, but when he offered nothing in return, so lost in his own thoughts, she quickened her pace and huffed away.

Wow, I really am an idiot.

He tried to remember the last time he had sex. Not since before Paris. Jesus, if that wasn't a record, he didn't know what was.

Returning to his cell, he entered the passcode and found a waiting voice message from a number he didn't recognize. Switching to speaker, he clicked play. A distraught Joel flooded the line, the grad student's voice shaky and stabbing.

"She's dead. Do you hear me, asshole? She's dead. Kate should've been your patient, not Melissa's, and now my girlfriend is dead. I hope you die too. I hope you die the same horrible, miserable death. You ..." Joel's voice drowned out in a sob and disconnected.

The phone, wet in Ben's hand, fell to the grass. The bandage hung loose on his sweaty palm, blood pooling around the unhealed papule. He stared dumbly at it, not even remembering to blink.

Melissa. Dead. Couldn't be.

Suddenly he was in her upscale apartment, slouched on a Williams-Sonoma couch, watching her dance the robot, trying to distract him from the B minus he'd just gotten on a histology exam. Despite his frustration over the low (for him) grade, he'd laughed out loud at her ridiculous moves, and when he did, she'd hopped onto his lap and whispered in his ear. "I love when you laugh. Do it more often."

A trio of bikers rolled past, breaking his memory. Sweat dripped into his eyes and blurred his vision. He swiped the moisture away, knowing tears were there too. His hands shook. The bloody bandage on his right palm flapped like a useless sixth finger. He ripped it off, squeezed it into a ball, and whipped it into the air.

"Fuck you," he yelled as it landed in a bush across the pathway.

Somewhere behind him a man said, "Watch your language, buddy." Ben didn't turn around, just stared at the skyscrapers off in the distance.

Kate was dead. Melissa was dead. Harmony would be next. Sophia was still in the hospital, her high blood pressure buying her a heart echo and a kidney ultrasound. Their newborn son couldn't maintain his body temperature and still fell asleep while eating. Were those things Ben's fault too?

And Willy. Willy had been dosed with Ben's blood.

Oh, God, please don't let it be my fault.

He buried his head in his hands and sank farther down the tree. After his initial shock subsided, he realized passersby were staring. One even asked if he needed help.

He shook his head. No, he needed to get a grip, that was what he needed. He needed to get his shit together. He wiped his eyes again, the salt and grime stinging.

When he could focus again, he scooped his phone from the grass. He opened to *Favorites*, took a big breath, and called Laurette.

Before she even finished her French-sounding hello, he cut her off. "This divination thing. How soon can we do it?"

23

"You don't trust him either, do you? That's why you brought me here to see the mambo." Ben bounced his thigh against the edge of a round table, its burgundy tablecloth flapping against his chinos. "Where is she, anyway? Mixing up her witch's brew?"

Laurette pressed her lips together but said nothing. Ben's leg banged the table and toppled one of three lit candles grouped together in the center. Laurette righted it before its flame could do any damage, then put a firm hand on his thigh to stop its motion. A clot of hot wax hardened on the tablecloth.

Behind them a faint wedge of sunlight streamed in from the room's arched entryway, and in front of them thin strips of light peeked behind heavily draped windows. A Tiffany-style lamp in the corner and dozens of lit candles provided the rest of the illumination. In the center of the room stood a red pole with two intertwined snakes painted along its length and offerings decorating its base. Laurette had called it a *poto mitan* and said it was integral in calling the Lwa.

Cloth-covered buffet tables lined three of the four walls. Each was decorated with brightly colored scarves as well as an elaborate display of candles, masks, dolls, statues, skulls, beaded necklaces, mixed nuts, dried fruit, chocolate, and bottled beverages. Cones of patchouli- and spice-scented incense burned on metal stands in the center of each table. On the brick-hued walls hung wide-eyed statues and masks, as well as paintings of animal sacrifices.

Nestled among them were crosses bearing a crucified Christ. To Ben, the eclectic mix was unsettling.

But the *pièce de résistance* was an enormous wooden statue hanging in the center of the front wall, a four-limbed creature with human arms, hoofed feet, and a horned goat face. The arms opened in a creepy welcome; the hooves crossed at the ankle; and the bulging white eyes with their blackened centers focused directly on Ben. Although its human torso was female, complete with purple-bikini-clad breasts, the rest of the statue radiated masculinity, even with its genitals hidden by a mass of colorful snakes coiled around a golden staff.

Thank God for small favors, Ben thought, trying hard not to stare at the hideous thing. From a lifetime of stored mental images, he recognized the icon but knew little about it. Laurette had told him it didn't belong there, no more than a pentagram belonged in a Christian church, but she suspected its presence was a reminder of the dark forces out there. "We must never let our guard down," she had said.

He shifted in his chair, his pants and dress shirt sticking to his skin, his tie hiding the bulge of the amulet. The lack of air conditioning made him wish for summer clothing, and he longed to kick off his shoes and socks and roll his bare feet on the area rug.

Laurette had called the place a *peristil*, the name for a Vodou temple and all its rooms. To Ben, despite the Halloweenish decor, the place looked like an ordinary row house on the north side of Philly in a rundown neighborhood.

"I do not know if I trust him or not." Laurette's response came so long after Ben had posed the question he forgot he'd asked it. She spoke in a whisper, as if worried someone would hear.

But who? They hadn't seen a soul since they were ushered into the room by David Alcine, the nervous looking man with scarred arms Ben had met at the pharmacy.

Laurette continued. "My auntie feels I should listen to my brother and take you to Jean Miot, but I think we will start with Mambo Tina instead." She played with the shiny clasp on her purse.

"Your aunt will blame *me* for not following Guy's advice. She prefers the dog who keeps pooping in your yard to me."

Laurette's lips formed a tiny smile. "She does not hate you. She just does not …"

"Trust me?"

Ben took the forthcoming silence as a yes.

"You sure you know what you're doing?" he asked.

With a startling suddenness, Laurette pivoted toward him. "Of course I am not sure." She looked over her shoulder and scanned the doorway. Her voice lowered again. "But when I telephoned Mambo Tina's assistant for advice—"

"David?"

"Oui, David. He grew quiet whenever I mentioned Jean Miot's name. I could sense his fear, you know?"

Ben nodded, even though he didn't know.

"Jean Miot is a bokor. Perhaps we will need him later. But for divination, Mambo Tina is better. My gut tells me this."

Again, Ben nodded, but his own gut told him to get the hell out of Dodge. One o'clock lecture started in forty minutes. Fat chance he'd make it. Plus, he needed to get to the lab to get his blood drawn. He hadn't had time that morning, not with three sets of rounds and six patients to cover. No other student had six patients. Though perhaps a sign of Dr. Smith's growing trust in him, it couldn't have come at a worse time.

What am I doing here? This is insane.

Willy and Maxwell. That was what he was doing there.

Like an acid wave, the burn was back in his throat. "So, this Mambo Tina, she's our magic bullet? She'll, uh … fix things?"

The look Laurette gave him suggested he had demons coming out of his ears. "Fix things? Mon Dieu, it will take far more than simple divination to fix things. But it is a start. It will show what step we must take next."

"And it won't involve my son." Ben's response was more a statement than a question.

Before Laurette could answer, a figure walked into the room.

Together, Ben and Laurette stood and faced the room's entrance. A short, stout woman in a white sundress and a sheer, lime-colored shawl strolled toward them. "Good afternoon. I am Sabatina Dalembert. You may call me Mambo Tina." Her Haitian accent was thicker than Laurette's, but her English was just as solid. "Please, sit."

Around the cramped table, Ben studied the woman, her face flickering in the light of the candle flames. She appeared to be late-thirties to mid-forties, with thinly braided hair twisted into a bun on the back of her head. Two wooden pins secured the dark mass in place. Modest gold hoops dangled from her ears, and several strands of beaded necklaces adorned her neck and torso beneath the shawl. Though her apple cheeks rose in a smile, her small, hazel eyes suggested a trace of unease.

Seconds later, David Alcine slid into the remaining seat. Ben hadn't even heard the assistant enter the room. As before, the rubbery, protuberant keloid scars covering his arms caught Ben's attention, but he tried not to stare. The assistant appeared more relaxed in Mambo Tina's peristil than he had in the pharmacy. The collar of his polo shirt was flipped up in a casual manner and his smile more liberal, though still not the kind to put one at ease.

For a moment, no one spoke. Like a caveman in a penthouse suite, Ben was completely out of his element, not because of his skin color but because of the mystical elements surrounding him. The goatman's menacing eyes seemed to say, *Get out while you still can.*

Eyes downcast, Mambo Tina ran her hands over the burgundy tablecloth. Her mouth grimaced, and her rouged cheeks tensed. David's smile faded. "There is darkness about you," she said.

Ben released a hollow laugh. "Wow, you dive right in, don't you?"

"I must touch you to better tell, but fear holds me back."

In the growing heat, Ben rubbed his neck. Not exactly music to his ears.

The mambo spread her arms and then closed them, repeating the gesture several times while whispering foreign words. Though Ben didn't understand them, Laurette's death grip on her amulet suggested she did.

Unexpectedly, Mambo Tina clamped down on Ben's arms and pinned them to the table. Both Laurette and David snapped back to give the woman room. Pulling Ben closer, she continued to chant. The heat from the candle flames warmed his face, and the heavy incense in the air made him queasy.

Then, just as abruptly, she released his arms and stopped praying. He wondered if she'd been burned by a candle. "Oh no, you should not be here. You bring danger to all."

"I don't ..."

"Your friend tells David you carry a curse, a powerful curse. I did not believe at first, but she is right. I feel it." Though far from gaunt, her cheeks stretched over her facial bones in alarm. "I do not want it here." She shoved away from the table.

Laurette stood too and reached for Mambo Tina's hand. "Please, I beg you. *Aidez-nous.* Help us. Just a divination, that is all we ask."

But the mambo seemed not to hear. A second look of surprise lit up her face. "Ah!" She stared at Laurette's hand and then snatched the other one too. "You are connected to him, yes? You have a *koneksyon*. I feel it."

Ben's confusion matched Laurette's, but after a few moments, his skepticism kicked in. He wondered what had taken it so long. He should be at lecture. Why was he risking his rotation for this nonsense?

But just as he stood to leave, he remembered Jean Miot near the newborn nursery. And then he remembered the man's demand in the park: *Bring me your son.* What was it Laurette had said? It didn't matter whether Ben believed or not. What mattered is that others did.

For the first time, he understood what she meant. Just because he walked away didn't mean they would. He closed his eyes and swallowed a mix of frustration and fear.

"Please," Laurette said. Mambo Tina had released Laurette's hands but hadn't yet retaken her seat. "Help us see what to do next. We will consult Monsieur Miot if needed, but—"

"Jean Miot, yes, David told me of his ... involvement." The priestess seemed to struggle to find the right words, her face pinched in trepidation. She sighed and sat back down, followed by David and Laurette. Ben remained standing, his emotions all over the place. At least they were speaking English.

To Laurette, the mambo said, "I know of your brother. He is a very good houngan. If he says a bokor is needed, well ..." her voice trailed off. "But understand I want no part of the bokor. I offer no ceremony. No spells or treatments. No *wanga*. No offerings to the Lwa other than to keep my own people and peristil safe. If I help you today, that is it. Finished. *Konprann?*"

"Yes, I understand," Laurette said, her relief palpable. "Thank you."

Mambo Tina held her warning stare for several seconds. Then she gave a slight nod to David who stood and left the room. Moments later he returned with a deck of cards and a flat basket.

When Ben saw the fate of his future depended on ordinary playing cards, he suppressed a groan and eye roll. Laurette had told him cards were used, but he'd expected tarot, not Bicycle.

Do it for Maxwell.

For his son, he took a seat.

Diving right in again, Mambo Tina prayed and called out to an invisible presence. From Laurette's earlier explanation, Ben knew the priestess hoped to invoke the Lwa—or spirits—best suited to explain the clusterfuck he'd gotten himself into. How the cards were sorted depended on what the Lwa dictated.

Biting his lip in restraint, he watched the mambo take the king of spades and place it face-up in the basket.

"This is you, yes?"

Luckily she didn't wait for an answer, because Ben had none to give. What he did have was a healthy dose of scorn.

She shuffled the rest of the cards and asked Ben to cut them. After he did, she placed the deck in front of the basket. From it, she laid eight cards face-down around the king of spades, forming a square. On top of the king, she placed a ninth one. Two more cards were laid in the basket to the right of the square.

One by one, she started flipping cards over. Every so often, she paused and whispered a prayer. At her side, David watched in silence.

The sixth card she flipped was an eight of spades. Nothing special about it to Ben, but Mambo Tina's forehead wrinkled in concern. "Have you lost something? Has someone taken from you a personal item? Clothing, grooming tools, a favorite book?"

"No, not that I know of."

The mambo looked unconvinced. She turned over the seventh card and then tapped the eighth with her index finger, as if hesitant to reveal it. When she finally flipped the six of diamonds, her cheeks sagged. "You are losing control."

"Well, I'm not sure I'd—"

She raised a hand to silence him and flipped over two more cards. The tenth one was the eight of diamonds. A small cry fluttered from her lips, and she stiffened and turned toward David. "*Ou wè?*" she asked him. He nodded and heatedly rubbed a thick keloid.

"What?" Laurette asked, her voice hurried. "What do you see?"

Mambo Tina leaned over the basket of cards toward Laurette. Above the dancing candle flames, her face was a flickering mask of shadows and light. "He seeks his *Lwa Met Tet.*"

Laurette's hand flew to her chest.

"My what?" When no one answered, Ben rotated his neck and started bouncing his thigh again. The heat in the room had grown unbearable.

The priestess turned to Ben, her face so sober his stomach twisted. She wiped a line of sweat off her brow. "He has something of yours. He seeks to control you."

Though she spoke English, it might as well have been Haitian Creole, so clueless was Ben of her meaning. Before he could ask for clarification, she flipped over the next card. Her eyes bulged like the goatman's behind her. She shoved back her chair and almost slid off it. "*Yon ti bébé?*" When Ben didn't answer, she repeated herself in high-pitched English. "There is a baby?"

Ben froze, unsure what to say. Though David looked as shocked as his mentor, Ben refused to believe the information came from the cards. Laurette must have told David about the baby, who then told the mambo. Whatever game they were playing, as soon as his son was brought up, he wanted no further part in it.

As if reading his thoughts, Laurette shook her head, coiled hair dancing around her chin. "I never told them. I promise. You asked me to keep him secret and I did."

She looked sincere, and Ben knew her well enough to believe her. Or at least he thought he did. But maybe she told her Aunt Marie, who then passed the news onto her pharmacist husband, who then passed it onto David. God, it was like six degrees of Haitian Vodou. Ben almost laughed out loud at the absurdity. However they'd found out about his son, it sure as hell wasn't from playing cards. No way.

He puffed out his cheeks and exhaled slowly. "Yes, I have a son. Maxwell."

"Mon Dieu." Mambo Tina rose from the table, lit another candle, and stood in front of one of the colorful altars against the side wall. David followed suit, choosing an altar in front of the goatman.

Several seconds ticked by while they prayed. Ben pushed off from his chair. "Sorry, Bovo. Can't do this anymore."

Laurette put a restraining hand on his thigh. He stood anyway, but before he reached the door, Mambo Tina rushed toward him and gripped both of his forearms and turned his palms upward. She tore away the protective bandage and stared at the dark papule below. Beneath her scrutiny, Ben swore he could feel the thing throb.

"I got cut. By an old bone. You already know that."

The priestess stared at him, her shoulders hunched close to her neck. "The Lwa say you carry evil. Grave evil. Old evil." She lowered her voice, but Ben still heard the tremor. "He has something of yours that he will use to learn your Lwa Met Tet. If he—"

"Will somebody tell me what a goddamn Lwa Met Tet is?" Ben practically crawled out of his skin.

"It literally means 'master of the head,'" Laurette said, her hand on her amulet. "It is like your personal guardian."

"Yes." Mambo Tina cut back in. "And if he succeeds, he will control you. He wants what you have."

"Who does?" Ben's palm lesion pulsed in time with his racing heart. Sweat dripped down his back, and he wanted desperately to flee the oppressive room. "Jean Miot?"

Mambo Tina shook her head. "I do not know. I do not see. Monsieur Miot? Perhaps. All I can see is he is a dark man. Darkness all around him." She turned to Laurette, her words tumbling out. "An *iliminasyon*. That is your next step. To receive messages from Monsieur Oris's ancestors. To find out why he was chosen." She clutched Laurette's hands. "You must help him. There is danger all around him. You as well."

"Will you not help him too?" Laurette's fright nearly matched that of her catacomb meltdown, and out of all the lunacy Ben had just witnessed, her fear unnerved him the most. Aside from himself, she was—or at least she used to be—the most rational person he knew.

The mambo shook her head emphatically. "Too much danger, I cannot get involved. You can perform a lamp service. It is simple to do."

"Enough," Ben interrupted. "Tell me what's going on."

Mambo Tina continued to address Laurette as if Ben hadn't spoken. "Whatever you do, do not let this dark man near the bébé. You must protect the bébé."

Desperate for an explanation, Ben put a hand on Mambo Tina's arm. His touch was a lightning bolt. Her chin shot up toward the ceiling, and her back arched. The thin shawl fell from her shoulders, and the fabric of her sundress strained against her torso. She shrieked as if burned, the terror on her face unlike anything Ben had ever seen save for Laurette in the catacombs. David rushed to the mambo's side, put his arms around her, and spoke soothing words. Eventually, her body relaxed. When her gaze found Ben's, she started backing out of the room, David holding her protectively.

"Wait," Ben called out. "What does he want from my son?" The room with all its candles, statues, and incense caved in on him, and soon he could barely breathe.

"Mambo Tina, please," Laurette pleaded again.

Just before the priestess exited the arched doorway, she grabbed her throat and whispered, "Blood." She choked and coughed, and tears sprang to her eyes.

Holding his breath, Ben waited for her to say more, but when she managed to finally speak again, it was the last thing he wanted to hear.

"He wants your son's blood."

24

The rest of the afternoon flew by in a blur. Patient duties, radiology rounds, pathology rounds, buzzing by L&D any spare moment to make sure Jean Miot wasn't stalking Sophia and Maxwell, obsessing over why Sophia and Maxwell were still in the hospital, grieving over Melissa's death, fretting over Harmony's new seizures, panicking Willy would be next. Never had Ben felt so discombobulated, as if he were straddling a fence, one foot planted in reality and the other in a dark and horrifying world.

Dr. Smith dropped by the ward late afternoon but said nothing about his skipping lecture. Maybe she thought he'd been visiting Harmony, whom she had since learned was his mother, and decided to throw him a bone. After all, their relationship had thawed a degree or two. She merely pimped him on hemophilia A and B, which was what the missed lecture had covered. When he answered every question correctly except one, she pressed her lips together, gave a slight nod, and moved on. Though he was grateful he'd read up on the topic the weekend before, he'd hardly opened a book since.

Skipped lectures and missed readings weren't how his third year was supposed to go. He had a plan. He had a schedule. He had to be at the top of his game. If he wanted to get into orthopedic surgery, he couldn't be running around like a chicken—no, make that a goat—with its head cut off.

At four thirty, with his throat burning and his stomach in knots, he stopped by Labor & Delivery one last time. He had to hurry if he wanted to make it to the outpatient lab before they closed. That meant running to the

Talcott Center and then back to the main hospital for the blood draw, but Ben had to know his son was safe first.

Tanisha was in the supply room, gathering IV tubing and catheters. He squeezed into the small space beside her and asked for an update.

"Partial good news." The young nurse's smile was hopeful. "The pediatrician said Maxwell will be ready for discharge soon, but the obstetrician wants to keep Sophia a little longer. Keep an eye on her blood pressure and stomach aches. Plus, today she has a low-grade fever."

Blood drained from Ben's face. He tugged at his tie, the bone amulet shifting beneath his shirt. "Do they think she has a uterine infection? Or a virus?"

Or a freaking Vodou curse?

The nurse shrugged, her dark ponytail shrugging with her. "They're checking a CBC today."

Fingertips danced up Ben's spine. Sophia's previous eosinophil count had been normal. He'd scoured her chart to be sure. Had it changed?

With an anchor on his chest, he thanked Tanisha and headed down the hall toward Sophia's room. Finding the door ajar, he gave a sharp knock and went in.

Sophia was nursing Maxwell. Ben apologized for barging in, but Sophia seemed not to care. "He's feeding much better now. You can hold him when he's done if you like."

Ben ran the back of his hand across his mouth. "Wish I could, but I have to get back to the hospital before five."

"Will you be here tonight?"

"Sorry, I have something I need to do."

Though her smile remained, disappointment showed in her eyes.

"I'm not pulling away. Really. I meant it when I said I was all in."

She nodded and stroked Maxwell's head, but Ben could tell she didn't believe him. Longing to step closer but not daring to take the risk, he squeezed the bell of his stethoscope hanging around his neck. Brimming with frustration, he wanted to break something with his bare hands. From across the room, he drank in Maxwell's dark shock of hair, his contented swallows, his tiny arm resting against Sophia's gown. He'd do anything to protect his son. Anything and everything. In this whole stupid nightmare, that was the only thing he was sure of.

"I promise I'll be back tomorrow."

Before Sophia could respond, he slipped out and hurried to the lab to get his blood drawn. Time to face the music and find out if he was responsible for Kate's and Melissa's deaths. For Harmony's downward spiral. For Sophia's prolonged hospitalization.

Then, after getting his blood drawn, he'd meet up with Laurette. They had an *iliminasyon* to perform. Whatever the hell that was.

25

After sunset, back in his basement apartment, Ben heard Mrs. Sinclair's doorbell chime just as he stepped out of the shower. *Crap.* Laurette was early. He'd hoped to get to her before his landlady did.

In the humid bathroom, he whipped a towel over his torso and practically tripped into a clean pair of boxer briefs and shorts. Before pulling on a T-shirt, he grabbed the bone amulet from the vanity and slipped it around his neck. Stupid, he knew, but no sense in abandoning it now.

As Laurette had instructed, he'd dressed in all white, minus the red Nike logo on his gym shorts. When he opened his apartment door, he heard his friend's condolences to Mrs. Sinclair. From his position at the base of the stairs, he saw two sets of legs, one dark and toned, the other a pale kaleidoscope of varicose veins in a house dress. Izzy the cat threaded through both of them, prompting cooing words and a quick pet from Laurette. He imagined his landlady's pinched expression at Laurette's evening visit, but better she think they were hooking up than learn the truth. Premarital, interracial sex paled in comparison to a Vodou ritual.

After entering Ben's crypt, Laurette said, "She still does not like me much." Tote bags hung from each shoulder, and sleeved cups of tea filled both hands. Her fresh, clean scent suggested a recent shower. "But it is clear she adores you. Says you bring her groceries and you fixed her washer, no?"

Ben took the proffered tea and closed the door with his foot. It was true he'd finally silenced the machine's earthquake rattles the night before.

After Melissa's death, the repair had given him a reprieve from his tortured thoughts.

"I do what I can."

"You are a good man. A kind man."

Blushing, Ben entered the kitchen and set the tea on the table before joining her in the living room. She stood in front of the desk, both tote bags on the floor next to her flip-flops. The larger bag's pink stripes clashed hideously with the burnt-orange carpeting.

He took in her white shorts and tank top. "What's with the all-white look, anyway? It's like we're headed for gymnastics camp."

"White is sacred to the spirits. A sign of modesty and purity. We must be clean too." Plopping to the floor, she pulled a stainless-steel basin from the smaller tote bag. "This is a *kivet.*" She pronounced it *key-vet.* Knocking on its base, she added, "Fireproof. That is important."

"I'm sure Mrs. Sinclair would agree."

Laurette smiled, but the levity was brief. "A lamp service, or *iliminasyon*, is a simple ceremony. Anyone can do it. With it, we hope to receive messages through our dreams, messages that will offer guidance."

"*Our* dreams?"

His friend tapped the smooth base of the kivet. "Mambo Tina said I am part of this, yes? What we do not yet know is why. Now go get the tea. It's herbal. It will soothe us."

When Ben returned with the cups, Laurette was emptying the large tote bag of its contents: two white sheets, a white plate, a white candle in a white ceramic holder, matches, a gallon of water, soft bunches of cotton, a bottle of olive oil, four coins ranging from pennies to quarters, a plastic sandwich bag full of herbs, and a small bottle of perfume. She held up the last two items, one in each hand. "Basil leaves and lilac perfume."

For the millionth time, Ben questioned the sanity of what he was doing, but what other choice did he have? If his lab test came back with a high eosinophil count, Dr. Smith would forget all about medical-studentitis and lock him in quarantine faster than her shiny pumps could travel. And then how would he keep Jean Miot away from his son?

Mouth going dry, he took a sip of tea. Though never his favorite beverage, it tasted more bitter than usual. Regardless, he choked it down and shifted his focus back to Laurette and her mountain of supplies. "For someone who doesn't practice Vodou, you seem to be a pro."

"Just because one does not slit the goat's neck does not mean one has never watched it."

Jesus. Ben missed Laurette's stupid goat jokes, but that was one he could have done without.

"My auntie practices daily. Many of these items are hers." His friend stood and scanned the small room, hands on hips, bare arms sculpted.

Ben sipped his tea. Watching her do this for him made his voice grow thick. "Thank you, Bovo. For helping me. If it wasn't for you, I'd be—"

"There is no need to thank me." She stepped over the white sheets toward him. "You and me, we were drawn to each other, yes? Like a magician and his wand." She reached out to grab his free hand, but he jumped back before she could.

"No, don't touch me."

Seeing his look of horror, she laughed. That sunburst of a smile he so missed lit up her face. "Oh, my friend, do you think if you could make me sick, I would not be by now?"

Still chuckling, she left him and returned to the floor, where she picked up the clumps of cotton. After pulling off several small pieces, she twisted each into a point at one end. "Wicks."

Ben joined her, his fear of infecting her retreating. "Participating in this lamp service doesn't mean I believe. You know that, right? I wish I did, but I still think it's bullshit."

Laurette placed the last of the five wicks on the floor. She glanced at the bulge under his T-shirt where her bone amulet lay. "Oh really? Then why am I here?"

"Because I don't know what else to do."

"Then let us get started. We do it for Harmony, yes?" Her expression softened. "And for Willy and Sophia. And your bébé."

Ben inhaled deeply. He nodded, and for the next several minutes, he watched her work and listened to her explanations, periodically sipping his tea at her prompting. First, she put the four coins in the bottom of the steel basin. Then she filled it partway with water, placed it in the middle of the living room, and sprinkled shredded basil on top. After that she grabbed the plate and drizzled it with olive oil.

Next she took the two bed sheets and spread them open, one on each side of the basin. With barely enough room in the living room, the sheet she crouched on bunched up against the desk legs, and Ben's caught on the La-Z-Boy recliner. He pulled the chair toward the kitchen and spread the sheet out all the way.

"Our beds for the night." She indicated Ben sit down on his.

"Comfy."

Laurette wrapped a white scarf around her head, tucking in the coils of hair that refused to cooperate. From the smaller tote bag, she pulled out a potpourri of items and created an altar of offerings: apples, bananas, oranges, ears of corn, small bottles of oil and salsa, a jar of olives, several bottles of alcohol, a small plastic skull, a wooden rattle with brown and white beads around its head, and what looked like two party hats. Unable to help himself, Ben shook his head.

"Tonight we honor the *Rada Lwa* and the *Gede Lwa*."

"The who?"

"The Rada Lwa are the oldest Lwa whom the slaves brought to Haiti from Africa. They are calm spirits who protect the Vodou tradition. Among them is an herbal warrior whose war is on sickness. That is good, yes?"

"How do you know all this? David Alcine? Your aunt and brother?"

She nodded. "The Gede Lwa are the spirits of the forgotten dead. They bring messages from our ancestors—Haitians greatly value their ancestors, you know—but the Gede Lwa can be outrageous. Funny too, so these things are for them." Laurette held up the party hats, the toy skull, and a jar of spicy salsa. Her voice took an ominous turn. "But we shall avoid attracting the *Petro Lwa*."

"Do I want to know why?"

"The Rada Lwa represent pre-slavery times, but the Petro Lwa lived through the horrors of slavery, and they continue to live through the terrors of today. That makes them wild and unpredictable. Some suggest they are evil spirits, but that is not really the case. Still, no need to invite them tonight, oui?"

Oui indeed, thought Ben, polishing off his tea, wishing it were spiked with whiskey.

Grabbing the perfume bottle, Laurette sprinkled fragrance on her neck and wrists and urged Ben to do the same.

"Great. I always wanted to smell pretty."

Ignoring him, she lit the white candle, said what sounded like a Hail Mary (though Sophia would be a better judge of that), and, with her gaze on the ceiling, prayed to Bondye, who Ben remembered was the main God. "I ask that Bondye, our ancestors, and the Lwa bless this ceremony."

After her prayers, she put the lit candle in its holder next to the basin. Then she gently placed the cotton wicks onto the plate with the pool of oil. While she did that, she informed the Lwa of what she and Ben would like to learn from their dreams, including what Ben carried within him that made the women sick and what could be done about it. They also wished to be assured Maxwell would be okay. Finally, they wished to know the identity of the dark man who had terrified Mambo Tina. The one she claimed had something of Ben's in order to divine his Lwa Met Tet and control him. Despite his skepticism and warm tea, a shiver ran through him.

When all five wicks floated on the plate of oil, Laurette lifted it and moved it in four directions. She repeated the act with the basin containing water and basil. Then, carefully, she put the lightweight plate inside the basin where it floated on top of the water. Once assured of its stability, she lit the wicks and said to Ben, "To be safe, set your phone alarm for five hours. Longer than that and we risk a fire." Then she sat back, drank her tea, and stared at him.

"Now what?" he said.

"Now we sleep. But please, though you say you do not believe, try to keep an open mind. If you do not, we risk learning nothing."

Ben's heavy exhalation flickered the flame of the candle near the basin. He hoped he could do that.

"Now, please turn off the lights."

Ben stood but then paused and rubbed his forehead. He felt a little light-headed. "What did Mambo Tina mean about a dark man wanting my son's blood?"

It was several moments before Laurette answered, the sound of her tea swallowing audible in the still night. "I don't know, but blood is very powerful in Vodou. When an animal is sacrificed, it is to appease the Lwa and bring good fortune. The slaughter is humane, and not a shred of meat or blood is wasted. You Westerners roll your eyes, but do you not kill to get your meat? Are your slaughterhouses not worse? But ..." When her voice trailed off, Ben urged her to continue. "Perhaps some Lwa—or bokors who practice dark magic—seek certain blood for a darker power."

"Certain blood? Whose? My son's? Mine? Jean Miot is a bokor, right?"

"Yes, but that does not mean he wishes you harm. It is *because* Monsieur Miot is a bokor that he is a better choice than Mambo Tina. This is what my brother Guy says. Monsieur Miot knows how to deal with these ... these matters."

"I don't care. I don't want him near my son."

"Let us get started then." Laurette's determination hardened her pretty features.

Ben turned off the overhead light, and they each lay down on their respective sheets. Though they'd folded them over to use as light blankets, Ben reached up to the sofa and grabbed the Philadelphia Eagles coverlet for Laurette in case she got cold. After a few seconds of listening to Mrs. Sinclair creak across the floor above them, he said, "So, in five hours we'll have answers?" He wished he could erase the sarcasm in his voice.

Raising her scarf-covered head, Laurette looked over at him, her face a flickering mass of shadows in the candle light. "Let us pray to Bondye we do. Because what other option remains?"

26

So much heat. Outside and in.

Where am I?

Lust flooded his veins. Heat baked his body.

Home.

No, not my home.

Where was she? How dare she hide from him?

All around him flames snapped and licked, fiery tongues of reds, oranges, and yellows.

She's mine.

Trees burning. Crops burning. The acrid scent of scorched sugar cane.

There she is.

He grabbed her and pulled her by the back of her hair, her face hidden by dancing flames. An unbearable craving pulsed through his blood.

What am I doing?

Just a dream.

Yet there he was, cinching her hair, laughing as she tried to escape, the sticks and stones in the soil cutting her bare feet.

Her screams fueled him. He ripped the dress from her flesh and ran his fingers down her skin, ignoring the cracking flames surrounding them. They were alone, and she was his.

She writhed and kicked. He gripped her more tightly. So powerless she was in his arms. A belt appeared in his hand.

Stop. Wake up.

Leather snapped bare calves. Her skin welted and oozed. His lust grew thicker.

No, please. This isn't me.

He went back to watching. No, participating. He would have her. With a fistful of coiled hair, he yanked her head so hard her neck almost snapped. And so what if it did? There were others. So many others. But she was his favorite. So innocent. So warm.

No!

Ignoring her pleas, he whipped her over and over again, her back a grid of red weals. Her fighting ceased. Bending her limp frame over, he took what he came for. When he finished, he dropped her to the ground, where her body curled like an infant's, her tender flesh torn and bloody from his belt. She lay quiet.

But still he heard screaming. Whose?

Slowly the girl rolled onto her back. Her face came into view.

No. I don't want to see this. Please.

Moisture bathed his body. His heart hammered like a drum.

Wake up. Wake up!

But it was too late. Dark eyes of fear and pain stared up at him. Hatred too.

Who was screaming? He scanned the purplish night, the burning crops, the flaming home. So hot. So much heat.

His gaze returned to the girl, but it was no longer the face of an adolescent. It was someone else. Someone he knew. Those deep eyes, those arched brows.

Was he mad? What had he done to her?

Wake up. Wake up. Wake up.

Vengeance in her eyes. Bared teeth. Snarling lips.

No, it wasn't me, he tried to shout, but nothing came out, his lips drier than the leather belt in his hands.

He backed away. The woman—his friend—stood and advanced toward him. No longer naked, she was cloaked in a white gown. From her mouth poured screams. Shrieks. Wails.

Shh, please, I'm dreaming, we're dreaming, please, stop screaming.

Howling, her mouth formed a deep, black oval. She pulled a knife from her gown. He backed up but something stopped his escape. Though the knife plunged forward, something else stabbed his back.

No! Don't!

Ben's eyes shot open. He blinked and flailed to orient himself. Something poked his back. He tried to call out, but cement sealed his lips, and teeth trapped his tongue. A smoke alarm shrilled, and someone was screaming.

When he finally cleared his mental fog, he realized it was Laurette. He also understood the source of the heat: fire flickered in the center of the room.

"Shit." He leaped up from a seated position. The poke in his back had come from the corner of the desk, though how he'd ended up on the other side of the room he had no idea.

Small flames danced in front of him. From their light, he saw Laurette writhing on the floor, her screams meshing unbearably with the wailing smoke alarm.

When he ran to her, his feet twisted in the sheet, and he tripped, his face inches from the glowing flames. Frantically, he freed himself. "Laurette, fire! Help me put it out." His shouts seemed lost on her.

Balling up his sheet, he batted the flames that engulfed her own sheet as well as the carpet below. Finally her shrieks lessened, only to be replaced by foreign words he didn't understand.

Then he remembered the gallon of water she had brought for the cere-mony. He lunged for the jug near his desk and doused the remaining fire. At last, the flames died out.

He ran to the entryway and flicked on the light, then switched on the living room lamp. "Laurette, be quiet." His plea went unheeded.

The fire was out, but the smoke alarm still shrieked. He rushed to the kitchen, grabbed a chair for a footstool, and ripped the alarm from the ceiling. He supposed the act was pointless. Mrs. Sinclair would have already called the fire department.

Returning to the living room, he found a quieter Laurette rocking and chanting. Burnt carpet, smoldering sheets, spilled water, and strewn altar paraphernalia littered the area.

He dropped to the floor near his friend. With the fear of the fire behind him, a new fear enveloped him. Self-loathing and disgust, too. He wrapped an arm around Laurette, forgetting about the infection he might carry.

"Bovo, wake up. Pull yourself together. The fire department will be here any second." He imagined Mrs. Sinclair's reaction to Laurette's screaming and added, "And probably the police too."

At his touch, his friend quieted. She also tensed, and when her eyes caught his, she jumped up and backed away, her terrified silence worse than her shrieking.

His mind went back to the disgusting dream, though it wanted to be anywhere but there. He ran a hand over his mouth and then through his tousled hair. How could he dream something so ugly? So vile? It made him want to puke.

He approached his friend. She backed up until she hit the wall, a framed print of Pink Floyd's *The Wall* rattling near her head. Contempt replaced fear on her face, and if he hadn't known better, he would have sworn she'd witnessed his dream.

"What did you do?" she asked.

Before his muddled mind could make sense of an answer, a new wailing materialized.

Sirens were on their way.

For the next thirty minutes, Ben and Laurette tried to convince two police officers—one male, one female—that they were merely performing a lamp ceremony. A fuming Mrs. Sinclair hovered nearby on the stairs. Having to admit the Vodou practice was humiliating enough, but having to swear he hadn't hurt Laurette, nor would he ever, was the real kick in the balls. Luckily, she had returned to her senses and backed Ben up. She claimed she'd merely sleepwalked through a nightmare and accidentally started the fire. She apologized for causing a stir.

After the police made sure Mrs. Sinclair didn't want to press charges for the fire, they thumped up the wooden stairs. During their departure Ben heard the male cop say, "Well, that was a first." Once they left, the landlady stormed inside the apartment, her terrycloth robe spilling more cleavage than Ben cared to see. Despite the charred scent in the air, he could smell her drugstore cold cream and mentholated chest rub.

Her sallow eyes narrowed, and her gaze darted around the debris, starting with the burned and wet sheets and ending with the party hats and alcohol. Thankfully the liquor bottles were intact and had not fueled the fire. Plump cheeks flaming, she pulled the robe tightly around her. She couldn't have looked more repulsed than if she'd stumbled upon a mangled body. She scrutinized Laurette. "Voodoo? You brought voodoo into my house?"

Knowing it wasn't the time to differentiate voodoo from Vodou, Ben intervened. "I'm sorry. Don't blame Laurette. She was just helping me out. The fire was my fault, not hers." He started to explain further, but then stopped. What could he possibly say that wouldn't sound nuts?

Ignoring him, Mrs. Sinclair pursed her lips and shook her head. She pointed to Laurette. "Get out of my house. I never want you or your disgusting ways here again."

"Hey." Ben stepped forward, his forehead vein throbbing.

"Hey nothing, mister." The landlady shifted her focus to Ben, index finger still stabbing the air. "You have two weeks to find another place. I won't have devil's work in my house again, you hear me?" Before Ben could launch a defense, the woman flew out the door in tears.

For a moment he stood rooted to the spot. Finally, he shuffled back and sank to the couch. He folded his hands on top of his head and exhaled slowly. Laurette joined him and put a supportive hand on his shoulder. "I'm sorry. I should have known better. This room is too small."

"This isn't your fault. Not by a long shot." Like dripping sap, he lowered his fingers down his face, pulling his cheeks and lips with them until his hands plopped onto his lap. "I have no clue what's going on." He turned to his friend, found he couldn't face her, and pressed the bandage on his hand instead. "My dream. In it, I hurt you." His voice cracked. "Oh shit, it was awful."

To his surprise, she murmured agreement. He remembered the feeling he'd had earlier of her seeing his dream. His muscles tensed, but he dismissed the paranoia. It wasn't possible.

"There is more you need to know," Laurette said. "But I could not see it all. Something, or someone, tried to block my messages."

"Who?"

"I don't know. A man? A woman? I don't know. I only know there is darkness." She paused when she saw his slight head shake. "I know a part of you still believes this is silly, but you cannot deny your own dream, can you?"

He swallowed, his eyes glued to his bandage. "No."

"Then listen to what I tell you without scorn. I must hurry. Your Mrs. Sinclair will come and pull me out by my hair." She scooted to the end of the sofa cushion, grabbed his chin, and forced his eyes back to hers. "I believe, at least for a moment, I was Nasicha Boro in my dream."

"Who?"

"Nasicha Boro, the priestess who cursed her slave owner centuries ago, the Frenchman who raped and impregnated her daughter. Do you not remember my email?"

Ben remembered. He also remembered his horrific dream. He wanted to dropkick himself to the moon.

"In my dream I saw her curse come to life. The right person has finally come along. You."

Ben rubbed his eyes. His body craved sleep, but his mind rapid-fired. He kicked an orange near his foot and watched it roll to a stop in front of the overturned metal basin. Spilled basil dotted the orange carpeting. "Are you saying my getting infected wasn't an accident?" He refused to use the word *cursed*.

"Not an accident, no." She hesitated and wiped ashes off her white shorts. "I believe the bone has been waiting centuries for a descendant of Pierre Marcel's to come along and receive the curse."

He banged his thighs with his fists. "Oh, come on. So now I'm related to the slave owner?"

"I don't know. I am only telling you the messages I received from the Lwa tonight."

Cursing under his breath, he got up and collected scattered items off the floor. Whatever wasn't ruined by fire or water, he tossed into Laurette's tote bags. When he grabbed the plastic skull, he studied it. "I'm sorry, but this is too effed up for me. This is where I get off the crazy train."

Laurette rose and plucked the skull from his hands. "Look at me." When Ben didn't, she once again grabbed his chin and forced him. "There is something else you must know, but I am afraid to tell you."

He barked a sharp laugh. "Why stop now? You're on a roll."

"You are in danger. The dark force I sense is trying to learn your Lwa Tet Met, just as Mambo Tina divined. He wants to control you. Vodouisants do not willingly share their Lwa Tet Met for that very reason."

"But I'm not missing any personal items, remember? How could he—" Ben froze. A wet sheet fell from his grasp. "Oh shit. I *am* missing something. A baby memento my dad had in his store. A lock of hair and a bronzed shoe."

He leaned back against the desk, his legs going weak. With all the chaos of the last couple weeks, he'd forgotten about the theft. Jesus, every time he convinced himself this whole mess was a farce, something new came along and punched him in the gut. "You don't think … God, this is unreal."

Despite the warmth of the room, Laurette hugged her arms. "I do not understand. What baby piece?"

Ben relayed the story of his missing infant keepsake, discovered by his father after the chocolate shop's break-in. His agitation rose, and he pushed away from the desk. "Come to think of it, when I was repairing the shop window, I saw a weird guy outside the store. He'd helped my dad carry in boxes a few days earlier. He sounded Haitian, or Caribbean, anyway."

"Was it Jean Miot?"

Dreadlocks flashed in Ben's mind. "No, definitely not."

Footsteps creaked above them. Their gazes shot to the ceiling as if Mrs. Sinclair would somehow appear there. Laurette hurried and stuffed the basin, unburned food items, and alcohol bottles into her bags. "I wish you had told me about the stolen baby memory. This is not good."

"If it even *was* stolen. How was I to—"

"Yet the dark force needs more. I saw it." Having cleared away as many items as she could, Laurette hefted both bags onto her shoulders. "He wants your blood." Footsteps started down the steps, pausing halfway down. Laurette spoke more quickly. "This will be difficult for you to hear, but—"

A voice bellowed from the stairwell. "I want that voodoo woman out of here in two minutes or I call the police again. And this time I *will* press charges."

Ben hustled Laurette to the door. "Go. I'll sort this out with Mrs. Sinclair. No way will I let her treat you like this."

But when he went to open the door, Laurette planted herself in the entryway and whispered in urgency. "Wait. You must hear this."

Ben shook his head. He didn't want to hear it.

"You are not the only one in danger."

"You think I don't know that?" Saliva sprayed his lips. He wiped them off and thought of the two women who'd died and the people who could be next.

"No, you don't understand. If Nasicha's curse is in you, then it is also in your son." A tear slid down Laurette's cheek.

Ben fell limp as a thread. He'd never seen her cry, and the act weakened him as much as her words. "Hey, Bovo, it's okay."

Footsteps boomed down the rest of the stairs, and a hammering pounded the door. "Now. She is to leave this instant."

"Give us a second, for Christ's sake." Ben's landlady must've been as surprised by his outburst as he was, because after a moment of silence, her feet clumped back up the stairs.

Laurette wiped her eyes. "I'm sorry, my friend, but you do not understand."

"Understand what? That Jean Miot has some weird fixation on my son? Yeah, I got that."

"No. You do not understand that to a dark force such as this one—whoever or whatever it is—the blood of your infant is even more powerful than yours." Her jaw slackened, and her own helplessness grew apparent. "I have seen it. In my dream tonight, I have seen it."

A mass the size of a walnut closed off his throat. "Saw what?"

"Oh, my dear Benjamin, this dark being plans to sacrifice your son."

27

Early morning light peeked through the basement window and signaled it was time to get up. Given Ben's few hours of panicked dozing, which were horrifically punctuated by dreams of assault, curses, and infant sacrifice, he was more than ready. But how he'd survive a day with one foot in medicine and the other in Vodou remained to be seen.

Swinging upright, he shifted his legs over the bed, cotton boxers the only barrier between him and the sweat-soaked sheets. The urge to vomit hit hard, and he had to lean forward for a few minutes before he could stand. A sluggishness beyond fatigue depleted him, as if he'd popped too many antihistamines the night before. Eventually he stumbled to the bathroom and flipped on the shower. Rather than waiting for the water to heat up, he slid beneath its icy stream. He gasped, but the chill had the desired effect and his level of alertness rose.

By the time he stepped out and toweled off, it was ten after six. Plenty of time to get to the hospital.

But he had a stop to make first.

Something Laurette had said after the lamp ceremony disaster had been circling his brain in an endless loop. Until he put it to rest, he'd never be able to concentrate on work. *The bone has been waiting centuries for a descendant of Pierre Marcel's to come along and receive the curse.*

The concept was preposterous, he knew that. He also knew there was a way to prove Laurette wrong. The idea had struck him in the midst of his turbulent dreams.

Body barely dry, he wrestled on a pair of chinos, a light blue dress shirt, and the least cheap of his ties. He brushed and gargled away the funk of Vodou dreams and smoothed his dark hair. The stubble went untrimmed another day.

With nothing but a chug of water for breakfast, he exited his basement apartment and locked the door behind him, not having the energy to think about where he'd live in two weeks or how he'd find time to move. The only thing he could concentrate on at the moment was proving Laurette wrong.

And he was relying on his dead father to do it.

The aroma of freshly brewed coffee and burnt toast filled Willy's foyer, but to Ben's surprise, his father was not in the kitchen. He was in Max's study. Like a sacred mausoleum, the room hadn't been disturbed in three years. Yet there Willy was, beyond the French doors, sitting cross-legged on the middle of an African rug. To his left a coffee mug steamed. To his right two overturned desk drawers spilled pictures, papers, and small-business magazines. His hands gripped photographs, his eyes leaking tears.

Ben's throat closed. His heart cinched. He entered the room and knelt next to his father. "Dad, you okay?"

Startled by his son's presence, Willy swiped a hand over his eyes and waved off Ben's concern. "I'm fine, just fine."

Ben reached up and snatched a tissue from Max's oak desk. A plume of dust rose in the air. Taking it, Willy honked his nose a few times, then tossed the wadded tissue into a wastebasket near the desk. "You were right. It's time to get to these things. Max would be mortified to see all this dust, wouldn't he?"

"He'd be mortified to see you back in that flannel shirt." At that, both men laughed, easing some of the heartache in the room.

"You can go through his closet if you like," Willy said, studying the photographs. The top one showed a decked-out Max at a community gala, a plaque for volunteer work clutched in his hand. "He would want you wearing his stuff."

"Maybe." Ben shifted back on the rug, not wanting to risk touching his dad with his so-called cursed body. "But our styles aren't exactly simpatico."

Another chuckle from Willy. "Hey, why are you here?" He peered at his watch, as if just realizing the time of day. "Shouldn't you be at the hospital?" His face grew paler. "Is it Harmony? Did she …"

"No. She's okay." Ben doubted that was true. The last time he'd checked on his mother was before the lamp ceremony the night before, and she hadn't been okay then, not with her new seizures and confusion. Worrying his father was not in his game plan, however, so he shifted gears. "The reason I came is because I want to see Max's genealogy studies."

"Why in the world do you want that?"

"I don't have time to explain. I have to get to the hospital, but it's important."

Willy frowned and scratched his cheek. He waved a hand at an oak file cabinet near the window. "I think they're in there. He was still working on my family tree when he …"

Willy's voice trailed off, and his hands shook when he lowered the photographs to the floor. Harmony's illness obviously had him spooked. Probably the reason he sought solace in Max's den.

Ben wondered if he should tell Willy about Sophia and Maxwell. A grandson might console the man, give him something to look forward to. But he held back. It wasn't the right time, not with the baby at risk. For the umpteenth time, he reminded himself it didn't matter whether he believed in Laurette's theory or not. Jean Miot did, and that was all that mattered.

"How 'bout if I fix you some breakfast?" Willy stood and left before Ben could object. The thought of Jean Miot hurting Maxwell destroyed any appetite he might have had.

With his father out of the room, Ben opened the file cabinet and flipped through Max's colored and alphabetized folders. Filed under "G," the genealogy documents were easy to find. He plucked them out. One was marked *Oris,* the other *Towner.* The *Towner* folder was empty, but that didn't matter. Ben needed information on *his* biological bloodline, not Max's. Then again, there was only a fifty-fifty chance of finding what he needed. Harmony most likely had never researched her roots.

Flipping open the *Oris* folder, he glanced at his watch. Morning report started in forty minutes. Even if he made it in time, he wouldn't have a chance to pre-round on his patients. He had so much to do on them. All were complicated cases.

The acid in his throat returned, first as a burning pebble and then as a growing wave. If he didn't get his stress under control, his esophagus would be a corroded pipe before the end of the month.

Just get what you came for, Benny Boy.

Still standing, he pulled the large, folded genealogy from the file and covered the desk with it. Max's closed laptop bulged beneath its center. It was a typical family-tree chart with solid lines connecting clusters of colored rectangles. Though perhaps easier to do online, Max had preferred the old-fashioned way, and penciled-in names and eraser marks covered the thick, beige paper.

Taking a moment to get his bearings, Ben scanned the sheet and found Willy's name in a rectangle near the bottom. Above him were two more rectangles, one marked *Dennis Oris* and the other *Donna Perry Oris*, *Perry* being Willy's mother's maiden name. No other children.

Quickly scanning upwards, Ben saw Max had researched all the way back to the 1600s. Several boxes were empty, filled only with a question mark. Willing himself to calm down, Ben rolled his neck and loosened his shoulders.

He returned to the bottom of the genealogy and perused upward again, but this time more slowly. Nothing stood out in the 1900s or 1800s. When he found the 1700s, the time when the Haitian slave revolt took place, he slowed even more. A Juliette Oris, dated 1745 to 1817, was married to a Claude Oris, dated 1742 to 1796. No Marcel.

He looked up and exhaled. So far so good. Surely this was a waste of time. He returned to the tree line. Both Claude and Juliette were listed as living in Paris, at least at the time of their deaths, but when he followed the line up from Juliette Oris to her parents, his stomach dropped to the floor.

Juliette's father's last name was *Marcel*. His first name, *Pierre*.

"Not possible." Ben spoke out loud, his voice cracking. "Not freaking possible."

His legs no longer supporting him, he sank into Max's desk chair. He read the name again, certain he'd made a mistake.

Pierre Marcel—1722 to 1772.

He couldn't breathe, couldn't think, couldn't process the name before him. The desk, the walls, the French doors, everything blurred in his vision.

Pierre Marcel. A vile, slave-owning rapist. In Willy's family tree.

And Ben was his descendant.

28

Someone was messing with him. Someone had combed through his family tree and concocted the whole thing. Ben's mind could simply not conceive the alternative.

But who?

Thunderbolts blasted his brain, and a heaviness rooted him to Max's chair. He massaged his skull but to no avail.

Could Laurette be playing him? Just making all this up to—to what? Torment him?

No, she wouldn't do that. What would be her motive?

Jean Miot? He'd been lurking around the hospital. Could he have been responsible for the chocolate store break-in? Stolen Ben's infant memento and then broken into Willy's place and found the genealogy? Ben glanced at the dust on the file cabinet and desk, undisturbed until his actions that morning. A break-in seemed doubtful. Could Jean Miot have known about Ben's family history some other way? It wouldn't be that difficult to find out.

What about Laurette's Aunt Marie? She'd never cared for Ben. Could she have crafted a ghoulish fiction to disarm and unravel him?

Another thought surfaced, though more far-fetched than the others. Joel. Could the disgruntled grad student have invented the whole thing as part of a scheme to get Ben tossed out of med school?

Ben squeezed his eyelids together until flashes of light strobed behind them. One fact derailed all his conspiracies: people associated with him were getting sick. They were dying. How does someone fake that?

But the alternative? A centuries-old curse materializing in a descendant? Evil beings wanting to harness that power for themselves?

Ben swore and burst up from the chair. He threw his arm over the genealogy, sweeping it to the floor. A leather pencil cup flew with it, and pens and markers rolled across the rug.

"Are you okay?" Willy called out from the kitchen. The scent of sautéed onions and sizzling bacon drifted into the room. Ben felt only nausea. His stomach swirled, and his mouth grew thick with coppery saliva.

He stared at the family tree on the floor. Felt it mocking him, taunting him to believe. Picking it up, he laid it back on the desk and pulled out his phone. He snapped four pictures, one of each quadrant.

But only one section mattered.

The one that showed his ancestor was a slave-owning rapist.

Haitians greatly value their ancestors, Laurette had said. So what did that mean for Ben?

Repocketing the phone, Ben closed his eyes and pressed clammy hands over his face. He had to get to the hospital. Had to see if his CBC was back. If his lab test was normal, then someone was just messing with him, though for what reason, he had no clue.

Willy appeared outside the French doors. "Got an omelet and bacon ready for you on the counter. Med school's making you thin." His father glanced at the scattered pens and markers on the floor and then back at Ben. "What's wrong? You look weak." Willy stepped toward him, but Ben backed away.

"No, don't touch me."

Willy stopped, his feelings obviously bruised, but Ben could not risk touching him. He'd already bled on the man once. He would not make that mistake twice.

"Is it your rotation? Is that internist lady still giving you a hard time?" His father stared at him, worry in his eyes, waiting for Ben to speak.

The need for Ben to confess was excruciating. He longed to spill the story. Longed for someone else, someone who didn't believe in Vodou, to hear it. He needed to see a look of *don't be ridiculous* on another person's face, a look that would put Ben's own fears at ease.

His father leaned forward but kept his distance. Broken capillaries coursed through his sclera, and dark circles shadowed his eyes. "What's eating you, son? You're scaring me."

Ben pried open his parched lips. A croak came out. He cleared his throat and tried again. "I'm … I think I …"

Think I'm what? Behind Kate and Melissa's deaths? Behind Harmony getting sick?

As much as he wanted to share his story, he couldn't. He couldn't do it to Willy. Didn't want to burden his father with the news that he might carry a lethal disease or, at the very least, was mentally cracking up. His dad had been through enough. Instead he blurted, "You're a grandfather. I have a new son."

Willy's mouth fell open. Shaky fingers flew to his lip, and his hooded eyes blinked like he'd come into bright light from the dark. Then his parted lips curled upward, forming the most genuine smile Ben had seen on his father's face in months. And though Ben couldn't explain it, for the first time in the past couple weeks, he felt hope.

"What's his name?" Willy whispered, as if speaking too loudly would make the news untrue.

"Maxwell. His name is Maxwell Diaz-Oris."

29

After delivering the bombshell news about Maxwell, Ben couldn't bring himself to rush out on Willy, so while the new grandfather chattered on about baby-proofing the home, Ben choked down a hot breakfast he had neither the time nor appetite for. When he finished, he thanked his father and promised to talk later. As he fled Willy's condo, even walking proved difficult. Somehow he made it to his car in his frazzled state, and then to the hospital, drawing only one fist shake and two horn honks.

Inside the parking garage, he swung the Mustang into the first available spot, up on the fourth level. He wasn't thrilled about another parking fee, but stopping at Willy's had made biking impractical.

Grabbing his backpack and white coat from the passenger seat, he hopped out of the car. If he hurried, he might catch the last half of morning report. And maybe only half of Dr. Smith's disapproval.

He shifted his backpack from one shoulder to the other and squirmed into his lab coat. Alongside him, a few other employees shuffled toward the garage's stairwell, heels clicking on concrete, voices jabbering on cell phones. Ben pulled out his own phone. Paying little attention to his surroundings, he texted Laurette the pictures he took of Max's genealogy and told her to call him ASAP. No doubt he was disrupting her life as much as his own.

He pocketed the phone and stepped into the crossway, the stairwell just up ahead. Could Laurette really help him? Would she—

"Look out!"

Someone yanked Ben back by his white coat. A nanosecond later a dark sedan with tinted windows roared past him. Wind lifted Ben's hair, and his backpack flew off his shoulder. Flailing, he struggled to remain upright. He stumbled back and landed with a *thud* on his side. Pain shot through his hip and torso.

"Are you all right?" A breathless woman with a purple streak in her hair reached down to help him, her eyes wide and her mouth an oval of alarm.

Ben extended his bandaged hand but then snatched it back before making contact. Keep your curse to yourself, he thought, a bit hysterically. Wincing, he righted himself. The sulfur of burned rubber hovered in the air. "I'm okay." He dusted off his chinos and retrieved his backpack. "Jeez, you saved my life. Thank you." His voice shook as much as his limbs.

"I was coming up from the other side." The woman pointed to a row of cars one aisle over. Her other hand pressed against her heart, as if, like Ben's, it threatened to bound out of her chest. "That same car was driving slowly behind me. I started to get nervous, you know? Like it was following me. I couldn't see in the windows. I had just crossed over when you stepped out. That's when the car sped up." Her voice rose in the acoustic space. "If I didn't know better, I'd say the driver *wanted* to hit you."

The eggs curdled in Ben's stomach. "That's a cheery thought." After a couple beats of silence, he motioned toward the stairwell, and the two crossed over to it. Hoping his voice didn't betray his true feelings, he said, "I'm sure it's nothing."

"Are you really okay?" She passed through the entry door he opened for her.

Ben patted around on his torso and grinned. On the inside he was chewing his nails to the quick. "I seem to be in one piece. Thank you again. I mean it. If it wasn't for you I'd be a pancake right now."

She blushed. "I'm just glad you're okay."

Together they trotted down the stairs to the second level walkway, but not before Ben stole one last glance at the parking ramp. He pictured his body lying broken and bruised on the pavement, blood smeared across the hood of the car that killed him.

Blood. His blood. The idea made stolen baby hair look like child's play.

30

"Benjamin."

Ben glanced up from his computer charting and immediately straightened. Dr. Smith stood on the other side of the counter, her pale blue suit as soft as clouds.

"Would you please meet me in the ICU in fifteen minutes?" Her tone held an unfamiliar softness. "Harmony Claxwell has been asking to see you, and I'd like an update on her course as well."

Before Ben had a chance to nod, the internist turned and clicked her way down 6 West's hallway. She'd been in a hurry since before rounds, a good thing since it meant no time for pimping. Between his near collision in the parking lot and his still-pending blood test, he might have withered under her usual onslaught.

After informal rounds earlier that morning, Ben had phoned the outpatient lab, his heart beating somewhere behind his Adam's apple. Though it was his own blood test, he doubted the lab would fork over results to anyone but the ordering physician, so he claimed to be calling on Dr. Smith's behalf. Like the overworked tend to do, the tech had snapped at him. "We have a bunch of stat CBCs to run first. It hasn't even been twenty-four hours since Dr. Smith's routine order was drawn." Then, in a fading voice that suggested she was already hanging up the receiver, he heard, "Check back later today."

It may have been less than twenty-four hours to her, but it felt like twenty-four years to him.

Scratching his plans to check in on Sophia and Maxwell, he pushed his chair away from the ward counter and headed to the ICU instead. Two nurses smiled and waved goodbye. In his haze, Ben managed nothing but an unfocused nod in return. He wanted to call Laurette. They'd been playing phone tag since he'd texted her the genealogy pictures, which, based on her voice messages, had spun her into a tizzy. She'd said she was in class until noon.

What would he do if his eosinophil count was high? Worse, what would Dr. Smith do? Probably quarantine his Typhoid Mary ass. He'd do the same were it him in her fancy designer shoes. But he couldn't be locked away, not with so much to sort out and so many people to watch over.

A suffocating force squeezed his chest. One of those people was wasting away in the ICU. His mother. He realized it was the second time in five hours he'd called her that instead of using her name. Would this be the day she died?

When he entered the ICU, his pace slowed and his body tensed. The charged environment still made him uncomfortable. He worried his inexperience in the unit flashed on his forehead. Ventilators popped and hissed inside patient rooms, and cardiac telemetry blipped behind the counter. But the place also energized him, and he hoped to one day charge through its doors as confidently as the residents and nurses buzzing around him.

At the center of the circular corridor, rooms radiating outward like a giant pinwheel, Ben spotted Dr. Smith leaning against the guardrail near a patient's room. She was talking to a nurse and flipping through papers on a clipboard. When Ben approached, he saw Harmony through the window, her eyes closed, her skin sallow. Blood crusted around her nostrils, and pink urine drained from a catheter looping beneath the bed sheet, its collection bag partially filled.

Upon seeing him Dr. Smith handed the clipboard back to the nurse. Given her kind eyes and sad frown, Ben knew it was bad news. "I'm sorry, but she's in DIC. They're having trouble controlling her bleeding. She's lasted two days longer than Melissa, but I don't think your mother is going to make it."

Ben tightened his jaw and sniffed. Willy flashed in his mind. He nodded.

"I'm going to get an update from the ICU attending. Why don't you visit her?"

After gowning, masking, and double-gloving—the latter now required by the infectious disease protocol team given the illness's ongoing mystery—he entered the room. Not having much in the way of body fat to begin with, Harmony seemed little more than a twig in a bed of blankets. Her cardiac monitor traced a tachycardic rhythm even the greenest of premed students would identify. Beneath it, her oxygen reading hovered around a borderline ninety percent despite the high-flow nasal cannula. The nasogastric tube maintained its bloody suction.

Taking care not to kink the IV tubing dangling from her bruised arm, Ben pulled the chair close to the bed and sat down. "Harmony," he said. When she didn't respond, he raised his voice and repeated her name a few times.

Her eyes fluttered open. At first she didn't register him, but then a smile formed on her crusted lips. "My son, coming back to see me." A cough cut her off, and she craned her neck as if to avoid choking. Ben elevated her head and grabbed tissues to place at her mouth. The white fibers soon bloomed to red.

When the coughing subsided Harmony flailed her hand until she found Ben's. Her fingers wrapped around his gloves. He returned her squeeze, wishing he could discard the years of distance between them as easily as he would discard his gloves when he exited the room.

"Always so proud of you," she said, her voice raspy. "Always loved you so much. Please don't hate me."

Ben bit down until his molars ground together. "I don't hate you. You should rest. You don't have to talk."

"No, there are things I still have to say." She tried to push herself up, but the attempt was feeble. The gray gown slipped off her shoulder, revealing a bony lump. When Ben adjusted it, she gestured for him to raise the bed. Once he did, she continued. "Couldn't keep you. My father … a cruel man. Evil. He did things to m—" More coughing consumed her.

Ben exhaled and squeezed her hand. He both wanted and didn't want to know what followed. "Shh, it's okay."

"You … So much better with Willy …" Straining, she lifted her head an inch. Trapping him in her jaundiced gaze, she said, "Take care of your father. Heal him." Her gaunt body erupted in a coughing fit so strong, the oxygen prongs dislodged and her heart rate monitor wailed.

Ben, caught between medical student and shell-shocked son, elevated Harmony so she wouldn't choke. Outside the door a nurse whipped on a gown and gloves. Holding his breath, Ben cradled his absentee mother in his arms, her heaving and wracking body weaker than a child's. Gently he wiped the frothy, pink discharge from her lips.

God, I think I did this to you.

"Love you," she managed to squeak between sputters. "Please for …" Her voice gave out.

An unbearable ache blossomed inside Ben, crippling him to his core. He whispered in her ear. "It's okay. I forgive you." He paused, then added, "Mom."

Her head turned toward him, and for the first time he thought he saw peace in her eyes.

Five minutes later Ben shed his personal protective equipment and exited Harmony's room. Trying to keep his emotions in check, he cracked the knuckles on one hand. When he started on the other, Dr. Smith appeared, her eyebrows drawn and her arms folded. Ben wondered why she was still in the ICU.

Then it hit him. The blood test. Had the lab called her? Was he officially the grim reaper?

A sheen of sweat dotted his forehead, and his neck muscles spasmed, but when she spoke, it wasn't what he expected. "I've got a consult. My outpatient resident is on vacation, so you'll come with me if you like." The internist headed to the exit before Ben could respond.

A consult? As a med student? What about the patient notes he hadn't finished? What about sneaking away to see Sophia and Maxwell? If he didn't get to L&D soon, he'd rupture an aneurysm. Jean Miot could be lurking there that very moment.

Ben hurried after his attending. Refusal was not an option.

"You'll be interested in the case," she said, allowing him to press the automatic door release for her. "Another patient with a high eosinophil count."

"Wait, what?" Ben gripped the edge of the door as it opened. *Oh, God, not Dad, please not Dad.* "Who? Where?"

"A woman." Dr. Smith smoothed the lapel of her suit. The furrow in her forehead deepened. "A woman in Labor & Delivery."

31

M oments after entering the second-floor walkway, on the way to the L&D consult, pinpricks of anxiety danced down Ben's spine, and tightness encircled his chest. Vertigo and a rapid heartbeat followed. Stumbling, he pressed his hand against the glass enclosure. The wave of claustrophobia was so unexpected, he nearly cried out. He crossed through the skywalk every day, sometimes repeatedly. But never like this.

The suffocation grew so strong, the outside street traffic blurred. In its place, images of the catacombs' limestone quarries shimmered and then faded.

"What's wrong? Ben?"

He heard Dr. Smith before he saw her. Slowly she came into view, concern and surprise on her face. Passing hospital staff seemed ready to intervene but moved on when they saw Ben had recovered. As quickly as the outside street traffic had vanished, it returned, as did the sunny, blue sky.

"Are you ill? Do you need to rest in the student lounge?" The internist grabbed his arm as if worried he might stumble again.

He pulled back gently. "I'm fine." The words came out a dry croak. "Just worried about my mother, I guess."

"What was I thinking? You don't need to come with me. I know you and your mother are estranged, but you can spend the day with her if you like."

"No, I'm good. Really. It's better if I stay busy." Translation: nothing could keep him from the L&D consult.

Dr. Smith scrutinized him and then nodded. "Yes, I find that too. I admire your work ethic. It seems to be a thing of the past for many of today's students and residents."

Ben doubted that was true, but he was relieved to be walking once again. "So, tell me about the consult." But inside he already knew, and the thought almost sent him back into a tailspin.

Sophia.

"An OB resident paged me earlier. They have a postpartum woman with ongoing hypertension, muscle aches, and abdominal pain. Some diarrhea, too, though not bloody."

At the Talcott Center Ben held the door open for his attending, his knuckles blanching on the handle.

"Worried about infection, they ran a CBC. The woman's eosinophil count was high, though it hadn't been at the time of admission nor on a follow-up a few days later. The OB resident happened to be in the ED the night Harmony Claxwell came in. He remembered her strange eosinophilia, so his attending told him to call me. Odd, isn't it? Fortunately, her baby's eosinophil count is normal."

Ben said nothing. Couldn't. Despite the building's air conditioning, his shirt stuck to his chest like latex.

When they passed through the L&D waiting room, Dr. Smith raised her electronic tablet and swiped a few times. "Her name is …"

Ben braced himself.

"Ah, here it is. Diaz. Sophia Diaz."

Another wave of vertigo. Ben loosened his tie. His limbs moved like rubber. He needed to sit. Needed to get his bearings. Instead he opened the door to the ward and waited for his attending to pass.

Oblivious to his mental state, Dr. Smith forged on down the hall. Meanwhile Ben fretted about what would happen when Sophia identified him. Not only would Dr. Smith find out about Maxwell (and assume the infant would derail his work ethic), she'd figure out he was indeed Typhoid Mary, no lab test necessary.

He realized his attending was speaking. "What's interesting is that if Ms. Diaz has the same infection, she's been sick for several days but hasn't progressed like the other women. What might that tell you?"

Stifling the tsunami in his gut, Ben forced rational thought. "She has some innate immunity?"

"Excellent. What else?"

"Uh …"

Dr. Smith showed him her tablet, having to hold it up near her face given their height difference. A list of Sophia's medications popped up. "What if Ms. Diaz received a medication that blunted the response?" she asked. "For example, she's been on magnesium. What if antibiotics and antivirals are not what these patients need at all?"

The excitement in the internist's voice was palpable, and for a moment Ben felt his own hope rise. Could she be right? Could it be that simple? If so, that implied a treatment existed. Maybe they could cure Harmony after all. And if there *was* a medical treatment, that meant he wasn't the source of the outbreak, at least not through a curse, anyway.

The more he thought about it, the more it made sense. Why had he been so stupid?

"You're sure you're all right?" She slipped the tablet under her arm. "Did you get your blood drawn yet?"

Ben nodded.

"Good. Seeing normal results should put you at ease. Nothing's come my way, but we should have the test result soon."

And once again, the tsunami of uncertainty returned.

Outside Sophia's door, Ben's mind reeled. How could he get her to not let on she knew him? The moment Dr. Smith learned Ben had been in contact with Sophia, he'd be linked to yet another infection. Just when the attending finally seemed to respect him, too.

"Oh good, someone's on the ball. They put out the personal protective equipment I requested." From a nearby cart Dr. Smith grabbed a gown and mask and indicated Ben do the same. Evidently thinking his hesitancy was due to fear of contagion, she added, "Don't worry. Whatever made these women ill is clearly not airborne. It appears to require extremely close contact to spread. If we cover everything, we'll be fine." Her last words were muffled by the mask as she slipped it over her nose and mouth and tied it in place.

Ben put on his own and tugged on two pairs of gloves. Maybe with the mask Sophia wouldn't recognize him.

Right. And maybe a spider wouldn't notice a fly in its web.

Announcing their presence with a perfunctory knock on the door, Dr. Smith entered the room. Ben followed behind, the synthetic scent of the mask heightening his disequilibrium. Sophia lay elevated in bed, flipping through TV channels. She turned to greet them, and immediately her eyes locked on Ben's.

Behind Dr. Smith, he shook his head so swiftly his cheeks rattled. Sophia looked confused but said nothing, and for once Ben was grateful for his lowly place in the hierarchy so his attending couldn't see his warning. After Dr. Smith introduced herself as well as Ben, Sophia tore her gaze away from his and answered the internist's questions about her symptoms, but the hurt and misunderstanding in her eyes was obvious.

She thinks I'm ashamed, he thought, his heart once again getting skewered.

He tried not to think about her falling ill. Tried not to think of her bleeding from every orifice like Kate, Melissa, and Harmony. She hadn't beaten cancer only to die so horribly. Instead he tried to focus on what Sophia was telling Dr. Smith. "They say he's well enough for discharge now."

Who, Maxwell? From the secured and locked-down nursery? Leaving Jean Miot with unfettered access?

Ben turned to stone. A rush of blood flooded his head, and his palms blazed inside the gloves. If he got quarantined and Sophia remained hospitalized, who would care for Maxwell? Sophia's family wanted nothing to do with her, and he suspected she felt the same about them.

A strange sound came from him, making both women glance his way. When he cleared his throat to cover himself, Dr. Smith resumed her questioning.

He had to get that lab result. Had to get it before Dr. Smith did. Because if it was abnormal and she found out first, she'd have no choice but to shut him off from the world. And then who would protect his son?

32

In an obstetrical consultation room decorated with framed photographs of birthmark-kissed newborns, Ben sat on the edge of a twill sofa, cell phone in hand, its *Send* button one push away from proving or disproving he'd killed two women and infected two more.

Ten minutes earlier Dr. Smith had left the L&D unit, but not before ordering Ben to write a consult note. "I'm trusting you to handle this. Don't disappoint. I'll review the note after lunch and sign off on it."

As a third-year student, Ben knew she was granting him an honor few got, and the thought of effing it up made his throat burn. But he had to get to his blood test before she did. So the second she departed, he'd fled to the consultation room to call for it.

And yet his phone remained inert in his hand, its only activity a recent text from Laurette, probably fired off during a class break. In it she said she'd seek advice about the genealogy find from her Aunt Marie and Guy as soon as she could. Their involvement only fueled Ben's fear. They'd again recommend Jean Miot, a man Ben wanted nowhere near his son.

But what if Miot was the answer?

Ben flicked at his temple. Never had he felt so conflicted. Until now his entire life had been mapped out like a spreadsheet. If his blood count was high, he had two choices: turn himself in for evaluation and quarantine, or flee the hospital and head to Vodouland to protect his son. The first choice meant continuing on as a medical student; the second one spelled his academic demise.

Cursing, he puffed out his cheeks and pressed *Send*.

"Outpatient lab, Kim speaking."

"Um, hi. I'm a med student working with Dr. Smith. She asked me to check if the CBC on Benjamin Oris is back yet."

"Oh yeah, you called earlier. Good timing. I was just about to phone Dr. Smith's nurse. We have to do that for all critical values."

Ben closed his eyes. His body collapsed.

"The patient's eosinophil count is crazy high. That's why we ran it again. We thought the first result was an error." Kim's voice carried the hushed excitement of medical staff faced with the unusual. "Get this, it's twenty-five thousand five hundred. That's *sixty percent* of this guy's total white blood cell count. Normal is less than five to seven percent. Can you believe it?"

Ben's mouth felt like Nevada soil in hundred-and-ten-degree heat. "Wow," was all he managed to say.

"I know, wild, isn't it? So you'll let Dr. Smith know? We'll fax her a written report but this way I can document she was notified. What was your name again?"

Ben disconnected. An animated group of student nurses passed down the hall, commiserating over a practicum they'd just completed. In Ben's mental state it sounded like gibberish.

So there it was. Question solved. He'd killed Kate and Melissa, killed them as surely as if he'd strangled them with his bare hands. And now he was killing Harmony. And probably Sophia too.

He leaned back and let the couch swallow him whole. His core resisted contraction, his limbs refused extension. A grain of self-preservation shouted at him to act, told him to get moving before Dr. Smith got the report, but he remained rooted in place, his fists opening and closing, the bandaged papule mocking him like a melanoma of death. In his mind's eye he grabbed a scalpel from the supply room and sliced the motherfucker right off. Just another chunk of tissue tossed out with the rest of the biohazard waste.

Rubbing his face, he tried to pull himself together. A blip of rationality settled in, and he wondered why Sophia wasn't as sick as the others or why Maxwell wasn't sick at all. According to Laurette the infection touched everyone he was close to. An eighteenth-century priestess had made sure of that. Was actual blood contact a requirement? After all, he'd never bled on Maxwell, only held him. Or, as Ben's son, did the infant have some sort of immunity? Maybe that was what made his blood so valuable to the lunatic in Laurette's dream.

Or maybe Dr. Smith had the answer. Maybe the magnesium in Sophia's blood stream had blunted the infection, an infection no more cursed than whooping cough or strep throat, just simply the result of a nasty old bone.

But if someone meant his son harm, did the source of the disease even matter?

Using every muscle fiber he had, he rose from the couch and headed back toward L&D. There really was no choice. He knew what he had to do.

33

"I'm sorry I acted like I didn't know you, but it's not what you think."
Ben's bare hands gripped the safety rail on Sophia's bed. A few moments earlier he'd slipped into her room unprotected. No need to waste time on gowns and masks when both of their eosinophil counts were stratospheric. But he couldn't leave the hospital without first warning her to keep Maxwell safe.

Sophia twisted the gold cross hanging over her satin pajamas. Her usual cheer was gone. "What's wrong? You look scared."

Ben glanced at the door behind him. "There's so much I'd like to tell you, but I don't have time. You'd never believe me anyway."

"What's happening?"

"I have to go. You might not see me for a bit." Ben's pager vibrated against his hip. Even without checking the number, he knew it was Dr. Smith. Knew it like he knew the sun would set that night. His speech sped up, and his underarms grew sticky beneath his shirt and lab coat. "Don't let anyone near Maxwell other than you or the nurses. I mean it."

"You're freaking me out. You can't just tell me something like that and leave."

"I don't have time to explain. Please, Sophia. Trust me."

"But you don't understand. They have me in isolation. They won't let Maxwell in here since his blood test is normal. Of course I don't want him to get infected, but I can't bear being away from him." Sophia blinked several times. Her voice shook. "He's ready for discharge. They want me to contact a family member to take him home. I was hoping it would be you, but now you tell me you have to leave." She bit her lower lip, as if trying not to cry.

"I'm so sorry it turned out this way." Ben felt more pulled than taffy, but he had to get moving. God, she'd hate him forever now.

"But I can't give him to my mother," Sophia said, her voice rising to a wail. "My parents and sister think I'm a whore who got herself knocked up. In a one-night stand no less. Do you think I want my son around that? My only supportive relative is an aunt in San Francisco, and that doesn't do me any good right now."

"I wish I could help, but—"

"You can. Please, take Maxwell home with you. Just until they let me go. Your father can help."

Tormented, Ben's mind raced for a solution. His pager buzzed again, every vibration reminding him how little time he had before Dr. Smith saw the lab result and connected the dots. He wanted nothing more than to take Maxwell home, keep him safe, protect him. But that couldn't happen because Ben would be put into quarantine, and he'd be no use to his son sequestered away. Jean Miot, or whoever it was, wanted Maxwell. Ben had to stop the man while he still could.

Even if he somehow managed to break Maxwell out of San Quentin nursery in the next few minutes and run off with him, he'd still be putting his son in danger. Who knew what Jean Miot might do? Although Ben hated the thought of Maxwell staying with Sophia's mom and dad, he doubted they'd let Miot anywhere near their grandchild. Besides, Willy wasn't a possibility. He'd have too many questions, none of which Ben had time to answer.

"Your parents will understand. Babies change things, right?"

"Please, Ben. I won't ask you for anything else regarding Maxwell, but I'm asking you for this."

A knife sliced his heart. "I'm sorry, I can't." He moved closer and stroked her short, dark hair. "You have to trust me. Something terrible is happening, something I can't explain, but I have to stop it."

"Oh dear God, does it involve my baby?"

Ben withdrew his hand a little too quickly. "Maxwell will be safe with your family until I can get him. When this is over I promise I'll tell you everything."

But would Sophia still be around to tell? Or would she end up sick and bleeding like the others?

Bile rose in Ben's throat. "I have to go. I have to leave the hospital." He locked his anguished gaze on her own. "But when this is over I'll be a good father to Maxwell. I promise."

"Are you in trouble?" she whispered.

"I don't know yet." He took a pen and small notebook from his lab coat pocket. After ripping out a sheet of paper, he jotted down Laurette's number. "I won't be using my phone for a while, but if you need to reach me, you call this number. Laurette is my friend, and she'll help either one of us." Then, not knowing whether he should or not but doing it anyway, he bent down and kissed her cheek. "It'll be okay."

When he pulled away, Sophia stopped him. "Wait." She removed her necklace, brought the cross to her lips, and then hung the gold chain around his neck. "I think you need this more than me."

Ben couldn't help a weak smile. A cross and a bone amulet. On Benjamin Oris. Realist, pragmatist, skeptic. He headed to the door, but when he opened it and poked his head out, he froze. Down the hallway, just in front of the exit doors, a nurse and a doctor huddled with Dr. Smith, the attending waving her hands in an agitated manner.

She knew.

But something else choked off Ben's airway. Dr. Smith wasn't alone. Next to her stood her stepson, Joel (though why, Ben had no idea) and behind him, an armed security guard.

It didn't take a Mensa scholar to know who the guard's target was.

34

Ben whipped his head back into Sophia's room. He leaned against the door, his heart rate matching his racing thoughts. Escaping to the stairwell near the nurses' station was a no-go. Even in the unlikely event Dr. Smith and the security guard didn't spot him from down the hall, someone at the ward counter would. Plus, running only made him look guilty. It wasn't like he'd purposely infected the women. But if he turned himself in, he'd be no good to Maxwell. Or anyone else left in his orbit.

"Tell me what's going on." Sophia's voice shook with worry.

Ben could only stare at her.

Voices approached. He recognized Dr. Smith's among them.

On instinct, he darted to the bathroom in the back corner. Before he closed the door, he looked at Sophia with a flushed face. "Please don't tell anyone I'm here," he implored. "I'm begging you to trust me. Maxwell's life depends on it."

Before he got an answer from the alarmed mother, he closed the bathroom door just as the main one opened. Breathless, he backed up toward the combination shower and sitz bath. Absorbent maxi-pads, drying breast pump parts, and scented body washes and lotions cluttered the small space. He stepped into the shower and pulled the curtain closed.

Trying to make out their voices above his hammering heart, he wondered why Joel was there. Had he been in Dr. Smith's office when she received the lab report? Then he remembered. Joel had seen him entering Labor &

Delivery the week before. With Sophia sick, maybe Joel had made the link between them and was there to prove it.

Nausea washed over Ben. In the claustrophobic shower space, the perfumed body wash magnified his lightheadedness. He gritted his teeth and forced his focus on Dr. Smith's words.

"… just had a few more questions. This is Joel, by the way, one of our … students."

Ben heard a rustling and imagined a pissed-off Joel stepping forward in his personal protective equipment. Ben couldn't believe he'd been allowed in.

Dr. Smith continued. "The medical student I rounded with earlier, Benjamin Oris, has he been back to see you?"

There was a pause, and Ben wondered if Sophia would give him away. Who could blame her? But he sagged in relief when she said, "No. Why?"

"It's come to our attention that you know Mr. Oris. It's important we talk to him."

"Me? I don't know him."

"That's not true," Ben heard Joel say. "A nurse told me he's visited you several times."

"I'm sorry, I think you're confused." Sophia's tone was so syrupy sweet Ben almost believed her.

A pink razor fell from the lip of the tub to the protective mat. Against the rubber the sound was negligible, but Ben froze, worried someone had heard it. Sweat plastered his shirt to his torso like cellophane. If only he'd taken off the stifling coat.

"She's lying," Joel said. "I told you something weird was going on. Ben's like the angel of death. One of those doctors or nurses you hear about who—"

"Joel." Dr. Smith's rebuke halted her stepson's rant, but the damage had been done. What would Sophia think of Ben after hearing that?

The mother of his child said nothing. Ben wrapped his hand around her cross in gratitude, his palm sticky and hot.

After a few moments of silence, Dr. Smith spoke again. "Thank you, Ms. Diaz, but just in case Ben does come back to see you, could you please have the nurse page me or your doctor? He hasn't been answering his pages. We're worried he's contagious, and we want to be cautious, that's all."

"Contagious? With what?" Even from his hiding place, the fear in Sophia's voice was obvious. Yet no betrayal followed.

"We're not sure yet, but we'll let you know when we have more details. Please, have the nurse call us if you see him."

Dead air followed, then shuffling and the shutting of the door. Finally, just when he thought he'd go mad in the confined, heady space, Sophia said, "You can come out now. They're gone."

Ben stepped out of the tub, deeply inhaling the open air. His relief was short-lived. Only fear and uncertainty lay ahead.

35

Under a blazing midday sun, Ben speed-walked the one and a half miles to Willy's house. The temperature had topped ninety degrees, and with each step his adrenaline-fueled stench hit him. At least he'd ditched his white coat and tie, stuffing them into Sophia's overnight bag in the closet.

Too worried security would apprehend him at the gate, he'd left his car in the parking garage. Paranoid? Maybe. But with each passing minute he grew more convinced it was the safest position to take. He'd been equally careful slinking out of Sophia's room, checking every hallway and stairwell until he'd finally cleared the building.

Wanting to avoid fellow students or hospital staff returning from lunch, he chose Spruce Street over Walnut. In doing so, he passed a Jewish temple on his left, its gray stone a sharp contrast to the red-brick buildings around it.

Judaism, Catholicism, Vodouism—religions and practices as foreign to Ben as Mars. Beneath his drenched shirt, Sophia's cross twisted around the bone amulet, their tips snagging his neglected chest hair.

"Don't shave it all off," Melissa had once said in the bathroom, wrapping her arms around his torso as he clutched a hair trimmer in his hand. "If I wanted a bare chest, I'd date a woman."

Melissa.

Melissa was dead.

He moaned, barely aware he'd done it. Sweat dripped down his cheeks. He should've caught a cab. He'd be there by—

A few yards ahead a nurse Ben recognized was looking at a designer handbag in a store window. Ben lowered his head and held his breath, not daring to exhale until he passed her. Witnesses were a development he didn't need.

Again he wondered if he was being paranoid, and again he told himself no. He'd learned enough from his epidemiology class to know public health officials had the right to invoke police powers to protect the public, and that included arresting a carrier of a lethal disease who refused to go willingly. In other words, a fugitive.

Was that what he was? A fugitive? Though unspoken, the word tasted foul in his mouth.

Yet he barreled on toward South 22nd Street, avoiding eye contact with any of the other pedestrians. Once at his dad's place, he'd fetch Max's Mazda, but before that he'd grab Willy's old cell phone from the kitchen drawer, the prepaid phone his dad used until Ben saved his pennies and got him a better one last Christmas. The old one had a year-long plan so there should still be some minutes on it. Worried the police would track his own cell, Ben had already powered it off.

He pulled his key chain from his front pocket and jingled. The key to the silver Mazda was still there, right next to the one to Willy's condo. When he got there he'd call Laurette. No way could he do anything without her.

=⊨=

"Thank God you're here. I've been trying to call you." A distraught Willy jumped up from the kitchen table and in his haste to hug his son, he practically pulled Ben down.

Ben fended him off with outstretched arms, fearful of what a bear hug might do. Though the cooling relief of Willy's air-conditioning was welcomed, the image of his father bleeding in the ICU was not. "Dad, what's wrong? Why aren't you at the store?"

"She's going to die, Benny. They called me." Dark circles under Willy's eyes suggested he'd had no sleep for days.

"When?" Ben tried to keep his voice calm.

"Just a while ago. A doctor from the ICU." Willy stumbled to the living room and paced the area rug. "I should've visited her. I should've been by her side." He punched the wingback chair, and then gripped its wooden frame and shook it.

Though hesitant to touch his father, Ben went to the trembling man's side and lowered him into the chair. Willy emitted a heartbreaking moan, and in the sunlight streaming through the Palladian window, Ben noticed his dad's skin was too sallow, his lips too dry, his tone too flaccid.

Oh, Jesus, no.

Ben choked down a spasm. "Don't blame yourself, Dad. I was with her this morning."

Willy nodded dumbly, his hands shaking on his thighs.

"I'll get you some water." Ben took a step toward the kitchen. "Hang tight, okay? We'll figure out what to do."

Again his father nodded, and when Ben was sure the man wouldn't crumple onto the floor, he hustled to the kitchen and poured two glasses of water from the fridge's dispenser—one for himself and one for his father. As he gulped the cold water, he prayed for a next step to materialize. He couldn't leave Willy in his agitated state, but he desperately needed to call Laurette.

Crossing to a drawer next to the sink, he rummaged for Willy's old cell phone. He found it, along with its charger, and plugged it into an outlet near the stove. When he returned to the living room, Willy was slumped back in the chair, his legs extended at odd angles, his shoes abutting a patterned rug.

"Dad." Ben rushed to his father. Water spilled over the sides of the glass and splashed onto the floor. "Here, drink this." With urgency, he put the glass to his father's lips.

Willy obliged, barely. After a few sips, he said, "I don't feel so good." He put his hands on the arm rests and leaned forward, but instead of standing, he toppled over and rolled onto his back. His eyes blinked wildly.

"Dad!"

Ben dropped to his knees near his father, right before Willy vomited.

"Oh shit." Ben turned his father onto his side so he wouldn't choke. Willy's body trembled in Ben's arms.

His father's eyes blinked open. He no longer retched, but soupy vomitus soaked his chin and puddled around his head. "Sorry, Benny Boy. Looks like I made a mess."

Ben gently pulled his father away from the pea-green puddle. He ripped off his own vile shirt and used it to clean his dad's face. "I'll call an ambulance."

Trying to hide his mounting panic, he stood and wiped vomit off his hands and onto his slacks.

"No … no need … I'll be …" Willy's voice faded off, as if the act of speaking required more energy than he possessed.

You'll be dead.

Choking off rumbling sobs, Ben dashed to the kitchen and clutched the landline. He pounded the handset in his palm three times. "Goddammit," he cried. Then, with fingers quivering worse than his father's, he dialed 9-1-1.

Ben had grown up confused and angered by a bipolar mother who flitted in and out of his life like a butterfly. He'd worked tirelessly in construction to save money for med school, postponing the start of classes until an age when most students had already graduated. He'd studied until his eyes nearly bled, achieving mostly As. He'd watched helplessly as one of his fathers wasted away from cancer and the other one silently grieved.

But the hardest thing he'd ever done was abandon his hospital-phobic dad in an ambulance that afternoon.

"Benny, please, stay with me. I don't want to be alone."

Willy's pleading and poorly veiled terror would forever burn in Ben's brain, as would the ambulance siren and lights speeding away in the distance.

But Ben couldn't go with him, no matter how deep the rip in his heart. Even if he wasn't immediately recognized by the ER staff, the moment it became known yet another person linked to Ben had become ill, Ben wouldn't see freedom for days. And during that time his newborn son would be discharged to a family Ben knew nothing about, leaving the infant exposed to a charismatic, chisel-faced Vodou practitioner hell-bent on making the baby's acquaintance. And though the bokor claimed only a desire to help, Ben's instincts warned otherwise. Then again, his instincts seemed to be crap lately. He'd touched the catacomb bone, after all, even when Laurette had pleaded with him not to.

Still shirtless and sweaty, Ben tore himself away from the curb where he'd abandoned his father and trudged back to the condo. The first thing he did was call Laurette, using Willy's prepaid phone, its charge already at fifty percent.

She answered immediately. "Why have you not called me sooner? I have been frantic to reach you. We must talk about your family tree."

Rolling his neck but failing to release the tension, Ben made his way into Willy's bedroom. "We have a shitload more than that to talk about."

Ben filled her in on his day, starting with his high eosinophil count and ending with Maxwell's impending discharge and Willy's ambulance ride.

"I can meet you at Willy's at three." Laurette didn't hesitate, nor did she sound surprised. "I can't break free before then. We will go to Mambo Tina's."

"Is that what your aunt and brother suggest?"

A pause. "No. They insist for such a curse a bokor is needed. Auntie Marie says Jean Miot is trustworthy."

"But you don't think so." In the bedroom Ben rummaged through Willy's closet, looking through Max's clothes. Despite his shell-shocked state, he was clear-headed enough to know he couldn't traipse around in vomit-stained pants or go bare-chested with a bone amulet and a Christian cross twisting against his flesh.

"Let us try Mambo Tina again. Maybe this time she will help us. I listen to my gut here, Ben. Is that not what you Americans say?"

If only his friend sounded more hopeful.

"But what if I infect you too?" He ran his hand slowly over Max's faux-cashmere coat, inhaling its woodsy, amber scent.

"I have told you, you will not make me sick. I don't see it in my dreams."

Ben was about to ask how she could be so sure, but Laurette had already hung up.

Turning to Willy's oak dresser, Ben emptied his pockets of keys, wallet, and smartphone and went back to rifling through Max's clothes. A pair of black jeans with a thirty-two inch waist and thirty-four inch inseam was closer to Ben's size than Willy's thirty-six by thirty-two. He pulled them off a hanger along with a form-fitting T-shirt. After plugging the prepaid phone back in, he headed to the shower. When he finished, he found a pair of Max's boxer briefs in the dresser and slipped into the fresh clothes, replacing keys and wallet in his pockets. He'd add Willy's old cell phone after it charged longer. He then discarded his vomit-stained clothes in a plastic bag for later cleaning, the shirt still in the living room where he'd left it.

If there is a later, he thought, swallowing his mounting dread. For either him or his father.

After cleaning the vomit off the floor, he hopped in place and pumped his arms, hoping the physical motion would sharpen his focus. He'd acted on logic and reason many times. His gut reaction of what to do had rarely failed him. He needed to channel that again. Needed to ditch the fear and emotion.

Of course, that was when his world had been black or white. Right or wrong. Logical or illogical. In this new world, all bets were off.

36

"Do you think she'll agree to see us?" Ben asked Laurette an hour later. They stood on the berm near Max's Mazda, the silver car so grimy from misuse neither one dared lean against it. "She made it pretty clear last time I was about as welcome as a boa constrictor."

"I don't know." Laurette tossed her own keys into her Parisian purse, its canary yellow the same color as her skirt. Defined deltoids pressed against her capped sleeves, and her elegant fingers reached for the passenger door handle. As always, she remained fresh in the summer heat. She studied Ben for a moment, apparently aware of his distress. "Try to relax. I know you feel you have forsaken your father, but you are of more help to him breaking the curse than sitting at his bedside."

"Assuming it can be broken," Ben mumbled. A plump bee buzzed drunkenly in front of his face. He swatted it away, but with as tight as his throat felt, the insect might as well have stung him.

"I called her assistant, David," Laurette continued. "I claimed to be Claudette in need of a *wanga*. I was afraid if I used my real name, Mambo Tina would not see us."

"What's a wanga?"

"It is a talisman of sorts, a magical charm. Objects within a small packet that serve as a home for the Lwa we serve." Upon seeing Ben's skepticism, she added, "It may sound foolish to you, but you would not be here now if you did not think you needed help from a Vodouisant, oui?"

Touché, Ben thought, squinting into the sun, wishing he had his sunglasses from his car.

Rounding Max's vehicle he opened the driver's door, but before he got in, Laurette said, "I must tell you, Dr. Smith called Dr. Khalid, not only to update her on Sophia, but to tell her of a medical student who appears to be a carrier. A student who—how did she say it?—oh yes: a student who has gone AWOL. As my advisor, Dr. Khalid passed the information on to me. She is aware I know you, but I told her I did not know you well, nor did I know of your whereabouts."

Ben ran the keys through his fingers. "So they know I'm patient zero. Typhoid Mary. They'll want to quarantine me." A glimmer of hope flashed in his eyes. "Dr. Smith thinks magnesium is slowing it down."

"You know magnesium will do nothing." Laurette gave an abrupt wave in the air as if shooing away another bee. "The infection will never be gone. They can lock you up for twenty years and pump your blood full of magnesium, but as soon as you are released, you will infect another person close to you."

A Dodge truck barreled by. Ben watched it disappear, along with his tiny sliver of hope. Then he dropped his tense body behind the wheel of his dead father's car and took one step closer to the unknown.

Mambo Tina's short, stout body blocked the entryway of the peristil, a title far fancier than the rundown, North Philly row house deserved. Like unwanted Jehovah's Witnesses, Ben and Laurette waited on her awning-less step, the sun baking their scalps. Ben's thoughts cycled to Willy and the terror he must be feeling all alone in the emergency department.

Behind Mambo Tina, David Alcine rubbed his keloid-scarred arms, a reaction no doubt to the reprimand he'd just received from the priestess for booking the false "Claudette" an afternoon appointment.

"I told you yesterday, I do not want you here." The mambo's pellet-like eyes narrowed in disapproval, and her rouged cheeks glowed like two shiny apples. "*Li pote sa ki mal van.*"

"But those evil winds he carries are why we need your help, Madame." Laurette shifted her purse, the bag thumping Ben in the side.

David whispered something in Creole, and Mambo Tina leaned back to hear him. Within the foreign speech Ben heard Jean Miot's name.

"No, you must not consult him." Mambo Tina sprang forward so quickly one of her wooden hair pins shifted. "David already arranged for you a meeting with the bokor at the pharmacy." The mambo glowered at her assistant, prompting him to lower his gaze and rub more ferociously at his scars. "But that was before he understood your danger. You cannot seek Monsieur Miot's help now. His dark magic cannot be trusted." She lowered her voice to a hushed baritone, and her fingers tapped a string of jingling beads over her heart. "He takes souls for payment."

Ben swallowed a scoff and shifted his attention to a homeless man toting a bag stuffed with cans.

Laurette moved a step closer to the shawled woman. "What do you mean?"

The priestess hesitated. Her brow moved in and out of a frown, and she tightened her lips. Finally, she sighed and waved the two of them in, signaling David to close the door behind them. Halfway down the dim hallway she approached a small altar. Jumbled upon its velvet covering lay a cross, beaded jewels, candles, and religious statues. Holding her hands to her lips, she whispered a prayer. When she finished, she turned back to them.

"Monsieur Miot does not work alone. There is a deeper force within him."

"What force?" Laurette wrapped her arms around her torso, as if seeking warmth in the already overheated dwelling. "A person? A spirit?"

Mambo Tina raised her hand. "I do not know, and I will not speak of it other than to say it has not been seen, only felt." With obvious reluctance she turned and led them down the hall into the same dark room they had visited before, its heavy drapery once again closed to block out the sunlight.

The three Haitians and the lone American sat down at the round table with the burgundy cloth where the card divination had taken place the day before. Assuming their same positions, Ben was once again trapped in the leer of the goat-headed statue. As before, long, cluttered altar tables lined the periphery, and multiple candle flames cast the room in a shadowy glow, probably in anticipation of the fictitious Claudette's appointment. The quiet was thicker than the heat.

Upon Mambo Tina's go-ahead, Laurette relayed the events of the lamp ceremony the night before. Holding nothing back, she spoke of a slave girl's violent assault at Ben's hands, burning dwellings, and curses cast but not activated.

Hearing the fiasco repeated out loud filled Ben with the same revulsion he'd felt before. Dream world or not, no part of him believed he was capable of such vicious acts. A foulness coated his tongue, and he bit his lip to keep from spitting the taste out.

Laurette also told Mambo Tina and David what she'd learned about Nasicha Boro, the eighteenth-century priestess who'd placed the curse on Pierre Marcel after the Frenchman had impregnated her daughter. "But the curse did not take hold before the girl died. Her bones were—"

Mambo Tina cut Laurette off with a raised arm. In the flickering candlelight, a deep line creased her forehead, and her hand flew to her heart. "Mon Dieu, you told us of a curse, but you did not tell us you think it is that of Nasicha Boro." David's worry matched his mentor's, and his scar-rubbing hands fell still, as if too alarmed for motion.

"I … uh …"

It was the first time Ben had ever heard Laurette trip over her words, and like the others he waited expectantly.

She chewed her lower lip before trying again. "I worried you would think me fou. The woman is a myth, no? So I mentioned only a curse. I hoped, perhaps, you would divine it. But after last night's iliminasyon, I now know it is the truth, whether others believe it or not. I swear this to you."

In the silence that followed, Ben's apprehension grew. Once again he was the odd man out, but although he didn't completely understand their fear, he felt it just as acutely.

Mambo Tina inhaled deeply. "We know of this curse. It is said Nasicha Boro was a very powerful bokor. To this day many believe she lives on as a dark Lwa. They fear the curse's rebirth, so they appease their own Lwa to keep it away. But as you say, others wonder about its truth." She turned to Ben. "Just as in your culture, we too have our urban legends."

Laurette leaned forward, her refined nose inches from the candle flame. "But this is no myth. The Lwa showed me last night. I felt the woman's fury and pain. I saw her plant the curse. Only it did not go as planned. Her daughter died before the curse could pass to Monsieur Marcel."

"And so that is where it stopped, no?" Mambo Tina's expression suggested she wanted to believe her own words but didn't.

"No, it is not where it stopped." Laurette's tone grew fiery. "The curse did not die. It lay in wait in the dead girl. Waited as her poor body decayed in its mass grave. Waited as her bones were disturbed and moved to the catacombs. Waited to be released so it could finally wield its power."

"But how?" the priestess asked.

"Through a descendant."

Nobody spoke. The goatman glowered at Ben. David Alcine's heavy breathing nearly extinguished the candle flame, while Mambo Tina's entwined hands pressed against the burgundy tablecloth. With a tight nod she motioned for Laurette to continue.

"From the moment we boarded the Paris Métro to the catacombs, I felt darkness. The closer we came to the slave girl's bones, the stronger that darkness grew. I resisted going forward, but …"

She didn't have to finish her sentence. Ben knew it was because of him they had charged on. He lowered his head and picked at the bandage on his palm.

As if reading his mind, Laurette said, "But it does not matter why we kept going. Stopping an earthquake would have been easier than stopping Ben from touching that bone. He was chosen. I see this now. And when it cut him the curse planted its seed in his blood, where it grows stronger with every beat of his heart."

If Mambo Tina doubted Laurette's words, she made no sign. Instead she shifted her hands to her cluster of necklaces, closed her eyes, and mumbled a prayer.

For the first time since they'd sat down, David spoke, his nervous gaze on Laurette. "Are you telling to us now this man at our table has connection to Pierre Marcel?"

"Oui." Wasting no time, Laurette pulled her phone from her purse. "Here. I will prove it." With tightly pressed lips, she opened her photos and showed them the pictures Ben had sent her earlier. In them was the proof they needed of his shameful family tree.

With the self-consciousness of an illiterate man in a bookstore, Ben watched Mambo Tina and Laurette pray in front of the peristil's candlelit altars and make offerings to the Lwa. David had slipped out moments before. Ben understood none of what they said. All he'd absorbed was that Mambo Tina would, reluctantly, perform a ceremony that evening, one that would allow better understanding of the curse. But she'd made clear there were no assurances of its cure.

Stepping away from the round table, Ben ached to rip open the drapes and bathe the room in light, a splash of sunshine to brighten the darkness within him. His mind shifted back and forth between his son's impending discharge and his father alone in the ER. What a shit son he was.

I must be insane, he thought. A few weeks ago his only concern was surviving his internal medicine clerkship. How paltry that goal seemed now.

He could still turn back. No one had a knife to his throat. He could turn himself in, test Dr. Smith's theory of magnesium treatment, and abandon all talk of Vodou ceremonies and black magic. But as much as he pined for the familiar, for textbooks and patient notes and even pimping by Dr. Smith, was he willing to risk Maxwell's fate for it?

With a start he realized David had returned and was speaking to him. The assistant priest extended a scarred arm and held out a small, clear bag containing yellow powder. "Keep it in your pocket, but be very careful." David crinkled the skin of his nose, his pores large and sebaceous. "Do not sniff. Do not let it touch your eyes."

"What is it?" Ben asked, accepting the bag but holding it at arm's length.

"Protection. Against your enemy should he appear." David skittered away to join Mambo Tina before Ben could ask more.

Ben studied the tiny resealable bag. His knowledge of pharmaceutical powders, assuming that was what it was, would barely fill a Post-It note. He was about to give the packet back, but then he hesitated and slipped it into the front pocket of his jeans. As he did so, something poked his right flank. He jumped. Looking over his shoulder, the goatman looked back. Ben had backed right into the ugly thing. The beast's bulging eyes engulfed him, and Ben imagined it laughing at his naiveté. With a shudder he moved away and joined the three Vodouisants near one of the altars.

"I am not a bokor," Mambo Tina was saying. "No black magic here. Through me, you can only seek help from the Lwa. But I will need the bébé."

Ben's stupor broke. "Uh-uh, no way." His abruptness startled them, and all three shifted his way. "I'm sorry, but that's not possible. Besides, my son is still in the hospital. At least I think he is." Yep, shit father, too.

"Nothing can happen without the bébé." Mambo Tina steepled her fingers as if the issue were settled. She moved closer to Ben, and a quiver worked its way into her voice. "Now I must ask you, have you been unsure of the things you have done?"

"I don't know what you mean." A drop of sweat trickled down Ben's forehead, and he wiped it away.

"Laurette tells me your baby hair is taken. I do not know if it is enough—blood would be stronger—but this dark being seeks to learn your Lwa and control you."

Ben still didn't completely understand. Things were moving too quickly to process. But he assured her all of his actions had been his own. At least he hoped they were. His absent-mindedness in the parking garage that morning had almost gotten him killed.

In a fugue-like state he listened to the priestess relay items needed for the ceremony. Laurette riffled through her purse for a pen and paper to jot them down. "It is the seeker of services who must collect the supplies," Mambo Tina said. "I am merely the means through which you seek your solution." Then to Ben's chagrin, she added. "If there is one."

Ben struggled to listen to the rest of what she said, but her speech was too fast and too peppered with Haitian Creole for him to grasp it all. When Laurette asked about a *pwen cho,* explaining to Ben it was a receptacle to enslave a spirit, his muscles tensed so firmly, he worried they'd rupture.

Mambo Tina shook her head, and her nostrils flared. "Oh no. I do no such thing. That is the work of bokors like Jean Miot." She leaned over the first altar and started blowing out candles. In her haste she missed most of them. She stood up and started twisting a ring on her finger. "But I need the bébé," she added.

Skeptical, exhausted, terrified. Each one of Ben's emotions gave way to the next, only to repeat the cycle again. There was no way to get Maxwell out of the hospital without turning himself in, nor was he sure he wanted to. Though he trusted Mambo Tina more than Jean Miot, he wondered why he should. He knew nothing about the woman. All he had to go on was Laurette's guidance. He'd have to hope that was enough.

37

Two hours after leaving Mambo Tina's peristil, Ben returned to the same back room he'd visited twice in as many days. The grim-lipped priestess had ushered him down the hallway to drop off his armfuls of ceremonial supplies, requesting he spread out the goods on the table. "I have invited many people to the ceremony," she said. Then she took off, leaving him to fend for himself, wondering who the people would be.

Doing as he was told, he emptied the bags and deposited the items next to the unlit candles on the burgundy tablecloth: fruit, nuts, salsa, chips, chocolate, toys, party favors, and alcohol. Lots and lots of alcohol, the bottles clinking together as he unloaded them from their brown bags. Apparently the spirits liked their spirits. From what Ben had gleaned from Laurette, so did the participants, making Ben question how much of the ceremonial outcomes depended on inebriation rather than Vodou.

After completing his task he stood ill at ease and made eye contact with the goatman. Unhappy with that exchange, he shifted his gaze to the snake coiled around its golden staff. Finally, he took in the center pole followed by the altar tables lining three of the four walls. All were draped, adorned, and crammed with items just as they'd been before. At least someone had opened the curtains in his absence, lessening the creep factor of the place by about half.

Reflexively, he patted his front jean pocket. David's plastic bag of yellow powder crinkled beneath the denim. He wondered again what it was. As a medical student he had studied pharmacology, but a whole host of herbal medicines existed beyond his knowledge, some that were toxic in small doses.

He thought back to the lamp ceremony the evening before. No alcohol or drugs in his system to explain his heinous dream, nor the fact Laurette had shared it. In fact, other than a cold sandwich for dinner, he'd consumed little before the service. Only Laurette's herbal tea had followed.

A wriggling suspicion taunted his brain. He shook it off. Laurette wouldn't drug him, would she?

Maybe I should go to Jean Miot after all.

Ben's head jerked. The thought was so unexpected, he froze.

"You bring everything, yes?" Mambo Tina's voice broke Ben's paralysis. He spun around to face her. Rummaging through the items he'd arranged on the table, she nodded and repositioned her shawl. "I need time to prepare," she said. "You will come back at eight."

It was a statement, not a question, so Ben took his "bad wind" and departed her peristil.

Behind the wheel of Max's Mazda, he rolled down the windows and waited for Laurette to call. After making the ceremony purchases an hour earlier, he had driven her back to Willy's where she retrieved her Subaru. The plan was he'd deliver the goods to Mambo Tina while Laurette checked in on Willy and explained as best she could why Ben wasn't at his side. Then she would visit Sophia to pass on Ben's new phone number and find out whether Maxwell had already been discharged to his grandparents. Ben hoped Laurette's mentee status to the epidemiologist would grant her access to Sophia, who was being kept in isolation. Luckily, no one knew Laurette and Ben were good friends. At least he didn't think so.

A heavy cloud cover rolled in and prematurely darkened the sky. With it came a cooler temperature. Good thing, too, because the gas gauge was low and he couldn't afford to let the car idle with the air conditioning on. He closed his eyes and relished the light breeze lifting the hair off his sweaty scalp. A whiff of a nearby grill and its charbroiled meat reminded him it was dinner time. He longed to be with Willy in the condo's courtyard, barbecuing a steak, using Willy's special sauce that made even a vegan drool. Instead, Willy was in the emergency department, alone and scared. Hopefully Laurette had put him more at ease.

Sitting there, alone with his thoughts, waiting for his friend to call with the next step made Ben antsy. He needed to be doing something. But what? Where could he go? Not to his apartment. The police probably had it staked out. Thanks to Ben's fleeing, he looked guiltier than he actually was, as if he'd deliberately infected the others, just as Joel had suggested. Did Dr. Smith believe that too?

He couldn't risk going back to Willy's either. By now Dr. Smith must know the newest infected patient was Ben's father. So, stuck in geographical limbo, Ben sat in the car, tapping his fingers on his thighs and his feet on the floor. For the zillionth time he checked his watch.

Leave. This is a waste of time. Go to Miot.

Ben shifted toward the passenger seat. He half expected to see someone there, so unexpected was the thought.

Rattled, he shook his head. Lack of sleep and little food was messing with his mind. He remembered the protein bars and water he'd bought when they picked up the ceremony supplies, along with two energy drinks to power him through what could be a long night. Digging through the plastic bag on the passenger seat, he plucked out a nut bar and a small bottle of liquid caffeine. Halfway through the snack, Laurette called the prepaid phone.

He snatched it from the dashboard. "Yes?"

"She is gone."

"Who's gone?"

"Sophia."

Ben bolted up in the seat, his thigh banging the steering wheel and the protein bar flying from his hand.

"She fled the hospital. The moment her baby was discharged to her mother. Did not even stop to sign one of those forms for when patients leave early against the doctor's wishes."

Despite the seriousness of Laurette's news, Ben sighed in relief. Hearing *she is gone* had conjured something far more terrible.

"I should have seen this coming," he said. "Sophia was distraught over Maxwell staying with her mom, and I'm sure she knew the hospital would never let her leave isolation." Ben cracked his neck. "Maybe this is a good thing. Maybe we can get her to bring Maxwell to Mambo Tina's. You know, assuming the mambo can stop this." Though Ben still had enormous doubts about a curse only Vodou could break, he was trying his best to believe. Otherwise the night ahead would be a bust, and he would be back to square one, whatever the hell that was.

"Yes, if public health officials do not come for her first."

Ben cracked his knuckles. He couldn't let his mind go there. "How's Willy?"

A brief silence followed, broken only by a bicyclist whizzing by the open car window. Ben grabbed the energy drink and squeezed.

"He is okay," Laurette said. "I explained to him what I could, that you are caught up in something with this infection and it is not safe for you to see him."

"And he accepted that?"

"Not at all. He looked worried and scared. Did you expect otherwise? But our conversation was broken when the staff came and took him to 6 West for admission."

6 West. Ben's floor. The ward he'd abandoned that afternoon, patients and colleagues alike.

Poof. Just like that his career was over. He banged his skull against the headrest.

"And Ben?"

A deep exhale. "Yes?"

"Your father's eosinophil count was very high."

Ben dug his fingernails into his palms. Though he'd expected the news, hearing it out loud walloped him with such remorse and fatigue, he wanted to curl up in a ball and cry uncle.

"They have started him on magnesium." He knew she didn't believe that would help any more than he did, but he wanted to. God, did he want to.

Jean Miot popped into his head, the bokor's dark eyes as mischievous as the goatman's. A numbness washed over Ben. "We have to get to Sophia's. We have to find out where Maxwell is. Make sure he's safe."

What if the police were coming for Sophia too? Or what if Jean Miot was? Jesus, he'd never meant to put her in such danger. At least in the hospital she was safe.

He put the energy drink between his knees and whipped out his wallet, looking through it until he found the sticky note he'd jotted Sophia's address and phone number on when he'd snooped through her medical record.

Based on the location, Laurette was closer than he was in North Philly. With renewed energy and purpose, he barked at her to go straight there. He'd be at least ten to fifteen minutes behind. "I already told her she could trust you, so she should let you in."

Laurette agreed and they disconnected. Ben uncapped the energy drink and chugged the syrupy sweet liquid. Then he started the car and squealed away.

Twenty-five minutes later Ben pulled onto Sophia's street. Parked cars on either side left little room to navigate. Much to his agitation he'd taken three wrong turns. It had been over eight months since their one-night stand, and without his smartphone or GPS in Max's car, he had to rely on memory. A rather drunken memory. All he remembered was a small, main-floor apartment in a three-story row house, nothing more than a living room, kitchenette, bedroom, and bath.

When he spotted her unit, he kept driving until he found a parking spot two blocks down. Maneuvering the Mazda into a tight space, he fought the urge to ram the cars in front and behind to speed things up. It felt like a clock was ticking inside his head, each second another second too late to get to his son. When the car was finally parked, he jumped out, locked it, and jogged toward the unit. The clouds had thickened and grayed even more, and he worried a storm would follow.

Halfway to Sophia's door he spotted Laurette's dented Subaru. Seeing it empty, he relaxed a bit. Good. Sophia must have let her in.

Slowing his pace, he covered the last bit of sidewalk and trotted up to the complex. Upon reaching the building's main door, he noticed it wasn't closed all the way, its wood warped near the bottom. Same way it had been eight months before. Ben made a mental note to fix it. Though it offered convenient access for him now, he didn't want strangers getting in so easily. Not with his son there.

Inside the musty foyer he headed to Sophia's door on the left. It, too, was ajar.

His spine prickled. "Laurette?" he called through the tiny crack.

No answer.

He pressed his palm against the faded wood. "Sophia?" Just as he was about to identify himself, he clamped his jaw shut. What if Dr. Smith was in there? Or the police? Or Joel, who was convinced Ben and Sophia were connected? Maybe they'd set a trap for him.

But the only sound beyond street traffic was the muffled television set of a neighboring apartment.

Ben pushed the door open a few inches, his heart rate picking up. "Sophia?"

Still hearing nothing, he shoved it wide and stepped inside. When he did, an involuntary cry escaped him.

There, just beyond the door, near a sand-colored sofa, lay Sophia in maternity leggings and a gauzy top, limbs sprawled out over a crimson rug.

No part of her was moving.

38

Ben kicked the door shut behind him and rushed to Sophia's side. Dropping down, pain shot through his kneecaps, the threadbare rug a poor cushion for the hardwood floor.

"Sophia."

No response.

He placed two fingers against her neck. A strong carotid pulse beat, and her chest rose with steady, albeit slow breaths. He exhaled in relief. Assessing her body for injury, he ran his hands over her black leggings and loose-fitting top as well as her head and neck. Finding no obvious fractures or wounds, he gently placed her sprawled limbs in a more neutral position. Lavender-scented lotion wafted up to him.

"Sophia." He tapped her cheek and raised his voice. "Sophia."

Nothing.

He lifted her eyelids. Two tiny pupils stared back at him. He placed his lesion-free palm against her face and noted her warm and doughy flesh. Had her infection worsened?

But those constricted pupils …

A knot twisted in his belly. Had she been drugged?

Hurry. She is not where your focus should be.

Once again the thought was so insistent, Ben whipped his head to the side and looked behind him. No one was there.

But his thought was correct. He needed to find Maxwell. And where was Laurette? That was definitely her car out front.

Shifting from knees to heels he scanned the small space, ears pricked up for newborn cries or murmurs. Only the muffled sounds of the neighbor's television set filled the air. A dozen feet to his right, an empty infant carrier sat on the kitchen table. A diaper bag rested nearby.

Ben stood up, the abrupt movement deepening his cerebral ache. His heart thumped erratically, as much out of fear for his son as from the energy drink he'd chugged on an empty stomach.

Four strides across the small apartment landed him in the bedroom, a crowded but neat space with a double bed, white dresser, stacked plastic storage containers, and a bassinet. Like the infant carrier, it was empty.

Ben grabbed the door frame on each side and squeezed. Where was his son? Had Sophia taken him to her mother's after all? Doubtful, given the new mother had checked out of the hospital against medical advice.

He lowered his head in frustration, but something he spotted made him snap it back up. A new unease squeezed his throat. There, wedged against the dresser, was a yellow purse with a shiny metal clasp, a purse Ben well recognized. After all, he'd been in the Champs-Élysées boutique with Laurette when she'd bought it.

He reached for the purse. A sticky substance on the back of it moistened his fingers. After flipping the bag around, he saw it was blood. His attention shifted to the hardwood floor. More blood congealed next to the dresser.

With mounting dread he rushed through the small apartment, opening closet doors and cabinets, searching any place someone could hide. He found no one.

Returning to Sophia's side, a horrible scene reeled through his mind: Sophia letting Laurette in after Laurette had explained who she was. Laurette going back to peek at a sleeping Maxwell in his bassinet. Someone forcing his way in before Sophia had secured the door. Someone hurting Sophia and Laurette. Someone taking Maxwell.

Gently, he shook Sophia's shoulders, Laurette's blood still sticky on his fingers. "Sophia, who did this? Where's Maxwell? Where's Laurette?"

Sophia's eyes fluttered open briefly then closed. A whisper passed her lips, but Ben couldn't make out the words.

"Sophia," he prodded, squeezing her arms.

Her eyes opened again, and through those pinpoint pupils she tried to focus on Ben. "My baby … took our baby."

"Who? Who took him?"

But she'd closed her eyes and was back asleep.

A brick dropped on Ben's chest, and for a moment he sat paralyzed, unable to speak, unable to think, unable to focus on anything but the image of his son being carried away or Laurette injured. Or worse.

The last thought catapulted him to action. Gingerly, he lifted Sophia into his arms and placed her on the sofa. Another feel of her pulse confirmed a steady rhythm. The suspicion she'd been drugged grew stronger. Easier for someone to take off with the baby and keep her from calling for help. But what about Laurette?

Ben squeezed Sophia's hand. "I'll make this right. I promise."

Next to the infant carrier and diaper bag, he found a small handbag containing Sophia's cell phone. For the second time that day he dialed 9-1-1, and for the second time that day he knew he'd have to abandon someone he cared about. But Sophia would want him to put Maxwell first, of that he was sure.

After giving the emergency operator the address, he hung up before she could ask for his personal information. Returning to the bedroom, he grabbed Laurette's purse to take with him, but as he was about to leave the apartment, he realized he was unarmed. If he was going to track down Jean Miot, a man who wanted his and his son's blood, he'd need more than a yellow purse and a palm lesion. And he *was* sure it was Miot who took them. His mind practically screamed it at him.

Spotting a wooden knife block next to the gas stove, Ben grabbed a large-handled one. The blade was big and awkward and would be difficult to carry, so he put it back. He whipped open drawers, sweat dampening his hairline, his mental clock ticking way too fast. In a drawer next to the stove, he found a sheathed butcher knife and slipped it into the back of Max's jeans, which were just snug enough to keep it in place. He pulled his T-shirt over it.

Wanting to be gone when the ambulance arrived, he hurried to the door. When he opened it he jumped back in alarm. Someone he never expected to see was standing there, fist raised and ready to knock.

39

"What are you doing here?" Ben glared at Joel across the threshold. The guy's presence was an unexpected kick in the groin.

"Funny, that's what I was gonna ask you." Grim-lipped and less GQ-groomed since Melissa's death, Joel craned his neck to peer into Sophia's apartment.

Ben inserted his body in the door frame, blocking the view. "What's it to you?"

"I've been watching Sophia Diaz's place, asshole. After we learned you infected her, we had proof you two knew each other, though she lied about it. Then, surprise surprise, the *chica* fled the hospital." He seethed beneath the surface, and a lock of hair flopped onto his forehead. "Just like you."

"And what, you accessed her private medical records to get her address? That'll look good when you reapply for med school." Though Ben's mouth formed words, his brain hunted for a way to get Joel out of there. The ambulance would arrive any minute. Ben had to be gone when it did.

"It's called Google, dickwad. While the rest of the city searches for you, I figured I'd come here, you know, just in case you plan to kill Sophia like you killed Melissa."

It was Ben's turn to seethe, and when Joel pushed forward to get in, Ben tensed his body and shoved the grad student back with his chest. "No reason for you to be here. Go back to Mommy so you can hang on her lab coat."

"Screw you." Joel stuck out his own chest and braced his feet, meeting Ben's resistance. "You might have fooled my stepmom into thinking you're an innocent Typhoid Mary, but I know there's more to it. How come only people *you* know are dying?"

Ben's right hand tightened into a fist while the other squeezed Laurette's handbag. "Leave. Now."

"Not until I see if Sophia Diaz is okay."

Before Ben could respond, Joel caught him off guard with a hard shove, and despite their equal bulk and Ben's two-inch advantage, Ben stumbled back. Laurette's purse fell from his hands.

Joel stomped into the apartment. When he saw Sophia on the couch, he stopped. Then, as if scared of what he might find, he took a tentative step forward and leaned over her. "What have you done to her?"

"It wasn't me, I swear." Even to Ben's ears his denial sounded weak. "I've called an ambulance."

Joel glowered at Ben. "Save it for the police. They're on their way."

Ben's stomach flipped. Was Joel bluffing? He opened his mouth to speak, but instead, an unexpected rage enveloped him, and a vile thought stabbed his brain.

Kill the bastard.

With his limbic system trouncing all reason, Ben lunged forward and pulled Joel up by his polo shirt, nearly ripping the fabric off the stunned grad student's body. Then he slammed a fist into the guy's jaw. Joel stumbled backward and collided with Sophia's television.

Bewildered, Ben blinked and tried to process what had just happened. He needed to get out of there, but beating up Joel wasn't the way to do it. Before he could change tactics, Joel righted himself and plowed into Ben's torso. Both men went down and slid into the connecting kitchen, where Ben's head smacked the checkerboard flooring. Joel took a swing of his own, and Ben's cheekbone exploded in pain.

Ben bucked his body and pushed Joel off. He scrambled to his feet. "Listen to me. I'm trying to stop this. If I don't leave soon, more people will die." He reached out a hand to help the guy up, but a second vicious thought stopped him cold.

Kill him. Gut him with the knife.

"Jesus Christ," Ben said aloud. Before he could dwell on his inexplicable savagery, Joel was up and taking another swing. Ben ducked, but not in time. Joel's fist clipped Ben's ear, generating a sting in his cartilage like that of a hundred fire ants.

Sirens sounded in the distance. The two men suspended their fight, arms still drawn, Joel half in the living room, half in the kitchen and Ben less than two feet away.

The grad student pushed the hair out of his eyes. "Time's up, Mr. Angel of Death."

Motionless, gaze holding Joel's, Ben weighed his options. Stay and be quarantined. Leave and continue to piss away life as he knew it. The first risked harm to the people he cared about, because he wouldn't be able to look for them. The second branded him nothing short of a fugitive, because now that Joel had seen him, Ben could no longer claim ignorance if he were caught again.

He backed up to the table. Joel advanced an equal distance. Reaching an arm behind him, Ben grabbed Maxwell's car seat. Before he could think it through, he swung the carrier in a forceful arc and cracked the grad student's head. With a yelp, Joel tripped and fell. His skull thumped the refrigerator. Hard. He crumpled to the tiled floor and lay blinking and dazed.

Heat flushed Ben's face. His heart raced, and his throat burned like a torch. I hit him too hard, he thought. He dropped down next to Joel and sighed in relief when the grad student attempted to speak. The refrigerator kicked in, and above its hum Ben apologized to Joel, sickened by his own brutality.

The sirens grew louder, seemingly right up the street. Having no choice but to leave, Ben rushed up and snatched Laurette's purse from the living room floor. He fled the apartment and then the building via the back door.

Outside, beneath pendulous clouds, he sprinted down an alley, nearly colliding with a dog walker who moved away just in time. At the corner he skidded to a turn, his elbow scraping a blue mailbox. He ran down the sidewalk until he was back on Sophia's street. When he reached Max's car, he got in and sped away, hoping to elude the police and ambulance in front of Sophia's building, their flashing lights drawing the attention of drivers and pedestrians alike.

Sighing in relief, he figured he was in the clear.

Until he spotted a cruiser pulling out behind him.

40

A swirl of red and blue lights lit up the rearview mirror. Having no time to wonder whether they were for him or not, Ben gripped the steering wheel and shot through an intersection just as the light turned red. Hoping the crossing traffic would slow the police down, he accelerated and took a sharp left onto Broad Street. Unfortunately, the heavier traffic forced him to slow down, and behind him the siren wailed, its rhythm matching that of his pounding heart.

A sudden thought of where he could hide came to him, at least until he could figure things out. Jerking the steering wheel to the right, he squealed onto Snyder Avenue and then pitched a left onto South Fifteenth.

Hunched over, hands glued to the steering wheel, he continuously shifted his eyes from the traffic ahead to the scene in the rearview mirror. Though a siren still keened, its flashing lights were no longer visible. With neck muscles as tense as fiddle strings, he did a visual one-eighty of the upcoming intersection. At least a hundred feet separated him from the closest oncoming car. He shot through another red light, ignoring the blast of horns that followed.

Only a few more miles. Then he could collect his thoughts and plan his next move. After a couple more turns and side streets, the siren faded away. With the tiniest relief, he loosened his grip on the steering wheel, his fingers stiff and sweaty.

South of the Schuylkill Expressway a warehouse came into view. Back before he'd started med school, Ben had been part of its construction crew.

The gray, nondescript building stocked office furniture and bulk paper supplies. Deliveries were made via a large loading dock on the east side. Its seclusion would offer Ben a place to hide and clear his head.

Nearly taking out two parked bicycles in his haste, he swung the Mazda onto the loading dock. As expected at this hour, the place was deserted, and although the building would be locked, nothing prevented him from parking his car in the covered area. He just hoped he wasn't being watched on CCTV somewhere.

Shutting off the engine, he finally sank back against the seat. His nerve endings sparked like the shocks of an electric eel, and the rank scent of his own stress mixed with lingering diesel fumes. He closed his eyes and willed his heart to slow down.

Go to him.

His eyelids snapped open. Another sharply lucid thought. He intended to find Jean Miot, no doubt about that. The only question was where? If Ben wasn't simply being paranoid and the police had been chasing him, they could easily identify the silver Mazda.

He glanced at the loading dock's entry, focusing on the two bikes he'd almost crushed. He opened the car door and trotted over to them. A thick chain tethered the more expensive-looking bike. The other one stood free, its seat torn, its bar rusted and its tires thin. But it would do.

He sprinted back to the car and grabbed a bottled water from the shopping bag on the passenger seat. After chugging it, he stuffed his half-eaten power bar into his back pocket.

Snatching Laurette's purse, he started to remove anything with her name on it. If the police found the car and the purse, he didn't want them connecting his law-breaking acts to her. When he flipped through the wallet, a photograph fell onto the grocery bag. In it a younger, smiling Laurette embraced a man whose face was turned and partially hidden by his long hair, which was loosely secured by a leather strap. Given the high arch of his visible eyebrow, Ben guessed it was one of her brothers. Maybe Guy, the brother who'd given her the amulet to keep her safe.

Lot of good that did her, thanks to you, Benny Boy.

A visceral ache twisted his belly, and for a moment breathing was difficult. He hoped to God she was okay. He pocketed her phone and other identifying items, along with the picture, and then fished out her car keys as well.

Returning to the bikes, the air muggy and choked with mosquitoes, he reached back and patted the waistband of his deceased father's jeans. The sheathed knife was still there. He pushed it down deeper and hoped it would stay put while he biked. Though he regretted abandoning Max's Mazda (abandonment seemed to be his new MO), he knew it would eventually make its way home.

A bike ride back to Sophia's would be nothing for a cyclist like him. Assuming—hoping—the police were gone, he'd take Laurette's car to Mambo Tina's and pray she knew where Jean Miot lived. What would happen after that, he had no idea. He only knew his life, as well as the lives of the only people he cared about, depended on him to not screw it up.

41

Ben stood on the peristil's doorstep and waited as Mambo Tina opened the door. Like a turtle emerging from its shell, she poked her head out and scanned the impoverished urban neighborhood. The cloud-covered sun sat low on the horizon, and a lone street light tacked onto a telephone pole cast a thin cone of light. Once satisfied Ben was alone, the priestess pulled him inside and quickly shut the door. The familiar scents of incense and candles greeted him, and beyond the dark entryway, a dim glow flickered from the back room.

"Sorry I'm late, but things have—"

"Hurry, we have little time."

Before Ben could tell her he'd only come for Jean Miot's address, the mambo pulled him inside and pushed him toward a room on her left. A flip of the light switch revealed a darkly wallpapered den containing a paper-strewn desk, laptop computer, plaid couch, and blood-red artwork with various acts of ceremonial worship, including a goat sacrifice. As in the rest of the peristil, candles abounded, though none were currently lit.

The priestess urged him inside, impatience on her pinched face. A white, mid-sleeve dress accented by colorful beaded necklaces clung to her stout body. As always, two wooden sticks supported the braided bun in her hair.

One step into the study, a thought stopped Ben cold. *Do not trust her.* He wasn't sure why he thought it, and the uncertainty of that made him uneasy.

"*Vini*. Come." Mambo Tina waved him in, but then, perhaps sensing his trepidation, she widened her button eyes and let her arms fall to her side. "*Bondeye mwen*—dear God—he has found your Lwa Met Tet."

"I don't …"

"He is in your head, no? He is telling you not to trust me."

Ben clutched the door frame. "How could you know that?"

"Shh, no time. Danger for Laurette and the bébé."

Confusion and distrust clouded Ben's mind, and lack of food made him lightheaded and shaky. How could she know Laurette and Maxwell were missing? He'd picked up Laurette's car from Sophia's and driven straight over without calling the mambo first. Thank God the police had cleared out by then.

"Divination. This is how I know these things," the priestess said, addressing his bewilderment.

Ben tried to process her words. It wasn't possible. Someone must have told her. But who?

They lie. All of them lie.

An image of Maxwell sprang to Ben's mind, and despite his shakiness he darted out of the den and ran to the peristil's back room. Candle flames on the cluttered altar tables danced in the wake of his abrupt entrance. He called Laurette's name and, stupidly, Maxwell's too.

"Do not let him in." Mambo Tina had trotted down the corridor behind him. "You must trust me. Stay true to your own thoughts."

Ben swiped a hand over his perspiring forehead and studied her tense expression, her apple cheeks tight with worry and her hands fidgeting with the stringed beads swaying over her chest. In the graveyard quiet of the home, he struggled with who and what to believe.

"Where is David?" he demanded.

"Getting more supplies for the ceremony. We must find your bébé. We must try to stop this. There is little time."

"You don't think I know that?" Ben's bark echoed in the shadowy room. He squeezed his head in his hands. Think, he told himself. You know Laurette. You trust her. She trusts this woman.

But do you?

Mambo Tina put her hand on his arm, her head level with his shoulder. "Stay true to *you*, Monsieur Oris. Let all other thought go. He seeks to control you."

"Who's 'he'? Jean Miot?"

"I do not know. Maybe him, maybe someone else. Maybe not a man at all. But it is Monsieur Miot you must start with. He knows where your son is, of that I am sure, and I cannot help you without the bébé." Mambo Tina paused, and then, looking past Ben to the hideous goatman statue on the wall, said, "From father to son, the curse does pass."

Her words sent a chill down Ben's spine. "Can you stop this...this...curse?" Aloud, from his own mouth, the question sounded ridiculous.

Mambo Tina raised a hand. "I make no promise." She moved closer to one of the altars and picked up a crucifix. She held it to her lips, the movement jerky in the flickering candlelight, and mumbled a prayer. When she finished she pulled a slip of paper from the side pocket of her dress. Her voice dropped another decibel. "This is what you come for, no?"

After a beat, Ben extended his arm and took the proffered note. Written upon it in barely legible handwriting was a North Philly address, not far from their current location. "Is this what I think it is? How did you know I was coming for his address?" Once again, mistrust fogged his brain.

"Do you still have the powder David gave to you?" On her tongue, *David* was *Dahveed*.

"Yes, but I—"

"Go. Go now, boy. Get your son and bring him to me."

Do not trust her.

Again that intrusive, unexpected ding of a warning. Louder than a simple thought. His own and yet not his own. His throat tightened, and the sheet of paper trembled in his hand. Was he cracking up? Was that it?

Shaking his head, he backed out of the candlelit room. He turned and stumbled to Laurette's car. If only he knew what to believe, who to trust. Rational Ben took over and reminded Bewildered Ben that the intrusive thoughts were far more likely to be from low blood sugar and stress than from a mind-controlling enemy. Get your shit together, he ordered himself.

Clicking open the car door on the darkening street, he chided himself for getting sucked into their beliefs. And yet there was no alternative. It was either that or turn himself in and live out the rest of his days in notoriety, stuck with some repugnant nickname generated by the media, like Doctor Death or the Med Student Murderer.

He started the car. Belief or no belief, ridiculous or sane, he had to find Maxwell. Had to make sure Laurette was okay. Needed her to tell him what in the hell to do next.

But can you trust her?

Whether his own or someone else's, he couldn't dismiss the thought. Laurette was the one who invited him to Paris when her brother had backed out. She was the one who first mentioned the curse. She was the one guiding him through this nightmare.

Out of nowhere a warmth crept over his chest, subtle at first but then growing in intensity. Soon his sternum throbbed with heat.

Startled, Ben clasped the leather strap of Laurette's amulet and pulled until the sharp bone popped out the neck of his shirt. Though physically unchanged, the thing felt like it was on fire. He was about to lift the strap over his head to remove the amulet when he remembered Mambo Tina's words: "Stay true to you."

He licked his lips. He swallowed and wished for something cold to drink. Finally, with a sickening feeling he was choosing the lesser of two evils, he tucked the amulet back into his shirt, its heat down to a dull warmth. Not daring to delay another second, he drove the car into the deserted street and headed north.

42

Without his smartphone's GPS and not knowing the passcode for Laurette's phone, the route to Jean Miot's street was a maze of frustration, especially under thick, dark clouds that made the nine o'clock sky blacker than usual. At each corner Ben squinted to make out signs, well aware his slowed pace was attracting the attention of neighborhood youth. Clustered in packs on doorsteps and curbs, they eyed his vehicle with suspicion.

After a few wrong turns, he spotted the street name Mambo Tina had given him. Miot's house number matched a corner brownstone.

Nearly at a crawl, he rounded the block to scope out more of the area. In the beam of his headlights, graffiti splashed the brick walls and shutters hung from windows, many of which housed metal bars. Unlike the other streets, Jean Miot's was eerily deserted. Ben almost preferred the packs of intimidating kids. At least then he wasn't alone.

Returning to the original road, he hooked a left on the side street bordering the bokor's building. Free of parked cars, it was more a narrow, concrete alley than an actual road. On the right lay a weeded lot with two warehouses and a set of train tracks, and on the left, the side of Jean Miot's home. Surrounding the warehouses was a chain-link fence, slashed open in several places. Ben pulled Laurette's Subaru up to it. He doubted he was supposed to park there, but the spot offered the quickest getaway from both the front and back of Miot's house.

Not daring to make a sound, Ben climbed out of the car and gingerly closed the door. Though acutely aware his trespassing could land him in worse straits than a jail cell, like getting caught by residents who didn't take kindly to someone snooping around their turf, he approached the back of the bokor's house. Every atom of common sense screamed at him to get back in the car and leave, but the thought of Laurette and Maxwell inside, having who knows what done to them, pushed him onward. With a steeled jaw and taut muscles, he stepped into Jean Miot's backyard.

Despite the urban location, a surprising amount of vegetation separated the front and back row houses from each other, giving their yards a dense, almost forest-like appearance. Weeds grew thick from the ground, and leafy branches from tall trees crowded the windows and brick siding. Like the warehouses across the street, chain-link fencing separated one unit from the next. Luckily, given Miot's corner spot, no fence separated his yard from the alley. Escape, should Ben need it, would be unimpeded.

Making his way through the vegetation, Ben crept to the bokor's back door, glancing around to make sure he'd gone unnoticed. Few units had porch lights, the closest being the neighbor's on Ben's right, but its dim wattage did little more than allow Ben to see the door in front of him. That was probably for the best. What the foliage didn't hide, the darkness hopefully would.

Scents of cooking grease and laundry soap circulated in the evening air. Ignoring the pragmatic inner voice that told him to flee and call the police, he pressed his ear against the door. What would the cops do? Believe his story about a Vodou bokor kidnapping his newborn son for a blood sacrifice? Right. They'd lock him up in quarantine at best, jail at worst.

A sudden, pulsating rhythm cut off his thought. More palpable than loud, Ben felt its bass vibrating his cheek against the door. Leaning back, he looked through a window on his right but saw nothing. Nothing through the tiny basement window either. Both were blacked out, but whether from paint, fabric, or paper, he couldn't tell. He only knew their purposeful masking made his heart beat faster.

Standing on the doorstep, his insides roiling, he wondered what he should do. Knock? Break down the door? Smash the blacked-out window? Go around to the front instead?

He scanned the alleyway to his left and the backyards to his right. Were the neighbors watching him? Would they turn him into a zombie and force him to do their bidding? Laurette's laughter rippled in his mind, and he could see her smiling at his ignorance. "That's Hollywood voodoo. It is not our way."

Just enter.

The thought came out of nowhere.

A tinny fear coated Ben's mouth. He reached behind him to confirm the knife was still tucked in his pants. Before he could do anything else, the neighbor on the right opened his door. A pit bull sprang out of the house.

Ben didn't move. Didn't breathe. Even if whoever opened the door couldn't see him, the dog, who darted around the tiny lot sniffing randomly at weeds and bushes, certainly could.

"Hurry, you furry bastard," a deep voice called. "And don't even think 'bout escaping through that fence hole again."

Ben's heart hammered his ribs. If the mutt spotted him and started barking, it would be open season for a bullet in Ben's ass. Fight or flight kicked in, and the only thing keeping him from choosing flight was his fear for Laurette and Maxwell.

With a suddenness that made his bowels hitch, the dog halted, sniffed, and pointed its snout in the air. It circled its muscular body toward him.

"What the hell's wrong wit you? Hurry up." The neighbor paused and then stepped out of his doorway. "Who's there?"

Enter. Now.

Whether his own thought or not, Ben listened. He gripped the door knob and twisted, and though surprised and relieved to find it open, he'd later cringe at his own naiveté.

Without checking to see if the neighbor had seen him, he burst inside Jean Miot's house. Behind him the dog yelped a tirade so frenzied, it wheezed.

Ben closed the door and muted the dog. Once inside, his own senses went haywire. Blackness accosted him, as did a powdery haze, its scent so salty and fetid his eyes watered. He sneezed and coughed. At the same time, a rhythmic drumming vibrated the floor below his feet and drowned out all other sound. Whether a recording or live, he didn't know, but he thought he heard chanting as well.

As his eyes adjusted to the dark and the sting in his corneas and nostrils abated, he spotted the outline of a refrigerator. The bokor's kitchen. He held out his arms and took a step forward. At that moment, a strobe of red light sparked through a crack near the floorboard on his left. He jumped at its suddenness.

Blinking rapidly, he willed himself to calm down. He had to think clearly, plan things out. In the darkness of his own house, the bokor had the advantage.

But then, like in the catacombs, Ben lost control of his own movements, and any planning he'd managed to scrape together flew out the blackened window. Like an overpowering force, the pulsating light drew him toward it. He could no more resist its pull than he could resist gravity.

He approached the door. What he would find, he didn't know, but one thing was certain. Evil was expecting him.

43

Come. You are so close.

Ben opened the basement door. Strobing blasts of crimson light flowed up the stairs and blinded him. Drumming pounded his ears.

Come. Your son awaits.

Shielding his eyes with his hand, he called out Jean Miot's name. The drumming swallowed his words. Did the bokor really have Maxwell? Or was it a trick?

On leaden feet Ben descended the first step, going by feel rather than sight since his eyes hadn't adjusted to the pulsing red bursts. Nausea consumed him, and he swayed on shaky limbs.

"If you hurt my son, I swear I'll …" Ben reached for the knife tucked in his pants. He left the blade in place, but his face tightened in such anger and fear his lower lip split open, its membrane dry and cracked. He descended another step, one hand flat against the concrete wall for guidance. "Why don't you can the gimmicks, asshole?" he shouted over the drumming.

Whether the bokor planned to comply or not, Ben didn't know, because when his foot reached the third step, a vortex consumed him. To his astonishment the strobe light and drums disappeared. Silence replaced them, a silence so loud he widened his eyes in shock.

A cry caught in his throat. Panic incapacitated him. No longer was he in a humid basement stairwell. Instead, damp, stone walls surrounded him, their closeness sealing him off like a crypt. Looking down into the shadowy space, he recoiled in horror. A spiral, concrete staircase had appeared out of nowhere.

A bolt of recognition hit him. He was back in the catacombs. Back in that claustrophobic stairwell that had reduced him to a blubbering mess.

"What the—?" His voice cracked and cut itself off.

A hallucination. It had to be.

"Gimmicks?" A hearty laugh echoed in the long, gray space, though Ben saw no one. "You see what I can do, boy?"

Like a stone vise, the walls closed in on Ben. He wasn't sure how long he stood there, frozen, inhaling and exhaling in short, chaotic gulps, but a sound finally forced him to action. Weak and distant, but unmistakable.

An infant's cry.

Having nothing but stone walls to clutch for support, he held his breath and took a step down.

Think of Maxwell. Think of Dad and Laurette.

Laughter that wasn't his own erupted inside his head. His right foot faltered and his arms flailed. The walls seemed to collapse with each downward step. Unlike Paris, no lamps lit the way, yet something offered a shadowy illumination, enough to highlight the coffin-like space.

With each step he took, the walls crushed his chest and squeezed off his air supply. He knew it couldn't be real. Knew it was simply a trick. He recalled the powdery haze in Miot's kitchen that made him sneeze and cough when he'd entered the home. Was it more than mere dust? And yet despite that logic, he felt the cold stone on his skin. He saw the spiraling staircase. He sensed its claustrophobic squeeze.

Just as he had in the catacombs.

Downward he climbed, one foot after the other, replacing his view of concrete steps with an image of Maxwell. The baby's soft skin, his tiny feet, his sweet infant smell. Soon Ben achieved a rhythm, blocking everything out but his son, and after what seemed like hours, the stone evaporated and the walls returned to their drab dustiness. The strobe light once again blinked red, and the drumming flooded his ears.

His relief was indescribable. Pausing on the last step, he inhaled so deeply he thought his chest would rupture. Then, having no idea what or who he would find in that flashing chaos, he tried to recover his sanity.

44

In the pulsing redness at the base of Jean Miot's stairwell, Ben plucked Laurette's amulet and Sophia's cross from the inside of his shirt. Untangling them, he squeezed the smooth, sharp bone with one hand and brought the cross to his lips with the other, like he'd seen Sophia do. Stupid or not, he'd take any comfort he could get.

From father to son, the curse does pass.

Shaking off Mambo Tina's prophecy as well as the horrifying catacomb hallucination he'd just experienced, he tucked the bone and cross back into his shirt and forced himself to press on. Over a concrete floor, he shuffled toward the source of the epileptic light. When he reached the elongated lamp, he punched it, hoping to break the thing before it blinded him. Instead, it swung in the air, and he had to duck to avoid its return arc. A closer look revealed a cord tethering it to the ceiling.

He swore and kept moving. Thankfully, his visibility improved once the light source was behind him. In its blood-red blinking, a large, unfinished room crammed with clutter came into focus. Wicker chairs lined the sides, boxes were strewn about, and colorful, life-sized statues of people and animals populated the floor. Tall, short, fat, thin. Wood, plastic, stone, ceramic. In the flashing light they seemed to dance and sway, macabre faces grinning through painted eyes and toothless mouths.

But no Jean Miot.

Ben halted. He sniffed the air. The tangy, metallic odor of blood was unmistakable. He'd smelled enough of it over the last few weeks to know.

Refusing to acknowledge the fire in his throat, he pushed onward, shuffling with uncertainty in the crowded and seemingly limitless space. Over the drumming he yelled out to the bokor. "This is crazy. Just tell me what you want."

No answer.

Damp basement air cooled the sweat on his body and made him shiver, his T-shirt thin and wet. Looking back and forth, he negotiated his way around statues, their limbs and claws brushing and poking his body. When the top of his head thumped something, he reached for the knife in his waistband. Though he didn't remove it, he kept his hand gripped around the handle. Above, he saw a leering skull suspended within the pulsing light. Scanning the length of the ceiling, he noted other hanging objects as well: masks, naked doll parts, stuffed animals, and bones. Lots and lots of bones.

God, he hoped they were fake.

God, he needed Laurette.

With each advance the smell of blood grew stronger, and between the blinking light and the incessant drumming (though it had quieted, of that he was sure), his mind seemed disconnected from his movements. A few times he mistook a statue for a human being, and, thinking he'd finally found the bokor, he gripped the knife handle more tightly, his heart rate temporarily spiking.

After he rounded a cluster of stone statues, he caught his breath and froze. Through the flashing he saw candlelight ahead. Illuminated in its flames were two men facing an enormous altar, as tall as their chests. They stood with their backs to him, both dressed in dark tunics over dark pants. The altar, similarly cloaked in dark fabric, was crowded with skulls and long bones, their orientation not unlike that of the catacombs, a place Ben seemed unable to escape even in North Philly. In the center of the high altar, near the back, a bronze skeleton draped in a long coat and top hat grinned malevolently. Ben stared into its bony orbits and gaping nasal cavities, his legs growing weak.

Though he was close enough to hear the two men chanting, neither one turned around. Something on the altar occupied their attention. Something with blankets piled around it like a makeshift bassinet.

Maxwell.

The urge to call out to his son was so strong Ben could hardly contain himself, but he held back. If they didn't know he was there, he could maintain the advantage.

Yeah, you keep telling yourself that, Benny Boy.

He inched forward. Could he take them both? Candles flickered around the two men, the red strobing dulled to a benign blink at this distance.

The closer he got to the altar, the stronger the scent of blood became, and his nostrils flinched reflexively. When he was less than fifteen feet away, four silver bowls on the altar came into view. All were lined up single file in front of the bone piles. A thin line of blood dripped down the side of one and onto the altar's velvet covering.

The hair on Ben's scalp stood up. He suppressed a whimper, praying the blood wasn't Maxwell's or Laurette's. A few more silent shuffles forward revealed a small goat on the floor. The animal's neck yawned grotesquely, a bloody slit stretching ear to ear.

Ben choked on a cry of surprise, yet still the men seemed oblivious to his presence. From behind he presumed the one on the left was Jean Miot. Same height and closely cropped hair. The guy on the right was shorter and more muscular. Long dreadlocks hung down his back, secured loosely by a leather strap at the base of his head. Something clicked in Ben's mind, but in his angst to rescue his son, it vanished.

From what he could tell, the men chanted in Creole, their voices rising and lowering in spirited cadence. Less than ten feet behind them, Ben reached for his knife.

His hand never got there.

The man with the dreadlocks turned and looked over his shoulder. At the sight of him, Ben halted in horror. White paint masked the upper half of the guy's face, and black kohl circled his eyes, transforming them into large, black medallions. His hand clutched a knife, its curved blade similar to a weapon in a video game Ben had once played.

Still gazing at Ben, the stranger's freaky face lit up in a smile. Another glimmer of recognition hit, yet Ben still couldn't process it, not with that curved blade so close to his son on the altar.

"Welcome," the man said congenially. His manner suggested he'd been expecting Ben the whole time. Without another word he turned back toward Jean Miot, whose own large eyes and handsome face were free of paint.

When the eerie man nodded, Miot turned toward the bassinet and scooped out an infant. For a moment Ben stupidly thought maybe it wasn't his son. Then he recognized the Noah's Arc onesie Sophia had dressed him in, and his world disintegrated.

Like a morbid reenactment of *The Lion King*, Jean Miot lifted Maxwell up in the air. The infant whimpered but did not cry.

"No," Ben screamed, his body rooted in terror. When the dreadlocked man raised the knife, Ben found his feet and rushed forward so quickly he forgot about his own weapon.

But he didn't get there in time.

With barely a grunt, the painted man plunged the knife into his target.

45

The knife pierced its target, but the target wasn't Maxwell.

Ben watched in horror as the man with the painted face buried the curved blade deep into Jean Miot's belly. Like a record cut off mid-song, the bokor halted his feverish chanting, arms suspended above his head, a silent Maxwell still in his hands. His eyes widened in pain and confusion. When his grip on the baby loosened, the man with the dreadlocks snatched Maxwell and secured him in his left arm.

Jean Miot stumbled backward, the knife's handle jutting out of his gut. "*Poukisa, poukisa?*" he gasped. Though Ben didn't understand the word, the betrayed look in the man's eyes required no translation.

Maxwell started to whimper. Ben's chest heaved at the thought of his son in discomfort or pain. Trying his best to ignore the sickly sweet scent of blood and Miot's distressing pleas, he kept his gaze on the murderous man and stepped forward in an attempt to grab his son. Once again he was stunned into stillness when the shorter but more muscular man plucked the knife from Jean Miot's gut with his free arm, scurried behind him, and sliced the blade across the bokor's throat, silencing his cries once and for all. Jean Miot fell in a heap to the floor. Then, as if the bokor were nothing more than a goat, the painted man snatched a silver bowl from the altar and wedged it beneath Miot's throat.

As quickly as Miot's blood drained from his body, Laurette's reassurances of noble and compassionate blood sacrifices drained from Ben's mind. He could hardly believe what he'd just witnessed. A grisly nightmare, but it was real.

Critical seconds slipped away as Ben battled his shock and ongoing sluggishness.

Do something, he screamed to himself.

Hand shaking, he pulled the knife from the back of his pants and removed its sheath, tucking the plastic cover back into his waistband. Despite the weapon, he knew he was no match for the face-painted psychopath. What the killer had achieved with a baby in his arms defied a normal man's skill. Any rash move on Ben's part would only endanger Maxwell.

In the flickering candlelight, Miot's body shook and heaved and then fell still. The killer leaned over and picked up the bowl. Blood spilled onto his hand and splashed his black tunic. Neither seemed to trouble him. He replaced the bowl on the altar with an unsettling calmness. Then he lowered Maxwell into the bassinet, which was nothing more than a plastic tub stuffed with blankets.

Another whiff of metallic tang hit Ben, this time human. He gagged, not from the blood itself, but from the act he'd just seen.

Keep your shit together, he told himself. Just get your son and block out the rest.

As the murderer clutched the blood-filled bowl on the altar in front of Maxwell and chanted in Creole, Ben inched forward. He didn't get far before a figure dashed in his peripheral vision. He twisted his head to the right and saw something dart away into the flashing redness.

A person? An animal? Not daring to leave his son, he turned his attention back to the altar. Maxwell's whimpering had subsided, offering a morsel of relief.

Unless the baby was too weak to cry.

With fury trumping fear, Ben tightened his grip on the knife. "I want my son. Now."

The half-white, half-black-faced man set his blade on the altar and turned around. He pulled a cloth from the pocket of his tunic. Slowly, methodically, he wiped his hands free of Miot's blood, making sure to clean between each finger.

Ben took another step forward. When he was less than five feet away from his son and even closer to the killer, the man dropped the cloth, grabbed his own knife, and narrowed his dark glare on Ben.

Despite the eerie white makeup and kohl-lined eyes, seeing the Haitian so close triggered something in Ben's memory. The eyes, the dreadlocks, that black tunic. Then he remembered. Jesus, how could he have been so stupid? "You're … you're …"

I am the man here to save you. You will not hurt me.

Ben blinked and slowly shook his head, trying to clear his mental fog. The thought was not his own. Impossible or not, he swore it was not his own.

Queasy and disoriented, he did his best to look past the murdered man on his left and the sacrificed goat on his right. He focused on the man at the altar, whose blood-soaked tunic and bizarrely painted face were hideous. Maxwell remained quiet in the bassinet behind him, but the infant's silence was now more alarming than reassuring.

When he found the strength to speak again, Ben said, "I've seen you before." He breathed through his mouth to lessen the stench of fresh blood. "At my dad's store. You stole something of mine. Have you really been inside my head?" The question seemed too ludicrous to articulate.

Yes, it is I.

The knife nearly slipped out of Ben's hand. He tightened his sweaty grip. The intrusive thought had been the loudest one yet.

No. It was just another hallucination. Whatever he'd inhaled in Miot's kitchen was making him see the catacombs and hear internal voices. That was all.

"*Oui, c'est moi.* It is me," the man repeated, as if confirming Ben's doubts. "We finally meet *face à face*, Monsieur Oris."

Ben recognized the words as French, suggesting a higher Haitian education, but who the guy was he had no idea.

"I am sorry for the—how did you call it? Gimmick?—on the stairs, but it was necessary to make you understand my power, oui?" Faint flashes of red light still pulsed back by the stairwell, casting the man's dreadlocks in an ethereal glow. His fingers traced the velvet covering of the altar and brushed against the blankets in the bassinet.

Seeing the murderer's hand so close to Maxwell made Ben's face burn. He raised the knife a few inches, but if the killer seemed worried about the weapon, he didn't show it.

"I just want my son," Ben said. "Miot has nothing to do with us if that's what you're worried about."

With a feather's touch, the man rested his palm on Maxwell's stomach. Then he folded the blankets around him. Ben's jaw twitched, and he stepped forward, hoping he wouldn't slip on the blood-soaked floor. He nearly closed the gap between them.

"Monsieur Miot had evil plans for you and your son. Do you not see that? That is why I stop him."

You can trust me.

Ben swayed on his feet, his body trembling with adrenaline. He had to keep it together, keep his thoughts focused no matter how difficult. Once again he wondered about the powdery haze in the kitchen. He swiped the knife-free hand over his mouth, the split in his lip reopening. Could he overtake the guy and grab Maxwell?

"It is true, I only want to help you, but you must trust me."

Trust me. Trust me. Trust me. Trust me. Trust me. Trust me. Trust me.

Turmoil swirled inside Ben's brain. He no longer knew what to think or who to trust. He just wanted to get his son and leave.

Trust me. Trust me. Trust me. Trust me. Trust me. Trust me. Trust me.

Another thought fought its way to the surface, this time his own, but something Mambo Tina had said. *Stay true to you.* He mentally repeated the words over and over again, and a bit of calm began to return. No, he did not trust this man. Could not trust him after what he'd seen him do. If Miot was indeed the threat, there were less violent ways to subdue him.

He swallowed and stepped up to the altar. He was so close to the killer now, the man's tunic brushed his left arm. Ben glanced at his swaddled son, his heart breaking. The infant was asleep and seemingly okay, but how long would that last?

With a voice far steadier than he felt, Ben looked at the man's curved blade and said, "I'm getting my son and leaving. If you want to deal with me, we do it without him." *Son.* Such a new word to Ben, and yet it rolled off his tongue without pause.

The Haitian reached out his arm. Ben flinched, but all the man did was grab the leather strap around Ben's neck. He pulled until the bone amulet popped out and then rolled it gently in his hand. For the first time, uncertainty clouded his two-toned face.

"You wear Laurette's amulet." His voice was quiet, his expression perplexed. Then he nodded, as if coming to an understanding. "Ah, oui. This explains my challenges. But it also means you believe. That is good. You will need to."

Like a candle from the altar, the killer's face flickered, and he gripped the bone tightly and tugged. To his obvious frustration, the leather strap held. Ben jumped back before it could be pulled again, and when he did, the bone slipped out of the Haitian's hand. The guy yelped and brought his palm to his face. Blood dripped from where the bone tip had sliced his flesh.

After his initial shock, he licked the blood from his hand and smiled in delight, his teeth glowing in the pulsing light. "*C'est ironique, n'est-ce pas?* It is ironic."

Ben shoved the amulet back inside his shirt. "How did you know this belonged to my friend? Where is she?"

The man's glee faltered, and his expression told Ben he hadn't meant for that to slip out.

Trust me. I am here to help you.

"Bullshit," Ben said. He reached for Maxwell, careful to keep his knife away from the baby. He'd had enough of this freak show.

Before he could scoop the infant up, the killer grabbed his arms. "I cannot let you take him. First we must—"

Something slammed behind them. Both men jerked their heads at the noise, its reverberating crash overtaking the drumming.

Two people appeared from behind a toppled Virgin Mary, one stumbling, the other propping her up. The first person flooded Ben with relief. The second one stunned him.

46

"Laurette!"

Though desperate to run to his friend, Ben didn't dare leave his son's side. Not with a killer nearby, a man who had slit a human throat as casually as a fisherman might slice open the belly of a trout. Instead, in the pulsing redness, he watched Laurette and a tall, bespectacled woman weave around Jean Miot's bizarre maze of life-sized statues. Skulls and doll parts dangled from the ceiling above them.

The woman was Laurette's Aunt Marie, but why she was there, Ben had no idea. Was she the one he'd seen dart away after the bokor was murdered?

When the two women reached the altar, Ben replaced the knife in his waistband and embraced Laurette with one arm while keeping his other hand on Maxwell's bassinet. She sagged against him.

"God, I'm glad to see you, Bovo," he said, keeping his gaze on the killer. The man took a step back, his expression beneath the face paint unreadable.

Ben fought the murkiness in his brain. He didn't dare pick up his son yet. He'd never make it past the killer without a fight, and that would put Maxwell at even greater risk. Nor could he leave Laurette alone with the psychopath.

"Grab one of those chairs," Ben said to Marie, raising his voice above the drumming, which seemed to be coming from a speaker at the back of the room. When she returned with a wicker chair, Ben guided Laurette onto it, keeping himself near Maxwell's bassinet. The soles of his shoes stuck to the blood-bathed floor.

Cupping his friend's chin, he pulled down her lower eyelids one at a time, but in the blinking redness and dim candlelight, gauging her pupil size was impossible. Dried blood caked her forehead where a lump had formed.

Frustrated, he glared at the dreadlocked man on his right. "Turn the goddamn lights on so I can see her injury." Like one of the ceramic statues, the man simply stood there, mumbling something Ben couldn't hear.

"Laurette." Ben tapped her cheek. "Laurette, can you hear me?"

She groaned and nodded.

Thank God, he thought. Still, he wasn't sure the head bump was the only reason for her lethargy. To Marie, he said, "Where was she? Has she been drugged?"

"In Jean's bedroom." Marie's eyes were dark orbs beneath her wide-framed lenses. "I bring her down to see what Guy is doing."

"Hush, woman." The killer stepped forward, and Ben instinctively wrapped his entire arm around the bassinet. Then it dawned on him what Marie had just said.

"*Guy*?" Ben stared at the painted man incredulously. "What are you talking about?"

With effort, Laurette lifted her head. "*Mon frère.*" Her words came out thick and garbled. "Please, tell me it is not true."

Ben knew the word *frère* meant brother. He'd heard Laurette use it before. And he certainly recognized the name Guy as Laurette's Vodou priest brother. After all, the man had been advising Laurette on how to deal with Ben's situation. But discovering Laurette's brother was the same man who'd brutally murdered Jean Miot minutes before was inconceivable.

"Oh shit," he mumbled, finally piecing together what he couldn't place earlier. The leather strap securing Guy's dreadlocks. It was the same thing he'd seen on the man in the photograph in Laurette's wallet, back at the warehouse when he'd removed her identifying papers.

But he still didn't trust the guy. *Stay true to you*, Mambo Tina said in his head.

As if her strength had run out, Laurette slumped deeper in the chair. Her head plopped onto her chest. Ben's heart flipped, and he dared take one step away from Maxwell to make sure she was okay. As soon as he saw she was still conscious, he turned to Maxwell, but with the same swiftness with which Guy had killed Jean Miot, the man got there first and scooped the infant up in his arms. Moments later his murderous fingers stroked Maxwell's scalp.

Despite his lightheadedness and shaky limbs, Ben lurched forward like a rocket, using anger as his fuel. He gripped Guy's muscled arm. "Give me my son."

With alarming strength, the priest shoved him backward, and by the time he found his footing, the knife was back in Guy's hand, its blade pulsing in the dim, red light.

"Don't you fucking hurt him," Ben cried.

"Shh, shh, shh." Guy's tone was calm. Soothing. He stroked the dull side of the knife over Maxwell's dark hair, just as his fingers had done moments before. The infant stirred but didn't wake.

"Please." Ben's voice cracked and his chest swelled with such intense misery he couldn't breathe. "He needs to go back to the hospital. It's too cold for him here. He needs to eat."

"Guy, *arrêtes*. Stop." Marie inched forward but recoiled when Guy took a step toward her. "I am sorry," she said to Ben. "As soon as I see what my nephew is planning, what he do to Miot …" Her eyes darted to the dead man, and she bit her lower lip. "I go upstairs and get Laurette. I was here to help, you see? That is why I work with Jean Miot. Because Guy tells me to."

Ignoring his aunt as if she weren't there, Guy strolled toward Laurette, Maxwell still in his arm, knife in his hand over the infant's head. Ben followed, his heart hammering his ribs like the drumming hammering the room. Reaching behind him he retrieved his own knife once again. He would stab the fucker in the back if he had to, without a shred of remorse.

As if reading his mind (and maybe he was?), Guy spun around and pressed the curved blade against Maxwell's cheek. That was all it took to make Ben lower his knife.

Guy cradled Maxwell and bent down to his sister, keeping his attention partly on Ben. A look of regret befell his painted face. "I am sorry, my sister. Monsieur Miot was not to hurt you. He only went to seek the baby from its mother, but you surprised him." Guy reached up and ran a hand over her coiled sprigs of hair, his weapon's blade pointed upward so as not to cut her. "Do not worry. The drug will wear off soon."

A tear slid down Laurette's cheek. Marie, normally stern-looking, wore the face of a frightened child. Wringing her hands, she seemed to want to tend to her niece, but Guy's foreboding presence kept her at bay.

"You," Laurette said, her voice weak. "You are the dark force, not Jean Miot. You are the dark presence Mambo Tina saw and yet did not see."

"*Oui. C'est moi.*" Guy slipped into French, but Laurette made him stop.

"English. It is not only me you must explain to." She looked Ben's way, and he was relieved to see her regaining some strength.

The bokor abided her wishes, cradling Maxwell closer to his chest. "I do it for us, my sister. Monsieur Miot served his purpose, but he is a tool I no longer need. Only his blood helps me now. To fulfill the curse the Lwa demand the blood of dark magic."

"Fulfill the curse?" Laurette's words came out a low rasp. "We are trying to stop the curse, not fulfill it. I don't understand." Her eyes pleaded, and Ben could tell she was desperate to trust her brother. He knew how much Guy meant to her. But he only half listened to their words. All of his focus was on getting to his son.

"Do you not see, sister?" Guy grew heated, and he stood and shifted Maxwell to the other arm. "Nasicha's curse should be ours. Its power should be ours. Our ancestor wishes for us to avenge her. Avenge the terror this white man's family unleashed upon her own." The words spat from his mouth. Violent emotion the man hadn't yet displayed twisted his face into a macabre, half-white, half-black mask.

Sucker-punched again, Ben caught his breath. Laurette was the slave woman's descendant?

And Ben was the slave-owning rapist's.

No. Not possible. The odds were astronomical.

"With this power, the power due us, think of the good we can do for our family, for our country. We can finally stop our enemies. Our country's enemies. Now it is our turn to take from *them.*"

Laurette shook her head, eyebrows furrowed, mouth agape. Her hands gripped the wicker armrests, and she managed to find the strength to push herself higher.

"This is why I brought the two of you together."

"Brought us together? What?" Laurette's voice faded. She took quick, shallow breaths, as if unable to catch enough air. "But, this is not possible."

Guy shifted his knife to the hand supporting Maxwell. With the other he grabbed the bronze amulet around Laurette's neck and ran his thumb over its embossed star and emerald. "Do you not see? I gave you this charm. To bring you and Marcel's spawn together. For years I have planned. For years I have worked to make it come true. To finally transform our great ancestor's curse into the power it deserves. Finally she will see her revenge." He bellowed the last words, and the shout stirred Maxwell into arousal, though it still wasn't enough to wake the baby fully.

He should be crying, Ben thought. He should be wailing by now.

"What have you planned, brother?" Laurette sat up straighter, almost to full height.

Marie stood motionless to Ben's left, mumbling prayers. Though she'd claimed innocence, Ben felt nothing but fury that she'd let things play out as they had.

Guy glanced Ben's way. He pressed the knife back against Maxwell's head, its blade just above the infant's delicate scalp veins. "*Le sang. Leur sang.*"

Ben didn't know what the words meant, but given the shock on Laurette's face, he knew it was evil. She shifted forward and, to his astonishment, burst up from her chair and shouted, "Grab your son, Benjamin." Then she pushed herself onto her brother.

Ben lunged for Maxwell, but Laurette's shove had been too weak. Guy merely staggered on his feet, knife and baby still in his grip.

"You defy me, sister?" With a sandal-covered foot, the priest booted Laurette back. The kick was not hard, but it was enough to make her stumble and fall against a statue of a lion. Her head thumped off its stone base.

"Laurette!" Guy strode to his sister's side. He nudged her with the hand holding the knife, but she didn't budge.

Though desperate to go to her, Ben froze, his eyes pinned to his son.

Guy turned his kohl-lined gaze up to Ben, his eyes narrow cracks and his jaw a tight scowl. He shot up and unleashed his rage. "See what you make me do to my sister? You have evil in your blood. Generations of wickedness run through you. And *pourquoi pas*—why not? You are the descendant of a slave owner."

His hateful glower traveled from Ben to Maxwell, and with the swiftness of a leopard, he sprang past two statues and returned to the altar. He put the baby back in the bassinet. Then he turned around and faced Ben. "Now, you will give me your *sang*—your blood—or I will take it by force."

47

"If you do not wish to see your son die, drop the knife and come to me."
The combination of addled thoughts, shaky limbs, and disorienting setting made Ben a weak opponent. He knew this. Had the two of them squared off in a school yard or construction site, he might have stood a good chance. But here? In this gruesome place? With his panic mounting over Maxwell and Laurette? Aunt Marie had better odds.

Dropping the knife on the concrete floor, Ben held up his hands. "Fine. Just don't hurt my son." Tensing his muscles, he did his best to block out fear and instead focus on what he'd have to do to overcome the man.

"Bring me his knife," Guy barked at Marie. When Laurette's aunt complied, Guy tossed the blade, its flight cut short by a nearby statue. Then he said, "*Apportes-moi la corde.*" When she only shook her head, Guy shouted, "The rope. Now."

As Marie hustled off, the dark priest turned around and faced the too-quiet baby on top of the altar. Nestled among the altar's skull and long-bone displays, candle flames flickered and wax dripped onto the black velvet. Behind the altar the bronze skeleton in the long coat and top hat maintained his maniacal grin.

Guy raised his arms and bellowed what seemed to be some sort of incantation. The sudden noise startled Maxwell in the bassinet. At least the infant was alert enough to startle. That afforded Ben some comfort.

To Ben's left, Marie shuffled forward with a yellow rope, her knowledge of its location making him wonder whose side she was really on. She refused to meet his eyes.

The rope could only mean one thing: time was up. Rash or not, he had to act.

Do not fight it. You must let this happen.

"Get out of my head, you bastard." Channeling his confusion into anger, he charged at the man.

Guy spun around and smashed a fist into Ben's gut. Air whooshed from his lungs, and he stumbled backward. Before he could regain his footing, Guy punched him in the face. He went down, his head landing next to Laurette's unmoving foot on the concrete. Guy yelled at Marie in French, probably demanding the rope to immobilize Ben. Somehow he staggered to his feet as Guy's demented face pulsed in and out of the red strobe light, the upper half flashing white. Behind him Maxwell finally started to cry.

The dark priest gripped the knife in his hand. "You cannot win, boy. This is not a fight of physical strength. Do you not—"

Ben plowed into Guy, wary of the knife but throwing punches just the same. Though Ben felt the impact of the blows on his knuckles, they seemed to have no effect on Guy. As if amped up on something, the priest fended them off and landed harder ones in return.

When Ben threw a left hook, Guy raised the knife-wielding hand to block the blow. A sting shot across Ben's exposed upper arm, and a warm dripping followed. The fresh flow of Ben's blood momentarily slowed Guy, and hunger flashed in his eyes. Ben took the opportunity to punch him in the solar plexus.

Apparently seizing her own chance, Marie cried out and wrapped the rope around her nephew's midsection. Before she could trap him, Guy's right arm slipped out and whacked Marie in the face. The woman dropped. Her glasses flew off her face and disappeared into the pulsing red beam.

A blow to the temple took Ben down next, his skull narrowly missing a ceramic statue of a two-legged beast. Once on the floor, the frenzied priest straddled Ben and pinned his arms with granite thighs. The rage on his face was unmistakable, his black-rimmed eyes wild with hate and revenge. White makeup laced with sweat streaked down his cheeks.

"It is over now. There is nothing for you to do but accept your fate, just as my ancestor was forced to accept hers." Guy ogled the blood seeping from the cut on Ben's arm. He ran a finger over it and brought the fresh liquid to his lips. His body quivered. "Power runs through you, and I will make it my own. Those who cross me will rot from inside out." Guy smiled, blood staining his teeth. "But the blood of your son is *plus fort*—stronger. The blood of a bébé. It is all I need. You are extra." Guy raised his chin to the ceiling and brayed in a foreign tongue.

His arms going numb, Ben bucked and twisted. The priest's strength was shocking. What had he taken to make him so strong? Nothing Ben did seemed to affect him. From behind Guy, Maxwell's wailing grew louder, finally overpowering the fanatical drumming.

Ben roared and tried again to shove the guy off. He had to get to his son. Guy wouldn't stop until he had both Ben and Maxwell's blood sloshing in his shiny bowls. Even if Ben was sure of nothing else, of that he was certain. Yet no matter how hard he bucked he couldn't shake Guy.

And then he remembered. David Alcine's powder. The powder he'd warned Ben not to sniff or get in his eyes. The packet was in his front pocket, so close to his fingers, and yet, with his arms pinned, it might as well have been across the room.

Guy chanted, repeating the same incomprehensible words over and over. He raised the knife.

A raging scream echoed in Ben's ears. It took a moment to realize it was his own. With all his might, he bucked and writhed again, twisting his body beneath Guy's bulk. The man was clearly angered to be jostled about, but Ben's frenzied corkscrewing finally allowed him to slip a hand into his pocket and grasp the plastic pouch.

Despite Guy's unsteadiness from Ben's struggle, he raised the knife higher. He lowered his chin, Ben's blood still smeared on his lips. "For Nasicha and Kalifa," he said. His voice shifted into a ghoulish ululation, a noise far more terrifying than the drums or chanting.

Ben summoned every ounce of strength he had. Just as Guy lowered the knife, Ben heaved his torso and lower body. Although the pitch didn't topple the priest completely, it was enough to lift him off Ben and cause the knife to miss its target. It scraped off the ceramic creature with a raking sound. Ben pulled the plastic bag from his pocket and wriggled out from underneath the painted man.

Both arms free now, he ripped open the bag. Flecks of the yellow powder spilled into his hands. He held his breath. As Guy bellowed and lunged forward, Ben squeezed his eyes shut and blew the contents into the priest's face. When Ben dared to reopen his eyes, Guy was blinking in confusion. Though Ben's injured left arm felt weak, the cut perhaps deeper than he'd realized, he wrestled the knife from the priest's hand.

He struggled to his feet, his jaw, cheekbone, and temple throbbing from Guy's punches. As he waited for the powder to take effect, Ben wondered if he'd been duped. The powder was useless. He should have—

The priest's eyes widened. Yellow powder clung to his smeared makeup, creased his lips, and shimmered in his dreadlocks. Staccato coughs erupted from his throat. He fell back onto his tailbone, and his hands flew to his throat. Seconds later he collapsed on the floor.

For a moment Ben stood motionless, the chaos of drumming, flashing red light, and infant wailing clamoring around him. Slowly, Marie rose to her feet.

Her movement propelled Ben to action. Not knowing if Guy was dead or merely sedated, he ordered Marie to tie her nephew up. He refused to spend another second away from his son. Wiping his hands free of the powder, he hurried to the bassinet on the altar. "We have to get Maxwell and Laurette to Mambo Tina's," he bellowed over his shoulder to Marie. Looking at his wrist, he saw his watch had vanished in the fight, but even without knowing the hour, his gut told him time was running out. If Mambo Tina couldn't help him, Willy would die, a thought Ben refused to accept.

When he finally scooped up Maxwell with his uninjured arm, Ben sobbed with relief. He took a moment to comfort his son, tightening the blankets around him. After the infant's cries tapered off to a whimper, he went back to Marie, making sure she'd secured Guy's hands to the heaviest statue near him.

"Is he alive?" Ben asked.

Marie nodded. Ben checked the knot. Though satisfied with her work, he was not satisfied with their options. Leaving the dark priest alive could come back to bite them, but no way could he kill an unconscious man who wasn't an immediate threat. He'd have Marie call 9-1-1 in the car. Miot's dead body should keep Guy busy with the police for a long while.

With one last look at Laurette's brother, the man's eyelids weepy and dotted with powder that shimmered in the pulsing light, Ben weaved his way to Laurette, still unconscious on the floor. A part of him was relieved. At least she hadn't witnessed what her brother had tried to do.

Soothing Maxwell with soft words, Ben reluctantly handed the infant to Marie. He hefted Laurette over his injured shoulder, grunting with the effort and using his good arm to hold her body in place.

As they made their way in the huge unfinished room toward the stairwell, both the drumming and red flashing intensified. If Ben's arm had been free, he would have broken the freaking light once and for all. Instead he called out to Marie. "Do you think Mambo Tina can help before it's too late for my dad?"

Relentless drumming was the only reply.

48

With Laurette laid out in the back seat of her Subaru and Marie in the passenger seat holding Maxwell, Ben sped away from Jean Miot's house of nightmares and headed toward Mambo Tina's peristil. His face throbbed, and his left arm was a combination of tingling and stabbing pain. With the bizarre incident behind them, Ben's mind kept replaying Miot's murder, the bokor's final expression as shocked and horrified as Ben's. That moment would haunt him for the rest of his life.

Flying through an intersection, his hands trembling on the steering wheel, he did his best to shake the image and focus on driving. He couldn't risk an accident. Maxwell wasn't in a car seat. Once again random groups, mostly young males, milled around on the sidewalk. The heavy clouds had since dissipated, and a near-full moon cast silvery light on the dilapidated neighborhood.

Maxwell had quieted, the humming engine and driving motion rocking him back to sleep. According to the dashboard clock, Ben had been at Miot's for over an hour. Maxwell had been away from Sophia's for at least three. The infant needed to eat. In the hospital Sophia had been nursing him every two to four hours, and even then his blood sugar hadn't remained stable.

Like an ever-tightening zip tie, worry cinched Ben's chest. Newborns didn't always wake up for a feed, even when they needed one; that's what the pediatrician had said. Reaching over to Marie, Ben patted his swaddled son. "Hang in there, little man."

In the rearview mirror he saw Laurette sprawled in the back seat, still passed out. From being drugged? From head trauma? Ben's throat grew thick, and his thigh bounced up and down on the seat. She should go to the hospital. Maxwell too. An image of Willy alone and scared on 6 West popped into Ben's head. His eyes burned, and his jaw clamped down so tightly his teeth hurt.

To Marie, he said, "Laurette and Maxwell need medical attention. I'll drop the three of you off at the ER and then drive to Mambo Tina's."

"I am sorry. That cannot work." Marie readjusted her seatbelt strap and released a trapped edge of Maxwell's blanket. "She need the bébé. And Laurette too. The mambo need all people to help."

Like misty fog, doubt settled over him. Maybe he should just turn himself into the police and explain the situation himself. Did he really think Mambo Tina could fix this? Did he even believe there *was* something to fix? He'd allowed himself to get sucked so deeply into their madness he no longer understood truth from fantasy.

But a man had been killed. It didn't get more truthful than that. And someone had almost taken him out in the parking ramp that morning. He still wasn't sure it was a coincidence or if it was meant to get him out of the way. *The blood of your son is stronger,* Guy had said. Maybe Ben was just a bonus bleed at this point. So truth or fantasy, it didn't matter. Until this Vodou shit was resolved, his son would never be safe.

Once he felt far enough away from Miot's house, he dug into his pocket and handed Marie the prepaid phone. "Call 9-1-1 and let them know about Jean Miot and his killer. Then hang up before giving them your information." When she started to protest, he said, "We can't risk Guy coming after us. For Christ's sake, if he tracked me down through my ancestor, he can certainly figure out we're headed to Mambo Tina's."

With that she acquiesced. When she finished the call, Ben flipped on the radio for distraction. Anything to quiet his mental anguish. Finding it set to an AM news station, he thought about changing it but instead put his focus on getting to the peristil in one piece. In his state, self-combustion was moments away.

Paying little attention to a blaring political ad, he veered left at a stop sign. By the time the news came back on, he reached Mambo Tina's street.

And that's when self-combustion took place.

Hardly believing his ears, he turned up the radio, one hand shaking on the knob, the other on the steering wheel, fighting to keep the car on the road. Together he and Marie listened.

"We've just received an update on the AMBER Alert for Maxwell Diaz-Oris, an infant abducted from his mother's home earlier this evening. Ms. Diaz is recovering at Montgomery Hospital, and although she reports no memory of the incident, an anonymous source with inside knowledge claims Benjamin Oris, a medical student and father of the infant, has abducted the child."

Ben squealed the car into an open spot in front of the peristil. Now his whole body was numb. He couldn't move. Couldn't breathe.

Kidnapping. He wasn't looking at quarantine. He was looking at prison.

Joel, Ben thought, jaw sagging open. He was the only one who could have placed Ben at Sophia's apartment.

Marie placed a hand on Ben's arm. "Soon this will be over."

"Do you really believe that?" Ben's question came out a sarcastic croak. Panicked, he tuned back into the news announcer.

"Benjamin Oris is currently being sought by public health officials as the source of a fatal blood infection. Officials believe he is patient zero and requires immediate quarantine before he infects anyone else. Pictures of Mr. Oris can be found at our website or Facebook page. It is advised that anyone who might have seen Mr. Oris call the police or the health department immediately at—"

Marie turned off the radio.

"Jesus," Ben said, his body weighted to the seat, arms and legs useless, his brain a muddled mess.

So much for turning himself in and clearing things up with the police. Not with a kidnapping charge hanging over his head. The only way through the fantastical nightmare now was forward.

Ben turned off the car. He squeezed circulation back into his muscles and rolled his neck, wincing at the pain in his left arm. Then he exhaled so loudly Maxwell stirred.

Time for his next fight.

49

If Maxwell was disappointed it wasn't a breast nourishing him, he didn't show it. Nestled in Ben's arms on Mambo Tina's plaid couch, he sucked at the bottle of formula like a barracuda. Perhaps it was hunger, perhaps it was simple instinct, but whatever the reason, Ben felt the relief of a man rescued at sea that Maxwell was vigorous enough to feed.

Earlier, in anticipation of the evening, Mambo Tina had sent David out to fetch formula, a bottle, diapers, and wipes. She'd also recruited a client who was a new mother to bring over clean blankets and white onesies. The fact the priestess had thought of those things when Ben hadn't mired him in self-doubt. What did he know about being a father?

But as he watched his son feed, heard the suckles and swallows, cradled the blanketed body in his bruised arms, he thought his heart might burst.

Mambo Tina joined him in her darkly wallpapered den, its ceremonial artwork as disturbing as before. Dressed in a more formal white gown than her usual summer dress, she looked every bit the Vodou priestess. A delicate white shawl draped her shoulders, pearled pins held her bun in place, and chains of white beads swayed around her neck. Although her small eyes sparked in anticipation, they flashed fear too. Smelling of Ivory soap and lilacs, her aura emanated cleanness and goodness, and for the first time since the horrible lamp service the night before, Ben felt a moment of peace. Laurette, too, was safe in one of Mambo Tina's bedrooms, though he still worried about her head injury.

"Thank you for getting these things for my son. And for helping us." Gratitude pinched his throat.

The mambo took a seat on the couch next to him and Maxwell. "I have not helped you yet, son. I pray that I can." At that she said a short prayer before continuing. "Although all priests and priestesses know dark magic, we do not choose to practice it. It is not...how you say...of the ethics. My *magique* will only work if Bondye, God, is willing. You also must understand that the rightness of what we are to do does not fall on my shoulders. It falls on yours."

"What does that mean?"

"It means I am not responsible for what happens. It is you who is."

Ben wondered if that was the Vodou equivalent of medical consent, like a patient signing off on the possibility of death. The thought did little to comfort him.

They watched in silence as Maxwell chugged the last of the formula. Ben slouched in exhaustion, while Mambo Tina sat ramrod straight on the edge of the couch. It was nearing ten forty-five, and Ben knew the Vodouisants were eager to get things started. He had no idea who or how many people were present, but nervous voices, chairs scraping tiles, and shuffling footsteps floated from the large room at the end of the hallway.

"You must burp him now," Mambo Tina said.

"I don't know how."

"Here. It is simple." The priestess scooped up Maxwell and laid him upright against Ben's left shoulder. He grimaced at the pressure on his wrapped-up laceration—another act of kindness by the mambo—and held his son in place. He patted his back as she had demonstrated.

The baby felt so small and light. So vulnerable. Ben stared at the papule on his hand as it touched Maxwell's blanketed back. He still worried about the lesion's contagiousness, but Mambo Tina had assured him the protection of a glove or bandage was not needed. "There is no one here you will infect, and the bébé carries the same curse as you," she had said.

A burp punctuated the silence. Mambo Tina smiled, displaying widely spaced incisors. "See? He is happy with you. You will be a good father, Monsieur Oris."

Ben returned Maxwell to a supine position in his arms. He leaned his head back against the plaid cushion, closed his weary eyes, and prayed to a god he'd never before acknowledged that she was right.

=╠

The next thing Ben knew he was being roused by Mambo Tina, David Alcine by her side. Marie was seated on the sofa's armrest, two cushions down from Ben, texting something on her phone. She held the device inches from her eyes, her glasses still in Jean Miot's basement.

It hit Ben that Maxwell was no longer in his arms. He shot upright, wincing at the stab of pain in his left arm. When he saw his son lying on a bedding of blankets on the floor, he relaxed. The glass-encased clock on Mambo Tina's desk told him he'd dozed for thirty minutes.

"The room is ready," Mambo Tina said, her voice calm but her hands wringing. "But first, David will take you to prepare yourself and the bébé. Get you something to eat too."

"Where's Laurette?" He wiped his eyes and blinked away grogginess.

"She is still resting in my room, but she shows signs of waking up."

"Why didn't Guy try to drug me too? Would have made his job easier." Then again, he probably had. Ben pictured the hazy air in Miot's kitchen. That would explain the stairwell hallucination, his addled brain, and his subpar fighting.

The mambo smoothed the fringe on the end of her shawl. "Untainted blood traps the fear of the sacrificed. Perhaps he did not want to lose that." As if the statement were not at all creepy, she gave a quick nod and said, "Let us begin. David will bring Laurette to the ceremony. We will need her as much as we need the bébé, I fear."

"Why?" The dread Ben had carried around for days crept up his spine and obliterated any calm the short nap had given him.

"Marie tells me about Guy. About their family ties to Nasicha. Marie did not know of this before. If she had, she would not have asked David to arrange a meeting for you with Monsieur Miot. But like David, she believed Guy's advice to contact the bokor was in your good interest."

Laurette's aunt looked up from her phone, squinted at Ben, and nodded. Her somber expression matched the mambo's. David's was even more pronounced, his gaze darting back and forth to the den's doorway and his hands scratching his keloid scars as if he had poison ivy.

The priestess retrieved Maxwell from the makeshift bed on the rug and laid the sleeping infant in Ben's arms. "Laurette is a part of this curse, just as you are. Yesterday I felt the connection between you two, but I did not understand it. Today I do."

"And if Laurette can't wake up enough for the ceremony?" Ben hugged Maxwell closer to his chest, ignoring the discomfort in his left arm.

"Then we must hope her auntie will be enough." Though the words sounded assured, the mambo's pinched countenance suggested otherwise.

Ben studied Marie. Though she had helped him escape Jean Miot's basement, she hadn't gained his trust.

"Go. You must prepare yourself and your son." Mambo Tina waved her arms and ushered him up from the couch. "David will take you to the kitchen where you will clean your son and dress him in white." She examined Ben's dusty jeans, torn at the knee from his struggle with Guy, and his sweaty, blood-stained T-shirt. "Then you will clean yourself. David has white clothing for you."

For the next fifteen minutes, Ben bathed, diapered, and clothed his son, grateful for David's assistance, who Ben learned was a father of three. Maxwell's eyes remained open, and he seemed to enjoy the bath. Each time his gaze connected with Ben's, Ben's heart swelled to the size of the opal moon outside the kitchen window.

As he rinsed the soap off Maxwell's smooth skin, Ben prayed he was doing right by his son. A Vodou ceremony? He must be insane. But he'd die before he'd let Maxwell get hurt. At least the police should have Guy by now. One less stone to weigh down his chest.

When he finished with Maxwell, Ben devoured the sandwich David had made for him and chugged a large glass of water. Then he carried his son to an upstairs bathroom and cleaned himself up. A glance in the mirror revealed clumped hair, a cut chin, and a swollen bruise near his right eye where Guy had clocked him. A few minutes later someone knocked on the door. "It is time," he heard David Alcine say.

Ben rolled his neck and cracked his sore knuckles. He picked up his son and opened the door.

50

No need to check a clock. Ben could feel the midnight hour. It clung to him and Maxwell like a dark cloak as they made their way behind David to the ceremonial room. Barefoot in white pajamas an inch too short, Ben felt foolish and awkward. David, too, wore all white, but his linen pants and button-down shirt were more dignified.

Nonbelievers can't be choosers, Benny Boy. The stupid thought made him choke off a nervous laugh. Holding Maxwell's swaddled form close to his chest, he kissed the infant's powder-scented forehead. Drumming flowed down the hall, but unlike at Jean Miot's, it sounded lively and animated. None of that relentless monotony.

When they entered the large room, Ben's mouth dropped open. The space, so dimly lit on his past visits, burst with light from a string of decorative lamps. In the corner, a wiry man squeezed an oblong drum between his knees and tapped its taut membrane with enthusiasm, his head rolling back and forth to the rhythm. A dozen other people, all dressed in white, populated the room. The women wore dresses and head scarves, the men loose pants and shirts. The room had been cleared of Mambo Tina's divination table along with the area rugs, stone tile left in their place. Chalk drawings to invite the spirits covered many of these tiles, all of them encircling the decorative center pole, which Laurette had called the *poto mitan*. A few attendees sat in chairs pushed against the back wall, but the majority hovered about or attended to last-minute details.

Beyond the human element, visual stimuli abounded. The same three altar tables lined the sides and front of the room, and the serpent-toting goatman still hung in its place above the far one. Draped with colorful cloths, the tables overflowed with bounty: fruit, corn husks, oils, salsas, chips, chocolate, skulls, small statues, dolls, vibrant masks, party hats, and alcohol. Ben had purchased and delivered many of the supplies earlier, but he didn't recognize everything. Least crowded was the front table. Upon its ivory cloth, chains of silver and gold beads weaved around dozens of crosses. Big crosses, small crosses, metal ones, and plastic ones. Lots of lit candles too. In the center of it all lay a small bassinet draped with white blankets.

But what Ben saw flanking the bassinet disturbed him most: two metal bowls on either side, not unlike those he'd seen at Jean Miot's.

A wave of vertigo hit him. He inhaled deeply and hugged Maxwell closer, at least taking some comfort in knowing Mambo Tina's bloodletting would be more humane than Guy's.

Ben stepped farther into the room, the flooring cool beneath his bare feet, compliments of two large fans positioned near opposite walls. Above him, colorful ceiling streamers twisted and swayed in the draft. Though the drumming continued, the voices had hushed the moment Ben entered, and a collective gaze shifted his way.

He wondered what they must think. Did they pity him? Despise him for his ancestry? Truly believe he was cursed? Or were they just there for booze and a good show?

Ben turned to ask David who the other attendees were, but the assistant had not followed him into the room. Instead, Mambo Tina entered and approached Ben, offering a sweet smile to his dozing son. "David and Marie are collecting Laurette. I do not know how much your friend has told you about our ceremonies, but I do not have much time to explain. You will have to trust me."

So what else is new, Ben wanted to say but didn't. "She mentioned these things can get loud and hectic. Lots of chanting, singing, dancing."

"Yes, this is true, though some ceremonies are small like your lamp service. But tonight I invite many trusted Vodouisants. There is a *règleman* we follow. A set of rules. We begin with prayers to the different Lwa, the spirits. Then there is music. You see the *asson* and the *tcha-tcha* over there?" The priestess pointed to a small side table where several rattles lay, some shaped like a beaded gourd, others a stick with a rounded end. "Everyone participates. No observers allowed. After the prayers, the dancing begins. Many Lwa love a good party, and we have wonderful gifts to offer. If we are lucky, the spirits will take human form."

"So I've heard. Laurette said sometimes a person gets … possessed." The word felt ridiculous on his tongue.

An eye roll must have slipped out too, because Mambo Tina grabbed his forearm so swiftly, Maxwell startled. "I see doubt on your face. You must try to believe. If you do not, I fear we will fail."

"I'll try."

The priestess nodded, released her hold, and led him deeper into the room. "It is not possession as you know it. Instead a body is used by a Lwa. It is only temporary. This person is called a *chwal*, this is to say, a horse. Through the chwal the spirit can eat, drink, dance, and party with the other guests. But do not be alarmed. Once possessed, a human can do things he or she normally could not. The *gymnastique*, oui? Flip, contort the body, even swallow fire."

Ben grimaced, mostly out of disbelief, but a little out of fear.

"But the chwal does not know this and will remember nothing when it is over."

If her words were meant to reassure him, they failed. Retaking his arm, she led him away from the drumming and toward the front altar. The guests had resumed their chatting, and some even danced.

"If we are blessed," Mambo Tina said, running her hand along the white tablecloth, "we may receive a Lwa with the ability to heal. And to forgive. But will this end the curse? I do not know." A shadow crossed her face, and not from a candle flame. "For this to happen I most need Laurette to be the chwal. Because of her connection to you and Nasicha, who placed the curse so many years ago. But I do not know if your friend's injured body is strong enough to welcome the spirit."

"And if it's not?" Ben's neck and shoulders were back to their usual screaming. At least Maxwell was still asleep, gratefully oblivious to his father's anxiety.

"Then we hope the Lwa chooses Marie."

"But how can you be sure who gets chosen?" Scanning the sizable group in the room, Ben thought the odds seemed pretty shitty.

"We cannot. We can only hope through our prayers and offerings the Lwa will hear us. So tonight we must offer more than food, drinks, and merriment. Tonight we must offer your …" She hesitated, her trimmed fingernail clinking against a collection bowl and then a scalpel next to it. From her distasteful expression, Ben deduced the anticipated ceremony shot way past her ethical boundaries.

"You must offer my blood. And Maxwell's. But only a small amount, right?"

She nodded, and once again, Ben pressed his son to his chest, ignoring the shot of pain in his arm.

"Blood is the best food to serve the spirit." Her voice dropped lower, and Ben had to stoop to hear her. "The fresher the blood, the more life the spirit can absorb and the more powerful it will be. And with that power we hope it takes human form in Laurette."

All at once the chattering behind them quieted. Ben turned toward the doorway to see David and Marie helping Laurette inside. Somehow they'd managed to slip her into a white dress. Her eyes were open, but her sleepy lids suggested they'd soon close. Since she had been lucid enough to converse with Guy back at Jean Miot's place, Ben worried her ongoing lethargy was due more to head injury than drugging. As soon as the ceremony was over, he vowed to get her to a hospital, even if it meant turning himself in as a result.

Which, of course, it would.

But as much as it pained him to see Laurette injured, he knew she would want him to end the cursed infection beyond all else. Or at least to try. She'd chew him out and withhold her Haitian baked goods if he did otherwise. His lips curled into the tiniest smile, and the reminder of their friendship buoyed him.

"They are here. We must hurry." The priestess adjusted her head scarf over her bun, the tremor in her hand not lost on Ben. "We do not know if he will come. We must finish before he does."

His moment of levity vanished. "Who, Guy? But I had Marie call 9-1-1."

"Do not take this off." The mambo tugged on the leather strap around Ben's neck. Laurette's bone amulet slipped out of his pajama top and slid over Maxwell's blanket. "Laurette felt you must have it. We should never doubt the importance of what we do not understand."

She turned and walked toward the others. Ben followed on rubbery legs.

A short time later the ceremony began. Ben's comfort level hovered around zero. To him a mosque would have felt less foreign. As Mambo Tina had promised, a series of prayers in front of the serpent-decorated pole started things off, but what was said and to what Lwa, Ben had no clue. Other than a listless Laurette who remained slumped in a folding chair near the doorway, everyone stood around the poto mitan and participated.

David had planted Ben on a stool a few feet in front of the altar, leaving enough space for others to move around him. Though the air was cool from the fans, perspiration dotted his face and torso. Maxwell, however, remained asleep in his arms, no doubt compliments of the full belly and warm bath. Listening to the prayers and chants around him, in a language and culture he didn't understand, Ben envied his son's blissful rest.

After fifteen minutes of benediction, the drumming resumed and the musical instruments rattled and clanged. A flurry of white spun around Ben as participants danced and sang. Their jubilation was more celebratory than somber, but from Mambo Tina's earlier explanation, Ben understood the guests hoped to entice and invite the Lwa.

From his seat he watched Vodouisants yodel and chant, ululate and sing. Every ounce of his energy went into willing his mind to believe, but though he longed to get swept up in their hoopla, nothing but discomfort and worry took hold. Worry for his father, for Harmony, for Sophia, for Laurette. He stroked Maxwell's cheek, enormously grateful to have his son back in his arms. At least he'd done something right that day.

All around him celebrants shimmied and jumped, swayed and shook. David danced, and Marie twirled in a circle with a gourd-shaped rattle. Like the others, they were completely consumed, working themselves to exhaustion to entice the Lwa.

Before Ben's seeds of cynicism could grow deeper, Mambo Tina approached. Time for phase two, he guessed, his gut churning and his heart rate climbing. When he stood, his left arm throbbed in pain, as if an ongoing warning from the dark priest who'd stabbed him. Following Mambo Tina to the altar, Ben did his best to avoid the goatman's gaze.

The priestess reached for Maxwell, and, after a moment of hesitation, Ben relinquished his son. The mambo laid the infant in the bassinet on the altar.

She reached into a dress pocket and pulled out a pair of medical gloves. On either side of Ben stood David Alcine and Marie, both with pinched faces, their dancing joviality gone. Behind them, the music and partying continued.

Mambo Tina unraveled Maxwell's blanket and gently lifted his left foot. From the table she picked up a small lancet, similar to the kind Ben had seen diabetics use to check their blood sugar. After cleaning the infant's pink heel with an alcohol swab, she squeezed his foot in her gloved hand until the area purpled and flushed with blood. Maxwell roused and started to cry. The priestess looked up as if seeking final permission from Ben.

Swallowing a lump of uncertainty, Ben wondered what he was doing. Had he gone completely mad?

No. He had to believe. Or at least give it his best shot. He pictured Willy in the hospital, vomiting blood, going into organ failure, dying. He had to believe. There was no other choice.

Against every rational impulse in his mind and body, he nodded and watched as Mambo Tina pricked his wailing son's heel and squeezed blood into the smaller of the two collection bowls, which he now saw contained a clear liquid. Red droplets plopped onto stainless steel, and Ben fisted his hands to keep from reaching out to his son. He knew from Laurette the priestess had once worked as a nurse. She'd likely performed thousands of similar pokes, but it didn't make seeing his son get squeezed like a lemon any easier. He only hoped the small amount of blood would be enough. Though enough for what, he couldn't know.

When she finished, David held pressure to Maxwell's foot and applied a small bandage. He swaddled the baby back up and soothed him with calming tones. Ben reached for his son, but Mambo Tina frowned and shook her head.

She asked for his right hand. He proffered it hesitantly, not because he feared a blood draw but because he feared infecting someone. She gripped his palm, oblivious to his concern. Next to her, Marie's chanting intensified, and after David replaced Maxwell in the bassinet, he too picked up her cadence. Their combined voices so near Ben's eardrums emitted a ghostly echo, making the hair on the back of his neck stand up.

Foregoing the lancet, Mambo Tina wiped down Ben's palm with alcohol and picked up the scalpel. Without warning she slashed the blade over the meaty flesh of his palm, right through the purple papule that had plagued his last month. His quick intake of breath got swallowed by the chanting and music, both of which dizzied him.

Breathing more rapidly, he watched her milk a steady flow of blood into the larger bowl. Once again he asked himself why he was doing this, and once again he told himself to shut the hell up and believe. On and on the priestess pumped. In her exertion, a clump of braided hair escaped her headscarf and brushed against her firm jaw. Just when Ben worried she was about to bleed him dry, she nodded to David. The assistant pressed a cloth to the wound and applied pressure. Then he pulled gauze from his pocket and wrapped it around the cloth.

Picking up both bowls, Mambo Tina placed them on the floor at the foot of the altar. The slight tremor in her arms made Ben's stomach knot. If a Vodou priestess wasn't confident of their success, how could he be? She started praying, and David and Marie shifted their chants to match hers. From the floor vibrations caused by the dancers, the burgundy liquid shimmered and swirled in the bowls. The medical part of Ben's brain (seemingly shrinking by the second) wondered why the blood didn't clot, but then he realized the clear liquid he'd seen in the containers must have been an anticoagulant. Maybe David had taken some heparin from the pharmacy.

Wanting desperately to believe in the ceremony's power, Ben squeezed his eyelids together and focused on Maxwell. On Willy. On Harmony clinging to life. On Laurette and Sophia. He even tried praying, though with his areligious past, he expected God would laugh in his face. Despite the darts of pain in his left arm, he reached up with his non-bandaged hand and clutched both Laurette's amulet and Sophia's cross. Though he doubted he could remember all the words, he mentally recited the Lord's Prayer.

The singing and dancing escalated, and Marie got whisked into the middle of it. More frenzied drumming and rattling too. From the altar Maxwell resumed his crying, his shrieks adding to the chaos.

But nothing happened.

No Lwa came forward. No Lwa offered healing or forgiveness. No Lwa yelled, "Hallelujah you're cured." Ben opened his eyes and looked around. Despite the dancers circling Marie and offering gifts, the woman's body remained untouched. She merely danced and chanted around the poto mitan like the others, nothing to suggest she'd become a possessed chwal.

Ben's skepticism washed back like a wave. From Harmony or Max, he could understand such gullibility. Maybe even Willy. But from himself? Insane. He should be at the hospital with his father. Laurette should be in the ER. Good God, he thought, what kind of a shit-for-brains med student am I?

A shriek split the air. At the same time, an electrical current ripped through Ben's body. His hair shot straight up, as if being torn from his scalp.

He whipped around and sought the source of the cry. The tendons on his neck stood out, and he gripped the altar for support. A figure in a white dress leaped and twisted in front of him, knocking dancers and offerings aside like toy blocks. The body was so contorted and tangled he could hardly believe it was human. When he realized who it was, he let out a cry of his own.

Laurette. A Laurette he'd never seen before. One so crazed and rabid he would rather die than ever see again. Moments earlier she'd been nothing but a lethargic observer. Now she was a raving lunatic.

All around her objects flew. She leaped onto tables and kicked candles and skulls to the floor. She ripped the hideous goatman statue from the wall and flung him into the air. She smashed alcohol bottles against the walls. With her teeth she ripped the top off of a long-neck beer. Glass punctured her lips, and sprayed her face and ivory dress with blood. And yet she kept leaping. Yelping and flipping and contorting her body into inhuman positions.

Panicked ceremony participants ceased their dancing and fled to the back wall. The drumming and rattling halted. A few continued their chanting, and some even heightened it, but most cowered in fear at the beast before them.

Though visibly frightened, Mambo Tina, David, and Marie did not back away like the others. They raised their voices, screaming to be heard above the frenzied chwal. Marie especially was ululating and arching her back like a demonic circus performer.

Suddenly, the thing that was Laurette but wasn't fell quiet, so quiet even Mambo Tina halted her prayers. Only Marie continued, her face twisted and her eyes maniacal.

Like a silent leopard, Laurette pounced forward until she stood two feet in front of Ben. She lowered her head and cranked her neck to the right, rotating it to such an extreme it emitted a sickening *crack*.

From that twisted, downward position, she stared up at Ben. Frothy saliva dripped from her mouth. Blood stained her mangled lips. Sweat dripped from her arched eyebrows, and if not for those, Ben would have sworn on his dead father's grave it wasn't his friend.

A wriggling, snake-like finger pointed toward Ben. "*Vous,*" the lacerated lips spat, spraying the French word for *you* like poisonous venom.

Ben's bowels hitched. His heart pummeled his ribs. All thought fled his mind. Instinct kicked in, and he threw himself over his son's bassinet and prayed like hell.

51

Sweat dripped from Ben's forehead onto his son's blanket. The infant's wailing rattled his eardrums, but other than Marie's crazed chanting, everyone else hushed in fear. Even Laurette made no noise. But Ben felt her presence behind him. Felt the heat radiating from her quivering, contorting body.

He hovered over his son. Maybe if he didn't look at the thing that had consumed his friend, it would lose interest and find a new target.

A sudden pain exploded in his skull, its impact jerking him upright. The scent of burning wood assaulted his nostrils, and horrifying yet familiar images flooded his mind's eye. A burning shack. Whipping and shredding of bloodied skin. The brutal attack on a terrified girl.

Retching at the recollection, Ben squeezed his eyes shut and pressed his fists against his temples, desperate to block out the horrific scene of his dreams.

Another shrill cry split the air. Icicles studded Ben's spine, and before he could stop her, Laurette gripped the back of his shirt and tossed him like a beanbag across the room, where he landed painfully against the previously heaved goatman. Buttons popped off his pajama top and skipped across the floor. The bone amulet and cross flapped freely from his gaping neckline, and their sharp tips jabbed his flesh.

Mambo Tina rushed toward him. Laurette flipped through the air and pushed the priestess away. As the mambo went down, her expression widened in recognition and then shifted to disbelief. Scooting on her bottom like a crab, she backed away. "Not her. It is not possible." She prayed and made the sign of the cross.

Ben grunted to a stand. Laurette, her shredded lips salivating a foamy pink froth, circled around and kicked him in the flank. He crumpled back down.

She's too strong, he thought. Too freaking strong. Once again he struggled to a stand, his lower back burning, his legs threatening to crumple beneath him.

A rabid dog now, Laurette whipped around him. As he spun his body to keep track of her, he saw that most of the participants had fled the room. The handful that remained prayed alongside David in the corner near the abandoned drum. Mambo Tina had righted herself, and although she maintained her distance, her movements matched Laurette's in direction, as if preparing for the next attack. In front of the altar, Marie's chanting morphed into ululation, and Laurette grew even more agitated.

"Stop," Ben cried to Marie. "You're making it worse."

But the woman ignored his plea, and soon Laurette's leaps and bounds became nothing but a feverish blur. Every time he tried to dart past her to get to Maxwell, she blocked his way, her sneering, bloodied mouth howling in rage.

He held out his bandaged hand. "Bovo, this isn't you. You're having a—"

With a strength that made her brother's seem feeble in comparison, she grasped Ben's arm and twisted. He yelped, but before he could pull his hand away, she ripped off his bandage with her teeth and held his oozing palm to her face.

"Laurette, no." His words morphed into a howl as she bit a chunk of flesh from his palm.

Blood spurted from his hand, far more than from the cut Mambo Tina had made. Fueled by adrenaline and disbelief, he managed to tear his arm away. Looking at the wound, he felt his knees growing weak. A gaping hole gouged his right palm where the wine-colored papule had been. Blood poured around the muscles and tendons.

A gray veil slipped over his eyes as he teetered on his feet. Fighting it off, he clenched his jaw and blinked. Passing out now would doom them all. He pressed his hand against his pants to stop the flow of blood, his white pajamas reddening like the clothes of a murder victim.

Somewhere beside him Mambo Tina shouted, "David, get the bébé!"

While the thing that was in Laurette frothed and swayed in front of Ben, the assistant darted to the altar. Laurette's head shot up and her body stiffened. Before David could grab Maxwell, she leaped forward in two giant bounds and tossed the assistant into one of the side tables. Lit candles toppled over. Bottles of alcohol shattered on the floor. Despite Mambo Tina's warning of chwals' super-human stunts, had Ben not seen it with his own eyes, he never would have believed Laurette capable of such strength.

Isn't possible, has to be a drug.

Ben dashed to the bassinet on the altar. The odor of burning cloth singed his nostrils, and he became vaguely aware of David batting out a fire on his left. But there was no time to help with the flames. Maxwell's cry had exhausted itself into a sorrowful whine, one that tore at Ben's heart as viciously as Laurette's teeth had torn at his palm.

When he reached for Maxwell, the amped-up Laurette stopped Ben once again. Pulling him back, she spun him around and punched him in the jaw. Having no choice, he hit back, pain exploding in his pulverized, still-bleeding hand.

His blow had no effect on the woman. She merely shrieked and bounded away to the altar, where she snatched the scalpel Mambo Tina had used earlier to retrieve Ben's blood for the offering. With coiled hair flapping around her crazed and bloodied face, she sprang at Ben. Before he could duck, she forcefully stabbed him in the abdomen.

A wheezy gasp sprayed from his lips. He stumbled backward and looked down in shock at the growing circle of crimson. Like litmus paper, white fabric flushed to red. Still faltering, his left foot caught and twisted on something. The wooden goatman. Unable to free his heel from the statue's crossed hooves, Ben pivoted and fell. A sickening *pop* exploded in his knee.

Stars flashed in his vision. He writhed in agony on the floor, his blood smearing the tiles and his knee exploding in white-hot pain. Even worse was his helpless horror when the chwal approached Maxwell on the altar. Though Mambo Tina and David made another attempt to stop her, they were met with a swift punch to the priestess and a swipe of the scalpel toward the assistant.

Just as Guy had done in Jean Miot's basement, Laurette scooped up Maxwell and lifted him toward the ceiling, letting his blankets fall to the floor. Her body twisted and quivered, arms squirming like snakes in the air.

"Laurette, please." Ben's voice was weak with pain. Blood poured freely from his belly and hand. His knee couldn't support his weight. "Maxwell," he whispered, dragging himself across the floor. A few feet in front of Laurette, his eyes teared. "He's my son, Bovo. My son."

The cold air rejuvenated Maxwell's crying to a full-out wail, but when Ben spoke, Laurette swiveled her head in his direction. With the infant held high, her mangled lips opened and closed as if preparing for speech. A throaty, hissing voice emerged. "Hurting your child," she said, the accent different from her usual one. "What about what you and your kin did to mine?"

Mambo Tina had scurried to Ben on the floor. At Laurette's words the mambo's button eyes widened. "It is as I thought," she said, waving her frightened assistant over. "It is not a Lwa we invited into your friend. It is Nasicha." Though David looked like he wanted to flee, cradling his bleeding arm where Laurette's scalpel surely had slashed him, he joined his mentor.

The chwal stared at Ben. In his onesie, Maxwell shivered and wailed in her quivering arms. To Ben's surprise, Marie approached and danced around her niece. Together they chanted. Together they danced.

Mambo Tina started to weep. "Marie. She has done this."

Ben moaned and tried to push himself up to his knees. Stars erupted again in his eyes, and he fell back down. Blood flowed from his wounds, and a foggy weightlessness consumed him.

Maxwell. Have to get Maxwell.

Like a wolf in a trap, he dragged himself forward, shaking with pain, weak from blood loss.

Abruptly, the chwal stilled. Her transition from quivering cyclone to solid stone startled everyone, including Maxwell, who grew quiet in her arms. The vengeful gaze beneath Laurette's superb eyebrows shifted to the doorway.

A terrifying coldness froze Ben to the spot. He knew without looking what awaited him at the back of the room. Because somehow the chwal had told him.

The dark priest had arrived.

52

At the sight of Guy in the doorway, dreadlocks neatly secured behind his squarish face, skin now scrubbed free of ritual paint, Ben's body gave out. He halted his agonizing crawl toward Laurette and his son. Though the others in the peristil stood motionless, the room itself swayed and bobbed around Ben like a raft at sea.

Next to him, Mambo Tina's and David's prayers hushed, their expressions stiff and wary. As soon as Guy stepped into the room, the remaining few participants fled. The scent of burned linens and plastic masks hung in the air, the odor too dense for the fans to clear.

Though the dark priest had washed up, his eyes remained red and swollen, a residual gift from the powder Ben had blown into them. The black pants and tunic were also the same, their dusty scuff marks evidence of the earlier battle.

Marie moved forward and stood at Guy's side. Ben gaped at her. It took a few tries, but he finally sputtered a hoarse wheeze. "9-1-1. You never called them." That was all he could manage. Her betrayal and his fading grasp on reality left him too weak to continue. A fleeting recollection of Marie texting on her cell phone in Mambo Tina's den fluttered into his mind. Had she been informing her nephew of their plan?

Guy approached his aunt and embraced her. "You have done well, *ma tante.*"

Ben struggled to pull himself upright. He had to get to his son. When he got as far as a seated position, he retched. The left side of his abdomen felt bloated and tight, blood still seeping from the wound.

You're going to bleed to death, Benny Boy.

No, he had to get to Maxwell. In his mental fog, the infant's cries had faded to a muted wail, as if coming from far away. But the sound was enough to tether Ben to reality, and he focused his remaining energy on getting back to his son.

Guy left his aunt's side and strolled to his possessed sister, stepping over the fallen goatman on his way, its big eyes and long snout smirking in delight. Then he kissed the top of the chwal's head. Her body still writhed and quivered, as if not comfortable in her skin, but she maintained her hold on Maxwell.

Guiding Laurette to the altar, Guy lowered the infant into the bassinet.

Ben dragged himself closer. A shock wave of pain swept through him, prompting a new round of nausea. When he paused to catch his breath, a burst of shaking rattles and chanting animated the room. He startled and looked behind him, confused by what he saw. David was shaking instruments, his voice a fiery pitch, and Marie was whispering something in Mambo Tina's ear. When she finished, the short, squat woman nodded.

No, don't trust her, Ben tried to shout, but it only came out in his head. Marie's duplicity both baffled and terrified him.

The priestess hurried to one of the side altar tables, her eyes on Guy and Laurette. She picked up a heavy cross that had been knocked to the floor during the chwal's feverish outburst and handed it to David. Then she joined him in his ceremonial dance, soon accompanied by Marie.

Ben tried to get them to stop, his ashen face grimacing, his wheezy words swallowed by their clamor. After a few seconds he gave up and threw his remaining energy into inching forward. A part of him knew it was hopeless. Useless. He was as good as dead and so was Maxwell. Another part of him, one so primitive he hardly knew it existed, would not stop until he had freed his son.

Out of nowhere, fire lit up his chest. Stunned, he looked down, but other than the amulet and cross, nothing was there.

And yet his skin was on fire.

Ignore it. Get Maxwell.

Ben lifted his cement skull back up. At the same time, Guy grabbed the scalpel from the altar table. Ben could see his own blood congealed on its blade. The dark priest nodded to the chwal, who, in Ben's messed-up mental state, could have been Laurette, Nasicha, or Darth Fucking Vader at that point.

He knew he was losing it. Knew he might pass out at any moment. He pressed his thumb into his blown-out knee. Tears sprung to his eyes, and he almost lost his breath, but the jolt of pain bought him a few more seconds of consciousness.

The chwal erupted into a ululating dance, her howls drowning out the other three Vodouisants. With an expression of lustful revenge, Guy brought the scalpel toward Maxwell.

"No," Ben roared, and with the last of his strength, he rose on one leg, the other limp and useless. The room spun like a tornado, sparks flashing in his eyes. He swallowed vomit and hopped toward Guy who chanted above Maxwell's head.

The heat over Ben's sternum grew unbearable. He tried to ignore it, but the attempt was futile. It was like searing light burning through his chest.

Mambo Tina shouted something in French to David. Before Ben could process what was happening, David burst forward and smashed the heavy cross over Guy's head. Though momentarily stunned, the dark priest didn't go down. He charged at David with the scalpel and lashed the man's chest. Though blood spread through the fabric of David's shirt, the assistant didn't give up. He kept Guy distracted enough to allow Ben to trudge to his son's side, dragging the bad leg behind the good one.

The infant had quieted, probably from exhaustion, no cries left to give. With arms as flimsy as noodles, Ben wrapped himself over the bassinet. Too weak to even pick his son up, he had no idea how he'd get him out the door on only one leg.

A shriek erupted behind him. Leaning on the altar for support, he shifted his position in time to see Mambo Tina fling a wooden chair at Laurette. Marie didn't stop her. Though crazed, the attack was enough to make the chwal lose her balance. Marie pushed her the rest of the way down to the floor. Though Laurette was tall, so was her aunt, and despite Laurette's bucking, Marie held her down long enough for Mambo Tina to plant the chair over the rabid chwal. The priestess then sat down and started bellowing a different chant.

To Ben's right, Guy stabbed at David again. Then again. Finally, David went down.

No, Ben shouted inside his head. But he couldn't help the assistant. He would not leave Maxwell's side.

David lay on the ground, blood pooling around him. Mambo Tina sat on the chair that trapped the chwal. The demon inside Laurette bucked and writhed but inexplicably stayed put, as if incapable of escape. "Hurry, the spell won't last long," the priestess wailed.

Marie was back to a frenetic chant, shaking rattles and shrieking so fever-ishly that sweat flew off her face.

Guy left David's body and stomped toward Ben. Another burst of fiery heat erupted over Ben's chest. He looked down at the amulet. Its bone flamed redder than molten glass.

Unable to bear it any longer, he lifted a shaking left hand—the right one a mangled mess from Laurette's bite—and pulled the blazing necklace over his head. Before he could discard it on the altar, which was the only thing holding his trembling body upright, an ear-splitting howl stopped him cold.

Ben's gaze shot to the chwal trapped beneath the chair. Her battered body fell limp. At the same time, less than a foot away from Ben, Guy froze.

Something shifted in the air. Ben felt it as surely as he'd felt the amulet burn his chest. He clutched the leather strap below the scorching, sharp bone and stared at the motionless priest.

With a suddenness that made Ben totter on the altar table, Guy's eyes widened, his back arched, and a gurgling bubbled in his throat. A fire lit up his eyes, and the same crazed expression Laurette had worn moments before flooded his face.

As if from a hundred miles away, Ben heard Mambo Tina yell, "She is in Guy now. Monsieur Oris, you must hurry. It can only be you." When he didn't move, she cried, "Use the heat."

Ben didn't understand. He was so weak, her screams seemed to come through a reverse megaphone. He could barely lean against the altar. So weak. *Must lie down.*

Guy's immobility ceased, his transformation apparently complete. He lurched toward Ben.

"Use your fire, Ben. The amulet. It must be you. Now!"

Finally, he understood.

53

Guy stood inches from Ben's face, his breath foul and his weeping, irritated eyes bulging. His hands, sticky with David's blood, reached out and wrapped around Ben's neck. He squeezed until Ben's airway closed and his eyes widened in panic.

Still sitting on the chair trapping Laurette, Mambo Tina cried for Ben to act while Marie knelt over David. Beside Ben, Maxwell whimpered.

Light dazzled Ben's eyes. The lack of oxygen thickened his confusion. Focus, he told himself, but even his inner command sounded weak.

Goddammit, Benny Boy, do something!

Whether from hypoxia or divine intervention, Ben didn't know, but the faces of Willy and Max loomed over him.

With a shaky left hand and a residual strength he hadn't known he possessed, he shoved off the altar and stabbed the sharp tip of the amulet into Guy's neck, aiming right for the carotid artery. He pulled the bone out with a sickening *thwuck* and rammed it back in again, this time going for the trachea, where the bone lodged in the cartilage.

His A in anatomy class paid off.

Guy's head snapped up, and his hands fell from Ben's neck. As soon as they did, Ben sucked in a gallon of air. He coughed and sputtered, his chest heaving.

Blood gushed from the dark priest's neck. With slippery fingers, he plucked out the pointy-tipped bone and looked at it in shock, as if unable to grasp that the amulet he'd bequeathed to his sister had been used to take his life. He stumbled back, gurgling and sputtering from blood flooding his windpipe. After a few moments of struggle, he slumped to the ground and fell silent, his body surrounded by broken bottles and colorful Lwa offerings.

Ben blinked, knowing, but unable to process, that he'd just killed a man.

His eyes darted to Laurette, still lying under the chair. Groggy and with a slack jaw, she looked like she'd just woken up, her bewilderment a far cry from her maniacal display only minutes before. Tentatively, she crawled out and scanned her surroundings, pausing when she spotted Guy's lifeless body. How would Ben explain to his best friend he'd just killed the brother she adored?

Before he saw her reaction, his vision blurred and his supporting leg finally gave out. He went down with a thud. A second later someone grunted and heaved him back up to semi-standing.

"Quick, we must finish," Mambo Tina said.

Finish? Finish what?

Hazy thoughts and a din in his ears prevented him from hearing the rest of Mambo Tina's words. Though her lips moved in front of him, nothing but muffled tones came out.

So tired. Got to sleep.

His body slipped again, but once more he was propped up. By who, Marie?

A hand gripped his face. "Do not sleep, Monsieur Oris. We must finish this. I need more of your blood and more of Maxwell's."

His son's name roused him to speak, but the words came out slurred. "No, only mine."

He felt himself being slung over the table and landed hard on his back. Pain shot through his injured knee and slashed belly, causing another round of lucidity.

Through bleary eyes he saw Marie step away from the altar. Though haggard and disheveled, she resumed her chanting and praying. When he blinked he saw a limping Laurette join her.

He tried to call out his friend's name, tried to explain. Nothing came. With his head lolling back and forth on the table, he felt a sting in his mutilated hand, milking of his flesh, and then the cool metal of the collecting bowl. So sticky. His whole body so sticky. A tangy tincture of sweat and blood.

Maxwell. Where's Maxwell?

A trio of praying voices blended inside his head. Three women swaying in front of him. Three became six became three again. Nausea welled within him, and his hand fell free from the collecting bowl and flopped over the side of the table.

He saw his son lifted by dark arms, his tiny heel drained of more blood. *No*, he shouted, but his lips were cemented together. The three women chanted and danced, prayed and circled, a silent Maxwell somewhere in their web of arms.

And then it hit him. They weren't there to help him at all. They were simply waiting for him to die. To use Maxwell's perceived power for their own gain.

I'm sorry, my son. So very sorry.

From a thousand miles away, Marie leaped into the air. She whooped and hollered, much like Laurette had earlier, and in his fading state it sounded like pure joy.

Another voice, gleeful too. "*Bèl bagay Bondye*, it is working. *Ogou Balindjo* has entered her." And then a more somber, "Mon Dieu, we are losing him."

Please, don't hurt my son.

A tear rolled down Ben's cheek. The last thing he saw before he closed his eyes was Marie holding his child.

Sorry, Maxwell. Willy. Harmony. I failed you all.

After that, there were no thoughts at all.

54

Blinding lights. Motion. Shards of pain jabbing his body. Voices buzzed in his ears, some of them shouting.

Be quiet, he told them.

"Ben, can you hear me?" A man's voice. "... to surgery. You've ... lot of blood."

Words and questions assaulted him.

Sleep. Just let me sleep.

A bump jolted his leg, and he surfaced once again.

"Keep him in isolation." A woman's voice. "... highly contagious."

Dr. Smith? Ben tried to speak but failed, his tongue a desiccated sponge.

Something compressed his face. Humidity dampened his nose. Warmth flooded his body, and the pain dissolved. He giggled. A Japanese woman named Smith.

He was flying, Maxwell in his arms.

Hey, little guy, where should we go?

"Get him under as quickly as you can." The man's intrusion angered Ben. "Miss ... have to leave now. You did good."

"Ben?"

The voice was familiar. He was jogging, a woman with beautiful eyebrows by his side.

The pleasant sensation faded, replaced by fear. *No, she's not what you think.* He tried to open his eyes and warn them, but nothing on his face seemed to work.

"Miss, you have to leave."

"Ben, Maxwell's okay," the woman's voice called out and then faded.

Euphoria returned.

He let himself drift away.

55

*B*lip, blip, blip.

Ben's eyes fluttered open. Blurry whiteness greeted him, followed by a paneled ceiling. Machines hummed by his side, and awareness of pain settled in. Head, jaw, hand, abdomen, knee. Everywhere pain.

An IV line snaked from his left arm, and oxygen prongs plugged his nose. Through the cerebral haze, recognition finally surfaced.

The hospital.

A clock near a mounted television read a quarter past three, and sunlight streaming across the bedding suggested the afternoon. Blinking, Ben tried to orient himself, but the last thing he remembered was passing out on Mambo Tina's altar table.

Maxwell.

The heart-rate monitor sped up, and his throat closed. When he raised his head to call for help, thunderbolts shot through his body and leveled him once again.

"It is okay. You are safe now."

Ben turned toward the right, his jaw throbbing in protest. A white hazmat suit materialized. Sharp cheekbones, distinctive eyes, and a bandaged lip lay beneath its plastic face guard.

"Laurette," he said, grimacing at the chafing rasp beneath his vocal cords.

"Shh, it is okay. Your surgery went well."

"Maxwell?"

"Your son is good. He is with Sophia in an isolation room."

"And Willy? Harmony?"

"Your father is okay. He had only one day for symptoms so Dr. Smith feels he got the magnesium in time. But Harmony … I am sorry. She has bled into her brain and lies in a coma."

"I don't. What? I …" Too groggy to comprehend her words, he gave up.

"Yes, magnesium. That is what the doctors think is treating you all, since Sophia was on it and did not get so sick as the others. They believe it to be a miracle drug for this," Laurette made quote marks with her heavily gloved fingers, "unknown virus. Your eosinophil counts are dropping. Harmony's, too, though for her I fear it is too late." Laurette put a thick paw on Ben's arm above his bandaged hand. The plastic odor of polyethylene fibers wafted to his oxygenated nose.

"Magnesium," Ben said, his tone one of disbelief. But it also carried a hint of hope, because if it were true, then the whole thing had never been a curse after all.

"Yes, magnesium, but we know better, do we not?"

Though he wanted anything but, Ben's distrust of his friend returned, and he pulled his arm away. An image of her biting a chunk of flesh from his palm surfaced. Alarmed, he looked at his wrapped hand. Would he still be a surgeon?

Would he still be a med student?

Beneath the suit's plastic shield, Laurette's expression suggested his dismissal stung. "I know you are confused, my friend, and that you no longer trust me." Her eyes moistened. "Please forgive me. Although I remember nothing of my possession, Mambo Tina has told me of my horrible acts."

For a moment neither of them spoke, the cardiac monitor blipping in the chasm between them.

Ben moved on. "Why'd they let you in here? Aren't they scared I'll infect you?"

"At first they did not allow it, but after your surgery, you howled about Vodou and blood sacrifice. You were so upset, they allowed me to come calm you, but only if I dressed like this." She pointed at her protective suit. "Silly, no?"

Jesus. He didn't remember any of that. Like a drunk after a blackout, he panicked over what he might have said to the hospital staff. "So we've already had this conversation?"

"Twice." Laurette smiled, and the genuineness of it calmed him. "You were like a monkey cracked over the head by a coconut. But you are now more awake so let us hope you will remember this time."

"Great. Dr. Smith must think I'm insane."

"Do not worry about your preceptor. She believes you suffer from viral … how do you say? Induced, yes, viral-induced encephalitis. The epidemiologist agrees this explains your behavior over the past twenty-four hours."

"You mean my running away? So I'm not in trouble?"

Laurette smoothed the front of her bulky suit. "That I do not know."

The squeeze in Ben's throat returned. As if fearing the room might be bugged, he lowered his voice. "Did the ceremony at least work?"

"Oh yes, Ben, yes. Do you not remember that part too? A healing Lwa entered my auntie, and through her, Mambo Tina broke the curse. She drove it back into the soul of …" Laurette studied her hazmat-covered shoes and shifted from one foot to the other.

"Of Guy?"

His friend nodded.

"I'm very sorry about your brother, Bovo." Ben swallowed, relieved her gaze was not on him so he didn't have to look her in the eye. "It was him or me, and he would've killed my son."

"Oui." Laurette blinked and moved her focus to the IV pole near the bed.

"Wait. Your aunt." Remembering the woman's deceit, Ben lifted his head and torso. A surge of pain knocked him back against the pillows. Sweat dotted his forehead, and a chest lead pulled loose, the heart-rate alarm beeping in warning. He flattened the sticky pad back against his skin, not thrilled to see his chest had been shaved. The bone amulet, too, was gone, no doubt plucked from Guy's hand by the medical examiner and secured in an evidence locker.

Holy shit, I'm screwed.

"It is not as you think. Auntie thought Guy came to Philadelphia to help. At his advice, she arranged the meeting with Monsieur Miot. Not until last night did she learn Guy's true plan."

Ben scoffed. "She sure didn't waste any time helping him."

"No, you do not see. She had to pretend or he would have harmed her like he did Miot. She knows enough dark magic to play along, yes? Make it work in our favor. But to do so, she had to trust you could escape Jean Miot's basement and flee with your son to Mambo Tina's peristil."

"Which I did, thanks to David's voodoo powder. What's in that stuff, anyway?"

"While you tended to Maxwell, Auntie Marie slipped your knife beneath Guy's thigh. She found the weapon near a statue as he had not tossed it far. She did not call 9-1-1 in the car like you thought. She knew Guy would cut the binds and come to the peristil. Since she helped you in Jean Miot's basement, she had to try to convince Guy she was still on his side. So she texted him and told him you were at Mambo Tina's and his ceremony could be finished there. She knew the only way to stop the curse was to call forth Nasicha. Even Mambo Tina did not understand at first."

"But why would she risk that? You were wild. You almost killed me."

Laurette frowned at his bandaged hand and beat-up face. "I am sorry. It was not me, I promise you this."

Unsure what to believe, Ben stared at the clock, wishing he could turn back its hands to when Laurette had first offered the trip to Paris. Knowing what he knew now, he never would have gone.

Then again, who was to say he hadn't simply been infected with a deadly organism, one that *was* being treated with magnesium? Nothing more, nothing less. Everything beyond that was fantasy and make-believe, conjured by people with mind-altering powders and Vodou powwows.

"I can see the disbelief in your eyes. Still, after all this." Laurette exhaled, her plastic face guard fogging. "Auntie Marie knew if she could invite Nasicha's spirit into Guy's body, she could bring both of them to their end. Once the mambo understood Auntie's plan, together they called Nasicha out of me and into Guy, making sure to curse the chair that trapped me so I could not escape. Once I was useless to Nasicha, her spirit moved on to Guy. Yes, it was risky. There was no guarantee Nasicha would go from me to Guy. But there was no other way."

He rolled his eyes, but Laurette ignored him.

"After you killed my brother—and the evil priestess within him—Mambo Tina invited Ogou Balindjo, a strong healing Lwa, into Auntie. He took the curse away. You are free now. You and Maxwell are free."

Despite his struggle to accept her explanation, he hoped to hell she was right.

"Soon you will all heal and go home. Dr. Smith and Dr. Khalid will become famous among their peers. The work of Auntie, Mambo Tina, and David will never be recognized, but they do not care. You and your son are safe. That is all that matters to them."

At the mention of David, Ben's heart sank. "David isn't, he didn't die, did he?"

"No. He was badly injured, but he will live."

"How did you explain it to the police? Bet that was one heck of a chat."

"There will be an investigation, of course, but for now they accept our story that Guy ..." Laurette's composure once again faltered, but she cleared her throat and continued. "That Guy tried to kill you and David, so you killed Guy in self-defense. And really, is that not the truth?"

Ben raked the unbandaged hand over his mouth, the stab wound in his arm twinging. He longed for a shot of whiskey. Or three. "I don't know what to believe anymore. How could Guy foresee all this? How could he *make* you and me come together? That's utter bullshit."

"Guy is a masterful Vodou priest. He knew of Nasicha's curse. He knew of our heritage."

"How?"

"He must have traced the Marcel line down to you. It is he who steered me to a public health degree in Philadelphia, yes? Told me of the good I could do for my country, especially after the earthquake."

"But how could he know we'd be friends?" Though Ben wanted nothing more than to believe her, distrust still plagued him.

"He gave me the charmed amulet and it drew me to you. Do you not see? He wanted the power of the curse for himself, and it did not matter how long he had to wait for it. I believe that is why he killed Monsieur Miot when he no longer needed him. It was not only to offer the bokor's blood to the spirits. It was so he would not have to share such power."

Ben stretched his neck and shifted his torso, triggering another bolt of agony through his belly. His heart rate climbed higher.

"Push your button." Laurette pointed to the morphine pump.

After pressing the knob, he waited for the medicine's sweet release. When it came, his body slackened and sleep beckoned. Coherent speech required concentration he no longer had. "Doesn't make sense … better leave … need time to think …" His voice trailed off, and his head sank into the pillow.

Laurette squatted down in her bulky suit and met him at eye level. "I am still your friend, Benjamin. Though my brother may have forced it, I am still your friend. On this, you must trust me."

When he didn't respond, she stood to full height and left. Before she even closed the door, he drifted away, away to a world where he'd killed a man and witnessed the murder of another, a world where two women were dead because of him and another one was in a coma. A woman who, like him, had only wanted to protect her son. He just hadn't seen it at the time.

56

"Hey bud, now that your quarantine's lifted, how about a stroll today? Don't want blood clots, do we?" A nurse with a navy scrub top and long sideburns untangled Ben from the IV tubing.

With a grunt, Ben pushed himself up on the bed. Wincing, he stood and shuffled like an old man to the adjustable vinyl chair next to the window. The RN followed behind with the IV pole.

"Maybe we do," Ben said. "Might get me past my massive deductible." Ben's sarcasm was unwarranted, but after a week in the hospital, he was climbing out of his skin.

Still buried in bandages, his right hand was useless, and the twenty stitches in his left arm had made that limb as incompetent as his swollen, wrapped knee. Two other dressings covered his abdomen, one in the left upper quadrant from a partial splenectomy, compliments of Possessed Laurette's scalpel, and the other in the midline from an emergent surgery three days later for a ruptured bowel hematoma.

"Bet they'll stop your fluids today. Then you can get rid of this thing." The nurse tapped the IV pole with his fist, and when Ben didn't respond, the guy added, "Hey, at least you can leave the room. That's something to celebrate." He planted a pillow behind Ben's head and waited for a nod of approval before exiting.

The nurse, who Ben made a note to apologize to later, had a point. With Ben's eosinophil count back to normal, hospital staff had returned to standard infectious disease precautions. Visitors would be allowed too, and the thought of finally seeing Willy, Maxwell, and Sophia dissolved some of Ben's surliness. Like his own, Willy's and Sophia's counts had returned to normal, and they had been discharged the day before after a seven-day course of magnesium. For reasons Ben didn't understand, Maxwell's count had never been high, but the pediatrician had still observed him in the hospital until an agreed-upon incubation period had passed.

Ben stared out the window at the roof of an adjacent building. Discarded beer bottles littered a small strip of artificial grass, and two lawn chairs glinted in the sun.

In the last eight days, Ben had flip-flopped back and forth on who'd actually cured his infection: Mambo Tina and her Lwa, or Dr. Smith and her miracle magnesium. Funny how quickly the brain gravitated to the easiest and most comfortable explanation.

A knock on the door broke his trance. Willy peeked in, and for the first time in days, Ben felt lightness.

"Dad, come in." Ben sat taller in the green chair, the pillow slipping down to his lower spine.

His father stepped inside, thick hair disheveled, jeans frayed, Philadelphia Eagles T-shirt faded. He halted at the sight of his son's bruised and bandaged body.

"Ah, it's not so bad," Ben said. "Better than the time Max socked me in the face with the baseball."

They both laughed. "Yeah, Max wasn't much of a pitcher, was he? Cried more about that shiner than you did."

Again they chuckled, and despite the pain it caused Ben's incisions, he considered it well worth the discomfort.

"At least Max would've remembered to bring you flowers or somethin'." Willy looked at his empty hands as if expecting a gift to appear. "Sorry about that."

"I don't need flowers. I just need to see you."

At that Willy closed the distance between them, bent over the chair, and embraced his son as best he could among the intravenous tubing and abdominal drain.

When he pulled away, he sat on the bed, and for the next quarter hour they talked about his improved health as well as Harmony's ongoing coma. They danced around the Vodou elephant in the room, until finally, Ben couldn't take it anymore.

"Dad, I need to tell you something. It's going to sound crazy, but just hear me out."

Willy raised a hand. "Laurette came to see me after I was discharged. Told me everything."

"Everything?" Ben's expression was a mixture of uncertainty and embarrassment. "As in…?"

"As in your injury in the catacombs, the curse, the ceremony to stop it."

"When you say it out loud it sounds so stupid."

"She also told me Dr. Smith's version: an infection from an ancient bone, treated not with an antibiotic but with a mineral. Who ever heard of such a thing?"

Ben picked at a tuft of foam escaping the chair's binding. "I suppose that sounds equally messed up, doesn't it?"

Willy half-smiled, half-frowned. "You're too damn pragmatic for your own good, Benny Boy. If there's one thing Max and your mother taught me, it's that there's no black and white in this world. There's only endless shades of gray."

"Yeah, but how can I accept what happened?"

"Let's move forward, son. I've been living in the past for too long." Willy scratched his stubbly chin, voice sagging with emotion, hangdog eyes tired. "The only thing I know for sure is this thing wasn't your fault. You got caught up in something, and you did what you had to do to stop it and protect your son.

"But Kate and Melissa died because of me." Ben stared out the window, sorrow weighting his chest. "And who knows what'll happen to Harmony?"

"Harmony would've chosen to die ten times over if it meant her son and grandson would live. She'd want you to take care of your boy in a way she never could you." Willy cleared his throat but said nothing more.

With his thoughts on Harmony, a memory pinged in Ben's brain. "When I last talked to her, she mentioned something about me not judging you. What was that about?"

Willy looked up in surprise. His expression became mournful. "Oh, that's a conversation for another day, son."

Before Ben could query further, someone rapped on the door. A female voice followed. "*Hola chicos.*" Sophia walked in with an infant carrier. "Thought you might like a special visitor." Dressed in capri jeans and a pink tee, Sophia placed the carrier on the floor and scooped up Maxwell. "Time to meet your papa."

Upon seeing his grandson, Willy's face lit up. He moved to the edge of the bed and took the infant in his arms.

Watching Willy hold Maxwell made Ben's throat swell and his chest ache, so much so he worried the nurse would bring back the cardiac monitor.

Willy's Adam's apple bobbed up and down, and he sniffled twice before speaking. "I swear he looks just like Max. I know that's not possible, but he does."

Sophia sat on Ben's armrest, her personal boundaries more intimate than his own. A bouquet of lavender radiated from her skin, and a collection of bracelets jangled against her wrist. Tucking her short hair behind her ears, she asked Ben how he was doing.

"I'm okay. And I'm so sorry. I—" He started to elaborate then bit down. He had no idea what to say. Had no idea how to explain why she'd been drugged and Maxwell taken. There was so much ground to cover between them. Did she blame him? Hate him? Did she think he was nuts?

"Always so serious," she said. "I can practically see the thoughts swarming behind your eyes. We can talk later, okay? For now let's just enjoy the moment."

Her exuberant smile cast more rays than the late morning sun, and for the next half hour, Ben listened as she and Willy talked babies, diaper brands, and sleep schedules. The effect of their happiness on his pain was better than the morphine. When Sophia finally got up to leave, she promised to bring Maxwell by Willy's later. To Ben, she said, "If you feel the need to apologize to someone, make it Laurette. She's upset you've avoided her calls all week."

Ben's happiness bubble popped. Sophia was right, of course, but the longer he'd been in the hospital, the more time he'd had to consider Laurette might have cooked up the whole scheme from the start. Guy bringing them together seemed too far-fetched to believe. And just because it ended in Ben's favor didn't mean that was how she'd wanted it. "I'm still not sure I can trust her," he finally said.

"If not for Laurette, you wouldn't be here." Sophia's tone suggested she'd have no trouble managing their son's teenage years. "She kept you from bleeding out. She monitored you until the ambulance came. She risked her own arrest to make sure you got treated. Does that sound like a woman you can't trust?"

She left him with that thought, but before he could ponder it, Dr. Smith hustled in, cloaked in a lemon sheath dress and white coat. A balding man in a suit followed. Willy seemed to take that as his cue to leave, but not before he cast a don't-mess-with-my-son look on his way out.

Ben stared at the somber couple. Not once while he'd been ensconced in his isolation cocoon and Dr. Smith in her hazmat gear had the woman brought up Ben's flight from the hospital. Or his dodging of the police. He'd eventually deluded himself into thinking they might overlook the whole thing.

But apparently not, because his attending introduced the sour-faced man as Detective Finley, and in that moment Ben understood his penance was about to begin.

"Do you have any questions before we start?" Dr. Smith asked.

"Um, do I need a lawyer?"

57

Arms full of clothes, their fabric still heady with Max's cologne, Ben stepped out of the closet and dumped the newest batch onto Willy's bed. Goodwill pile on the left, Ben Oris pile on the right. Max had amassed an impressive wardrobe, and Ben figured his own attire would now drastically improve. Though Willy had helped Ben sort through Max's things, including those in the den, the clothes proved too much. So Ben sent his father out for an afternoon with Sophia and Maxwell instead. Even for Ben the project was laced with melancholy. Each item of clothing transported him back in time, the memories of his other father still very much alive.

An occasional wince from a stretched incision slowed his progress and his injured knee still gave him grief. It might even require surgery down the line if rehab didn't work. But for the most part he had healed well, and, like Willy, he was moving on, eager to get back to his exercise routine and the rest of his life.

Luckily, he hadn't needed a lawyer for long. Given his clean record, strong academic history, and the bizarre sequence of events in his twenty-four-hour flight from the hospital, an investigation chalked his behavior up to a "neuropsychotic episode induced by an unknown pathogen." Or at least that was what his medical record said. To his surprise, Dr. Smith had supported him, testifying to the police there was no way a practical student like Ben would have been involved in a Vodou ceremony if he had been of sound mind. "He's one of our best medical students," she'd told the detective in the hospital room. "I suspect the stress of his son being kidnapped pushed him over the edge."

Ben had practically popped his stitches in shock. He hadn't expected her support, especially since he'd fought her stepson at Sophia's apartment, leaving the grad student mumbling and dazed. Shortly after Ben was discharged, he'd gone to Joel and apologized. Although the guy had threatened to sue, he never followed through with it. Ben supposed Dr. Smith had something to do with that as well.

Furthermore, Ben's killing of Guy was ruled self-defense, with no charges against him, Mambo Tina, or anyone else at the peristil that night. Things might not have resolved so smoothly if the police had been told the whole story. Certain events had been left out, such as Laurette's wild stint as a chwal and Mambo Tina's bloodletting of Ben and Maxwell. The focus was on Jean Miot's stalking of the infant—backed up by the hospital's security cameras—and his drugging of Sophia, his abduction of Laurette and Maxwell, and Guy's psychotic plan for revenge. Mambo Tina, David, Marie, and Laurette had apparently synced their stories while waiting for the ambulance. When Ben's version varied from theirs, his lawyer was quick to point out that Ben had been experiencing disease- and drug-induced hallucinations on the night of the events. He had the medical records to prove it, including a positive blood test for an herbal hallucinogenic inhaled in Jean Miot's kitchen.

Given Ben's injuries, Dr. Smith had helped him rearrange his schedule, assigning him to the less grueling psychiatry rotation once he was well enough to work. Though he'd missed four weeks of internal medicine due to his recovery, she agreed to let him make up the time during his four one-week vacations throughout the year. That way he would be able to begin his fourth year with the rest of the students.

Whether her leniency stemmed from pity, respect, or the highly anticipated journal article she was about to publish on her discovery of a cure for the unknown pathogen, Ben didn't know. But given that she'd tried to convince him to pursue internal medicine rather than orthopedic surgery, he figured respect fit in there somewhere.

"We need minds like yours," she had said during her consult on a psych patient he'd been following. While Ben had suspected Wilson's disease in the patient, the psychiatrist had dismissed Ben's suggestion and diagnosed schizophrenia instead. It later turned out Ben was right, and though the psychiatrist had mumbled something about "beginner's luck," Dr. Smith had praised Ben's astuteness. In reality, his diagnostic pick-up probably stemmed from the extra study time he'd had while recovering at home.

Thankfully, home was still Mrs. Sinclair's basement. The woman had taken pity on him after his trauma but warned him there would be no more "funny stuff" on her premises. No doubt his handyman skills played into her decision. She might have been crusty, but she wasn't dumb.

Smoothing out a blazer he planned to keep for himself, he opened and closed his gimpy right hand, the skin graft still devoid of full feeling. A wave of despair washed over him. Dr. Smith might want him in internal medicine, but orthopedic surgery had always been his dream, and he prayed it remained an option. The hand surgeon said it was too soon to tell.

Before he could descend into a black cloud about his future, the doorbell rang. Knowing it was Laurette, he plodded to the foyer to greet her, anxious about their first face-to-face interaction since the hospital two months before. He'd learned through the grapevine her advisor recommended she apply for a spot in the CDC's Epidemic Intelligence Service. Not only would she make a great disease detective, the position would give Ben a few more years with her in the U.S. Assuming she still wanted him in her life. After his recent distrust and dismissal of her, he wouldn't blame her if she punched him in the face when he opened the door.

But she didn't, and after escorting her back to his father's kitchen, he grabbed them both a beer, and together they sat at the granite island bar.

"Thanks for inviting me," she said, her body perched on the edge of the barstool, as if she too were unsure how to proceed. Her usual glow was absent and her affect flat. Ben recognized the bereft look. He'd worn it himself after Max's passing.

"I've been an ass long enough. I've missed you," he said.

"Me too."

They fell into awkward silence as they sipped their drinks. Even though he had much to say to her, he didn't know where to begin. It was Laurette who finally spoke up. "Mambo Tina tells me you stopped by the peristil to thank her. She says you fixed the damage I did to her walls. You even hung your friend, Monsieur Goatman, back up behind the altar table."

"That thing is creepy." Ben allowed a small smile before his expression sobered again. "Mambo Tina is a good woman. What she did for me? Well, I can't ever repay her. You either." He forced himself to make eye contact. She needed to know he meant it.

Never one to accept praise, Laurette averted her gaze, crossed and uncrossed her legs, and changed the subject. "How's Maxwell?"

"He's doing great. So big already, you should see him."

A hint of her characteristic smile broke through. "I'd like that. And Sophia?"

"She's good. Never got that sick. Dr. Smith says it's because of the magnesium. Mambo Tina says it's because she shared Maxwell's blood. He was the only one fully immune to the illness, and that's why his blood count was normal."

"That's good, but that is not what I meant." A slight pause and a smoothing of her skirt. "How are you and Sophia together?"

Ben shrugged and took another sip of beer. "We're just co-parenting, that's all. She's cool and she's a great mom, but we have a lot of differences." What he left unsaid was: *she's not you.*

"Maybe so, but I see you still wear her cross."

Ben glanced down at the glimmer of gold peeking out from his sweatshirt. "Can't hurt, right?"

Laurette picked at the label on her bottle. "Does that mean you now believe?"

"About what happened?" Straightening his posture on the backless stool, Ben puffed out his cheeks and exhaled. "Hell, I don't know. When I play it back now, Dr. Smith's theory makes the most sense. Old bone. Nasty infection. Surprising cure. And you and I simply linked up because we were in the same epidemiology class and we're older than everyone else."

"And so my brother died for nothing?" Pain filled her eyes. "He was just a crazy man and the rest was coincidence? Misguided or not, he was still my brother."

"Oh jeez, I'm sorry, Bovo." Ben rushed to explain himself. "I didn't mean it like that. I know how close you were to Guy. The fact I was the one to end that makes me sick. I can't get that moment out of my head. Taking another man's life, well ... it's ..."

"My brother brought it on himself. I do not blame you. It's what had to be. But it is still very painful."

Ben saw Laurette's jaw tighten as she choked off emotion. He closed his eyes and did the same. When he opened them, she was staring at him.

"If you do not believe, how do you explain Guy's mind control, or my possession, or Mambo Tina's and Auntie Marie's skills?"

He rubbed his palm where the skin graft was healing. "I don't know. Maybe the rest just played out because our minds created it. Not to mention that special *tea* you slipped me the night of the lamp service." Not expecting her to confirm or deny, he merely sipped his beer and continued. "It's like Occam's razor, you know? When confronted with two explanations, the simplest one is most likely. But then I think of the other stuff—our ancestors' connection, the burning I felt from your amulet, you raging around like a rabid animal, biting the neck off bottles and tossing grown men like dolls—and, well, that's a little tougher to chalk up to coincidence."

A heaviness fell over them as they silently replayed that dark night, both lost in their own thoughts. Finally he said, "To answer your question, I don't know what to believe."

"All one can do is have an open mind, yes?"

Ben grimaced. "Oh, my mind's been opened all right. I now see those shades of gray Willy's always talking about." He swiveled his stool to face her. It was time to man up. The events of that horrible month had taught him control was an illusion, so he needed to seize the moments he *did* have power over. Like this one. "Look, I asked you to come to Willy's today because—"

"Because your bigoted landlady will not have me?" She tilted her head and raised an arched brow, and for a moment the old Laurette returned. What he wouldn't have done for a goat joke too.

"Ha, no. Well, maybe. We'll deal with that later." He allowed a brief smile before he continued. "I owe you an apology. A big one. From the start you did nothing but help me, and if it wasn't for you, I understand I would have died. And I thanked you by telling you to piss off, at least in so many words." Laurette waved him off, but he continued. "No, I need to say this and you need to hear it, even if it's difficult for both of us. I'm sorry. From the bottom of my heart, I'm sorry. That was no way to treat the best friend I've ever had."

"You simply needed time to sort things out. I understand."

"But if it wasn't for you, Maxwell and I wouldn't be here. Or Willy. Or Harmony. Coma or not, at least she's not dead. How can I ever adequately thank you?" His voice choked off, and he had to swivel his stool forward again to collect himself.

She put a hand on his arm. "You just have, my friend. That is all you need to say. You are welcome. It is in the past."

He turned back to face her. "But—"

"No buts. Let us move on, oui?" Her eyes implored him, and he obliged. Her ability not to dwell on matters was one of the things he loved about her.

In fact, so many compatibilities and similarities linked them, it was no wonder they got along well. Even if Guy *had* forced them together, Ben knew one thing with absolute certainty: the dark priest deserved no credit for the friendship they'd fostered.

That was all them.

THE END

ACKNOWLEDGMENTS

First of all, I would like to thank you, the reader, for giving me your time. Knowing you enjoy my stories is the most gratifying part of being a writer.

In addition, I'd like to extend a sincere thank you to my early readers. Your input is like gold. My gratitude also goes to Brittany, who helped affirm I was being respectful to Haitian Vodou and the people who practice it. Also to Andra, Audrey, Larry, and Gina. Two more big thank yous to my editor, Kevin Brennan, and my cover artist, Lance Buckley, who knocks each book cover out of the ballpark. Another huge heap of gratitude goes to ScienceThrillers Media for taking my words and transforming them into a polished product. It's an honor to work with you, and I value your input and keen eye. Lastly, may my family know of my ongoing, daily appreciation of their support of my writing, especially my husband, whose encouragement means the world to me, and my sons who never sugarcoat a thing.

Even when I might want them to.

AUTHOR'S NOTE

My research on Haitian Vodou took me into an exciting and intriguing world. Although I made every attempt to remain respectful of the practice, *The Bone Curse* is fictional, which means liberties were taken, particularly with my antagonist's actions. There could be no thriller without a bad guy, one who goes beyond the moral and acceptable.

Readers interested in learning more about Vodou practice and culture will enjoy *Haitian Vodou, An Introduction to Haiti's Indigenous Spiritual Tradition* (Llewellyn Publications) by Mambo Chita Tann, as well as The History Channel's DVD *Voodoo Secrets*. Both served as valuable resources to me. Additionally, more detailed information on the Paris catacombs can be found in *The Catacombs of Paris* (Parigramme) by Gilles Thomas, photographs by Emmanuel Gaffard and translation by Diane Langlumé.

Montgomery Hospital is fictional, as are the other businesses named in the novel. However, were Willy's Chocolate Chalet to exist, I would certainly frequent it.

About the Author

Carrie Rubin is an award-winning author, physician, and public health advocate. Her other medical thrillers include *The Seneca Scourge* and *Eating Bull*. She is a member of the International Thriller Writers association. She lives in Ohio with her husband and two sons.

Connect with Carrie Rubin

Facebook (facebook.com/carrierubinauthor)

Twitter: @carrie_rubin

Amazon

Goodreads

To hear about Book 2 in the Ben Oris series or other upcoming releases, sign up for the author's infrequent newsletter at

www.carrierubin.com

Online book reviews are greatly appreciated. A few sentences go a long way in helping other readers decide if they might like *The Bone Curse*. Thank you for leaving a review on your favorite social media, or on GoodReads, Barnes & Noble, amazon, or Apple iBooks

If you enjoyed *The Bone Curse*, you might like other titles published by ScienceThrillers Media.

ScienceThrillers Media specializes in page-turning stories, both fiction and popular nonfiction, that have real science, technology, engineering, mathematics, or medicine in the plot.

Visit our website and join the STM mailing list to learn about new releases.

ScienceThrillersMedia.com
publisher@ScienceThrillersMedia.com